Walter C. Dendy

Legends of the Lintel and the Ley

Walter C. Dendy

Legends of the Lintel and the Ley

ISBN/EAN: 9783337151737

Printed in Europe, USA, Canada, Australia, Japan

Cover: Foto ©Andreas Hilbeck / pixelio.de

More available books at **www.hansebooks.com**

LEGENDS

OF THE

LINTEL AND THE LEY.

BY

WALTER COOPER DENDY.

𝔎e moste reherse as neighe as ever he can,
𝔒r elles he moste tellen his tale untrewe,
𝔒r feiner thinges or finden wordes newe.
GEOFFRY CHAUCER.

LONDON:
BELL AND DALDY, 186, FLEET STREET.
1863.

PRESCRIPT.

 URING the progress of this little book, I have been conscious that its abrupt transitions, and the desire of avoiding the profusion of expletives which swell the fashionable novel, will tend to *compress* the story,—that the fragments of history may here and there be deemed *exotic*, and the wilder legends pedantic : yet, even with this foreshadowing, I trustfully cast the little book upon the waters.

W. C. D.

Legends.

LEGENDS

OF

THE LINTEL AND THE LEY.

———◆———

> " Giving each rock its storied tale,
> Knitting, as with a moral band,
> Thy native legends with thy land ! "

THROUGHOUT merry England there is many a beauty spot, blushing in quiet loveliness, or frowning in its wild magnificence, illumined and enriched withal by the charm of tradition. There are few more worth the gleaning than the leys and the hills and the moorlands that lie along the centre of the fair land of Surrey, almost at the threshold of London city. There bright flowers are blushing, and filmy winglets flitting, and Zephyr, wanton with the blossoms, is waking up the wildest madrigals with the songbird and the honeybee. All this is special for the pilgrim of nature, who, with fresh and grateful heart to the Creator, loves to revel among her blossoms and her butterflies, or "couched in the woodbine coverture," to listen to some choice scrap of truthful history, or a story from the rude gossip of the by-ways, or a legend from the antique, or even to some romantic myth, chime they in with the lone haunts or ruined walls around us.

B

You must know that this central belt of Surrey is teeming with legend-lore : and although it is not hallowed with the monastic shrines of Iona, or the seven churches of Glendalough, or graced with the more majestic adornments of the East, yet along these velvet brows that hang over Holmsdale once travelled many a sandalled devotee from Wynchestre to Canterbury. The *Pedlar's* or *Pilgrim's Way* here crosses the tesselated fosseway, *Stanestreet*, the route of Jute, Saxon, Roman, and Norman, whose incursions blend primæval Britaine with imperial and papal Rome, and there is a Bury on many a brow, a link of the chain of forts from Folkestone to Farnham. We may light, too, on many a holy fane, noted even before Domesday Boke, beneath the lintel of many a mouldering ruin, once resplendent with feudal glory, and on many a modern grange with family legend chronicled in England's history.

Let us contemplate and count our jewels from the lofty brow that juts like a bastion over the waterbrooks, they call it the *Stomacher* of Box Hill, which, with all its spoliation, is still dotted with the relics of a forest of box and yew and juniper that crowned it profusely even in the early days of Plantagenet. The *coup d'œil* is enchanting, there is beauty broadcast over three fair valleys, green as the emerald, and glowing with all the exquisite poetry of nature ! But a yet brighter glory is lighting up the classic ground : for around these valleys lies many a home of wealth and power, in which lofty intellect has loved for many a year to worship and adorn the beautiful. Yon frowning woods, indeed, embosom the villas of a Tacitus, a Demosthenes, and a Pliny of the past age.

There is Depedene, honoured by a triad of genius—
Howard, and Burrell, and Hope the brilliant author of
Anastasius, "full of marvellous fine things,"—Betchworth
was the home of Abraham Tucker,—in yonder quiet house
at Brockham, given, it is said, by his prince, lived Charles
Morris, the Anacreon of the Carlton House Symposia,—
near the dark spire of Dorking yonder, John Mason
studied self-knowledge,—Milton Court was the hermit
home of the philanthropist Markland,—the woods of
Wotton are hallowed by the memory of John Evelyn,—in
the Rookery, Malthus Englished Goethe and St. Pierre,—
Polesdon was the retreat of Sheridan,—Phenice and
Camilla Lacy of Fanny Burney,—in Norbury, William
Lock, the Mecænas of his age, strove to make all good
and wise and happy as himself,—in Mickleham dwelt the
Mills, the logician and the economist, and Daniell wrote
his essays,—to Conversation Sharp, in Fridley, came Horne,
Hazlitt and Macintosh,—Boxlands was the home of Singer
who edited Spenser, and wrote of Pope and playing cards,
—in Denbies herded artists, and poets, and songsters and
ballet-stars, in the time of Jonathan Tyers—in yonder grove
Mrs. Barbauld scribbled the stanzas on Nelson's victory,
and Juniper Hole was the retreat of illustrious refugees
from revolutionary France.   Hymettus in all his purple
glory looked not on a brighter galaxy of genius than this
poor chalk-hill, even in the palmy days of the Parthenon.

The green-laced chalk is here well-nigh perpendicular
over the Arcadian valley of Burford: across the bridge
the wayfarer may find the Hostelric, at this day a quiet
roadside inn, years ago the fashion.   It was oft the nest

of blushing brides in the flush of their honeymoon : it was haunted by grave senators, and golden citizens, and deep philosophers, and used-up libertines, and maudlin poets withal, whose rhapsodies were oft picked up by the spider brushes of the bedrooms, and intertwined with their ringlets, for maids gloried then in their mop of corkscrews. Fancy these present hours to be early in this nineteenth century, and that one of these dreamers of the light and loving lay, that worshipped and drew from nature, was wandering, as he was often wont, along these meadows of the Mole, watching the growth of flowers, that he confessed to be his "intensest pleasure," when they retired within the shade, and masked their beauty to the daylight—for they would, in his own phrase, "lose all their charm if, flaunting on the highway, they cried out : 'Admire me, I am a violet !'"

It was here he may have been first enslaved by, the vision of Madeleine, herself the very lily of the valley, sleeping among her kindred blossoms, and this is her picture sketched on a scrap of foolscap, and afterwards twisted among her auburn tresses.

> " Soon trembling in her soft and chilly nest,
>   In sort of wakeful swoon perplex'd she lay,
>   Until the poppied warmth of sleep oppressed
>   Her soothèd limbs, and soul fatigued away
>   Flown like a thought until the morrow-day,
>   Blissfully haven'd both from joy and pain,
>   Clasp'd like a missal where swart paynims pray,
>   Blinded alike from sunshine and from rain,
>   As though a rose should shut and be a bud again."

And in these lone meadows he would still wander on
until his large blue eyes were lighted up by the young
May moon that rose over Box Hill, and flickering among
the shadows, glistened on the ripples of the Mole. He
had thrown himself on the grass, and opening a page of
his Lemprière, he murmured in soft yet passionate accents :
" Endymion, Endymion ! "

" The very music of the name has gone into my being,
and each pleasant scene is growing fresh before me as the
green of our own valleys — " He was checked by a man of
thoughtful eye, who had come down from the grave of
Labellier on this very brow, with his quarto Chalmers
under his arm.

" Ah, foolish boy," he muttered, " mad and moon-struck
as young Percy Shelley."

" Shelley," exclaimed John Keats, " would I were mad
as he—oh, for the flash of Shelley's fine frenzy, that shames
my sandy scribbling !—oh, for the gush of deep and burning
passion that courses through his rich Saxon blood and bur-
nishes his downy cheek !—would I were stricken with midsummer madness like his. And yet I fear to know him : he
would mould me as his own, my poor faint heart would burst
with the bounding thought it would drink in from Shelley's
flood of glory. I will bide my time, for the angels have
whispered in my dream that Percy and I should slumber
side by side after death, though his name be writ in gold
and mine in water. I am withering fast like Kirke White,
e'en now the daisies are growing over my grave." (Who
knows not that this idea was realized ? In the Protestant
cemetery at Rome, on the *Honorian* walls by the tomb of

Caius Cestius, believed by Petrarch and others to be that
of Remus, are deposited the ashes of Keats and Shelley.)

"Endymion, hey," muttered Hazlitt, as he gazed at him,
"why the myth of the Moon on Latmos will madden
him outright. Hither boy—shut your Lemprière at once,
and leave Endymion on Latmos where you found him—
forget him—or if you must read stars, learn from the
Chaldæans or my Chalmers here, thou'lt drink more wisdom in an hour, than in a month of mooning. Yet if you
will sip Helicon, drink deep, 'drink deep,' as Alic Pope
sings, 'or taste not the Pierian Spring,' and *down* with
your dream of Endymion—nothing like scribbling to
lighten a loaded brain—and hark ye, we'll bring you out,
get Leigh to puff you in his ' Round Table '—and defy the
lashing of the *Quarterly*. " Keats shivered like an aspen
at the word, as 'twere, prophetic of his fate.

" Yet methinks," continued Hazlitt, arching his brows
like Fadladeen, "you're not further gone than Nat Lee, or
young Southey, or little Byron, or the fool who scribbled
this :—wilt guess where I found it?"

And Hazlitt read aloud the sketch that in her dream
had been untwisted from a tress of Madeleine, which he
had found upon the grass where she had been sleeping.
As he read on, blushes suffused the rhymer's cheek, and told
his secret, but Hazlitt spared his blushing, merely muttering to himself, " Guilty, by the brow of Erato ! " And
then, to cool his brain, the critic took the rhymer by the
hand, and walked him off to the spring in Betchworth
Park, that Hazlitt the waterdrinker called his Helicon,
and we the Lion's Mouth. What further parlance between

the sage and the suckling, whether John Keats on that midsummer night thought more of the beauty of Madeleine he has since coloured so highly in the "Eve of St. Agnes," or even sketched, to be polished up in Wight, his wild romance of the "Moon and the Sheepboy," we know not. It was long after midnight, however, that he ceased to gaze on the orb of night, as loth "to leave her behind him," and it was close on the dawn when Hazlitt saw him glide along like a ghost to his chamber, his lips yet murmuring in a low and wailing whisper, "Endymion, Endymion !"

Every river has its beauty spot, the Rhine at the Drachenfels, the Derwent at Matlock, the Clyde at Lanark, the Avon at Clifton, the Wye at Wyndcliff, the Mole in the leys around Box Hill and Norbury. No wonder that many a poet has hied hitherward to woo the Naiads of the Mole,—Drayton, and Milton, and Pope, and Wordsworth. Michael was so charmed that he made it the scene of the quaint allegory in his "Polyolbion."

> " The Mole, who, like some Earth-born giant, spreads
>   Her thirsty arms along the indented meads,"

is here, in Drayton's fancy, grown wanton, and like a love-sick girl is twisting and twining along the leys to get to her lover.

> " Her fore intended course the wanton nymph did run,
>   As longing to embrace old Thame's and Isis' son."

Her mother Holmsdale very wisely, as she thought,

> ·" ——— raised hills to keep the straggler in,"

but as love laughs at locksmiths, so, like her sisters Wey and Darent, the enamoured Mole

" Would *on,* though mountains interven'd,"

and managed to cleave the chalk at the base of the
Stomacher, and now meandering along the green flowery
meads, falls into the bosom of the Thames at Molesey.

Then sings another poet :—

> "The Mole glides on through quiet meadows rich
> In yellow cowslips and the tall foxglove,
> With its deep purple bells dew-laden !"

To make up the garland we may add many another
wilding, willow herb, ranunculus, hemlock, cardamine,
lychnis, angelica, soapwort, belladonna, clubrush, the
splendid *butomus,* and the orchids.

The phenomenon of the stream, the perforations of the
porous chalk, named it "mole" and "river swallowe :"
it is most prominent about Cowslip Farm, and Fridley,
Fred-ley, the meadow of peace, the largest swallow ab-
sorbing 260,000 gallons. In summer, except a *Holdwater*
pool here and there, it is often dry, especially from Cowslip to Lethered. In a hot season we have walked dry-
shod this bed of the river, then a gravel lane or pebble
garden, among coltsfoot and waterdock and dead water-
lilies. Yet even this has caught the fancy of the poets—

> " Sullen Mole that hides her diving flood."
> " Sullen Mole that runneth underneath."
> " Mole, that like a noozling mole, doth make
> Her way still underground."
> " Which, like a noozling mole, doth noozle underneath."
> " Mole digs herself a path by working day and night."

But we will forget awhile the poets and their pastorals,
and take up a theme of deeper interest.

It was about the dawn of this century that the sylvan solitude of this fair valley was sought as their sanctuary by a bevy of the choicest spirits of France, who had personally coquetted with courts and kings and swayed the policy of nations, and Fanny Burney was wont to call them

The Juniperes.

" We beth men wyde ydrive,
_ Aboute from contrey to contrèe."
R. GLOUCESTER.

THOSE long shadows of the cedars, that even now empurple the lawn of Juniper Hole, may be emblematic of the gloom that for awhile darkened the glory of "La belle France," and stained her temples with the blood of the innocents. An illustrious pair of these *émigrés* will give life to the scene.

There among those very cedars lounges the citizen, Charles Maurice Talleyrand de Perigord, the most astute politician of his age, very deep in thought, and there peering through the iron gates is Madame de Staël Holstein.

" *Voyez, voyez vous, monsieur*," she cried, " Madame Lock's ponies, and Fanny, to bear us to that *douce* Norbury, yet D'Arblay has been sighing the matin, so doth he jalouse her Aniella."

" Camilla, *s'il vous plaît*," whispered Miss Burney, waddling in, "we call her Camilla now."

"*Toujours gaie, toujours la belle*," whispered Talleyrand, drawing his chin within his magnificent cravatte, "and how *porte* themselves the Locks?"

"*Très bien*, and greet you Monsieur d'Autun or Augustodunum, for cutting the revolu—"

Talleyrand frowned away the other syllables : "There is no such word, mademoiselle, say ' policy.' "

"Hush," whispered Madame, "Fanny is a royalist, that very cheek old George of Brunswick hath kissed and called her 'good as gold.' "

"Royalist, hem, why *I was* one myself, *vous savez*, though now—*citoyen du monde*."

"Bah, bah, you are thinking even now more of a mitre and a princedom than *la liberté, n'est ce pas, n'est ce pas, monsieur ?* "

"Thoughts may not be spoken, madame, speech was given to conceal them."

"*Par example*, when you glorified Fanny's Evelina, and made me, your poor Corinne, so jealous."

"I may love Evelina, madame, yet worship Corinne— I may kneel to Juno, yet smile on Venus."

"Then give *me* the smile : love is dearer far to woman's heart than worship."

"Then, madame, wear your robe long to hide your *bas bleu*," and Talleyrand left the ladies together.

"Yet, I love him," murmured Madame, "and *you* shall love him too, Fanny."

"Nay, I love nobody for nothing, I am not so tinderly, yet is he *très comique*."

"*C'est vrai*, he is a study, so are we all. *Bien, bien,*

while the ponies rest you shall learn more of us. *Voila Narbonne, ci devant Ministre de la Guerre, l'Hermite de la chaussée d'Autin*, a cousin of Egalité, sprung from Victoire, *fille de Louis le Roi:* 'twere treason this at Versailles, 'tis truth at Junipere : his wife swore the child was her's, *taisez vous.* There are the Marquis and Marquise de la Chatre, le duc de Montmorency, and *triste* little Clarke, in silk, la princesse Hennin and Lally Tolendal, who cleared his sire's memory and reversed his attainder : he made that brilliant speech on Lafayette in *l'assemblée législatif*— there is Madame de Broglio and Sicard, and de Jaucourt, the most learned of us all, he excels Vaublanc : then there is the fair pet of Talleyrand, Mont Morin, and D'Arblay as you know, Captain of Guard when Louis fled to Varennes : *voila les Émigrés.*"

" *Les Juniperes*, Madame! *eh bien, êtes vous prêt ?*"

We are *en route* with them all to a nest of gables and chimneys that hangs on the hillside—Mickleham, once called Littleborough :

> 'The loveliest village of the plain.'

Its church of St. Michael, where by the way Fanny was married and buried, is a fine Anglo-Norman relic, with a very rich western door-arch, and in the porch an old tomb-slab inscribed with Longo-bardic letters : there are Norman arches and spandrils, and screens of more recent date, yet in perfect keeping. · In the Norbury chapel are richly ornamented tyebeams, and corbels, and bosses.

Yon ancient manor-lodge on the Mole was the home of the Stydolphs, to whom it was granted by the priests of

Mekylham, to *eat flesh on fish-days.* On the walls might be found *Asplenium viride.* The splendid demesne of Norbury rises before us, rich in beech and chestnut, and walnut also, of which one tree has yielded thirty bushels of fruit : there has bloomed the rare musk orchis, and the wild thyme, which heightens the flavour of the mutton.

The Locks received their illustrious visitors in the saloon, still displaying the taste of its master, of whom Rogers wrote in his note book,

> "Lock must do everything with taste."

The paintings of this room, so highly eulogized by Lawrence, are Barrett's landscapes, Cipriani's figures, the cattle of Gilpin, and the fruit of Pastorini. There was a dessert of Alpine strawberries and cranberries from the down, and very luscious cream, and sherbets cooled 360 feet deep within the well.

Mr. Lock, "the great and good," read to De Jaucourt his critic scraps on Milton, quoted by Johnson, while De Staël assured Madam Lock that it joyed her to have lived in *Junipere proche de Norbury,* and that she rejoiced her in the hope of spending a large week in her house.

"*Et vraiment,*" echoed de Broglie, "I cry my heart when I do leave you."

"*Ah, ce deliceux* Norbury !" chimed in D'Arblay, "*Oui, douce image de* Norbury *ma foi, bien voulez me rappelle q'une felicité vive et pure fait exister sur la terre.*"

Then Madame, pointing to a fat man who was poring over a manuscript, whispered Mrs. Lock, "Our French Cicero, madame."

"*Oui*," muttered Talleyrand, "*le plus gros des hommes sensibles.*"

The laugh of course was checked by Mrs. Lock's desire that he would read his "Strafford" to them. Lally, thus called forth, started from his reverie.

"Strafford, madame? I may blush at such a trifle. I will inflict on you my 'Pleadings for Emigrés.'"

"*Ce n'est bonne, cela,*" again muttered Talleyrand, "*un très honnête garçon, mais il est rien de plus.*"

Yet D'Arblay, in his rapture, cut a corner of his coat, "to be treasured" as he said, "with a *labella.*"

It was Madame De Staël's turn, and she gave some lines of Paradise Lost, but she paused and sighed, "*Hélas, pas assez bien!* yet I did learn to English by Milton, *eh bien,* my 'Tancred' were *plus apropos.*"

As she read on, Fanny Burney cried, "She blinks us all:" while Talleyrand raised his eyes and grumbled,

"*Bah, vous avez un chant en lisant, une monotone, n'est ce pas, bien du tout?*"

But his critique was checked in a moment: there was a buzz throughout the room, and De Staël whispered, *taisez vous donc, taisez vous,* letters from Paris be sure: look, look, Talleyrand is pale as death, and his lip is quivering: *eh bien!* he may deceive us with his tongue, but that scowl must be an awful truth: he is not acting now.

"*Diable,*" roared the accomplished senator, "Egalité of all men else to cry out 'Death,' *verrons, verrons, sacre Dieu!* Louis dead, the guillotine, and his family feeding in the Temple from one dish! *comment!—voila, voila Madame qui est ce que c'est.* Buonaparte—that boy—first consul—and

Chabôt denounce Narbonne, whose purse and power would weigh down all but the blood royal, *ma foi—ma foi !*"

"Narbonne ?" said Mr. Lock, " impossible, Monsieur, why, he is beneath my roof."

" So am I, monsieur, yet I am denounced as well—*voila*, Pitt, Fox, Sheridan, Grey, aye, e'en in your House of Deputies, Monsieur. In five short days, I must be in France : such is their graces' pleasure."

" Five days," cried Lock : " What ho ? who will ride post to Pitt ?"

" *Moi*," exclaimed Jaucourt, " Talleyrand saved. me in the Abbaye—my life for his. *Je suis prêt.*"

" Monsieur de Perigord disappeared—yet all remembered his last words : " *N'importe*, I'll rule 'em yet." Did he fulfil his threat ? the world answers " yes." On the arrest of Talleyrand, Jenkinson packed off the French *Papishes* from Juniper Hole, but D'Arblay lingered yet in Norbury, haunting the woods, and chopping off with his axe, very wantonly, the noble limbs of the forest trees.

The amphitheatre of hills inclosing the meanderings of the Mole in the vale of Mickleham forms an exquisite picture from the lofty brow of Norbury : the home-woods and combes and dingles, and the crests of Box Hill and Depedene and the Glory, are perfect. " From morn to dewy eve" we may prowl among the greenest glades prankt with oxlips, and violets, and thyme, and marjoram, breathing forth unconsciously something like the rhapsody of Harolde,—

" Here, in the sultriest season let him rest,
  Fresh is the green beneath those aged trees,

Here winds of gentlest wing will fan his breast,
From Heaven itself he may inhale the breeze.
The plain is far beneath him, let him seize
The pleasure while he can, the scorching ray
Here pierceth not impregnate with disease,
Then let his length the loitering pilgrim lay,
And gaze untir'd, the morn, the noon, the eve away."

The northern brow is looking on Thorncroft, that is
writ in the Boke of Domesday. On the bank in Lethered
is *the mansion* in which Bludworth concealed his relative,
Judge Jefferies, and in the Church sleeps Miss Chol-
mondeley, who was killed by an overturn of the Princess
of Wales' carriage. On this brow sat Fanny Burney
and General D'Arblay : he had *made insistance,* as she
said, to teach her Parisian, and she had in return, without insistance, taught him—to love her. Their very close
tête-à-tête was broken by Girardin presenting her a rose
from l'asile de Rousseau on Leith Hill, with which Fanny ·
began coquetting, and unconsciously strewing the lawn
with its petals. Marvel not at this, for D'Arblay had
just popped a very strange question that she had answered
by a smile and a sigh. She blushed, and looking on the
flower, she said, as if to change the subject: "Ah, poor
rose, how true an emblem of one as fair and beautiful as
thou, and like thee despoiled. Now guess you both of
whom I speak." Trust me her legend is worth the
telling, so I pray you one sigh of sympathy, one tear of
pity, for

The White Rose of England.

> " I knew, I knew it would not last,
>   'Twas bright, 'twas heavenly, but 'tis past."

CLOSE by the bridge of Lethered you may see a little
Inn that is known by the sign of "The Running Horse."
In the reign of the seventh Henry, the signboard of this
very humble cabaret bore this inscription,

> "Elynorr Rvmmin Alewyfe."

You may still see her portrait on the wall of the house.
It was immortalized by Skelton, subsequently the laureate
of bluff King Hal, who often came down here to angle in
the Mole.   He tells us that,

> " She dwelt in Sothray,
>   In a certain Stede,
>   By side Letherede."

There is an old book too, "The Pithy, Pleasant, and
Profitable Works of Master Skelton, 1568," thus prefaced :
" Here folloy the dyuers Balletys, and Dyties salacyous
divisd by Master Skelton, Laureat."   Nell's portrait is on
the title, and this is her motto,

> "When Skelton wore the lawrell crowne
>   My ale put all the Alewyves downe.

The eulogy is scribbled in a set of doggrel rhymes,
vulgar and indelicate to excess.   A long rigmarole of two
sheets and a half, 4to, running to eighty stanzas on the

bouquet and virtues of her ale. The seven "Passus" finish with

"Skelton's ghost to the reader."

One evening, in the Tudor reign, two gentlemen were engaged in deep converse at the door of this cabaret, while the buxom hostess stood by in waiting, and she was constantly curtseying low with a very coquettish smirk, as they chucked her under the chin.

"Your counsel is a puzzle, noble Surrey," said the younger of the two : "my hope call you it ? I do believe you are jesting."

"It is your only hope," responded the other : "look you, Edward, here is the third counterfeit turned up. Simnel, 'tis true, who aped your lordship, is raised from the scullery to be the King's own falconer, but there is Ralph Wilford the cordwainer's son, just now hung at St. Thomas Waterings, and now comes on the third, this Jew brat, Osbeck, for that is his real name, starting up to challenge your rightful claim. Now the only way to save yourself is to uphold this Peterkin or 'Pretio' Perkyn, as the girls call him, coward though he be, and i' faith you owe him a lift for plotting with Digby for you, when you were both in limbo yonder."

"So I must be a cypher then, and Perkyn, that I know not, graced with *my* crown !"

"Crown, fudge ! why old Stanley found that bauble on a hedge in Bosworth Field but t'other day: the *throne*, man —follow my counsel, I will kick you up to the kingship, my word on't."

"Read me your riddle."

"Thus—King Henry may defy your giant arm: let Perkin e'en play King for a little hour or two, and you may floor the puppet with a maid's finger, and then, up with the white rose at once. ' Show him at the cross, he'll take but for awhile, — see you not how like he is to Edward, and whispers float in the air that the royal rake was, night by night, at Osbeck with his fair mother, Katheryn de Faro : no marvel he's as handsome as his real or royal father, when cast in such a mould."

" Yet I would fain—

"Hear me out: there's Madame of York calls him her nephew, the White Rose of England—him, forsooth, not *you*, Earl of Warwick — gives him thirty body-guards, and foists him on old Margaret of Burgundy, who is to fling her new *ydoll* in the arms of Charles of France : creditme, she is a very Juno, a goddess of *mischief*.   Now do you give the land-louper but a lift, and then the gibbet."

" But how if young Edward still breathes, 'tis buzz'd about—"

"Pooh, Deighton and Forrest and Tyrrel take oath of their *bolstering* in London Tower, and their *earthing* by the Bloody Gate, though faith, they were but dead monkeys with their tails off, ha, ha ! Farewell, and 'ware Effingham, Warwick,—my William lacks advancement, High Admiral of the Red Rose, gramercy,—and keep your ring there out of sight, 'twill betray your royalty,—good night."

The most killing leer ever lighted up Nell's face when she was *alone* with a gentleman, and as Warwick kissed her cherries, she murmur'd softly, "Such a gentleman as you, 'tis a glory sure for Nell Rummyng to be—"

"Kiss'd by a lord," said Warwick, as he smacked her ruddy lip again, while Nell curtsey'd low and muttered, "For what we have received, the Lord make us truly thankful: but here is Master Skelton, my lord."

"So, *tête-à-tête* with Surrey, Nell," muttered the new-comer: "may I be bold with you, royal Warwick, and counsel you to cut him from this hour. Your ear, Prince Arthur and I were sporting but yesternight, and in his closet lay an order to attaint this Howard—"

"How say you!"

"Why, carried he not the crown at two coronations, Henry knows it from his Dam—look ye here, 'tis a woman's hand: 'To the King, youre faythfull newe bed-woman and humbell modyr, Margaret R.'"

"So," said Warwick, reading, "from Madame of Richmond: when she writes thus, she means to sting—she hopes 'to get God by the foot, as she had the devil by his taylo.'"

"Joke an you will, my lord, but know the cornets are abroad, and even the godson of Edward, as you are, must wear a loyal brow before Lancaster, so let your rose blush red for the nonce: as for your friends, there's Pole and Stanley in limbo, Humphrey of Stafford hung, drawn and quartered, and Walter Geddynges stark and stiff in Fingham aisle yonder. Who may be next? Aye, bite your own nails, Sir Earl, an you will; but snap not at

Richmond, or you'll rue it. An you would hope his favour, trick yourself in masquery by this 'Boke of Curtusye,' thus: 'A clene sherte and breche, a pettycotte, a doublette, a long cotte, a stomacher, and hosen, and socks, and schone.' Such was Richmond's own garb when, at his coronation, he and Toisson d'Or buckled the garter on King Philip at St. George's."

But the magpie's mouth was stopped by Warwick calling for his groom, and starting for Slyfield, and by Eleanor's screaming out, "not here, not here, fair sirs, not a corner or a loft for love or money: why Margaret Milk-duck, you foggy fat, you loosefish, show the gentles to the Crown."

"The Crown, nay we're safer here, hey, Heron?" cried the first cavalier who enter'd, "so a bicker of your ale, sweet dame—aye, spicy by the Lord."

"Choice," said the other, "so for a night or two."

"Nay master," said Nell, "'tis time to close, 'twere curfew, hark, thou look out,—the lights are dous'd at lynk-house, and the cresset blazing on the tower, and—"

But the cavalier slipped a ring on Nell's finger, and silenced her lips by a kiss. "Certes," said he, "if Des-mond saw us beating up for quarters thus, the laugh were his when we meet him at Shene."

"What, would you to Richmond, cavaliers?" said Skelton, peering from his corner.

"Nay, to Shene, knave, that were the better name. We are for the House of Bethlehem, my master, the Priory I think they call it."

"So, so!" said Skelton aside, "I smell a rat, I will try

these losels," and then, winking on Nell,—"Come, the
very best of your tonynge, blithe hostess : I challenge you,
fair gentlemen, a toast—let me see—aye, Alyce Dacre."

"Alyce Dacre," cried the cavaliers, "what, the pearl of
Lethered ! the white rose-bush bears not a fairer flower.
Alyce Dacre !"

Skelton took his cue at once, and as the strangers sucked
in the ale, he scribbled a note, and Nell sealed it with the
ring.

"A signet, hey," whispered the rhymester saucily, "and
what, prythee, gavest thou my Lord of Warwick in change
for this, Nell, the old itch for royal lips, hey, thou wanton?"

"You make me blush, Master Skelton—you are out,
sir, in your reckoning, 'twas the cavalier."

"I guessed it, the cordwainers' clique, be sure : the
Court must know it, aye, and to-night. I'll wear the ring
an hour for thy sake, my pretty Nell, and now send me
the scout for Richmond, quick !"

The strangers had caught the word and exchanged very
significant looks : in a moment they had changed their
minds, so, calling for a guide, they drew on their cloaks.

"So you will onwards, my masters," said Skelton, bowing
very low, "trust, me 'twere a grief indeed to part with
friends so soon : yet, if you *are* for Shene, it is myself
will fetch you agoing on your way as far as,—let me see—
aye, the Red Rose, a'nt please ye."

"The Red Rose does *not* please us, fellow."

"Peace, Heron, peace," whispered the cavalier, "thy
blustering will betray us—close thy lips, or we are lost.
We are beholden to thee, friend, lead on."

Then, with a smack on Nell's lip, the cavalier and his equerry followed Skelton from the cabaret.

Master Edward Slyfield of that ilk was "a stout esqvier who allwayo sett Gode's feare before his eyes."

So is he sketched on his slab in the Slyfield chapel in Great Bookham Church.

It was in this very sanctuary for the wayworn that a noble-looking creature had fallen prostrate—a woman, feeble and foot-sore, her garb being most discordant with her seeming destiny. Her perfect form was attired in the richest, tho' now most tattered costume, and a faded tartan was clasped by a fine rose pearl at the breast. Some lofty mystery, 'twas clear, hung around her : for, at her feet, lay a dwarf, in motley suit, and wearing a Glengarry hoof, whose eyes were ever turning in adoration on his mistress.

The squire of high degree had discovered her in his chapel, and, after listening with wonder to her story and confession, he raised her with an air of courtesy more than her garb might warrant, and bore her off in his carriage to Slyfield.

On that very evening the richly carved and chiselled staircase was lined with lacqueys, and the chambers were strewed with flowers and rushes for the nonce, for there was high revel in the hall. The sunbeams were streaming across the noble gardens, and through the huge arched window, gilding the deeply bossed ceiling and the fine Ionic mantelpiece. There was a gathering of the high-born at Slyfield that night, Estcotts and Lelyes, Howards and Dacres, and Scynt Johns, and the Codringtons from Nonsuch, and Warwick in a black velvet mask.

Just as the lady was concealed by Slyfield behind a japanned screen in the oriel, there was a sudden hush and pause in the revel, and Skelton, in a rich tabard, stalked in most consequentially, for, like other court fools, he was free to all.

The strangers stood aloof, astounded at such splendour in a hostelrie, while Skelton, raising his wand, welcomed them to the Red Rose of Lancaster !

"And what's the crotchet now, Master Skelton ? " asked Slyfield.

"Marry, the court fool, I—know'st not we have *carte blanche* for all our folly, an thou call'st it so, and faith the fool may find you sport in plenty, Master Slyfield : for these are the mummers of our masque."

"And what your theme, your plot, hey ? "

"It hath the court smack, Master Slyfield, ' The White Rose, or Who'll be King.' "

No wonder the guests were startled at this sally : the cavalier whispered his equerry : but Heron only shook his head, while the dwarf on tiptoe plucked Skelton by the tabard, and Warwick was seen to steal abashed from the room.

"Methinks this were too close a joke," said Slyfield, frowning : " we've coats of all colours here."

Skelton heeded him not, but took a roll of paper and fashioned a quaint conical cap, and, pinning on it a white rose, placed it on the cavalier's head, and cried, " All hail, King Richard, of that name the fourth. Oyez, oyez, a thousand crowns on Henry's head."

"Treason, treason," echoed through the chamber, while

Slyfield was supporting the lady shivering on his arm, and Dacre exclaimed, "This is rank treason: Master Skelton, I arrest thee."

"Nay, call off your bulldogs, Sir Justice," said Skelton, "'twere a wrong scent, sir, what think ye of this rag— 'Richard, by the grace of God, greeting, he who takes Henry Tydder, one thousand pounds and lands to the yearly value of one hundred marks to him and his heirs for ever'? Aye, thou mayst well blush, sir King, yet methinks the white lily might grace thy cheek the better. But the joke is passed now, so listen to the fool: base Fleming, King Henry repays thee for thy love in kind—the cornets, ho!"

The guards were in the chamber in a moment, and tore the fool's cap from his head. Perkyn Warbeck saw his game was up. The light had flashed on Master Slyfield now, and, while the dwarf was pricking Skelton's legs with his dagger, he led the lady from her screen.

"One act of justice, Master Warbeck, one act ere thou dost abdicate: honour thy wife."

While Perkyn fell on his knee, Lady Katheryn Gordon rushed from Slyfield's arm, and, sobbing wildly, fell on his bosom.

"Thy wife, aye, in life and death, York," she cried. "Quick, quick, Richmond will grant my prayer for pardon."

"Nay, lady," said Slyfield, "this were beyond our venue—even the king himself were nought in this, his peers must judge him now."

From such slight incident in yon poor cabaret, "began

the fatall daye of the death of Perkyn Warbeck and
Edward, Earle of Warwick, to approache." Yet even in
the deepest dungeon of the Tower there was a bright
planet shining : the dark destiny of Perkyn only brought
out in more lustrous light the devotion of the White Rose.
Even when the confession of his Flemish birth set him
"in the stocks in Chepe," his head lay on her breast.
When Warwick suborned the warders to slay the governor
and proclaim Perkyn king, her prayer averted the crimes.
" He was strictly watched," writes Stow, "altho he seemed
to goe at libertie, lest through the slippery arts of his
tempting speech and bihaviour, hee might vanish into
forraine parts and raise freshe stormes in England." All
this while his wife was his guardian angel, and when
he was drawn on a hurdle to Tyburn, and hung with
O'Water, who had proclaimed him king in Ireland, there
was Katheryn Gordon at his side.

The judgment of the Earl of Oxford was the doom of
Edward of Warwick, the last of the Crown Plantagenets :
he suffered on Tower-hill and was buried in Bisham Abbey,
and not till then did Ferdinand of Spain decree the
betrothal of Katheryn of Arragon and Arthur Prince of
Wales.

And Katheryn Gordon was now the only White Rose
left in England, and, being of the blood-royal of Scotland,
by this name she was honoured to the hour of her death,
even by Henry Tudor himself, who, indeed, would fain
have been her lover. The blot on her scutcheon was
waived, and young Somerset records that, at the marriage
of Margery Tudor with James of Scotland, Katheryn

Gordon took rank next the royal family. After a time, she married Sir Matthew Caradoc of Wales, and her only child was Lady Herbert of Ewyas, whose lord was the ancestor of the Earls of Pembroke. The tomb of the White Rose of England may still be seen in Herbert's aisle in Swansea.

When we review the Protæan group of friends that revolved like satellites around William Lock, we may believe that now and then a bookworm would creep down to Norbury. It is hereabout that we should be sure to meet him, and if we listen a few moments to his lore, he will discourse to us thus :—

The sylvan glades of Norbury are blended with history of the very olden time. Hereabouts the High Comitia of 666 were held by Frithwald, the first Bretwalda, sub-regulus or viceroy of Sudseaxnarice, Sudergerne, Sudrie, Suthria, Sutherlye, Southsex or Supprzeland, and Cogibundus fixed the seat of his Segontii, and the Regni of Champagne fresh from Chichester, and the half-savage Cænomagni. Those who have dived deeply into the chronicles will be ever haunted in solitudes like these by the memory of many a learned scribe whose book has charmed them with the choicest English legends. It may be of Gildas, called Sapiens, son of Can, a Strathclyd Briton of the sixth century, of Nennius of the seventh, of Beda Venerabilis of the eighth, whose *Boc ledene* King Alfred the truth-teller translated into *Englisc*. Then there were Jeffry of Monmouth, alias Gruffudd ab Arthur, the foster-brother of Saxo-Grammaticus. His work was "a history of the kings of Great Britain from first to last,

from Brute to Cadwallader, son of Cadwallo: it was
"yntytuld Brut of Brenhyned," and was compiled chiefly
from a tome found in Brittany, by Walter Calenius or
Mapes, Archdeacon of Oxford and Bishop of Exeter: and
it was partly translated from the Welch copy of Guttyn
Owain, the book of Basingwerke Abbey. Then Asser or
Esser, who wrote the life of Alfred, Ethelwerd, Matthew
of Westminster, Hardynge, who fought with Hotspur at
Holmden, Fabyan, Rastell ("The pastime of the People,
the cronycles of dyuers realmys, and most specyalle of
the realme of Englonde breuvely cōpylyd and emprynted
in Chepesyde at the sygne of the Mearemayd next to
Pollysgate cᵐ privelegio"), Grafton, Alfred of Beverley,
Ingulphus, Abbot of Croyland, Richard of Cirencester,
William of Malmsbury, Henry of Huntingdon, Simeon
of Durham, Roger of Hovedon, William of Newburgh,
Gervase of Tilbury, Caradoc of Llancaroon ("Chronicon
Walliæ"), Polydor Vergil, Rapin, Speed, Stow, Camden.

In daring without leave to marshal on our pedantic page
this awful phalanx of British sages, we must not forget
the most precious chronicle of all, *Domesday, the Boke of
Judgment*, the gospel of the eleventh century, now treasured in the Exchequer Chamber in Westminster (Liber
Vintoniæ, being the *Winton* copy of Henry the First).

Apropos, in this "Great Terrar," as Ingulphus terms it,
is noted the glory of the chalk hills, this very *Druid's
grove*. Like the cedars of Lebanon, it may be a group of the
real scions of the forest primæval that was in leaf when
Mesech, fourth son of Japhet, came into Britaine. Com-
pared with these, the Parliament Oak, aneath which Edward

and John sat in council, were a mere sapling. To the
dullest wight that wanders thitherward there will be
inspiration in such a scene.

"These are the haunts of meditation, these
    The scenes, where antient bards th' inspiring breath
    Ecstatic felt, and, from the world retired,
    Conversed with angels and immortal forms."

It is with this inspiration we ourselves crave a grace,
while we jot down, still from the pedant's lips, a legend

of Egland Gildas.   Yet remember we dare not challenge
your faith in its truthfulness, as who should say—

> " Rede me frynde, and be not wrothe,
>   For I saye nothynge but the trothe."

The truth is this, for know ye that the chronicles of
Eld clash in many and many a chapter, and are too often,
we confess, gilded or shadowed by myth and fable.   So
do we pray you to spare your frown and take for what it
is worth—

The Mystery of Saynte Eleyne.

> " Ytt was both good and yonge,
>   Of hye wysdome and womanly conninge,
>   And these with all the fayrest yt men knewe,
>   More angelyke than womannyshe of hewe."

WHEN the third century was half spent, Cojedunus,
the lieutenant of Rome, held court in Cissanceaster, the
Roman Regnum, our own Anglian Chichester.

The Celts and Cymri in crossing Gaul into Britain
conferred on the Cantii and South Saxons, in the mari-
time counties of Kent and Sussex, a polish (*vide* Diodorus
and Pliny), and on the Segontii of Belgium, who settled
in Surrey.   The Britons, indeed, when Cæsar landed,
blended with the Gauls in birth and language and
manners, yet the soldiers, and even some of the more
noble, were *painted* like the Picts, tattooed with the
blue woad-y-glâs, so that the nudes somewhat resembled

Australians. In the interior, however, since the advent
of Agricola, A. D. 78, some wore the *braccæ* and the *gwn.*

Now Coyll, Coel or Cœlus was King of the Trinobantes,
glorying also in the titles of Erl of Gloucester, Duke of
Cornwall and of Caer Colvin, Colchester or Camelodunum.
His surname was Cold-Heburg, and he was sung in later
ballads as "old King Cole," though he was aught but
"a merry old soul" when he returned from the wall of
Antoninus to Caer Colvin.

It chanced that Allectus had killed Carausius, so Ascle-
piodotus killed Allectus, and he was killed in turn by
Coyll, for he had appealed to Rome against his blood
relations, a fashion of the wild Britons, often to their cost.

Constancyus the senator, called Flavius Constantius
Chlorus, from his yellow paleness, had just reduced Spain,
and he was sent to amend the ethnology, policy and reli-
gion of this "ultima Thule." He embarked at Gesso-
niacum or Boulogne, and landed at Portsmouth, and made
a road for his march from Regnum to Noviomagus—by
Halnaker, the Devil's ditch, Slindon and Bignor, where
he rested and built a villa most complete, even in our day
the finest tesselated relic of Patrician Rome in England.
Thence they marched along the *Proluses* or British road,
based on soft turf for the chariot wheels, into Surrey, and
halted on Ranmoor Common, for the vergobrets or heads
of tribes were hanging on his flank, and there Constancyus harangued his forces, for, like Cæsar and Hannibal,
he was a scholar. "So we are now in Albin, eastward of
Jerna, and close to the Belgæ and the Cantii, but where
is this Coyll the cruel? the heathen shirks us!"

Now Coyll had been besieged by the Roman cohorts in Caer Colvin, and dreading the power of Constancyus he opened his gates and sallied forth to meet him. The Romans were yet encamped, when came a herald to the hills, who unfolding a white banner cried aloud : " Hail, noble senator! Coyll waits your pleasure in Coed Nordburie, and craves conference with the glory of Rome."

" Conference, knave! we are armed for vengeance. Go tell thy master so."

" Mercy, noble Roman" ('twas the Druid spoke), "mercy may better grace thee than revenge : be it a bloodless peace. My lord the King is cut even to the soul by his kinsman's death : it is a thorn in his breast, Lo! the priests are prompt for any sacrifice Constancyus wills. Regard us, noble Roman, for we are Peace. Is it not even in your annals we once met Cæsar with slings and spears, and our covinus studded with scythes : look on us now, our chariots are peace, — the Mœda and Essedum."

" We tread not on the worm," replied Constancyus : "back to your leader, but we make no pledge, we sit in judgment here : be Coyll but true, we sheathe sword and close the fane of Janus."

Around the outposts of the Britons' stockades and watlings, stuffed with straw, were many a straggler, naked and painted and hung with bone-toys, and ragged girls, painted with devils, and with hair dishevelled, and half mad with their *uisge*, were shaking their firebrands like a gang of fiends, and brandishing spears and jingling bells to scare the Roman steeds. Beneath huge oaks, cut in the form of a cross, were the numerals Y. H. Z. also displayed, so that the sacred symbol of the Saviour, at the dawn of the conversion in Britain, was blended with that of Belinus and Taramis. Other soldiers were at games for coins of Carausius, bright and newly stamped with two emperors joining hands. Coyll was in conference with his Dryws in the grove of yews as the van of the Romans came up. Constancyus, despotic as he was, revered devotion even in a heathen, and he stood aloof, surrounded soon by Gaels and Scottish deserters, who, with rings round their painted loins, were practising with their rattling spears and with their studded *Cat*, which they threw with force and drew back by a thong.

Coyll sat like a Highland laird of the last century, by his cromleh, wearing an *Ysgynt*, or leopard's skin: his tiny battle-axe was of brass, the islemen not having yet found their tin and copper. His men, decked in braslets and torques, bore spears of black flint or of bone (now often found), set in a shaft of yew, and round targets full of brass nails. As his servitors heralded the Romans to his presence, he rose and bowed and said—

"Hail, Consul! we seek peace with the Romans,—our Vates has pronounced, and Helen shall be our Dove of Peace."

"King," answered Constancyus, "we accept your pledge. The fame of holy Helen hath been wafted to Rome, we seek no brighter hostage, a soul like hers would consecrate even a pagan rite."

"On then to the *Teml*," cried the King, "our rites await thy presence."

In the *Arlais* or temple stood the holy altar, and on it flamed the sacred fire, like that of the Persians and the Hebrews. A priest stood by the *Carn-Kound*, a crossed heap, like the carneian of the Greeks, and cried, " The sun is now in Taurus, and lo ! the sixth day of the moon is nigh." On the altar was laid the secret alphabet of the *Ogham*, invented, it is believed, by Hercules.

Around stood the three orders of *Drws* or *Deorbe*, an Erl bearing before them the written *Beth enis nion* that was got from Little Britain—the Arch-Druid in white, his robe looped through a ring of purest gold on the shoulder : the bard in azure, wearing a gold cap fringed with oak leaves—and the *Ovydd, Vates, Embages, Hargazer* or prophet. In a circle beyond were grouped the slaves, Picts and servitors, together with the white bulls for the sacrifice.

The Ovydds opened the rites with this chaunt :—

" We are Druids, witness our oaks, our holiness, our wisdom, our magic words.

" By the bright circle of the golden sun,
By the bright courses of the errant moon,
By the mysterious zodiac's burning girth,
By the dread potency of evening star."

The Arch-Druid then bled the white bull with a lance, and laid the golden bowls on the carn. Then glared the lightning athwart the temple,—the flash of a gunpowder which, like that of the priests of Delphi, they kept a profound secret. This was the *De lanach*, " the flame of God," and *Druilanach*, that you may read of in the rhymes of Dargo, the son of the Druid of Bel.

Again the Ovydds chaunted, " Hail to thee, *Taranus*

(Jove, Thor, or Thunderer), hail *Satales*, (Mercury), hail *Ardurena* (Diana), all hail Belinus : say, is it peace ?"

Two milk-white bulls were then led on wreathed with white roses, and the Arch-Druid proclaimed, "The new year is at hand, gather the mistletoe."

The priest then took the golden sickle, and clomb the oak, and cut the bough, and the Druid received it in a white woollen cloth,—and then was brought in the *Anguinium*, a nide of serpents' eggs.

"Why, proh Jupiter, royal King !" cried Constancyus, "this is true patrician."

"*En patriarchus, en Druidos*," whispered the Druid.

There was now deep and solemn silence for a moment, until Coyll, standing erect, cried out, "Druids, tell the noble Consul how speaketh the oracle."

The Arch-Druid answered, " *Wyf syw, wyf dryw :* I am a sage, I am a Druid : peace, peace, no war !"

A shout of "Peace ! peace !" pealed through the woods of Nordburic, and echoed among the hills and along the valley.

"Consul," cried Coyll, "sackcloth and ashes in this high congress were but a light and wanton mockery of thine imperial Rome : when she gives the kiss of peace to Britain, we will grace the gift with a nobler offering of our own blood."

"Blood ! thy blood !" exclaimed Constancyus, "Heaven forbid ! The gore of the battlefield may consecrate the turf it stains, the gods themselves may smile on it, but they loathe the bloodshed of the innocents : even so teach the apostles of the Nazarene."

"Belinus, the god of wisdom, teacheth us, Consul: we offer the richest and purest thing in all the land,—the daughter of our heart."

"Heaven of its mercy, King, thy daughter! 'Tis written, 'if a wife kill her husband she shall lick the flames, and if a father doom his daughter——' look to your law, Sir King!"

"A father's will *is* law, Roman: a Briton hath power of life and death over wife and daughter: say, prophet, is it so?"

The Vates stood forth and cried aloud, "*A fyn daw dydderfed*—What God wills, so be it."

"Then the white bulls, if blood must flow," cried the senator.

"It is *mine* to decree," said Coyll, "and behold she comes, the brightest maid in all the land, Saynte Eleyne! Look in the *Illywarck ken*,—'tis writ, 'Coyll hath four-and-twenty sons wearing the golden torque,'—they are dead, *all*, Roman, and this my only child: she is called 'prosperous,' nay, she is more, she is Britaine. Tell me, what did the heathen Abram, the faithful: bound he not Isaac on the altar? My faith shall beggar his, for I am Belus, Apollo Carneus I,—so the angel of my bosom on the *skearn*."

"Her's be the glory that John beheld in the Apocalypse in Patmos!"

Coyll shook off the grasp of Constancyus. "My oath! my oath! before the judgment-seat of Belus: like Jephthah, judge of Israel, in the books of your Vates, swore I, Coyll, to offer to Belus what first did greet me. The man of Israel repented: I *glory*, Roman. Yet Eleyne dieth not.

Lo, in yon white thing she hath nursed from fawnhood, her namesake, *Elain*, her soul will rest, and Eleyne still breathe and lie in Coyll's bosom. Hither, Sir Erl !"

At the word, an Erl brought the doe in his arms, over burning coals, his feet being smeared with sacred ointment: and then glided in, like a thing of radiant light, Eleyne herself, her jewels gleaming like planets on her fair body.

> "So looked the star of Beauty's Queen,
> Soft o'er a sky of storm."

"Thou art ready, bright one !" he said, as Eleyne stood by the knees of Coyll, holding aloft the symbol of the Cross.

"Father !" she cried, in a tone of inspiration, "I have dreamed of this, and I am Christian. Look! 'tis of the true Cross, of aspen made—a miracle,—for as I passed in yonder aspen-grove, the leaves did tremble, aye, for very shame, and then came the vision of the lifting up of the *Soter* of the world, and of his birthplace when Kymbelyn was king. It will be mine to find the cross on Golgotha and build a church and hostelrie over the manger, and Eleyne will be *Stabularia Hostelrice Mayer* of the Church of Calvary. See ye the Star of Bethlehem on my brow ? It is the life itself of Eleyne."

The golden knife gleamed in the hand of the Ovydd, but his arm was arrested, he knew not how.

"'Tis Claudia holds thine arm !" whispered the maiden, "hark ! her cmyn hymn, '*Joli Christ celi*'—that's for the sacrifice."

The white bulls kneeled before the karn as Constancyus clasped her hand.

"Profane not!" cried the Arch-Druid, and the golden knife was close to the Roman breast, but Eleyne rushed between the Ovydd and the Consul. And then she took a tiny basket from the neck of her fawn.

"Here," she murmured, "is yew, slivered in the Eclipse, that is *Yod, Iota:* here is elm, *Aleph*, and here *Beth.* Now—now to Calvary!" And she laid her symbol on the breast of Coyll, who shivered and fell to the ground, and groaned in his agony—

"Thou art not mine, Eleyne, thou art Christian : I did steal thee from the hostelrie for sacrifice—now the fire of Belus—in my own heart—I am dying, Eleyne —dying!"

In that hour Coyll slept with his fathers. The Roman soldiers closed around, and Constancyus folded Eleyne to his bosom, and hailed her, "*Venerabilis piissima Augusta.*" So peace was between Rome and *Flavia Cæsariensis*, and Constancyus, by his rites with Eleyne, sealed his conversion to Christianity. He was crowned King in the minster of *Ebora*, or York, and struck that medal inscribed *memoria felix.* And thus Christianity dawned in Britain.

It is written, moreover, in the Chronicles, how Constancyus went to *Iseur* (Saviour), and saw the holy vision in Aldborough : and how in due time was born Constantine the Great. His birthplace is yet a dilemma, whether it were Ebora, or Caer Coel, or Diepanum, that Constancyus named Heliopolis, in Nicomedia : Ammianus, and

Gibbon, gleaning from Eutropius and Procopius, fix on *Dacia.* He was, however, crowned in York, and after eleven years was there proclaimed Emperor, and went to Rome to avenge Maxentius, and became the first Christian Emperor of the World.

And it is writ by Fabyan how "Heline found the cross with three nailes that owre Lorde was nayl'd with," and how the Emperor "put two of the sayd nayles in the bridell of hys hors, which he used in batayll, and the thirde he caste as witnesseth Seynt Ambrose in a *sawalowe* of the sea called *Mare Adriaticum,* which swalowe was before that tyme so peryllous that vnnethes any shyp escapyd that daunger."

Thus endeth the mystery of Seynte Eleyne.

We linger yet in Norbury, a spell is on us. These sable yews, that form so fine a contrast with the russet green of the beeches, are the very Titans or grand crosses of their order, for, unlike the beech the oak and the ash, that *succeed each other,* the yew is perpetual in its soil. Yet they are but an atom of the gigantic yew-wood, despoiled long ago for the choice bows that played havoc at Creci and Azincourt, even as the chestnuts of this valley, cut down in the æra of the Tudors for gunstocks, when Sylva Evelyn again brought them into fashion. Even the feathered denizens that are now haunting these ancient woods of Norbury—the cuckoos—why may they not be in direct descent from the eggs of those very birds that inspired the first English chaunt, "The Song of Summer" of the Anglo-Saxon?

" Sumer is icumen in,
  Loude sing cucu.
Groweth sed and bloweth med,
And springth the wde nu,
     Sing cucu.
Awe bleteth after lamb,
Strouth after calve cu,
Bulluc sterteth, bucke verteth,
Merrie sing cuccu, cuccu, cuccu."

But we must not forget Camilla. It was in the golden autumn that we were threading the Norbury woods, while the dotted chestnut moth (*glea rubiginea*) was feeding on the scarlet yew-berries along this very footway of Fanny Burney, as she trudged between Norbury and Camilla Lacy. At the moment as we syllabled her name, a childish treble was trolling a very simple ditty, about the time—

" When merry went the click clack,
The shuttle and the plough,
And the honest man could live
By the sweat of his brow."

The voice was of an octogenarian, hacking wood, and he had looked on Fanny Burney in her girlhood. His ruddy cheek was a May-flower in December, his name, we believe, was May, and he was born in Mickleham yonder on a May morning, and he had fondled in his arms Master William Lock, who never talked of goodness, but always did it, and who, in after years, doted so on Miss Fanny Burney, bless her (he raised his hat). Ah, master, she *was* a woman! I was at her wedding, sir, and her burying (again he lifted his hat), aye, when she had

weathered a matter of ninety years. To light on one
who had chopped wood with General D'Arblay was a
rare incident, and, in our sentimental mood, it was like a
voice from the tomb to chat with one who had chatted
with Fanny Burney in her sunny days, and it haunted
us all the way to her home of Camilla Lacy, in the
hamlet of Westhamble hard by, and indeed we forgot
awhile all about Bishop Odo, and the Michaelhams, and
Aperdeles, and Clares, Despensers, and Lyndeus, and
Stydolffs, and Howards—once the illustrious lords of its
Manor—and we passed listlessly by the relics of an old
chapel cell, built after the alienation of the Priory of
Reigate by Westhamble.

The house of Lady Cavendish is not, however, the
rustic home of Madame D'Arblay: that, humble as it
was, was consecrated by poesy and genius. For there
consorted the learned and the lofty: and Fanny was ever
happy, for she was ever truthful, smiling on like a mere
child of nature, even when she was shining one of the
most brilliant planets in the galaxy of letters.

Fanny's honeymoon and the birth of her bambino
were at *Phenice*, on the hill,—and when they flitted to
Camilla, Lally Tolendal and Princess Hennin were her
cronies: and there came Mrs. Barbauld, and her sick
brother Aiken, with his MS. "Evenings at Home:" and
there, too, the emigrant Count de Narbonne found a
peaceful asylum. But soon shadows came down on this
humble home: one morning D'Arblay learned that all
his property was sold in France for the nation, and that
Talleyrand was in the Convention, with Robespierre, Tallien,

and Marat. And then, with 120*l.* a year, they chose for
a time to feed almost on hermit's fare, yet Fanny smiled
it off with a chuckle: " 'Twill make you laugh to see, though
cry to hear."

Mount we now another magnificent hill, Denby's, now
crowned by Mr. Cubitt's palatial villa. There once stood
a plain farmhouse, which was *beautified* by Jonathan
Tyers from the profits of Vauxhall. There was then a
dark wood, and a pair of skulls on pedestals, and a Christian and a sceptic, and Truth treading on a mask, with
verses by Soame Jennings. And here Tyers aired his
London people—Mrs. Billington, Mrs. Bland, Violante
the danseuse, and Faux the conjuror, and Cadman the
rope-walker, who was killed at Shrewsbury, and Frank
Hayman, who, with Hogarth, painted up Vauxhall.

'Tis sixty years since. *Polesdon,* that lies beyond those
leafy dingles of Ranmoor, was at that æra haunted by
creatures of the same order, but of a very different genus.
They were a clique of those choice spirits of the Regent's
court, that sported the blue-and-buff livery of the Whigs
of the Georgian æra. We know not if the " finest gentleman " himself was ever here to honour the symposia of his
satellite, but as we linger about the grounds of Polesdon,
in solitude,

> " Fond memory brings the light
> Of other days around us."

It is in her magic mirror we see reflected the forms of
a very choice brace of bacchanals, ensconced in the dining-
room : so, while we listen to

The Georgians,

"Let me throw on a bottle of champagne."

"ENCORE, encore!" It was the anniversary of the Beef Steak Club, and old Charles Morris was the guest of Richard Brinsley Sheridan. Looking on the scene, wo might almost believe that the shade of Anacreon was being feasted by that of Cicero at Tusculum. Before the veteran song-writer were the silver bowl and golden cup given him by the Beef Steak Club and the Harmonics, of whose symposia he was the very idol.

He had brought them from Brockham, for he never dined on this day without them. And now, after quaffing deeply from the golden cup, he sung out a verse from the rhymes he wrote in his green old age of ninety years—

> "When my spirits are low, for relief and delight
> I still place your splendid memorials in sight,
> And call to my muse, when care strives to pursue,
> Bring the steaks to my memory, the bowl to my view."

"Well carolled, Charles, yet faith your chaunt doth smack somewhat of the childish treble. Anacreon in his dotage, hey? but now warble, warble one of Molly Dacre, you were so sweet upon : but first, who is she, a Lais or a Phryne, hey, my bonny Charley?"

"A Galatea in beauty, a Penelope in virtue."

"And you her Acis or Ulysses, hey?"

"William Scott was one, Charles Morris the other, for

we were both dying for Lady Clarke : here is her last
billet, I wear it to warm the heart of an old man,
heigho, heigho ! "

" Pish, pish, fling away your cypress, boy, our wreath the
myrtle and the rose : are we not Roman and Greek for
the night ? "

" Aye, aye ! bravo ! bravo ! the true old genuine
Georgians yet, and this, Carlton House, hey Dick ? "

" Aye, was not George a blood of the first water, hey ?
Gad's life, a Hart-royal, boy, a buck of ten tine. Re-
memberest thou Charley Bloomfield and Tierney, and
jolly-boy Thornton, and Hanger, and Stanyer the parson,
and Knighton, and Jockey of Norfolk, and, ' though last
not least,' our brother of York ? Faith, you threw them
all in convulsions that night ! yet little Tommy Moore
beat you hollow, by the beard of Anacreon ! Gads me,
how the royal eyes and mouth twinkled and watered
at Fanny of Timmol, and how York hiccupped Mary Anne
Clark !—halloo, snoozing Charles : time was when Fanny
would have kept you awake : what ho, Molly Dacre."

Morris only answered by snoring an echo, "Molly Dacre."

" Fine times those, old boy : let me think, aye, 'twas my
Begum Speech night—why, Charley, you're worse than
Thurlow, who snored through Kemble's address of Rolla—
'twas in '98, yet the old cynic bravo'd Hamlet,—faugh !

" Well, well, no matter, ' Pitt's adjournment on the
Begum Speech would make two immortals,' so said
Charley Howard : what ho, rouse thee Morris, awake,
arise, or be for ever d—'hem."

And Sheridan dashed cold water in his face, and as it

streamed over his lips he grumbled forth, "Faugh, cold water: the first time for months. Maraschino, Maraschino."

And as he gulped the liquor, he roared out—

> "Then what those think, who water drink,
>   Of those old rules of Horace,
> I won't now show, but this I know,
>   His rules do well for Morris."

And he snored again spite of Sheridan's grunt—

> "If any pain or care remain,
>   Why drown it in ——"

"Brandy, brandy," shouted Morris.

"Well put in, Macheath: ha, ha, my Stafford cup reeking with Regent's punch—Nector, by Hebe's lips— nothing like brandy : why, when George was waxing low, or Fitzherbert turned her heel, brandy always cured him. Let me recollect, aye, the time winter, scene Somerset House, enter the Royal George shaking like an aspen bough. My Stafford cup were too much, so a rummer, for I did not care to fuddle the heir-apparent, or, by the Lord, another splash at the White House. But for the proof spirit, hark ye, Charley.

> "The prince came in and said 'twas cold,
>   Then put to his head the rummer,
> Till Swallow after Swallow came,
>   When he pronounced it Summer."

"Ha, ha, ha—what now, sirrah, ride out will she ? "

"My mistress is waiting for the coach, sir."

"No, no, drowned rats—go tell my mistress so. Well we've drained life to the dregs, hey ? Solomon was right,

—all vanity, even love: as poor Goldy wrote, 'the modern fair ones' jest.' Yet no," and he looked at a picture by Jackson: "by the Lord I lied: when Jackson painted that, what said the Bishop? ''Twas a connecting link between woman and angels,' sweet, sweet Linley. And her song! Her song, a seraph's chaunt, though Sam Johnson did decry it. She sang at Oxford once when North was chancellor.

" 'If I dub you Doctor, Sheridan,' says he, ' 'twere not *honoris*, but *uxoris causâ*.'

" I never got degree—morals, hem."

" She was beautiful, exceedingly ! "

" Aye, as Ninon, Recamier, Pamela de Genlis, and these three girls bid fair to match her :" and he pointed to the pictures of his daughters, Norton, Dufferin, and Seymour.

"But, look ye out—yon beautiful Norbury."

"Beautiful, fudge—Pall Mall, man—that for the country, town, town for me.

> " In town let me live, and in town let me die,
> In truth, I can't relish the country, not I;
> If we must have a villa in summer to dwell,
> Oh, give me the sweet shady side of Pall Mall !"

" But see how the sunlight chequers those glorious trees of Lock's, *chiaro scuro* as Gainsboro calls it."

" Fudge, again—

> " A house is much more to my taste than a tree,
> And for groves, oh, a fine grove of chimneys for me.

" Well, the old cock must crow no more, even on his own dunghill at Brockham, yet for that very song, Charles of Norfolk will have me up in stained glass in his Baron's hall—Almeric, Grand Master of the Templars, ho, ho ! aye, a choice spirit is Charley, every inch a duke : three bottles under his belt, and I, a ' lean and slippered pantaloon.' Well, as Shallow says, we are all mortal."

" *Im*mortal, man—your rhymes will immortalize your name, and give your widow a dowry for a second husband."

" 'Tis fine weather now, sir," whispered the valet.

" What ! the rain held up—enough for one but not for two. Yet, hold sirrah, for once we wait your lady's pleasure : I'll whisk you home, Charles."

" You with the ribbons—you ? "

" Jehu and Phaeton were muffs to me : played I not Jarvey to my own Linley from the playhouse night after night, in the dark : aye, after Charles Fox and I had boozed pottle-deep at the Kit Cat Club ? but come, we're off."

So the orator of the Begum Speech, that enchanted the Parliament at Westminster into immediate adjournment, condescended to drive Charles Morris the rhymer to his home in Brockham.

You will not marvel that art, enamoured of the beauty of nature around this accomplished spot, has graced the rich demesne of Depedene with a very noble pile, embosomed in green and gold and crimson leafage,—the Palace of Pericles. Evelyn, and Aubrey, and Cowley have scribbled their eulogy of old Dipden : what would they now write of classic Depedene, when the Hopes have shown us how the merchant princes emulate the nobles of the land. Within arcades, and halls, and

galleries, floored with native woods and marbles, there
are gems of Fuseli, Lawrence, Cipriani, Barret, and
Gilpin, and Flaxman, and Canova, and the crouching
Venus and exquisite Psyche of Thorvaldsen, types of the
most voluptuous and the purest love. There are copies
of Arabesque frescoes in the Loggia of the Vatican, the
Medici and Lanti vases, and the wrestlers and the boar
of Florence.

There are flowers around us, rich and rare, to charm the
senses—

> " Called forth every one
> Out of darkness, as if but just born of the sun,
> While the spirit of fragrance is up with the day
> From his harem of night-flowers stealing away."

There are flies, rare and rich as the flowers, that feed in
the gardens and roost in the forest-trees that encompass
them. There flits the brimstone like a golden-winged
blossom : the comma, the Io, the orangetip, the coppers
and the blues, the grayling, the ringlets, the fritillaries,
and even the clouded yellow in black and gold and lace
underwing—we may, by rare luck, even net the purple
emperor on the topmost boughs of the oaks and beeches
and the Camberwell beauty, for they have haunted these
woodlands. Each variety of butterfly has its favourite
flower, but we note that it is the *hymenopteræ* that
sip the pollen, while the *nymphalidæ* and *lepidopteræ*
are sporting around.

Within a wilderness of shade of liriodendrons, copper
beeches and Hungarian limes ascend the terrace, crowned
with an avenue of limes overlooking a demesne of twelve

miles in circumference. The chalk valley of the Mole, its green-laced brows and moss-fringed dingles, come boldly out on the north, toned down by the long shadows of evening into a deeper beauty. The Alcove, where, we believe, "Coningsby" was sketched, looks down on Chert Park, once the vineyards and the home of the Sondes and Talbots, fringed with pines, planes, cedars, and sassafras, and Turkey oak. We may descend beneath the pineclad brow of Dorking's glory, by water-worn sand lanes, among golden groves and festooning blossom boughs flinging wide their flickering shadows, and woodland banks rich in ferns and choice wildings—angelica, campanula, nightshade, campion, cardamine, oxalis, anemone, violet, cranesbill—all fresh and beautiful as at creation's dawn, when man, yet pure and innocent, had his birth-place and his home in Eden. The flowers that graced the paradise of Adam are yet growing in ours: the flower and the leaf are holy things, emblems of hope and heaven. The lily that eclipsed the imperial glory of Israel, was the wand of the archangel, and the palm-branch of the white-robed seraphs was the earthly sceptre of the Saviour.

But the rankest weeds will often creep among the roses, the death-adder coil round the lily.

There was a serpent once that haunted, in human form, this fair green mound between the woods of Depedene and the town. The story must be told: it is of one in whose breast was engendered a dark and dreadful sin, that blasted his boyhood's home, and desecrated the page of history with

E

The Curse of Cotmandene.

> " How sharper than a serpent's tooth it is,
> To have a thankless child."

It was while Oliver was ruler in Britain, a baronet and his heir sat in the library of the vineyards over the hill, and this was their theme :—

" My counsel hath been vain, my son, I now command you : it is prohibited of heaven—it is in Holy Writ : ' Thou shalt not approach to any that is nere of kin to thee : ' Anne is no mate for you."

" Yet I may love her, sir—the heart were an icicle that loves not one so sweet and so beautiful."

" A sin, George, a sin : sweet she may be, yet were it lawless to feed on honey, wouldst rifle the bee-hive, 'hey ? Anne is your cousin-german, boy—forget her."

" I cannot forget her, my father, we are—"

" Not wed, ha ! "

" We are—betrothed."

" Then your souls may yet be pure. So, your pledge, George, at once, that it shall go no further."

" I am a Cavalier, and have learned my duty : you are my father, sir, and I do swear, but 'twill be a fatal oath—till you consent, it SHALL go no further."

" I consent ! aye, at doomsday : why, look you here, too, Anne cottons with the Roundheads, the knaves who lured this madcap Freeman from his father, and sacked our chattels, and sucked our life-blood. Heaven and

earth ! 'tis monstrous ! my ships, aye, and myself, of the
high blood of Atto Sondes, in pawn at Upnoor—and
your sainted mother in her tomb, and now her treasures
filched, forty thousand in gems and plate, three fair houses,
all my lands for seven years gone, Schyldevic, too, the
gift of Raculfceastre, and Lees, and the vineyards : their
plea a fiction gross as their crime. Penance for my sins,
quotha—why,' twould madden a saint : and yet he will
trick himself out in leathern jerkin—and all for what ?—
policy—nay, perchance he is a dotard too !"

" Love ! he dare not love my cousin Anne."

" Dare ! he dare sell his father to the Roundheads,
George, but I've cut the dog from my will."

" He is my brother, sir, spare him : he may love you
yet."

" Love ! the wildfire, the scapegrace ! why, only yesternight, a cocking at the Chequers with the losels of the
town."

" He is my brother, father."

" A cool hundred lost to a bully on one main, and
Sydney College dubbed him loyal, too—the senate lied—
and yet, what have I pledged ? to wean the rebel back !
fool, fool ! but 'tis cancelled now, and all I have is yours.
So make you ready, we will be off to Lees to-night."

" And my cousin Anne, sir ?"

" Oh, I may trust you with her now, poor girl : an oath
is on your lip !" so saying, the baronet wended his way
to Depedene, to fetch the lady home.

For a moment George was alone, overwhelmed with
thought. " He loves her," he muttered, " else why his

moonlight prowling on Cotmandene—aye, Anne must be warned this very hour."

"So, brother," cried Freeman, bursting in, "*tête-à-tête*, secrets worth knowing, an outcast I guess—*n'importe*, I'll seek consolation at the Dene, farewell."

"Nay, go not thither, 'tis my counsel, brother."

"Your counsel! ha, ha!"

"Your honour—"

"My honour, that's safe and sure at Howard's: why, is not your idol, Evelyn, the ruling spirit at the Dene?"

"No, 'tis the rebel sergeant—"

"Edward Dendy, true—he were a trump indeed who could bone a tabard and a chancery mace to boot, ride rough-shod through the Painted Chamber, and proclaim the lopping of the Martyr. Yet 'tis not old Noll I worship, the mighty Fairfax is *my* friend, *voici* my cornet's helm and ensign."

"And yet a Royalist and a Cavalier."

"Pshaw, feathers and finery, I'm sick of 'em: I keep my leather, you your velvet, George: now, just for a trick, let's prove the lady's fancy."

"Brother, I—"

"Nay, 'tis a match, velvet *versus* leather—nothing like leather, George: I win, be sure: so, as Anne rules her sire, and Delaune toads the Protector, count me a colonel in the coming onslaught. But you haunt the Dene as well as I: come, a truce with you, George, go you not thither, neither will I: how say you?"

"To-morrow, to-morrow, Freeman, we will talk of this to-morrow," and George walked slowly from the room.

"To-morrow," growled Freeman, "I'll know to-night— yet he cares not for a lip as I do, poor liquorish fool—yet she smiles on him and frowns on me—her own lips shall tell to-night if he be traitor, as I guess—revenge shall go its depth—but do I not wrong him—yet, why to the Dene so late—aye, she may cheat me yet—she walks to-night,—aye, now or never." So Freeman started off to Cotmandene, and hovered beneath the wall.

An hour passed: "Ha!" he whispered, "I hear her footfall—'Sdeath, a man's tread, too—what, before me— faith, he's no laggard in his love."

As he spoke, through the wicket passed a man and a maiden.

"Whispering close too," muttered Freeman, crouching low, "see how his feather wantons with her cheek, none but a lover's plume may dare so much. Ha, her glove thrust in his bosom, and, hark, her name breathed softly and warmly, and, death! a kiss—a brother's curse be on him!"

Freeman felt for his dagger in vain.

As the Cavalier left the wicket, the glove fell from his bosom.

"Ha, by hell!" muttered Freeman, clutching it from the ground, "'G. A.' broidered in golden hair." And Freeman, re-echoing the curse, bolted to his home, and burst on his brother in the library.

"Hypocrite!" he exclaimed, "thou hast robbed me of a heart, two hearts."

"What now?" cried George, looking up in wonder.

"What now! her kiss still burning on your lip: I heard the smack on't beneath thy scarlet plume—well may it

blush for its wearor's shame—I saw it brush her cheek—
what now!"

"Now will I swear—"

"Aye, swear, and lose a soul, swear on this broidered
glove—it has felt the pulses of your heart—I saw it drop
from your bosom—nay, nay, 'tis mine now, I keep it as a
witness to your lie!"

George gazed for a moment on the fatal glove, then
rushed from the room, leaving the frenzied boy in a trance,
and when he awoke, a *cortége* was already on its way to
Lees Court as night came down on Cotmandene.

On learning this, Freeman leaped into his saddle, and
rode furiously along the Pilgrim's Way into Kent, some
bright thing gleaming in the moonlight at his saddle-bow.
By the wood-side at Easling he dropped from his horse,
and, as the wild thing galloped off over the Lees, he strode
across the waste, and was on Lees Court lawn an hour
before the dawn, then, unlocking a private portal, he
ascended the backstairs in silence.

"That," he muttered, "is George's room, and this,
Anne's chamber," and he started at finding them both
ajar. "So, he is sound asleep, and she—what murmurs
she in her dream? ha, *his* name! *his!*" and he rushed
like a maniac to his brother's bed. With a cleaver that
he drew from his cloak, he aimed a blow: the blood
welled forth, and George started up, stared wildly, and
uttered a low moan, then fell bleeding on the bed. For
an instant a flash of remorse came over the frenzied spirit,
he would fain recal the life he had menaced, but, Heaven
of its mystery, the convulsive throes so harrowed up his

heart, that, in his maudlin pity, he threw the cleaver out
of the window and then drew the dagger he had stolen
from his father's cabinet, and inflicted five deep gashes in
his brother's breast.

The dying youth knew not in life by whom that life
was taken, but, as the accusing spirit flew up to Heaven's
chancery with the charge of fratricide, Freeman was
conscience-stricken with this truth—that all was revealed
to the parting soul by the wondrous clairvoyance of dissolution.

The matin-bell had not yet rung, but Sir George was
risen from his couch, for he was a sleepless man, when a
pale unearthly creature, in her night-gear, her silken socks
dabbled in blood, and with dishevelled locks, glided in,
and stood like a statue before his eyes.

"What art thou, bright phantom?" he cried in affright,
"Anne, Anne, is it you? Christ of his mercy! What
means this mockery, girl?"

For a minute she stood ice-bound, then, with a vacant
stare and smile that mocked the dark reality of the scene,
she muttered :

"My dream, my dream, clear as the light of Heaven :
look ye, good people, there lies my—husband, stark and
bloody," and, touching the ring on her finger, she pointed
to George's chamber.

"Husband!" cried Sir George: "who, who, for mercy's
sake?"

"Nay, nay, be quiet, sir, 'twas but a dream:" so,
drawing on the embroidered glove, to hide her bloody
finger, she held aloft her dagger, and glided from the room.

"Tell—tell me!" exclaimed Sir George, as he followed her stealthy footsteps, "whence that bloody knife : is the deed thine?"

"Mine, mine!" bellowed Freeman, starting from the floor, "father, I cursed him on Cotmandene, and there stands the accusing spirit."

Anne was kneeling by the corpse, and, as her head fell on its bleeding breast, a gleam of consciousness stole over her face, but 'twere a mercy she lapsed again into her phantasy.

"So," she murmured, smiling vacantly on Freeman, and touching her bloody ring, "so you are come to the bridal, brother."

"Brother," he cried, wildly, "*your* brother!"

"Oh, knew you not?" she whispered, "hush, 'tis a secret yet, my bonnie George and I, thrice asked in the church and cried in the market—so—" and she drew off the glove and laid it on Freeman's hand.

He gazed on it wildly, and on her ringed finger.

"Madman, monster!" he screamed, "Cain was an angel of mercy to thee, Esau waited for a death, but I—Anne, Anne, Anne!"

We may not hope to paint this scene in its own deep colours, the mute agony of that dark hour were beyond us : even the justices who were assembled in the hall were bewildered and horror-stricken, and the formality of the law came out in mercy to sober down the bloody romance of the morning.

Anne went through the ceremony of the oath, but her only evidence was the pressing her ring to her lip, and pointing to heaven. The guilt was clear as light, and Livesay signed the committal to Maidstone.

At the assize Freeman at once pleaded guilty to Crook, who sat in judgment, affirming that "He looked on death as a droan with its sting out." He was doomed in twenty-four hours, but Ede, the sheriff, gave him respite "for his better penitence." Then came the baronet's plea for commutation, *sudden impulse:* and he daubed it over with Freeman's piety during his brother's nightly reading of the Bible in the hall. But the full confession to Crisp, and Higgins of Hanton, and Yates of Belmour, quashed the prayer at once, and his fate was sealed.

So to Penenden Heath, in August, 1655, Freeman, in deep mourning, rode on horseback, and, on the ladder, he craved the people's prayer, and begged, of course in vain, to share his brother's grave.

The tragedy was the theme of the sensation scribblers for a season. Among other rhapsodies issued—"To the Kingdom," Boorman's "Mirrour of Mercy and Judgment," "The Devil's Reign upon Earth," "An Elegy on the Death of George S." Sir George himself wrote "A Plain Narrative of the Death of my Two Sons, with Postscripts of Holy Men," and "Crumbs of Comfort" was found in Freeman's pocket. These doleful records fill nearly forty pages of the tenth volume of the Harleian Miscellany.

All this while Sir George kept open house at Lees, both for rich and poor.

On the turf among the daisies, in the graveyard of the Church of ——, sat weeping, for many and many an eve, a lady in the deepest sables: and the classic story of

Heres, whose tears spangled with white flower-stars the
grave of Cepheus, ever crossed the mind of the minister
as he wended homeward from his evening prayer.

Evening is fading into twilight, the vesper chime is pealing along the valley from yon dark spire of St. Martin's in
Dorking : it is an hour when illusive fancy is paramount.
Under her spell we are listening to the clang of the
curfew bell ringing out the fire and light of the Norman,
what time the Sæsnag Bretwalda, Harold—as his Saxon
forefathers would style him—fell on Hastings' field, and
when after Editha, Eddiva, or Eddid, the relict of the
Confessor, Gundreda de Warenne, the child of the conqueror, was manorial lady of Dorchinges, for so those
same Saxons called it.   It was the home of the *Dwr
Richingar*, or water-folk, lying, as even now, so prettily
on the *Dol o cyn dwr*—the mead of the springs—along
which you see still ripples the *Emlyn, Ymellyn*, or mill-
stream.   Those noble Warennes were the mighty lords
of the lands around Holmsdale, but their memory most
vividly haunts the demesne of Depedene, in its outlying
park of West Betchworth. Those sylvan skeletons of
four centuries, that rise in grotesque majesty before us
as we fling open the park gate, smack of the antique :
their spectral arms towering into the clear blue sky, like
relics of the forest primæval : their trunks richly clothed
with *sticta, parmelia*, and other lichens.   As we gaze on
them, we may almost marvel that there is no tiny dryad
astride on a boss, no dainty Ariel grinning, in concert with
Puck on his toadstool, from yonder cloven pine.   Who

loves not the archæology of the park and forest? Who
will not worship the Parliament Oak in Clipstone, the
Shambles in Birkland, the Gospel-oaks, the sepulchral
yews, the Burnham beeches, the Purley oaks, and, *par
excellence*, these Betchworth chestnuts? Were their
leaves to murmur the secrets that have been whispered

beneath their shade, how would they light up the pages
of history and romance! Even yon triple avenue of
lindens is Norman-arched by Nature, as in honour of the
child of Neustria, William Rufus, who held the rich
demesne, and they lead to the site of the antient castle,
or manor-lodge of the Warennes of Surrey. Of this
there was, probably, no relic in our age, unless it were

the mullioned oriel of the grey ruin on the bank of
he Mole.   In the past age it lighted the closet of Abraham Tucker, who, though "dark," like Milton, was
equally blessed with "a more vigorous light within :"
and before this, perchance, it graced the oratory of
Eleanor Arundel, who, in the fifteenth century, married
Brown, then embattled her house and empacted her
manor.   You may see it sketched in Watson's "Memoirs
of the Warennes," to illustrate a family legend, the fragments of which are as varied as the names of him who
was the hero of the story.   He was styled by Maddox,
in   Baronia   Angliæ,   Johannes   de   Warenne,   Comes
Surreiæ : by Wynkyn de Worde, Warine, Erl of Surry :
by Peter of Longtoft, Le Counte de Garenne : by Leland,
Syr John, Earl of Garen and Surreia : and by Lambarde,
Erl of Warran.   The "Erl with the carpyd hat," we
believe, had deposited the fragments of this family legend
in the Chartulary of Stanlawe Abbey, where Camden found
them.

Deeply engaged in arranging these fragments, the Lady
Eleanor Arundel is sitting on her window-sill, in Betchworth Manor, and she discovered how, in the olden time,
there was a monk of Malmesbury then indicting the
reign of Edward the Second, since published by Hearne.
He was sojourning in Westhamble Chapel, and one
evening, haunting the demesne of one of the king's satellites in search of incident, he lighted on one John
Lymden, Prior of the Holy Cross, who was rapt in
meditation by this Castle of Becesuworde.   Closer questioned, he said that yon oriel window haunted him ever,

as he gazed on it, with a dream of woman's worth and woman's will. The prior at once found that he had said too much, but the hint tickled the ears of the monk, who would not lose so precious a morsel for the lack of asking.

> " ' Sire preest,' quod he, 'now fair you befallen,
> Say what you list, and we shul gladly here.'
> And with that worde he said, in this manere :
> 'Telleth,' quod he, 'your meditation :
> But hasteth the sonne wol adown,
> Beth fractuous, and that in litel space,
> And to do well God sende you his grace.' "

Thus challenged, the prior—after a moment's pause, and with a right solemn enjoyment of secrecy until the actors in the scene were gathered to the dust—whispered the legend of

The Lost Game.

" Thus, with a kiss, I die."

JOHN, eighth Earl of Warenne and Surrey, was high and mighty, the bosom friend of Edward the King, and

Edward the Prince, with whom, and young Fitzalan, he
wended to Scotland in battle array against Walleys, or
Wallace Wight. In the north country this pair of lordlings won golden opinions, and soon after wedded noble
and golden wives, as writeth Longtofte,

> " The young Erl of Warenne with grate nobles was there,
> A wif ther him bikenne yᵉ Erl's daughter of Bare :
> The Erl of Arundelle his londes raught he then,
> And took a damyselle Williams daughter of Warenne."

So, by this marriage, the Earl was the king's cousin,
grandson by marriage with the grand-daughter of Edward
the First, and brother-in-law of mighty Arundel.

Soon after Bruce lost the field of Methven, where they
had sworn to avenge the dirking of Comyn, and the
young Earl of Gareyne, with three hundred other young
soldiers, was knighted in the Abbey of Westminster on
the Eve of the Vigils : and thus he was bedizened,

> " His bliau was alle of gold begann,
>   Well chrislite maked I understonde,
> Batones azured everilke ane,
>   From his elboth to his honde."

The Erl sat in his "praty castellet of Sandal, on a hill-
ing ground with ·a diche aboute it," a gorgeous clump
of round towers pierced with crucial loopholes, richly
machicolated with a heavy port-quilice on each of its
iron-studded gates. The building of so strong a pile set
the folk wondering,—for he held the castles of Lewes,
and Reigate, and Wakefield, and Conigsberg. But
Sandal was to be now the cage of a noble dame, whose
fresh beauty had inflamed his passion, even as early as

her ninth year. For Johanne, his wife, was childless, and he was sated with Maude, his leman, although she was a fruitful mother. But his new love—Alyce, of Lancaster—was said to be somewhat of a prude, and although she almost confessed she loathed her lord and loved Earl Warenne, yet she flouted the suit of a man who could not make her an honest woman. Her coldness made him all but desperate, and he had planned a stratagem.

"These galling links of Hymen," he muttered, "still locked around my heart—would I were free!"

"Thou art free!" cried a stately woman, bursting from the arras: "free as the wind, Erl of Warenne! Aye, marvel not 'tis I that bring you freedom—look you here," and she laid on his arm a roll of vellum stamped with the privy seal.

The Earl started as he read—"A motion of divorce betwixt Johanne de Baars vel Barre, the king's cousen, and her lord, John Erl of Surrey, enforced by Maude de Nereford, against the Erl for nearness of blood."

"And by what right come you, Mistress Maude, twixt Erl and Countisse thus," said he, smiling.

"Right!" she cried, "had I not a precontract to Johanne, that were enough, methinks. But have I not the nobler right of vengeance—aye, and of motherhood, withal? Bore I not your boys, Lord of Warenne?"

"And richly have I endowed them," replied the Earl: "manors, and villas, and castles, and the Priory of Thetford: for your soul, what crave you more?"

"More!—a wimple and a hoop of gold," she cried: "so only may we gag the priests of Kent and Norfolk."

" You forget, Maude, my right of Mercheta made you
mine, even on your bridal night—I can put you off as
easily. Nay, the Church doth enforce me, mistress. Look
you here—a counter scroll will match thine at odds ! "

" How ! " screamed the woman.

" Aye, verily 'tis the Arches' mandate to the Erl of
Warenne for his ' disordinate life in keepynge Dame Mawde
de Nereford against the laws of God.' So, 'twixt the
Arch and the Chancellor, the lawn and the ermine, I *am*
free—and we are quits, Maude. This holy Marplot hath
blessed me with his curse—and you, though you burst
one chain, you rivet not another. A hoop of gold—
no, no ! "

The Earl vanished from the chamber, and Maude stood
a moment erect and statuesque.

" So I have burst his chain—and for whom ? For her,
the viper ! Forbid it, Heaven and Hell ! "

A low voice echoed her words—she turned, and beheld a man muffled and wearing a light shirt of mail, an
anclas, a broad short dagger in his clutch.

" Richard San Martin, you ! " she cried, " in the very
nick of time, by Heaven ! Ha ! I guess."

" You shall *know* anon ! " and he whispered in her
ear.

" Alyce — she ! " cried Maude, starting, " the harlot of
Lancaster—Warenne wish for her ? No, 'tis slander,
Richard, and I scout it. Yet, bethink thee, Maude—it
may be true. If it be—'tis death ! Better Joan the
barren than Alyce the wanton. Ha ! a light flashes on
me !—have I not heard ?—hist, Richard, hither—'tis a

deep game—say, wilt play it out—is't a match? Alyce
is yours by right, they say—your wedded, if not your
bedded, wife—wilt play it out, I say?"

"I am here to play it out," he replied: "you and I
must hunt in couples, Maude: we are life and soul to
each other. The game is mine: I'll have a coronet and
manors yet in right of my lady-wife. For, look ye,
Maude, the seal of Lancaster—this opens Dorset to me,
and Warenne's woodreeves for my escort. We'll hunt
her up, be sure, but not for him: she is for Number One,
and I am he. I tell thee, the game is mine."

"Then 'tis won. I worship thee, aye, as I hate Lord
Warenne now. Joy, joy! cry havoc! the cuckold and
his fool may fight it out: 'twere food for vengeance. But,
my boys! my boys! Warenne must live for them—the
doom be hers. Quick work, Richard, and our game is
won! Let not the sun arise, and you in Sandal. Quick
—away! away! the Earl is here."

Richard San Martin for a moment clutched his dagger,
but a frown from Maude sent it again to its sheath: and
he directly stole away from Sandal as quietly as he
came.

And what is the real secret of all this? Speed will
tell you. The Earls had, either of them, a wife, but
neither cared for them. The one was the mate of a barren
bed: of the other, Walsinghame writes, that both to
Lancaster and Warenne she was betrothed even in her
girlhood, and yet she was wedded, in very tender years
of age, to Richard San Martin, Knight. Lancaster scorned
this as low scandal, but when every lip whispered that

Alyce smiled on Warenne, his pride revolted, and he
sued for a divorce, citing Warenne for trespass against
" *la ples notre Seigneur le roy.*"   Paramount in the state,
he razed Sandal, sacked Wakefield and Pomfret, and
"likeways De Conyngesburgh in Norray," and then, in
mockery, they gave him in lieu some poor lands of Alyce
in Dorset, and this very Dorking—Betchworth, and 700
merks a year.   This was enough to chafe the proudest
man in Christendom—so, crestfallen, down came the Earl
to the Holy Cross, for Reigate Castle was too hot to
hold him.

His first greeting in Surrey was his excommunication
from Chichester : this was the climax, and he dived at
once into solitude at Betchworth.   But the sense of his
degradation rankled like a thorn in his heart, and fever
was lighted up in his brain.   The Prior, John Lymden, a
very skilful leech, was ever at his couch during his peril
and his probation, while the monks prayed unceasingly for
his soul.   He awoke to life, his lofty spirit chastened and
purified.   But who can paint his wonder, when, the
moment his consciousness was clear, his burning cheek
was resting on a woman's arm, and a woman's hand was
bathing his still burning brow ?   It was the vision
realized that had hung o'er his couch at the acme of his
delirium, the very lip that had whispered him to sleep,
and called her sister-angels round his pillow.   As his
nurse glided from the room, and the Prior entered, the
Earl raised himself on his couch.

"Tell me, Holy Father," he muttered—"I looked for
cowl and cassock, nor knew I yet the Holy Cross did

cotton with serge and wimple : prythee, solve me the riddle, Father."

The Prior studied the fire awhile, and answered : "An oversight, my son—but thou hast seen too much not to know more. I will trust thee, Earl of Surrey: for I have watched thy slumbers, and heard thy prayer. It chanced, but now, this ruffled dove fled to the bosom of the Church from the clutch of the eagle's claw,—but we of the Holy Cross may not gaze on woman's beauty, so have we feathered her nest here, e'en in your manor-lodge of Betchworth. I will trust her with thee still, for thou art within the Church's pale, and she is pure and gentle as the south-wind that blows over the blossom-beds of Holmsdale. Yet I would crave your solemn word."

"My oath, my honour ! Oh, if the faintest blush ——"

"Content thee, Earl of Warenne, she blushes not : her thoughts are of the angels—her cheek is ever pure and pale as theirs, so thou wilt honour her wimple as the cowl of St. Gertrude, the beloved of the Saviour : forget not, she is here."

Days passed, and the lay-sister sat still, in her gown of serge, by the Earl's pallet, in perfect silence, according to the canon of the Holy Cross : yet the tremulous pressure of her hand, soft as a feather, on his brow, and her suppressed sigh, bespoke the deepest sympathy : and it was holy and eloquent withal, as if spoken by the lip of a seraph. And so the hours lingered on—but it is not in the nature of man's heart, when sanctified by sorrow, to take, unlovingly, a fair, soft woman's tender-

ness : and how oft have nurse and nursling even plighted
faith on the earliest dawn of convalescence !

Even so, the Earl loved as he had never loved before,
for there was nothing to taint the purity of his adoration.
Yet his secret was sealed from the ears of his nurse and
his priest. From his unconscious murmuring, however,
in his slumber, his nurse gathered the truth—for thus
he thought aloud :

"Oh, had I known the charm of woman's truth and
purity, ere I had sinned—even one ray of her radiance
to hallow my early boyhood! Alas, alas! I had scorned
the light in my madcap hours!" And then trembled
on his lip the whisper of a name, and he awoke. From
the emotion of his nurse, the Earl guessed she had
learned the tissue of his dream.

"The name, holy sister—tell me, didst thou hear it ? "

A slight bend of the head was her response.

"Then you shall learn all—I will confess."

She moved toward the door.

"Nay, fear not—my story shall be truthful and pure as
the confession of a novice. Listen, I do pray thee."

It was, in sooth, a delicate task for a lay-sister to listen
to the story of a life like his, but it was part of her
mission to soothe the sorrowing soul in any way : and so
his lips breathed in her ear the purest penitence for
daring to profane, with unholy suit, the heart of grace and
purity. The sister trembled ever while she listened, and
on his prayer for absolution, she kneeled with intense devotion by the couch, and bent her head, and pressed her
crucifix on his lip, as assurance that his prayer was heard.

John Lymden sat in the oratory in Betchworth Lodge, in a very brown study, for a mystery seemed closing around him. The confessions of the Earl and the sister, his steps ever crossed by a man in a masque from Holy Cross to Betchworth, and now a gipsy ever squatting at eventide beneath the oriel, were enough to account for all his abstraction.

No wonder, either, that one evening these shadowy beings confronted each other in the park.

"At length thou art here," the Sybil exclaimed. "Do I divine aright? you know all?"

"All!" he muttered—"all I know is, all is lost. A losing game we play, Mistress Maude."

"What! she hath slipped her leash?"

"Stolen, when I had her in my grasp. But whether Lancaster or Warenne hired those burly monks, I know not: yet, ere I measure swords with one, I will make short work with t'other, if, as I guess, he's hiding here in Holmsdale."

"Why, thou art more daft than I deemed thee, Richard," muttered the gipsy. "A losing game? I tell thee, the game is yet to be played—aye, played and won this very night. Hark ye, I am deeper, wiser than thou deemest me : the Sybil hath a keener scent than a craven fool like thee—a dolt who cannot cage his love-bird when he has caught her. But I have news for thee. A holy sister—pshaw ! she sucks in the gipsy's jargon like a green girl, and crosses my Sybil's palm with gold for charity, ha, ha ! But list ye, she will be ripe and ready for thee, Richard—here here is that will give us life on earth, a ring of gold—

mark'st thou : if she frown here is that will give *her* life in Gehenna, and good-night to Alyce of Lancaster."

"Alyce !" exclaimed San Martin, waking from his dream.

"Aye, in yonder closet, so dally not, San Martin—this hour will seal her destiny and thine : there is a hairline 'twixt life and death—this very hour or never—the ring, take it, be silent as death till my footfall on the floor : hush, hush !"

A wicket opened, and the Sybil was in the lady's closet.

"I am here, lady."

"Again, wild gipsy : wherefore art thou here ? Thou triflest with my faith : wherefore art thou here ?"

"To tell thee the hour is nigh."

"The hour !"

"Aye, the hour in which thou must choose a bride-sheet or a shroud."

"Avaunt ! thou dost profane mine ear—words so wild and wicked I may not listen to."

"Thou must listen, Alyce of Lancaster—aye, and obey. Look you, lady, one drop of this were death. Well may you start—yet, this ring may save you. Your oath to the man I bring you—nay, you know him well, *too* well, they say—your oath to him, you live : flout me, and you die—so deep and deadly is the vengeance of Maude."

"Maude ! you in Betchworth, and Lord Warenne—"

"Nay, it shall not be Warenne, lady : one that hath better right, methinks, to those ashy lips of thine, than Warenne, aye, or Lancaster. Wilt obey me ?"

Alyce dropped on her knees, and, kissing her rosary, addressed a prayer to Heaven.

"Nay," continued the Sybil, "thou must pray to Maude if thou dost hope for mercy. What, silent still! fool, fool fool! I would have spared thy life." Maude stamped her foot—in vain. "Still mute as marble, then the lips of mercy are icebound as thine own. The sluggard hears me not—nay, then 'tis time to do." She took a phial from her bosom, and as the venom that she dropped still hung on the lady's lip, the Sybil was glaring on her victim, dark and desperate as the shade of Atropos. The Countess was still kneeling, like the image of a saint, and Maude, as if spell-bound, clutched her hands over her throbbing eyeballs, when San Martin rushed to the altar, and, kneeling by her side, kissed wildly the livid lips of the Countess. At the moment Maude awoke from her trance as they were yet kneeling, still and mute as death. At the sight, her fury was wrought to frenzy pitch, and shaking the Countess roughly, she screamed aloud—

"Alyce, your oath, your oath! Why, what mockery is this?—the ring, Richard, the ring." But the Knight moved not, and Maude snatched the ring and pressed it herself on the lady's finger. The Countess started at the touch, and breathed a deep hysteric sigh, while San Martin shivered and rolled prostrate on the floor. Maude stood over them erect as a statue, glaring on the scene in utter bewilderment.

"What—dead, dead!" she groaned in her despair. "*He*, the man of all the world to save me : the lightning flashes on me now—he hath sucked the venom from her lip, and

she that I had doomed, is breathing yet : but she must
die ! Ha ! who comes ? "

As she raised her dagger to strike, her arm was clutched,
and a gentle voice pronounced, "Heaven for its mercy,
benedicite."

"Mercy !" she screamed. "Mock me not with *your* mercy,
hoary priest—I scorn your grace and you. And you, John
de Warenne, look on your wanton now, the bride — of
death—she will follow him home, be sure. Hold, hold !
kiss not her lip : yon blundering fool hath left enough to
kill—thou must not die, I'd have thee live : look, she
is dying now, dying," and Maude, unheeded, lapsed again
into her cataleptic trance.

"A grace, a grace from Heaven," murmured the Prior,
as he drew the wimple from the lady's brow, and the Earl
fell at her feet. "Alyce, thou hast confessed him once—
he will confess to thee again, *Benedicite.*"

The Prior drew the ring from her finger and laid it on
the Earl's illuminated missal, while the acolyte, with his
asperge, sprinkled the holy water on their brows.

Ere the moon rose, the vesper-bell of the Chapel of
Westhamble was tinkling for the espousals of an Earl and
a Countess.

A mystery long veiled the life of Alyce. It was even
believed that, although the wedded wife of the Earl of
Warenne, she was through life a holy sister still : and
indeed Isabel de Houlande, whom he married after her
death, is called his second countess, and strange to state,
their marriage was on the prayer of Maude de Nereford,
who, after years of solitude and despair at being foiled

in her own game, died in Isabel's arms, a penitent. A ring
was Isabel's only legacy.

The Earl's scutcheon—with this addition, *quarterly, two
bars in chief, two lions rampant sable*—was rich in blazonry,
yet poor in descent. Although thrice married, he had no
legitimate issue, and there was a fate in the house of
Maude : for although her line is not even now extinct, yet
her children died before their father.

Every hour of the Creator's day hath its glory, but eventide is the painter's hour, when

> "The sudden sun
> By its effulgence gilds the illumined fields,
> And black by fits the shadows move along."

These far-scanned Betchworth Beeches crown the fairest
brow in Holmsdale, now bronzed in gold against the green-
blue sky. Yonder over the hill lie the lone villages of
Headley (Hallega), once the manor of Harold's mother
Githa, and of Walton (Waldetone), in remote time a
Roman station, and erst the home of Anne of Cleves.
On the box still feeds the driveller snail, imported as a
remedy for consumption for the Countess of Arundel.
Yonder are the coverts of Kingswood (Wodesmeresthorne).
Below the hill lie the demesnes of Brome, East Betchworth, and Wonham, and old Moor Place, in one chamber
of which was a bed, once in Wolsey's Palace of Nonsuch,
inscribed, *Remember thy End*. To the fanciful, the words
may foreshadow something of the destiny of an ill-starred
youth, the heir of Egland Moor. In the church of
Betchworth you might note an antique charter-chest,

hewn of one block.   What curious Chatterton it was we
know not, who, peering, like him of Redcliff, into the
reliquary, unfolded a stained mothworn scroll of sheep-
skin, scribbled by a lay-brother of the Holy Cross.   The
classic who can master the monkish Latin, may decipher
thus much of the Rembrandt sketch of

The Automaniac.

> " For my single self,
> I had as lief not live, as live to be
> In awe of such a thing as myself."

THE lights and shadows of genius often mark a very
fine hairline between illusion and insanity.   Those who
taunted Michael Angelo as the divine madman, and Oliver
Goldsmith as an inspired idiot, sketched no fanciful picture.

Psychology will bear them out : it has proved that at
one point the skulls of the brightest genius may be *cracked*,
yet through the fissure may gleam a light, *le don du ciel*.
Who, listening to those inspired creations, the *Requiem*
and the *Sonata Diavolo*, will regret that Mozart and Tartini
were spirit-haunted ?

But far more deep and dark even than this, is the light
and shade of the *passions :* the worshipper of an idol, yet
pure and innocent withal, may become its willing slave
even to death.   The girl who sat gazing hopelessly on the
Belvidere Apollo, enfolding it with a veil of Ind fringed
with gold, and strewing its base with flowers, died raving.
The phantoms of the conscience are even darker still—the

preludes, often, of insanity, and the incentives of suicide.
To escape the umbra of his Cæsar, many a Brutus has
rushed madly into the Shades below. There is a phantasy
however, if it be lighter, yet far more strange than these—
a being without a deeper fault than doting may be haunted
even to its doom, by—itself: it is true as strange, that
man may be the idol and the phantom of his own worship
—the living soul may be the sport and wreck of its own
shadow.

Young Olliffe, of Egland Moor, was the glory of Holmsdale : he was beautiful as Narcissus, and, like that self-
enamoured boy of Aonia, was ever gazing on his beauty
in some translucent mirror. Even the pool in Wonham
Park was his looking-glass : it were a mercy if, like the
son of Liriope, he too had been changed on its margin
into a blossom. It was no marvel that his beauty was set
up as an idol before his doting eyes : millions have done
the like in a light degree, but he had gloated on it so oft
and so intensely, that his Eidōlon became at length as
palpable as reality. The radiant spectre was ever before
him, and even in the shade of night his double was the
phantom of his pillow : and he awoke only to drink in
fresh adulation, both from himself and the fairest girls in
Holmsdale—for all were his flatterers and his slaves. His
soul was thus brimful of one passion, even to overflowing—
his own self was his all-in-all, the very god of his idolatry.
The love of woman was a blank : even on the lustrous eyes
of beauty, that dazzled all beside, he gazed without a
sigh or wish—his bosom was cold as an icicle. Yet, while
he walked and talked with his shadow, his face was ever

beaming with a radiant joy : and when some sparkling
thought flashed in his eye, and was echoed, reflected by his
double, he would laugh outright at the fancy of himself
or *his self*—for even thoughts would radiate from self to
self. Like Tasso's familiar spirit, this phantom self
was his *lar*, his household god : and even in the social
circle he would keep up a brilliant converse with his
double, mindless of all around him. As yet, his Automania was innocent and unpolluted, if the ecstasy of self-
love can be so. With all his scorn of woman, however,
his beauty charmed the eyes and thrilled the bounding
breast of many a maiden endowed with birth and beauty.
Above all, he was deeply, madly loved by a fair young
creature, Florence of Wodesmeresthorne : yet in the young
spring of her passion, she but blushed and trembled as she
gazed on his beauty, and the secret of her love might still
have been kept. But the everduring thought of Oliffe
Moor at length absorbed her very soul, until, in the intensity of her pure idolatry, her whole life was but the
automatic dream of a sonnambula. She would follow
Oliffe Moor like a shadow, and oft from morn to eventide
she would sit gazing in his face, dark with the demon
glare of triumph over a bounding and a bursting heart,
as he lay by Wonham Lake, entranced by the fascination,
not of *her* beauty, but of his own, until the shades of very
night came down on the weald. The blossom of her love
was like that of an early lily frozen in its young spring.

And now they were once more in Wonham Park, and
the green light of the moon was gleaming on her icy
cheek : one long-drawn sigh, and she drew a scarlet

passion-flower from her bosom, and laid it on that of Oliffe Moor. It was the last moment of her conscious life : yet she stood awhile in her cataleptic trance, while Oliffe Moor looked wildly on that spectral form of Florence, but interblended and lying on the bosom of his self!

In a moment his *chœromania* was clouded—a wondrous change came o'er the spirit of his dream : in a moment his self, that had been his bosom-friend, his heart of hearts, was now his direst enemy—his rival : the green eyes jaundiced his passion, and, like all blighted infatuation, it changed to the extreme of deadly hate. Even unbidden, his phantom self now ever intruded on his solitude, and, by some mysterious glamour, the phantom was never alone: the spectral gleam of Florence seemed ever to be interblended with the shadow of his self: her smile was on his self, her frown on him. Have you fathomed the secrets of the human heart? Know you not that a thing of beauty, once unprized, uncared for, may be deeply, madly loved when its love and its charm-fraught caresses are lavished on another? It is no fiction : the passion, of Oliffe Moor deep and burning as

> "The lava flood
> That boils in Ætna's breast of flame,"

like lightning from earth to cloud, flashed from the phantom of his self to that of the love-lorn Florence: the shade of the beautiful, that was once his scorn, was now his adoration—his self a loathing and a hate. Desire, as rank and despairing as this, must work a deep and deadly change in a human nature, like the canker in a mildewed ear. So sudden and complete was this,

that Oliffe Moor became, in one little moon, an object
of pity and of loathing: with haggard look, his hair
matted and dishevelled, he wandered, day by day, over
the wild moor, from Bocland to Wodemeresthorne, and
scared not only the tender child but even the rough
boors of Holmsdale, who scuttled away like hunted
antelopes rather than confront Bocland Shag.

As to the Grange of Moor, it was deserted by all but
one idiot thing, who endured his slavery with sullen
apathy. The neighbouring folk were, for a time, utterly
aghast at the unearthly sounds that frighted the village
from its propriety: yet Moor was still a mystery so
wondrous strange, that the folk even believed that they
themselves were dreaming. The curse told hourly on
the visage of the haunted youth—every morning saw
another furrow on his brow, another livid spot on his
cheek : often with frenzied cry he would challenge his
self with the doom of Florence, and smothered whispers
were afloat touching the mystery—yet none spoke out,
or would impeach the innocence of Oliffe Moor. It was
clear, indeed, that some malignant spirit was haunting
his breast: for, while he would fight the air with his
clenched fist, epithets, not to be echoed, were muttered
by his parched lips : even those of his lighter ravings
were wild and withering fragments, like these—

"Thus is my passion scorned and betrayed—*mine*, who
called thee forth out of the womb of darkness, and loved
thee, aye, beyond the love of woman, even of myself:
thou *wert* myself, as radiant in beauty, for that I loathe
thee now more than wert thou utter deformity: more

radiant than the angels, thou dost reflect on me myself,
for thou didst steal my beauty from me. Off! thine eyes
do blind me with their light, that, like the glare of
Lucifer, is burning out my life, while they illume the
chancery of Heaven, where thou, accusing spirit, hast
sent up my sins before me : see how they recoil on
earth, each a death-stain on my breast, a beauty-spot on
thine ! Ha! hold not that mirror to my eyes, tormentor,
that blazons to my sight the curse of my own deformity.
Hence nightmare, hence! lest I grow desperate, and kill—
I care not which : hence, thou mockery of my soul, thou
deity or demon, one thou must be! I wave thee hence :
haunt me no more, thy master and thy fate."

While the foam of fury hung on his lip, he drew his
poignard from its sheath, and thrust it—whither? Through
the phantom of his self—then burst into a frantic laugh,
and in another moment started, shivering with terror
at his own unearthly cry.

Think you a brain thus tortured could endure? No!
The spirit of Oliffe Moor was at once the sport and wreck
of its own creation. A frenzy-fever lighted up his brain,
and laid him prostrate : and day and night he echoed his
moaning and his muttering throughout its course—his
only theme being the curse on his self.

The crisis came on at midnight. The moment that a
gleam of illusive consciousness shot forth, Oliffe seized
again a dagger (none knew how it had been secreted), and
transfixed—the Shadow.

"What!" he screamed : "no groan, no blood—a charmed
life, triumphant and defiant of revenge : and I, to linger

on and loathe for ever! No! by Azrael's dragon-wing,
the fiend shall never dare to mock me thus. There is
a shadow I may call up, yet to close around us, and
shroud the eyes of Oliffe Moor from the curse of his
own beauty's light—aye, the shadow of the tomb."

The wild words were still quivering on his lip: and
ere the terror-stricken crone could move from her chair,
the steel had impaled his heart, and in a moment he
was writhing on the floor in the convulsive agony of
self-doomed death—the martyr of vainglory.

Know ye not, even in your own circle, other instances,
faint or transient though they be, of the automania of
Oliffe Moor? Which of us will put in a denial?

Nature is ever displaying the chameleon changes of
her "dissolving views" among the hills and valleys of
Surrey: one moment the wealden woods are black as
jet, and twilight comes down on the hill—then, in a few
moments, gleams a streak of silver-light, and behold—

> " The rising of the moon, calm, slow,
> And beautiful, as if she came
> Fresh from the Elysian bowers below !"

Such is the glorious effect as we mount the crown of
Reigate Hill, that rises direct from the centre of Holmsdale! We must gaze awhile on this fair valley, for the
prowess of its denizens of old is still the glory of Mid-
Surrey. The limits of Holmsdale however, like the site
of Troy, are yet a topographic question, with all the
prosing of Camden, and Lambarde, and Sprott, and Aubrey,
and Hasted, and Manning, and the olden maps. We

believe they are far wider than moderns have marked them. In 'Magna Britannia' (4to. 1730), Holmsdale and Holmwood borough are mapped south of Darkin, and around Redland. Elsewhere we read, "Between Otford and Sevenoaks is Holmsdale, a vale running into Surrey." In 774 the Mercians and the men of Kent fought at Otford: "the greate fight at the Holme, 902, between the men of Kent and the Danes." "The name of an old castle and of countrye by Rigate, wheare the Kentish men fought with the Danische Pyrates, in the time of Edward the Elder." So, on the faith of these records, they proudly boast their "vale of Holmsdale, never wonne, ne never shale," and point to mounds rich in paterae and arms and coins, and to Battle-bridge, Battle-hill, War-coppice, War-field, Kilmanbridge, and Slaughter-Weke in Legh.

On the verge of this dale the Saxons built a church in the early days of Christendom: on this site of Kircesfeld, Cherchefeld, Curchesfeld, Churgesfelde, arose the street on the ridge, Rhizegate, or Reygate, where once stood the cells of A'Becket and of St. Laurence, in Bell Street, and the Holy Cross in High Street. The Norman church of St. Mary Magdalene displays some fine antique on its reredos: on the line of the "Pilgrims' Lane," coursing along to Ightham and Otford, there is a mound fifty feet above the town, of fine diamond sand, of divers tints, like that of Alum Bay. It possesses deep interest, being the site of the "*Hypogæum munificum*" of Camden, a Norman castle fort held in olden time by the Confessor's spouse Eddiva.

In the feudal era, when the baron was a king, Warennes and Fitzalans and Maltravers held despotic sway in Reigate Castle : their families were united in the Howards, whose lineage is thus blended with Jocelina before the Conquest. In course of time, the Dauphin held awhile this fortress from John : his *jettons* or coins have been found in the dry fosses. The castle was doomed by decree of the Derby House in the seventeenth century, and it became at last *neglectum* and *ævo caducum*, being thus chronicled by Lambarde : " Ruynes and rubbishe of ane olde castel, which some call Holmsdale, which Alfred of Beverley calleth Holme."

Its mound was still a post where, in 1698, Livesay and Audley routed the Royalists. Even sixty years since there was a bit of curtain-wall : now its sole relic is " the wonderful cave made of fire-stone, the special white sand of which the Lord's Castle was built." The descent on sand steps is eighteen feet, the cave twelve, brick-arched of the twelfth century, trending S.W. to an angle, then N.W., still descending twenty-six feet to the entrance of the ward-room, and then flat to the dungeon. The crypt, or barons' hall, is a curved cavern, 123 feet long, stone seats surrounding the northern end. This cavern is a memory of William, Earl Warenne, and of that glorious noon of liberty, the dawn of which may be traced even to the time of Alfred, when the nobles of the land weighed in the balance even the Lord's anointed and found him wanting. Within this sand-rock was that judgment given on—

𝕿𝖍𝖊 𝕰𝖛𝖊 𝖔𝖋 𝖙𝖍𝖊 𝕮𝖍𝖆𝖗𝖙𝖊𝖗.

> " What time
> Th' indignant barons ranged in bright array
> Their feudal bands, to curb despotic sway,
> And, leagued a Briton's birthright to restore,
> From John's reluctant grasp the roll of freedom tore."

THE scene is before us. In the guard-room of the rock
behold two sentinels, keeping the closest watch, for it
was dark as twilight and still as death, and you would
scarcely hear the footfall of a mailed knight, or the clang
of his iron heel, as he trod the soft sand to the Hall of
State. Each held a *ghizarme*, a spear like a shepherd's
crook, wherewith to hook the leg of a traitor, as a sheepboy would a bell-wether, and cross-bows, just then introduced, hung at their side: 'twas whispered John
honoured the weapon dearly, for an arrow in the breast
of his brother had seated him on England's throne. On
the dais stood a mighty lord, William, sixth earl of
Warenne and Surrey, seised of two hundred lordships
even in this county. He was in half-armour, wearing
his hauberk over his plastron, and sandals of purple
cloth, embossed with gold. His banner was waving over
his head, checky or and azure, the wivern his helmet-
crest: the same was the coat-badge of his vassals, on a
chapeau gules turned up ermine.

His sworn crony was Gilbert de Clare, and they were
in deep converse, when came in a very spicy youth, and

whispered to his lord that Cardinal Langton was at the
Holy Cross, and craved a conference.

"Then, I guessed right," said Clare: "yet do I marvel,
noble Warenne, that you, of all men living, do consort
with Fitzwalter and his friends, and show King John so
bold a front."

"My reason is before you, noble Clare. Look on that
fair boy: were he not so fair, he would belie his mother's
blood. His descent is no secret: my daughter 'witched
the eyes of John, as Arlotte those of Robert of Normandy: there is the fruit on't. But Lachland loves not
Richard Fitzroy, and, spite of the Queen and Mareschal
of Pembroke, this base-born must wear skin socks, forsooth, while other royal brats may strut in gold cloth
sandals and legbands. Have I not cause of quarrel?
A Norman brooks not such a shelving, Clare."

As he spoke, the iron gate was flung open that had
shut in the cut from the cellar of the priory, and the
barons were dimly seen in procession, each wearing the
long tunic beneath, and the long surcoat over the mail,
the wicket or aventaille of their flat steel cap being wide
open. The Cardinal Archbishop wore the simplest gear,
like the great lords of our day, shabby to a proverb,
while their lackeys were flaunting in gold and colour.
Then came Fitzwalter, the chosen chief, and William
Mareschal, son-in-law of the King, and De Vesci, in his
sugar-loaf, a helm just in fashion, and he presented the
train of knights, who followed him, and sat down on
the sand-seats at the north end of the cave.

First spoke the Cardinal:

" Hail to the noble Warenne ! We have knelt in the crypt of Netley Lane, we have prayed in the chapel of the Holy Cross, and said high mass in the public cell of A'Becket, and we have come thus unarmed and unattended into your stronghold to confer and determine how we may avert the peril of our land."

" You honour me in your faith, barons of England," said Warenne, rising from his seat : " I am your debtor and friend to all who trust me."

" We may wonder at our daring, noble earl," said Fitz-walter, " to pass the bristling fortalice of one who hath lived in the heart of the King, but that we had your word of honour." (The Earl bowed.) " Yet do we demand wherefore your threat to raze our castles, parks, and manors : and wherefore your league with Louis and with Philippe ! "

" For the first count, forget it, nobles : for the league, believe it cancelled. I have closed with France, for she hath sold my titles in her land for my fidelity to Plantagenet."

" In lieu of Bamborough and the Bailiwick," murmured De Vesci, as the buzz went round.

" Hear me, barons," replied the Earl : " if I have once leaned to Lachland's cause, am I not *cognatus regis ?* Isabelle, my mother, granddaughter of King Stephen, Hamelin, my sire, a scion of Anjou, his shield, *semée de la France :* yet take I pride, Lord Cardinal, my hand hath ere this been linked with thine for freedom. Was it not at my behest the King hath named you, noble Fitz-walter, *Mareschallis exercitus Dei et sanctæ ecclesiæ ?* So are we quits, General of the Barons."

"Birds of a feather," whispered De Vesci—"*quasi* Royalists."

"Granted, noble Warenne," replied Fitzwalter : "and with that proud rank I marshalled my host at Edmondsbury, and there on the high altar we did swear, ay, to renounce our fealty and pursue with arms until we had enforced consent to the charter of our liberty : and so, noble Warenne, may we claim thy pledge ? "

"Lord Cardinal, to you I speak : in the new temple of London City signed not the King at my demand the confirmation of the Church's rights—doubt you me now ? Your schedule, nobles."

An acolyte, kneeling, laid the charter on the arm of the Cardinal, who read the roll he had copied from a charter of Henry. "Thus challenge we the King," he said : " 'tis but in part his oath of absolution."

"Why, good Lord Cardinal," interrupted Warenne, "we have gone beyond you, Salisbury and I : his absolution *is* signed. But first, what answer to *your* suit ? "

"Why, faith, a promise, yet craving ungraciously time till Easter, on plea of holy wars and his crusades."

"Easter?—why Easter-day is passed already. Lord Cardinal, the King shall do it : but where your rendezvous ?"

"Bedford. The castellan, William de Bello Campo, hath oped to us his gate, and without stand the Londoners, ruined by exaction : behold the keys of their great city ! "

"The keys of the kingdom ! " cried De Albini : "ay, we'll lock the King out of his throne. See to it, Langton, with me, protector of the petitioners ! "

The schedule, written on vellum, was laid on the same shelf, and as Warenne impressed on it his seal, a clarion sounded.

"Is it the King?"

"Only one blast, De Vesci : none so high!"

Richard Fitzroy announced the Seneschal in the leather-room.

"The Chamberlain, so: my lords, remember there's blood royal in him, so be wary. Armed, sayest thou?— down with the port-quilice—and we *en déshabille?* 'Tis better so—yet, good my lords, 'twere best be secret still, unknown : ye're born for better things than gyves and fetter-locks. So discretion be the word—guard the eastern outlet, so."

The Earl took from young Fitzroy his surcoat, "*violet in grinn,*" the mark of royal blood, and as the knights closed the wickets of their aventailles Hubert de Burgh stalked alone into the cave.

"Ha! in the wolf's den," he muttered to himself.

But Warenne greeted him with courtesy.

"And what from the King, Lord Chamberlain?" he asked : "I do hope a gentle and submissive—"

"Submissive! what, sir Earl, a challenge?"

"Ay, and we do echo it, Sir Hubert de Burgh!" cried Fitzwalter : "tell us in a breath: of this Earl John (so was he in Richard's time, and may be again) we demand our *charta magna* and *charta forestæ,* as this our schedule claims!"

"You bear it loftily, my lords incendiary." And De Burgh struck his heel so hard against the rock that he

bent at right angles the prycke spur upon it : maybe the
very spur found in the butts, 1802.

"Fair words, Sir Hubert," said Warenne, "or we close
our court. Your ear, sir Seneschal—that radiant boy—
pshaw !—your answer, Hubert, is it obedience ? "

"Obedience, trait—" and De Burgh bit his lip.

"Your answer : dally not ! "

"Here, then, is it writ in brief—read ye it : ' You maye
as well demande my kingdom as this charter.' The King's
great heart disdains a gentler phrase, you see : are ye
answered, lords—nay, then hear further : ' These your
exactions being grounded on no colour of reason, I will
never enslave myself by such a concession : ' this sware he
by Holy Cross."

"Hold, profane one ! " exclaimed the Cardinal : " I
condemn thee. And what says the Master Pandolfo ? "

"Why, that he gained thy pardon, Fitzwalter. What
says he ?—this—' the Pope swore by St. Peter the barons
shan't depose or oppose the king that has taken on him
the Holy Cross and is under the guard of the Holy See ! '
and, Stephen Langton, this for *your* ear, for that you did
refuse to excommunicate these rebel lords, *suspension !* "

The Cardinal answered with a smile, but Warenne
muttered :

"So he discusses with us. Seest thou that, De Burgh ?
We have a pile of such."

Hubert looked down on a round stone shot, one of which
is still shown in the cave.

"And where this conference, if we do grant it, as a
favour mark, at Windsor ? "

" The foxes' hole ? "

" No, no, we will meet in our shire of Surrey. So, nobles, with your leave, in this month of June will we wait John by the Thames : if he sign, 'tis peace, if not—"

" Ay," muttered Hubert, " what then ? "

" Then let rebellion rage. You know me, Seneschal. He swear by the Cross ? why, so have I : here, on the charter, my oath is sealed, that he should sign it and keep it true. A word in thine ear, good Hubert : my cousin, William of the Strong Hand, doomed by the Queen of France because he would not love her, tore out a lion's tongue—I will not shame my blood. Farewell, De Burgh : counsel well your king : save John of Britain as you did Arthur of Bretagne, when you did govern at Falaise. In one sentence, tell John from me 'twere better Arthur wore his crown than he thus flout his nobles. Farewell, De Burgh : look, when we meet again, 'tis peace ! "

Hubert bowed, and left the cave. So closed the conference and the eve of the charter, for Hubert's evidence left the King no hope of resistance.

In the Thames, by Wyrardisbury, in Buckinghamshire, there is an *Eyot*, or *Eight*, over against Yardmead, honoured by popular error with the name of "Magna Charta Island :" Matthew Paris will enlighten us :—" In Henry the Third's early reign, the rights of the charter were ratified with the *French delegates* in a certain island by the river Thames. Magna Charta was signed in Runnymead, *Runing mede*, ' the meadow of the rune,' or council :" *in præto quod vocatur Runimed.* It is recorded that, as he set his seal to the deed, John gnashed his teeth, while he gnawed the straws he had picked from off the ground.

AT this day the Holy Cross is a mere memory.   In the
hall of the Priory, now standing on its site, there is a
chimney-piece, we believe from Bletchingley, or Nonsuch,
well worth the showing—fluted Corinthian pillars, chairs
and canopies in niches, royal shields, and crown-bearing
angels.   May not the maiden Queen, who was often here,
have leaned on this marble, when with a regal frown she
counselled Essex to " keep his chamber " ?

If you chance to be spending Christmas in any of those
old manor houses that lie southward of Scal Hill, amid
the " russet lawns and fallows grey " of the Weald of
Surrey, and join the circle of the boors around the huge
hall fire, you may often gather many an old story, either
grave or gay, as their mood may be.

In Flenchford, by the Mole stream yonder, the ancient
Flenesforde, the demesne of Warenne, Fitzalan, Mowbray, and Sander of Charlwood, you might hear how
James Stuart, Duke of York, who had lost himself, as he
often did while out a-hunting, in the Weald, was rebuffed
by the yeoman's dame, who swore that no Catholic bigot
should ever darken her door of Flenchett.

Wander farther south a mile, and you will come to the
moated Grange of Leigh, the *Leghe* of the " Monasticon,"
the *Leght* of " Magna Britannia," the Lee, Ley, Lay, Leag,
Leigh, Legh, of others.   It has been the home of very lofty
families—Braose, Dudley of Northumberland, Shelley,
Cobham, or Copley, and Arderne.   In the moat we have
discovered an obolus of Domitian, coins of the Confessor,
and iron balls, the relics of Audley's skirmishes with the
royal guards.   The huge chimney springing from the roof,
the black-beamed hall, the carved staircase, the oaken

chest that closed in the wainscot (for Dame Cobham, like Lady Lisle, in the era of the Stuarts, had furnished a *priests' hole*), the chestnut arch, and the long black table at which we have eaten with the retainers of our own family, that sat below the Salt, all indicate antiquity.

In this very hall, many a year ago, a boy was listening, about midnight, to a pale and beetle-browed monk—but our quill has scribbled on too fast : so, if ye will shift awhile to London Town, remote and roundabout as the tradition will come before you, ye will learn from this boy, even then a wit of the first water, the strange, dark story of

The Bleeding Heart of Arderne.

"One without a tomb,
Call up Astarte."

IT was in the *Apollo* of the Devil Tavern, by Temple
Bar, that a trio of racy spirits were 'rousing : there was a
flash of joy sparkling in every eye, and pearls of wit hung
on every lip.   In the chair sat " O rare" Ben Jonson.
Apollo was his club-room, and, over the chimney, were
cut in marble Ben's *leges conviviales,* the laws of his Symposia, or Rules for the Tavern Academy.

Old Simon Wadloe, whom Jonson dubbed Sir Simon
the King, had just brought up a rich china bowl brimful
of nectar of the most spicy bouquet—canary, milk, sugar,
cloves, lemon, and rosemary.

As he rolled away, the fairest of the three took out his
pencil, and sketched, in a scene at the Boar's Head in
Chepe, something touching the fat of Falstaff.   Ben filled
his pipe-clay with the rich tabac vended by—the Abel
Drugger of the Alchymist, and cried out :

" Your goblet, your goblet, Michael Drayton, and yours,
sweet Willie : booze for Bacchus, by the foot of Pharaoh,
so pledge ye, camarados,

" ' Sack and the well-spiced hippocras the wine,
Wassail the bowl, with ancient ribbons fine.'

Ah, my eyes are clearer, my thoughts brighter, with
draining deep this poculum."

"Ay," responded Shakspere, "it hath a spell in't: it sets

the poet's eye in 'a fine frenzy rolling.' More things in heaven and earth than are dreamt of in our philosophy, Ben."

Jonson's eyes flashed darkly. "Ay, marry, there be shadow-truths eclipse our dreams: but replenish, replenish, and you shall hear one now, perpend. You must know, ere good Master Camden raised me from a brick-yard to Trinity on the banks of Cam, I lodged in Surrey, and there, in my chamber at Swain's, on my long table, spoiled many a quill plucked from the grey goose-wing. With my trowel in one pocket, and my Chaucer and my dog's-eared Horace in the other, I would wander, after labour, to Dame Cobham's at Legh, and there, after kissing the *Mawther* wench under the misseltoe, for she was *mortal elynge* without me, I would doze and dream in the dear old ingle nook till I was alone with the embers. One night, the bell then beating one, I was humming my chaunt in the 'Masque of Queens:'

> "'The owl is abroad, the bat and the toad,
> And so is the cat-a-mountain :
> The owl and the mole sit both in a hole,
> And frog peeps out of the fountain :'

when, lo! crept out of the wainscot a very shadow in human form. His scowl set me a-shivering, and I rose to leave, when he lured me back with a smile, and we cottoned in a moment, and I sat hour by hour, awe-struck by his hollow tones."

> "'Till each particular hair would stand on end,
> Like quills upon the fretful porcupine.'"

So chimed in Willy Shakspere.

"Well, trembling and etiolate, he pressed his hand on his brow, his eye glaring like lightning, and his long-drawn sigh like a distant thunder-peal. I was *hevy cherd*, as old Chaucer hath it, but, as he went on thus, my whole thought was exotic to him:

"In this great hall of Legh, a fresh and beautiful young widow, Dame Margaret de la Beche, the relict of Master Nicholas, had been sipping from a gold-mounted cup of the Ardernes.

"'Your cowslip, dear Mabel,' she said, sweetly smiling, 'is as fine as when my gossip of Arderne was in this life.'

"'Ah, mistress, would she were here still, sweet lady: such a pretty pair as ye were, with your merlins on your wrists,' twas special, sure, to see your ladyships lip your loving kisses. Alas! she is gone: and you so bonny, still in hat and feather.'

"'Ay, we can do it, Mabel, can we not? Look you, we've been lashing through the Queen's Wood in Walton, and Wonham swore I was match for Queen Lizzie Wode-ville, whose name the village bears. Look here, I've won the pads, Mabel. But look, the moon is up, and the dew on the grass, and my lacquey is not here, so good night.'

"'Alone, lady, and Sander prowling in Hart's wood?'

"'Fear not, I'm fleet o' foot—a Camilla, an Atalanta. I—I'll beat a lagging monk at any odds. Good night.'

"'Why, 'tis Bartholomew to-night, lady—loose fish on Legh Green, be sure,' exclaimed a man who entered un-observed. 'I'll esquire you home.'

"The lady quailed beneath his rolling eye.

"'We thought you at Wonham, sir.'

"'So was I, but now, and he has primed me with burgundy, for your suit and service.'

"'Then, I pray you, cross yourself, and swear to do my service fair and honest, Master Arderne.'

"'I swear, sweet Margery,' replied Arderne, tearing the breast-knot from her bosom, and setting it in the band of his beaver: 'by Jove, 'tis I must wear thee, Madge: head of the Homage of Shelwood my lordship may claim my Boro' English, faith. Shall we go ?'

"Lady Margery breathed quickly, and Mabel scowled upon her master. But there was no help for it, and the lady stood fumbling to clasp her light jacket with its jewel, and, as they crossed the drawbridge, the raven croaked ominously, and Mabel, a tear in her eye, looked after the ill-matched pair, and 'hoped her beauty would soon *get shut of him,*' for he smacked more of evil even than the monk.

"Margery de la Beche was less an Amazon than a Sylph, yet, as we have heard, she had a dash of Diana in her blood, and was the idol of the *Hawkery* on Epsom Downs, and had carried off a brush, yet her heart throbbed tumultuously as his eye gloated on her with most unchaste expression. As he lifted her over the stile, he pressed her so much closer to his bosom than need were, that she repulsed him in anger, and was right glad when they came upon the Mole.

"'Well,' she said, softly, 'here we are, at Flenchford Calceway Bridge, and Poynings will be close at hand, so I'll be safe. Good night, Sir Thomas Arderne.'

"The bridge was then a mere bridle-way, but wide

enough for one. Her long brown hair was fanned by the breeze, and rolled over her white neck in rich profusion, and so lovely looked she in her deshabille, that Arderne, half-reeling, pressed his lip on her cheek.

"She blushed deeply, and her brilliant eye flashed with fire. 'How dare you!' she cried, and tried to pass him.

"'Nay,' exclaimed he, 'no coquetting now, fair dame. By the brow of Venus, the Wonham burgundy hath made me too bold to be foiled by an angry beauty, so—'

"'How, Arderne,' she said, 'you forget yourself: you are—a—gentleman.'

"'Trust me,' he replied, 'and one that loves a lady: so, divinest Margery, while the moon smiles on us—and smile she would not, sweet wench, if we were wrong, you know. You are mine—mine!'

"But the moon smiled not: she hid her light and wept behind her cloud.

"The lady's head dropped on her shoulder, and she lay insensible on his bosom.

"But we are blind to the scene, and would fain draw a veil over her sorrows, yet the fate of Margaret is historic and the pith of our story.

"Arderne was for awhile lost in his wild delirium, and when his senses came back to him there lay on his bosom a form pale and cold as marble.

"She waked from her trance, and cried, 'Mercy, mercy! tell me, Arderne, tell me 'tis a dream, and I will bless thee! Ah, no dream, no dream!' and she uttered a piercing shriek, when a youth, with giant stride, leaped over the Mole, and caught Arderne by the throat. He looked on him and then on the lady with wild and speechless wonder.

"'You, you!' he exclaimed—'methought 'twas an outlying buck in rutting-time:' and he recoiled, as a tiger for a second spring—but in closing, a gold-hilt poniard was in his heart, yet he rushed away, exclaiming, 'I will proclaim thee in Reigate the ruthless boar of Arderne, ay, at the market-cross, Arderne the violator!' and he staggered along the lane, townward.

"Arderne was deaf to the accuser, but his conscience, stung by remorse, directly induced him, though his life was at stake and every moment precious, to bear his victim to Flenchford, and he laid her gently on his cloak in the porch : and so, pulling hastily the bell, he instantly disappeared.

"About eight o'clock that night, as the curfew was rung at the priory, a man staggered from the park-gate, and fell at the door of the old chapel of St. Laurence, in Bell Street. He told of a dark and dismal crime that he had witnessed : the prior sat to take his deposition, and a grim monk wrote it down : but ere he had named the homicide, his lip quivered and his limbs were convulsed, and so, deeply sobbing and muttering a prayer, he drew the dagger from his breast, and as the blood welled in torrents forth, in a moment he was dead.

"A man from the crowd, closely muffled, clutched the dagger and escaped, but the monk had seen its jewelled hilt and crest—a fesse checkie between three crescents. 'Twas clear, the cry was up, and the monk led the mob. The muffled man was found in the crypt, in Netley Lane :

H

he started away, but was caught in a dingle of the park, as he fled towards Leigh, by the monk, who whispered in his ear and glided stealthily away.

"*Pro formâ*, the crier called aloud '*Oyez, oyez!*' in Norman-French, and the prior sat in judgment. The evidence was circumstantial, for the witness was dead, and no malice could be proved against the Lord of Leigh (for so the lords of the manor were called by courtesy), and, indeed, the dead man had been the pet of Thomas Arderne. The half-damning evidence of the cloak found in the porch at Flenchford, and the state of Lady Margery de la Beche, told of some dark and suspicious mystery that the monk alone could unfold : but Chandler the prior, and William Howard the justice, were bosom friends of the accused, and prone to hush up and hide the shame of the prior's *cousin* Margery. The rich and great, you know, have ever the full benefit of clergy. So the capital charge was abandoned, and Arderne was, *pro formâ*, slightly burned on the hand by an iron far below the degree of white heat, and the crime was, for a time, well-nigh forgotten.

"Still, the dagger was a mystery not to be blinked : while the monk, they said, looked wondrous wise. His lip was sealed by the closest reticence, save a whisper now and then into the ear of the prior.

"One morning it was bruited abroad by the scribes of the Holy Cross that the lands of Leigh were yielded to Sir Richard Cobham, and Nature herself seemed to feel the blight : the twenty nightingales that were wont to charm even my rude ears flew right away, and, although they came back slowly, one by one, their notes were changed from joy to wailing, from chaunt to lamentation.

"Margaret, this while, brooded in deep seclusion at Flenchford, and the monk to whom she confessed dared, in that very hour, to insult her ear with his own burning passion, for oh, *he* had loved her long and despairingly. I may not paint her proud and damning scorn, as I held the dagger to her sight, nor my own deep and stony trance within my cell, yet thou knowest now who the monk was. Thou wilt not guess the miracle that followed —Margery de la Beche became the wife of Thomas Arderne! Marvel not: there were secrets deeper far. True, the murderous guilt of Arderne was writ in blood upon the dagger's blade, but *she*, the *wife* of him who once wore it—why, Scandal, ay, and Justice too, would bite their lips, and be silent.

"So the pensive widow was a blushing bride, and held her finger for a ring she scorned, her lip for kisses that she loathed.

"But her grief deepened hour by hour, why, *she* best knew : sorrow chilled and blanched her cheek to marble.

"The monk—look on me, boy, while I name him—the monk struck not: he swore a deeper vengeance. He threw the dagger in the moat, and day by day he haunted the soul of Arderne.

"The life of Margery was a blank : from her forced smile and fading cheek her husband turned in scorn : passion was dead.

"Oh, woman, woman, once fallen from thy sacred sphere of purity, who is to raise thee ? He who stole thy jewel ?

alas! his touch will but sully it with a deeper stain. He
who dragged thee down to earth? alas! the grave of the
heart is deeper, deeper still.

"Yet Margery was even now the love of all—of all but
one who had *sworn* to love her.

"To him she went through her cold and pitiless voca-
tion with patience and a smile.

"It was again the eve of Bartholomew.

"Arderne had chased a ringdove he had wounded, and,
like some special spirit, it led him to his wife's chamber,
and settled in her bosom. As she lay dreaming, something
she whispered strangely prophetic, for Arderne trembled
as he whispered "Mabel, I am off to Waldehache and
Hartswood—the Homage would cheat Mowbray of his
summons for Bidripe. So till midnight—and then, and
then—'

" 'And what then?' said Mabel.

" 'Why, then—ha! there's Mowbray. Good.'

"Lady Margery sat in her leaf-house by the moat: there
was a halo round the moon that night. Was she alone?
No, she was watched by one whose flame was burning still.

" 'Sleep on, sleep on, thou blessed one,' he whispered,
as he hovered over her: 'hopeless to death, I dare not
profane thy lips.' Ay, even a monk hath a conscience,
boy: but listen on.

"The curfew was booming over the ley when the lady
awoke, and kissed her kerchief that she had broidered, a
dagger impaling a heart blood-red.

"As Mabel approached, the monk had slunk away.

" 'Look, Mabel, look,' the lady exclaimed, 'how red the

halo round the moon, and mark how deep and dismal
peals the curfew !'

" 'Nay, brighter thoughts, dear lady,' said Mabel.   'Sip
your cup of cowslip, love.   What ! a dagger—a heart
blood-red ?   Prythee, work doves and roses, sweetheart.'

" 'Alas !' she murmured, smiling ghastly, 'my doves
are flown, my roses faded all !' (and she thrust the kerchief
into her bosom).   'Leave me alone, Mabel, with my ringdove in my lap : while I wake the thrush will carol to me :
and when you hear the nightingale, Mabel, be sure I
shall be quiet as a lamb :' and so, as Mabel with a sigh
retreated, Lady Margery fell asleep, and as her lids closed
the dove nestled in her bosom.

" And so all was still, until the midnight bell, when
horses came galloping over hedge and rail the Hartswood
way, and over the drawbridge they clattered like wild
jägers after a phantom stag.

" 'Welcome, gentles,' roared Arderne, ' to my poor house
of Leigh : 'tis all I have left : Cobham hath sacked my
land.   No more reels in Leigh Hall : so leave it will I, ay,
at the dawn.   The world is wide enough—no matter where
I wander.   Meg may live and die here, an' she will, and
brew her cowslip.   The king bar confiscation, will he ?
—ha, ha—and Cobham—But ho, Mabel, a bicker of
canary : 'tis all I can offer—ho, Mabel, ho !'

" ' My lady hath the keys,' muttered Mabel.

" 'Then I must mount,' grumbled Arderne.

" ' Nay,' interrupted Mowbray, 'Lady Margery is retired.
I'm off : farewell.'

" 'By the holy rood, no !' exclaimed Arderne.

" ' My lady is quiet now, poor soul,' said Mabel, holding his arm.   ' Hark ! she said she'd sleep when the
night-bird was singing o'er her bower.'

" ' Bower—sleep,' cried Arderne, ' when she should
smile welcome on her lord's guests ! '

" ' Let her sleep on,' said Mabel : ' she has not slept so
sound for many a night.'

" ' A time to sleep and a time to wake,' cried Arderne :
' she will wake when *I* call.   Ha ! she comes—I hear her
step along the gallery—and see how silently she glides ! '
and he looked wildly at the staircase.

" ' You are dreaming, Arderne,' said Mowbray : ' to bed,
to bed ! ' and as he spoke the nightingales were hushed in
a moment.

" ' Jove, this is fool's play ! ' exclaimed Arderne. ' Look,
look, to the garden, look ! '

" ' I see nothing,' said Mowbray as he followed Arderne.
' Yes see, still as a mouse in her leaf-house.'

" Arderne reeled into the leaf-house.   ' Wake, Madge,
wake ! ' he cried : ' the keys—we thirst for wine ! ' and he
shook her rudely : ' no sham, girl.'

The barn owls hooted strangely.

" ' Keep your owls quiet, Mabel. Ha, wine ?—so *this*
has set her sleeping, then ? Here, take the cup, Mowbray,
and drink while I shake the keys out of her.'

" Mabel snatched the cup from Mowbray.   ' Forbear,'
she cried : ' no lip shall profane the brim that hers hath
touched ! '

" ' Nay, then, we'll have it fresh : so wake, Madge,
wake :' and he shook her yet more rudely.

" ' Hold, Arderne, hold ! ' cried Mowbray, ' are you mad ? are you blind ? This is not sleep—for your life and soul, forbear.'

" ' Not sleep—not sleep ! ' exclaimed Arderne.

" ' 'Tis death, Thomas Arderne,' screamed Mabel. ' Death, death, death—do you hear ? '

" Arderne stood like a statue, his bloodshot eye glaring around, and he fell senseless to the ground as if a bolt had struck him, and his forehead fell against the yew stem that even now stands by the moat, and blood gushed out. The monk rushed forth and stanched the wound, for he was half a doctor, and bound the kerchief tight round his brow, and laid him on his bed. Listen, listen, boy. As they watched his couch at midnight, a soft voice was chanting in sweet though solemn tone, ' Mercy, Jesu, and graunt mercy.'

" Arderne started like a roused demon and rushed to the door, followed by Mowbray and—the monk. There was nothing there but a huge white owl that, as the chanting ceased, was flapping and hooting at the casement : to Arderne's conscience it was a ghost to his dying hour. In the lady's chamber Mabel had been watching, too : and when all was silent in Legh Place she folded in her apron a blighted and unchrisomed child, born after the death of its mother, and buried it in an earthen pot in yonder field. The monk watched her, and followed in the dark."

(The bones of an infant have been, a few years ago, exhumed by the plough.)

" In what unconsecrated ground the lady herself lies

they know not, for Mabel's lips were sealed. 'Twas rumoured her body was spirited away by angels, but the monk knows better, and could tell you where, to this hour, the lady lies inearthed, without a tomb.

"Arderne wore the kerchief round his brow until it dropped in rags : the wound had skinned over, but a deep *intaglio* of a bleeding heart impaled on a dagger burned on his brow even to his dying day.

"Christ of His mercy, that a dead wife's fingers should thus brand an erring husband's brow, and blazon for life his shame to all the world ! Ever after, on the eve of Bartholomew, Arderne was in deep seclusion : the veins of his forehead became like purple cords, and just at midnight a gush of grumous blood burst from the damning spot, and he sank from a state of frenzy to that of profound stupor : the while the monk, his leech, glared with the malice of a fiend on his agony, for the groans refreshed his soul, while each heard the cry of the Spirit of Evil from its unhallowed haunt, ' Live on, live on in loathing ! Part ye dare not : fate hath doomed your souls to that unhallowed fellowship where love itself is hate.' Thou seest, boy, what *I* am. He, too, was a woe-begone, maundering by day, and at night haunting his home a sleepless phantom. Vengeance was complete, so I flung into the moat the useless poniard. Like the Wandering Jew, Arderne outlived his hour, and one night I knew by the shadow on the wall that he was dying : it took a demon's form and then I knew that he was dead. The ghost ever haunts thus the next in guilt, as 'tis writ in the spirit-law of heaven's chancery. I know where to find him :

over his mother's vault in the chancel lay Thomas Arderne
stark and cold, his lip clotted with the gore that had
welled from his brow, pressed on the brazen scroll over
his mother's tomb—ay, on the mystic words that had been
ever in his ear, and were thereon inscribed, ' Mercy, J'hu,
and graunt mercy.' The monk had told his tale, and
starting from his seat he took a sandstone from his pouch,
and with a nail scratched a letter on its face. ' So one
letter more,' he muttered, ' would it were the last, of my
prayer for pardon.' This done, he crawled into his lair,
and I never saw Nicholas Sander more. Yet soon we
learned from the Green Isle that the Jesuit's death was
dismal as his life.

" ' He escaped the barre of justice, yet he was found out
by a raving phrenzie as he wandered succourlesse in the
waste mountains of Ireland, whereon lastele hee miserably
dyed.' 'Tis said the ghost of Margaret hovered awhile
over his corpse, and scared the vulture and the raven from
the carrion, for 'tis writ, that those without a tomb are
jealous even of the phantom of the dead regarding the
possession of the festering corpse. Ay, smile at my
phantasy as you may, my camarados, _I_ have seen, myself, too many ghosts to be a sceptic now. But your
goblets, your goblets : drown the ghost in this Red Sea
of the wassail bowl, for, good troth, my story hath been
a doleful penance for you both."

'Tis clear that Ben was in his richest vein that night,
but that night may be a sad, sad memorial : it may have
scaled the destiny of the " poet of all time," sweet Willie
Shakspere. In the library of the Medical Society of

London, we treasure a very quaint old MS. the diary of
John Ward, Vicar of Stratford, written about forty years
after Shakspere's death, and bearing the clearest marks of
veracity.   It is thus inscribed : "This booke was begunne
ffeb. 14, 1661, att Mr. Brooks his house in Stratford-
uppon-Avon," and it contains this record : "Shakspear,
Drayton, and Ben Jhonson, had a merry meeting, and
itt seems drank too hard, for Shakspear *died of a feavor*
there contracted."   This is the only allusion extant to the
dying of the Swan of Avon, the date of which was
about that of our story.

The tangled skein is not yet unravelled—Nicholas
Sander will be ever a dark and doubtful page on England's
history.   It was he who made Desmond a rebel, he who
wrote up the Holy Maid of Kent, and in his book (dated
by Holinshed, 1584), *De Origine et Progressu Schismatis
Anglicanæ*, affirmed that Henry's lust lay in the bed of
the Reformation—a sentence that brought down the Pope's
anathema on Elizabeth.   Camden dates his death 1583,
others his *burning* 1536, and others assert that Cromwell
himself endeavoured to save him.   It was believed, too,
that he desecrated again the scene of his legend, while the
mystery of the bleeding heart was whispered in many a
lone cottage around Leigh, how the ghost of Margaret yet
haunted the moated grange : and aged folk, even of
the last century, often heard the chant of "Mercy, Jesu,"
streaming across the meadows at midnight.

These myths are fading fast from the vicinage of Leigh,
yet there are relics even now that are strangely blended
with the tissue of our story.   There is Ben's table at

Swains : there is the brass in the chancel inscribed
" Mercy, Jesu, and graunt mercy :" there is the rudely
scored sandstone, a few years ago found in the moat, now
inlaid on a chamber mantelpiece : there is the dagger also
found in the moat, its rust believed to be the blood stain,
that has been often scraped clean away yet quickly re-
appears : and between the roof joists was discovered an
antique silver cup, cut with three rude letters $\begin{smallmatrix} & A. \\ R. & I. \end{smallmatrix}$, the
initials of John and Isabella Arderne, an heirloom of the
house, perchance, and the Lady Margaret's lip may have
been the last that touched its brim.

So endeth our dark and rambling fragment of antient
Leigh, that is now smiling in the sunlight of rural tran-
quillity.

Its meadows are now of brightest green, yet we must.
leave them for the rich down woods of Gatton yonder,
where old Gerard was wont to wander and study in the
air of heaven the choice wildings which the Creator had
flung around him.

The dwarf elder they call *Danewort*, for that it sprung
from the blood of the Danes mutilated by the Saxon
Amazons, and therefore never browsed by animals.

Napoleon's chimneypiece graces the library of Gatton
House, the manor lord of which once returned two mem-
bers of Parliament.

In the eleventh century, Hamo de Gatton, or De
Valeysne, held high state in the lodge with his bride, the
daughter of De Broc, *Ostiarius* of the King's Chamber.
Fancy may sketch this lord of Gatton, with his white wand

and golden key, as marshal of the maids : and here he was
wont to review his bevy of beauties, "*douze demoiselles à la
court die Roy*," whom he had hired for twelve or fourteen
centimes each.

Now, prythee, remember his name and his lineage, and
then, gazing on yon nameless portrait—copied, it is thought,
by Lely from one more antique—you may believe it to
portray the beauty of a young creature for many a year
the darling of King Edward's Court. Her name was
ever on the lips of the courtiers, and her story was
chanted far and near, both in hall and in hostelrie, and
this is—

The Romaunt of Ethel.

Oʜ, who that hath look'd upon Ethel Valeysne
Wolde nott drynke in ye sonnelite agen and agen,
Ye sonnelite that shotte like a star from her eyne,
And dreame alle of love and of heaven, I wene,
    And of Ethel, Ethel Valeysne.

Oh, her beauty was lite to the pourple Adour,
Ytte was deth to the Basque and ye Franche and ye Mor ;
Yette now never chauntys ye wylde troubadour,
Ne trylles ye chelaundre, ne blossoms ye flore,
    For Ethel, Ethel Valeysne.

Oh, Ethel, myne darling, why syghest thou soe,
Thy cheke ys as whyte as ye bloom of ye sloe,
Thy lips, once so flushing, as colde as ye snowe,
Oh, waste not thy morning yn wailing and woe,
    Myne Ethel, Ethel Valeysne.

For a maydene soe fayre 'twere a sinne and a shame
To spende her yonge lyfe yn ye armes of a dame :
There be lordynges yn plenty, of honour and fame,
Who would fly on love's wynglets to Waldinghame,
For Ethel, Ethel Valeysne.

Nay, mocke me not, ladye : oh, where ys ye worthe
Of an oath yt was broke yn ye hore of yts byrthe :
There ys joy for the slave, for the beggar there's myrth,
But oh, not a shadowe of hope upon yerthe
For Ethel, Ethel Valeysne.

Ah, the sprynge of my love yt was lucyd and bryghte,
Lyke ye glynterynge moon on a Midsummer nyte :
But ye shadowe of falsehoode came down on ytts lyte,
And ye budde, yt was burstyng yn beautie, ys blyte
To Ethel, Ethel Valeysne.

The dame watch'd yn silence ye teare yn her eye,
Lyke ye dewdrops yt deepe yn ye violets lye :
And she herde how her hearte breth re-echoed ye syghe,
And she whisper'd, "Ye angels, myne Ethel will dye !"
Myne Ethel, Ethel Valeysne.

Go, saddle ye palfreys, ye blacke and the graye,
We are off to fayre Gateton rigght sodainly,
To welcome home Hamo ye gallant and gaye,
He will charme ye darke hore wyth hys roundelaye,
From Ethel, Ethel Valeysne.

Lorde Hamo hed gone to ye falconie flyghte :
But theyre lye hys gems from ye londe of ye lite :

There be rubys so rede, there be pearlys so whyte,
Yet ye duste were as pretious as these yn ye site
                    Of Ethel, Ethel Valeysne.

What shadyth yonne courtaine of damasque and golde,
Oh, a tresore alle pryceless lys hydde yn yts folde :
Yet never Lord Hamo yts secrete hath tolde.
Why, Ethel, why gypsey, you shivere with colde !
                    Why Ethel, Ethel Valeysne.

Ytt ys here, when ye shadowes of twylyght are flone,
Lord Hamo will falle on ye Marmorie stone,
And worship hys ydol yn silence alone,
Noe marvel, her beautie ys bryght as thine own,
                    Ethel, Ethel Valcysne.

The dame drewe ye courtayne, ye maydene lokd rounde,
"Yt ys myne, yt ys myne, and the secrete ys founde."
Lord Hamo rush'd yn wyth hys hawk and hys hounde,
And he kneel'd, lyke a penytent kneel'd on ye grounde,
                    By Ethel, Ethel Valeysne.

And Ethel hath pillowed her cheke on hys breste,
Where she lay lyke a dove yn yts mother warme nest.
And she knew, as her harte to his bosome was prest,
Thro' alle ye greene Holmsdale noe maydene soe bleste
                    As Ethel, Ethel Valeysne.

O her lyf was a love-dreme ye nyte and ye daye,
And her cheke grewe alle roses lyke ghirlondes yn Maye :
But O, yt ys only herselfe that can saye
The wordes yt he breth'd yn hys roundelaye,
                    To Ethel, Ethel Valeysne.

We would travel far to witness such a bridal as that of Ethel, and we wonder if its record, like that of other Court beauties, was in the chapter-house of some cloistered abbey, or in the parish register of this fine old church of Gatton, where we are admiring those carved doors from Rouen, and stalls from Gend, and painted glass from Aurschot, a screen from Burgundy, and the altar of Albrecht Dürer from Nuremberg.

We confess that, for us, a village church is ever an inspiration and a study. There are few without some fragment of the antique. Yonder, in its pretty hill-solitude, is another of these rural temples, shadowed by its magnificent yew,—the cruciform fane of St. Margaret in Chipstead, of the twelfth century: the fine door-arches are early Norman.

As we descend across the belt of Firestone, we come on St. Katherine in Merstham, perched on a very charming site. The arms of Stuart surmount one arch, on another is a stone shield from old London Bridge. There are mural paintings of St. Katheryn and of the Virgin and Child, there is a crucifix-bracket, a double piscina, and a black marble font: there is the Newdigate tomb: and within a niche of the Albury chancel is that of Sir John Elmbrigge, or Ilanbridge, two wives and seven kneeling daughters, in brass, and indents for the sons, who probably fell in the Wars of the Roses. One of the bells is inscribed, "*Sancta Katherina, ora pro me.*" Told that bell a tale clearly as it tolled a knell, it might even now ring out a very strange story of the last

Plantagenet.

"Those evening bells,
Full many a tale their music tells."

AFTER the flight of Edgcote, when Fitzhugh beat Pembroke, Warwick the king-maker kept his pair of crown puppets under lock and key, and played them against each other, like chessmen, according to his humour. Edward was dragged from Olney to the "Byshoppe of Middleham," and Henry to the Tower of London, the Earl's son-in-law, Clarence, playing the spaniel at his heels. Gloucester, with other scared Yorkists that Warwick had "fluttered like an eagle in a dovecote," fled into Surrey.

In an oak closet of *Noak* in Chipstede were seated an old lady and a young soldier. Edward Stafford, Earl of Devon, had run away from Banbury to the quiet home of his aunt, the dowager of Wiltshire, lady of this manor, who, looking lovingly on the youth, assured him of his safety at Chipstead.

"Yet am I between two fires, sweet aunt," he said : "Warwick and limbo."

"Limbo !"

"Ay, fool that I was to split with Pembroke—he'll peach me, madam, to the King, so, 'twixt hawk and buzzard—hush !—hush !—who's here ?"

The groom announced three noble cavaliers, and the lady left the room.

"How!" exclaimed Stafford, "the noble Glo'ster! Wydville, Lovel, welcome to Chipstede!"

"Nay," said the Duke, "no names—their echo may cost us dear. By holy Paul! we know not if we walk on heads or heels while Warwick wields the scourge."

"And the king?" asked Stafford, eagerly.

"King!—which king? an' you mean Edward?" he added in a whisper, as Workworth tells us, "'By fayre speche and promise the kinge scaped oute of the By-shoppe's hands.' So we are bound for France, if the pale sun of York will light us on so far. No thanks to you for our roses, they blush deep for Edgcote, boy. Shame on you, Stafford—for the lips of a blowzy barmaid you have shut the fetterlock with a vengeance. Would Ned and I had been there! we would have fleshed our battle-axes in the blood of Wales, and Edgcote field had paled the ruddy glory of Towton. Well, let Neville crow awhile— *I* bide my time."

"The time is up," said Wydville, "the weather-cock is round again, and Clarence ratted."

"Ha! a spite to me," muttered Glo'ster, "Warwick will Queen his daughter, then."

"Not so: his Vice-admiral, the bastard of Falconberg, votes for Lancaster."

"Worse still," said Glo'ster, "but, red or white, number one for Richard. Cry havoc! I, and Warwick's blood! —nay, nay, all in peace! and Anne Neville is the dove that bears the olive. The red cockrell may crow—old Cicely work in the dark—and George cheat me of her lands—and let Warwick play suit as he will: Clarence

I

he shall drown in Malmsey for 't, or the white witch
Shore shall blast him, as she hath this withered arm of
mine. Would 'twere Ned's heart, it might have barred
a wedding. Aye, Anne *shall* be mine—plate, jewels, all.
I say so, Richard of Glo'ster! But who are these?"

"All game and true," said Stafford: "De Brewse of
Perefrith, and Quetche of Ihurst, and Passelew of the
Meadow in Alderstede, ye will cotton with us, we hold
a feast, this very hour. Say, how shall I herald your
Grace."

"Earl of Salisbury—my new style—an you will."

So was Richard hailed by these losels of Surrey.

Now the feast of St. Catherine was over at the Block
House in Merstham, the wine cups drained to the dregs,
yet Glo'ster cried, "Fill high! Nectar for the red lips!"

"Nectar *on* the red lips!" cried Passelew, "the lips of
Surrey are full of it. Whoop, Venus, come where the
love-birds roost, mellow as mother's milk, and ripe as
raspberries!"

"Whoop! for the sluts of Aldebury," roared all the
bachelors at once, and the madcaps rushed out in their
hot blood, and rolled and reeled like Comus' crew to
Alderstede. Lovel, *the dog*, at the very heels of his
master.

In their long Gothic chamber, at midnight hour, seven
fair girls were kneeling. The madrigals no longer echoed
in the music hall, and they were now breathing vespers
to St. Catherine.

"You Cicely," exclaimed Miss Elmbrigge, "you, mad
puss, profane Kit's cushion thus with unholy knees, with

the Romaunt of the Rose and a love-token dangling at your girdle. *Fi donc! fi donc!* your thoughts should be of heaven. Think you our saint will love you, and her angels bless your pillow, run your night-thoughts on rhymes and roundelays? But where *is* Kit?"

"Haunting the Pilgrim's Lane," said Cicely, "another holy walk, like nun in serge and sackcloth—hark! as I live ——"

A chorus of voices was borne on the wind.

"It is! it is! the roysters from the feast,—I know Brewse's twang among a thousand. Well-a-day! this comes of keeping wine and wassail."

As she spoke, the din was hushed, but there was a rush and rustle beneath the window. The six sisters were frozen to icicles, for the madcaps clambered on the vines, and leaped rudely into the room one by one.

"Ha!" hiccoughed Glo'ster, "the Prophet's paradise, by the Cestus of Venus!"

"And a houri for each of us," stammered Passclew, as he drew Clarice to his bosom, and imprinted a kiss on her cheek.

"Unhand me, sir," she exclaimed, "how dare you thus profane the sanctity of our chamber—Cicely, the bell!"

But Cicely Seyntcler was playing puss in the corner with Gloucester.

"Is this the noble Devon?" murmured Alyce, "on the eve of St. Katheryn, too. Shame on you, Edward Stafford! your aunt will blush for you, and your dishonour be trumpeted through the land. Think on your fair fame, my lord."

"Think on your own, beauty mine," he cried, "look, Venus shines on us through the casement, 'tis her hour of burning, bright one."

But we may not follow out the unblushing dalliance that assailed the maidens, while from their tremulous lips echoed through the chamber, "*Sancta Katherina ora pro nobis.*" The morning, it seemed, would tell a very dismal tale : but the Saint had heard their prayer, for the loud clang of the great bell in Merstham steeple peeled along the valley, and in a moment the village was alive, lights were dancing in the windows, and Aldbury House was wide awake.

The girls were in ecstasy—the hubbub sobered in a moment the wild thoughts of the intruders, even a sense of decorum came across them as they cooled—for remember they were still gentlemen born—they made a retreat as hasty as their assault, and when the chamber was entered, there were six maidens on their knees in prayer : and Sir John was consoled for his fright, by an assurance of its being a false alarm. They missed not Katheryn, who, indeed, had been absent, but who, as her sisters were offering up their thanksgiving, glided in like a Sonnambula, and, nodding good night, crept to her bed, unconscious of her state. A moment after a bright star fell from the zenith, and Cicely Seyntcler stole in trembling and flushed, and wearing a white rose-jewel on her breast. Why did Cicely blush?—time will tell. And who rung the bell?—for the Sexton searched the belfry o'er and o'er, and found no one. The gallants, whom the burgundy had made bold, rather than brave, slunk off home, glad to escape a drubbing from the lacquies. But it was an hour, or twain, ere Glo'ster reached Chipstead, in the flush of triumph, as Lovel set to his duty of robing his master for the night.

"A ring and a priest," muttered the Duke, "a ring and a priest, canst manage this, hey Lovel'? "

The equerry caught the subject at once, and, after two or three significant nods from one to the other, even the wild spirit of Glo'ster fell asleep.

The tolling of the bell was the mystery of the day in Merstham. The boors referred it to some lively soul of a certain old bell-ringer : the sisters to the influence of their own devotional prayer—and only Katheryn, whenever the bell was the theme, went off at once into a reverie.

And now it was the second midnight. At the altar, in Merstham, stood a cold and solemn group—Richard Duke of Glo'ster, Syr John Wydville, Lovel, and the sexton, dangling his iron keys, and fumbling the *golden* one in his pouch, without which the doors had still been closed. Lovel was, for the nonce, a friar in masquerade, and he gave away Cicely Scyntcler to Richard Plantagenet, as with his left hand he put the ring on a finger of her right, and, lo! another meteor shot across the sky, and by its light the eyes of Saint Katheryn, in the chancel window, seemed to glare upon the scene, and the sexton muttered, "Ah, me ! a fiery meteor never bodes a good ! "

At the moment a muffled bell was heard in the tower All looked aghast and glum.

"Heaven's mercy !" cried the sexton, " 'tis the ghost again—I thought it would come. 'Tis well I muffled St.

Katheryn for the nonce. The village is none the wiser,
and a muffled bell were best at such a wedding."

" Hush ! hush ! the ghost is here."

The heart of Cicely throbbed wildly, and she felt their
destiny was tolled out in perspective.

But the mystery was not faded yet : as the maimed
rites were slurred over, a form robed in white, with a
fleecy veil, glided in, and, with crossed arms, stood by the
altar regardless of all.

The sexton said 'twas St. Katheryn herself : he knew
her well enough—by hearsay. Glo'ster's cheek was wan,
for the Duke was mighty superstitious. Cicely was lost
in wonderment, and, as she hid her face, she felt the
pressure of a soft hand that led her to the crucifix, at
which they both kneeled and prayed, and then to the
font : but the phantom stopped, and shook its head, and
left the aisle, and when Cicely looked up she knew well
who was gliding from the chancel door, and she felt conscious that the lost pleiad—*her* star, had fallen.

Ascend the belfry in Merstham, and you will see on
one bell this motto, " *Sancta Katherina ora pro me.*"

Some said the saint herself inscribed the letters in
holy triumph : others believed it to be the devout grati-
tude of the seven sisters.

Now was this really the mystery of the bell ? No, Sir
John (whose effigy is lying in the south chancel, the merchant's pouch at his girdle) married one of these ladies.
One night he caught his sleep-walking wife in the belfry,
unconsciously ringing St. Katherine—and he learned the
secret in a breath.

At the *liaison* of Cicely Scyntcler who will marvel? for she was a wild and wayward puss, and her royal lover, though slightly stooping, was of very noble mien—indeed, a marvellous proper man.

True, the two portraits, in Walpole's *Historic Doubts,* present a poor picture, the right hand cramped. So, also, the engraved portraits of Houbraken and Vertue. According to Hardynge, Speed, Stow, and later historians, Richard was short, ill-favoured, and humpbacked : and even Rous, the chantry priest of Guy's cliff, who saw him at Warwick between his coronations, tells that his right shoulder was the highest, and a drawing on an illuminated roll of the Earl of Warwick in the library of the College of Arms, shows this deformity, and Shakespeare, the pet and sycophant of the Tudors, politically libelled the White Rose. *We* will believe the MS. of the Countess of Desmond, who danced with him, and who declared, that except the beautiful King, there was no finer man at Court than Richard.

Gloucester, after awhile, bore off his light leman to his Gothic halls in Crosby Place, and soon secrets of the cepest interest rolled along : the fight of Lose-coat Field, where the Lancasters cast their armour and fled, and the battles of Barnet and Tewkesbury. At the former fell Neville of Warwick. Then Devon, and Buckingham, and Wydville were beheaded—Henry the Sixth was killed in The Tower, Edward the Fourth died, and his two boys were killed or secreted—Clarence was drowned in Malmsey, they say—and, to crown all, victory and marriage blended the white and red roses. Cicely

Scyntcler the while prayed through her brief existence a penitent in the Abbey of St. Mary de Pratis in Leicester.

> Thus let me live unseen, unknown—
> Steel from the world, and not a stone
> Tell where I lie.

AMONG the groves of Eastwell, by yonder blue hills of Kent, a legend has been echoed from lip to lip, that shadowing forth the memory of remote days, is strangely blended with the incidents of our story—we will presume to glean from other chronicles more than was told by Heneage, Earl of Winchelsea, to Thomas Brett, in the library of Eastwell House.

While he was building his house, Sir Thomas Moyle, of Eastwell, saw on the table of his chief bricklayer, while sleeping, a classic volume he had oft been seen hastily to secrete. When he awoke, the Baronet returned the Horace, and questioned the man as to his source of learning. With a sigh the man confessed there was none more worthy to learn his secret than his master, though he meant to have hidden it in the grave. " I am not what I seem," he said : " For my learning, a fair and holy sister of the Abbey where I was born, taught me both to read, and to love her as if she were my mother, and I read with a Latin scholar too, and built baby-houses till I was fifteen. Then from time to time came a gentleman to Leicester and paid my quarterings, and once he bore me in a coach to a princely house in Bishopsgate, and there, in a Gothic corniced chamber, came in a nobleman in sable and fur, and wearing a star and garter, and talked

to me, and kissed and fondled me, and gave me a purse
with ten pieces of crown gold. I had heard of courts
and crowns, and my little heart beat at the tales of
splendour, and, lo! as I was longing, fate or providence
granted my prayer. A man of state, one John Kendall
by name, came to me, who said he was secretary to a
noble lord, and had just seen the coronation of King
Richard, by Bourchier, at Westminster. With him I
rode to York City, through streets hung with cloth of
arms and tapestry work, and there were southern lords
and men of worship in crowds about the streets, and the
clergy in their copes kneeled to King Richard, who
walked stately along in his surcoat and robe royal, bearing
his sceptre with his jewelled crown on his head. The
Queen, poor Anne Neville, was there too, and she led her
son Edward, who wore a demy crown. And so in the
Chapter House of York Minster, on the eighth of September, in the year of Grace, 1483, they were enthroned by
Rotherham, who placed on the King's head the costly
Abacot, or double crown of maintenance of Henry the
Sixth, which Edward the Fourth took at Hexham, and
with which he himself had been crowned in York, and
there, in York City, there were tilts and tournaments, and
revels and masques, and stage plays, and Edward of
Lancaster, in rich green velvet, in grand chapter, was
created Prince of Wales, and he held a golden rod and
wore a coronet.* And there was Jeffery de Sasiola, the
Spanish Ambassador—and I, a mere boy, walked by

* This we may learn from the Coronation Roll of Richard the
Third.

Edward's side, and there we were knighted by the King,
who struck the Ambassador thrice with a sword, and
hung a rich and costly collar of gold around his neck.
And then the heralds, who were much beholden to him,
proclaimed the King. And after all this, we went round
by Sheriff Hutton, to take young Edward Plantagenet,
Earl of Warwick, son of George Duke of Clarence, and
Elizabeth of York, daughter of Edward the Fourth, the
future Queen of Richmond the Usurper, and we left them
there in solitude, and then I returned to Leicester, where I
lived in some state—how and why the man told me not.

"And soon King Richard's throne was threatened. My
guide came again and took me to a tent on Bosworth
Field, and there was the nobleman, as I was told, now in
complete steel, with his helmet barred, and he asked me
what news from my school. I said that Richmond was
come over the sea to fight King Richard. 'Your news is
true,' he replied, 'and I am on the King's side, for I love
him as myself. Nay, I am here to fight for him and his
crown even to the death. Aye, by St. Paul, to the death,
boy. But hark—the clarion! Post you to yonder brow,
and watch the fortune of the day. If King Richard
wins, come to my tent, this man with his banner of
Blanc Sanglier will know you, and we will post to
London, boy, and there you shall herd and consort with
the noble and the mighty of the land—and your mother—'

"'My mother, sir! Have I one? My mother. Who—
where is my mother?—where, and what her name?'

"He whispered in my ear, 'Has not your heart told you,
Richard?'

"Heaven of its mercy, my heart *had* whispered, and I breathed the name Cicelè Seyntcler, the nun of Leicester.

"The nobleman then wiped away a tear with his .gauntlet, and continued—

"'If we fail, fly direct from the field—hide your head in solitude; for love and nature have stamped on your brow Plantagenet, my son, my son. But the morning dawns, the clarion sounds again, and here are Norfolk and Catesby, and—where's Stanley? Not here. Ha, ratted, like Buckingham. His son's head shall answer for't.'

"'He says he has other sons,' said Catesby.

"And King Richard frowned, and cried, 'White Surrey, ho!' and so he mounted, muttering, 'ha! my arm is palsied sure;' and then, turning to me, he said, solemnly, 'Remember, Richard;' and with that he gave me a purse with 1200 pieces of crown gold, and so we parted; and be sure I went weeping and awe-struck to the brow. All the world knows my gracious father died on Bosworth field; no parting kiss to my mother, no blessing on her boy. So I crept back in despair by the Bow Bridge, on the Stour, to the Abbey of Leicester, to kiss—to kiss my widowed mother, when rushed by a collier's hack, and, oh Heaven! my father—my father, stark, stark, lay across, trussed behind his own pursuivant ere he was King—Blanc Sanglier, Saint Leger, Senigleer, or White Bore—'like a hogge or calfe,' and blood, MY blood, welling from his breast. Heaven of its mercy, how the caitiff flung his sacred corse from side to side, 'chopping of it in and out, a myserable sight to loke on.'

"He dashed the gory head against the bridge, where crouched a withered hag that croaked in mine ear, 'I knew ye—both—Plantagenet: said I not where he struck his spear, there should his head be broke.' His corse lay exposed to scorn two days, and was then flung into a hole in the Grey Friars at Leicester. ["It was gode inough," writes Hardynge, "considering hys wretched levyng." The rude stone coffin has been since desecrated as a horse trough.] The gates of the Abbey were shut against me, so I wandered to York, and heard proclaimed by Wyndsore, at the Minster Cross, 'Richard, of Gloucester, late called King Richard, had been slayed at a place called Sandeford, within the shyre of Leicestre, and brought dede of the feld unto the towne of Leicestre, and ther was laide oppenly that every man might se and luke upon him.' After a time the Grey Friars buried him in church, and 'Henry the Seventh made a tomb over him of various colour'd marbles.' I dared not seek my father's friends: their houses to me were a fate—a charnel-house. So I sold my rich clothes and wandered south to London town, and learned to lay a brick. And, while in my rags, I crept into Westminster Abbey, and saw King Henry crowned with the *crown of my father*, in return for the rich Cap of Maintenance, or *Abacot* with a double coronet of Henry the Sixth, with which Edward the Fourth was crowned at York. Directly after Garter came Lancaster—a king when the Fourth Henry reigned, reduced by Edward to a herald, and now revived by the Tudor: and then came *Eagle*, so named from the crest of Edward the Third, King Henry's ancestor, and then Richmond, his robe

powdered with gold roses, and then Conk, Poursuivant
Extraordinary, brought over by Henry, and Rose Blanche,
a pet of the King, who knew his stronghold was as consort
of Elizabeth of York. Blanc Sanglier was not : his office
had died with my father : and there they strewed Rose
Nobles from my father's treasury : and so King Henry
sat on the throne. Now, mock me not, master of mine,
my soul longed to take up the gauntlet from the stones, but
I was disgraced and fettered, so I held my hand, bowed
my head to destiny, kissed my mother's holy church at
Titsey, and here I am a hermit in Eastwell."

Those who wandered in Eastwell Park even at the dawn
of the eighteenth century may have seen the relic of the
room built and tenanted by this man, and a levelled well,
both bearing his name : and half within the wall of the
church there is yet a raised tomb with indents for brasses,
which Parsons, in his " Monuments," assigns, on the faith
of tradition, to the son of Gloucester. Furthermore, if you
search the register at Eastwell, you will find a record
shown to Brett by Lord Winchelsea as "a curiosity,"
and which Brett has inserted in Peck's " Desiderata
Curiosa."

√ Rychard Plantagenet was buryed the 22d Desember,
anno 1580.

The mark is attached only to noble names in the
register.

Of this bastard there is yet much mystery.

Buckingham, and Drake of York, make him Captain
of Calais, while Rymer, in *Fœdera*, writes the name
John, and still asserts that he fell into the clutches of

King Henry, while many, with Walpole, have doubted
even his reality, from so slight a record. But, even the
legitimate son by Anne Neville was never heard of in
the reign of Richmond, although created in his first
year Earl of Salisbury by Edward, and years after Prince
of Wales by his father. In this dilemma we leave those
who read the records of Peck, and Parsons, and Noble,
fairly to judge whether this monument in Eastwell be
not the tomb of the bastard Richard Plantagenet.

THE transition of the sceptre from the clutch of York
to that of Tudor was sudden as our course back to
Surrey, from the diversion into Kent.

Ever after the demolition of the priories and cells by
the second King of that dynasty, the *Pilgrim's Lane*, as
this holy way is named about Merstham, has been a
solitude, especially along the Combes that dip down so
finely through the firestone into Holmsdale.

The lone ravine of the black bushes fringes a chalk-
pit 200 feet deep, on Whitedown, streaked with *sand-galls*.

In the Tudor time, ere the dawn of the Reformation,
this was the course of Kings and Cardinals, in all the
glory of Church and State, for it led to Becket's shrine.

On the site of the ancient may-pole, near the Harrow
yonder, is the mound of the Cardinal's Cap, not named
in honour, but in derision of the proud prelate, if the
chronicles be true. Great events will spring from little
things, and, however light this incident, the upshot was
momentous, indeed, to—

The Cardinal's Cap.

"Ego et Rex meus."

IN Tanrigge, yonder, is the site of the Priory cell of
the Austin canons, founded by Odo Dammartin, endowed
by Richard Cœur de Lion, and entrusted to God and
St. James, for paupers and wayfarers. Its only relics
now, are a few tiles beneath the chalk-down.

It chanced the King was coming to Tanrigge, and
the prior had an inkling of the spoliation of his rich
revenues—so, invoking his saint, he esconced himself
under a plea of penance in his sanctum, and securing
the consolation of a parcel-gilt cup, brimful of delicious
malvoisin, the orthodox monastic drink, he deputed his
hosteller to bestow *Pax vobiscum* on his illustrious guest.

Sir Thomas Carverden had greeted at the gate Sir
Nicholas Carew, of Bletchingley, a welcome from the
master of revels to his Grace the King.

"Thanks, thanks, Master Carden, but be sure 'twill
not be echoed by the King: the cold shoulder, hey! the
Tudor widow's mate Gaynsford of Chillows, and Crowhurst is the man now."

"Aye! High style at Crowhurst yesternight: but,
hark, a neighing of steeds: why, 'tis the Boleyns, from
Hever."

"We call him Rochford now," whispered Sir Thomas.

"A patent 'neath the petticoat, hey?"

"Nay, neighbour, I pray you, or myself, the warder of the rents, hayles, and toyles, must cite thee to York House."

"Ha! welcome Lord Rochford of Hever, fair Mistress Anne doth queen it early: faith, she doth grace her palfrey like an empress, but methought the apple of her eye was Percy."

"So thought I, Master Carden," said Rochford, "though we played for young Butler, but the boy was so hot on the Talbot and my Mary, Anne frowned him off."

As he spoke, a burly gentleman with one groom and one Pursuivant, Rouge-Dragon of Cadwallader, alighted at the gate: he was dressed in blue and crimson velvet, powdered with castles and arrows, the badge of Catherine of Arragon, and he wore the chapeau Montauban, a bright jewel of St. George gleaming on its satin lining. It was observed that he crossed not his brow at the piscina, nor made a venia at the portal of the guest-hall, and he rejected the kiss of peace and benediction of the Hosteller.

"No state, no state, master of the revels," exclaimed the King, as Carden kneeled to him, "break your staff, sir, no proud prelate we: a poor King, faith, on Cupid's errand bent, hey Rochford? But where's my sweetheart, will she coy it with the crown—her chamber, where? ha, she comes!"

A lady, about thirty, fresh as Aurora, entered the room, with two maids, Anne Saville and Anne Gaynsford, in a jewelled cap, with a pure white feather, a costly necklace, and embossed stomacher, and she leaned on two gallants—young Boleyn her brother, and her cousin-german the accomplished Surrey, who was clad in close dress of brown silk, richly embroidered with gold, a garter on his knee, and a jewelled dirk across his thigh.

As Anne Boleyn kneeled, the King clasped her waist, and kissed her lips, and saluted her Marchioness of Pembroke.

"I seal the patent, thus, on lips warm and red as the wax of the College of Arms, and sweet as the Rose of Damascus."

"Too gracious, Sir," whispered Anne, blushing, "the dungeon at Hever rather than a tuft, for that I have once slighted the suit of my King."

(She dreamed not she should after be nearly starved to death there by Henry's order.)

"I was a wilding then, hey puss? I am grown a man, and fling my toys away: so bring the robe of reconciliation my father sent to Bess of York, 'tis thine for holidays."

"Oh, what a jewel!" she cried, "let me see: look cloth of gold, ermined 'cross the breast, diamond and gold, silk kerchief, golden ropes, and golden knoppes."

Her joy was checked by the cellarer, who cried aloud, "the banquet waits my lord the King."

As Carden muttered a lame excuse for the Prior, Henry led Anne to the refectory, and there she sat enthroned on the dais, as our chronique tells: "In the place of honour sat the Phœnix, indeed, of his princely eye, and another Hester for England's salvation." The gold Apostle spoons were laid graciously for the Court,

K

and a huge porpoise was placed by the lay brothers at the top of the board.

The banquet over, the wassail-bowl, filled with Bourgogne wine, spices, sugar, and roasted apples, was brought in by the cellarer in great pomp, preceded by Will Somers the Jester, with his bauble and his bells. Surrey filled a golden cup, radiant with gems, a copy of the Holy Chalice of Valentia, that graced the Last Supper, and Anne Boleyn, like Rowena, kissed the brim, and, kneeling, pledged the King with *was-hael:* and this is the quaint chronique of Robert de Brunne—

> " The Kyng said as the Knyght gan ken,
>   Drink heille, smiland on Boleyne.
>   Anne she drank as hire list,
>   And gave the Kyng sine him kist.
>   Of that wassaile men told grete tale,
>   Of chamber Boleyne so gent.
>   Before the Kyng in halle sche went,
>   A coupe with wyne sche had in hand,
>   And her natur was well farand.
>   Before the Kyng on kne sett,
>   And on her langage sche him grett,
>   ' Lavered Kyng wassaile,' seid sche."

Surrey caught the cup from her hand, and *lipped* the kiss she had left on its brim.

" Ah !" whispered Anne, blushing, " mine are not the lips of Geraldine, Harry : my rebec, Anne Gaynsford, my rebec—now, listen to a lay of love, your own hearts' thought, fair cousin."

So Anne took her little three-stringed viola, and swept a symphony with the *six* fingers of her left hand, and then the Syren sung—

> "As ofte as I beholde and see
>   The soveraigne beautie that me bounde,
>   The nier my comforte is to me;
>   Alas, the fresher is my wounde.
>   As flame doth quench my rage of fire,
>   And running stremes consume by raine,
>   So doth the sight that I desire
>   Appease my griefe and deadly paine."

The King beat the measure as she sung, "and whose groans are these, rose-bud ?" he said.

"My cousin Surrey's, sir," she answered, with a leer.

"*He*, the traitor," cried the King, "that lymns the blazon of the Confessor with his own : *sat superest*, ha !"

"The King is frowning on us, Harry," whispered Anne in Surrey's ear : "can it be, then I must breathe a prayer for pity, or we shall rue it :" and, creeping to the King's side, she murmured forth her chaunt—

> "A breath will blur the ruby's blaze,
>   Will dim the diamond's light :
>   A moment, and their sparkle plays
>   As beautiful, as bright.
>   But if on woman's heart a stain
>   Is left by Slander's breath,
>   Alas, 'twill never shine again :
>   Her only hope is death."

"No more, no more of that, sweetheart," muttered the King.

"A dream, sir, but 'tis gone," she replied : "yet I would dare it all, bless but a royal bud my bosom : my head be your Grace's ever," and Anne laid her arm on his.

"Now, by the cloth of gold," he cried, "those sleeves of lawn deserve a crozier. A whim, a whim, Gentles, there was a Joan of Rome, why not an Anne of Durham ?

Mad monks and mitred priests—the church were safer
with a petticoat. For I will swear that little book that
dangles at thy girdle were a missal."

"Nay, sir, 'tis my *Tindal*, as you know, his rendering
of the Gospel into English: 'tis precious now, the only
one that's saved from the blazing pile at the Crosse of
Chepe. Wolsey denounced, condemned the whole, but
this one shall live to shame a Cardinal—wilt learn, gentles,
whence I got it? listen then.

"'Twas a priest from Geneva, a man of Martin Luther's,
did bring it down to Hever: on its revealings I have
purified my faith, reckless of pains and penance. One
night I did give it to my maid, Anne Gaynsford, that's
blushing, yonder, in the corner: your equerry, George
Zouch, aye, let him answer it, in frolic-mood, did filch
it from her purse, half out of spite, be sure, for it did
cheat him of his hours of dalliance. 'Twere wondrous
rich, thought he, and racy, too, to take her fancy thus:
so, first, he fell a reading on't, and then fell fast asleep.
By comes the Dean, 'twas in the Chapel Royal, and
bears my book to Wolsey, who denounced and locked
my treasure up. I wept and prayed, the scarlet priest
but laughed poor Anne to scorn: your Grace, a thousand
thanks, did bid it back, yet recked not of its worth:
read it, my lord, nay, *feed* on it, 'twill be the dearest
book that ever priest or Cardinal retained."

"Thou hast said it, sweetheart," cried the King: and
that moment was the dawn of the new faith in England.

"So," said Somers, archly, "the cockerell will crow over
the eagle."

And he whispered in Henry's ear—

> "Carolus, Henricus, vivant defensus uterque,
> Henricus fidei, Carolus ecclesiæ."

"The faith's defender, bah, send back your rose to Rome."

This *Rosa d'oro pontificia*, by the way, if we believe Holinshed, "was a tree of fine gold, wrought with braunches, leaves of flowres resembling roses, set up in a pot of gold, which had three feet of antike fashion. In the uppermost rose was a faire sapphire, *loupepersd*, the bignesse of an acorne." It was sent by Clement XVI., from Rome, to Windsor, in custody of Hannibal, 1524, for Henry's lash of Luther on the Sacraments.

The King smiled kindly on his fool.

"Thou hast dared to counsel thy King, knave," said Rochford, "canst counsel me how I may bear these blushing honours meekly?"

"That will I," replied the jester, snatching a book from Carden's pouch, "read this, 'tis the boke of noblenesse, that sheweth how many sortes and kyndes there is, and specially to those which doe followe the trayne and estate of warre, by John Larke, with the prologue of the Auctoure, and a treatise of nobility by his father's secretary, so know all."

"The masque, the masque," cried the King.

"What! maskers in a holy house," muttered Somers.

"Aye, and if the prior frown, unfrock him : ha! we, Henry Tudor, are Lord of Misrule in Tanrigge."

For the masque Anne had assumed the Boleyn coif of

velvet, but Henry drew out the jewelled pins and rows of pearl, and down fell the fair locks, in such exquisite disorder, that the King kissed her most lovingly.

"Have I not a mistress, sir?" she whispered, archly.

"Have not we *two*," he replied, "why, Martin himself will grant us a brace of lemans."

"That were loose moral, good my lord, I blush."

"*You*, maid to four Queens, and blush—nay, you shall be Queen yourself—"

"My lady, sir, you do forget—"

"Oh! Kate shall be dowager, content thee!"

'Twas a *point*, and the word *divorce* was on her lips.

"Divorce: nay, nay, a bull will do instead. Ho, Rochford, hither: to Rome, to Rome, aye, by the morning's light—and, for thy pains, rise Earl of Wiltshire and Ormond: and, Rouge-Dragon, hang the lesser George, on a black ribbon, round his neck."

"The Cardinal," whispered the Earl, as he knelt.

"Wolsey!" exclaimed Henry, "our cause is not in chancery, we have removed it to a higher court, my lord, the court of Cupid: there we are absolute, our conscience in our own keeping. Wolsey! 'tis Cranmer now. Ah! had he taught us Thomas Aquinas in our youth, we had been spared this shame with Kate of Arragon."

The hour of midnight struck. Sir Thomas Carwarden, with his white staff, marshall'd to the chambers, or the cells, through a rank of *rascals* from Crowhurst, Will

Somers, with the license of his Motley suit, proclaiming as a jest, "The Queen's maids of honour a chet-loaf, a manchet, a gallon of oil : in the King's chamber straw as at Windsor or York-terrace, coals only in the King's and Lady Anne's chambers."

On the morning after these scenes were played, a brilliant cortége from Hampton Court was ambling along the Pilgrim's Way, toward Canterbury, to kneel with a hundred thousand more at the shrine of the glorious martyr St. Thomas A'Becket in the Undercroft, on the anniversary of his enshrinement. After quaffing and crossing at the Holy-well under Merstham church, the mules, shaking their *Canterbury* bells, set off anew in the gallop therefore called a *Canter.*

They—

> " Ryde with gold all trapp'd
> In purpell and pall belapp'd,
> Some hatted and some cappy'd,
> Richly aud warm wrapp'd,
> God wot to their great paynes,
> In rocketts of fyne reynes,
> Whyte as Mary's milk,
> And tabards of fyne sylk,
> And styroppes with gold beglozyd."

Foremost rode a lofty prince of the church, on a Spanish mule caparisoned with crimson cloth, and saddle and stirrups silver-gilt. He wore robes of scarlet and crimson satin and sables, and shoes of silver-gilt inlaid with pearls and diamonds and silver crosses, his tasselled crimson hat and his pastoral staff, borne by Acolytes before him. Yet at this moment there is, in that man's heart, a worm,

deadly and venomous as the *palmer* that is feeding on
these yew leaves. It is an apt emblem, for the worm is
the larva of a very beautiful fly, the *golden porthesia*,
whose winglets might not be.outshone even by the broidered vestments of the Cardinal.

"I am sick and a'weary of this life," he muttered: "I
tell thee, myn owne enterly belowyed Crommwell, He
will give us the go by yet. Methought I had looped
his leading strings secure. Look ye, yonder is Garston,
the King's Exchange for Oatlands: there is a spring an

infant's hand might turn into Medway or to Mole, so mine
did turn the flood of favour to Windsor or Vatican. The
church's sacrament is strengthless now :—' Ave Maria,'
if *I* fail, good-night to Rome."

"Remember Okynage, my Lord!" said Cromwell (whom
he had taken from the forge) "remember the scarlet hat :
meet but the King at Hever and perchance "——

" The Tiara, hey : dignity *papelle !* No, Luther will
be all, and Thomas Wolsey nothing : I that whilome
was balm for the conscience of a King ! But this Night-
crow of Hever is his passion now, and seals his lips, as
she did those of Clement. His leman we had not feared,
but a Queen, a Queen ! "

" Queen, my Lord ? "

" No less, my Cromwell : would I had tricked her with
young Percy, but he jilted and turned to Alton Towers."

"Then Wyatt, sir," whispered Cromwell, " the love-
bird : she wears the lips of Phryne, and she'll melt, or we
will find her match, aye, witch for witch."

" What mean'st thou, Cromwell ! "

" An't please your grace. There is a slave of Cob, the
Primate's Steward, that haunts a cell in the convent of
St. Sepulchre. From her chapel of Courtatte Street, in
Aldington, she has maddened the mob with her oracles. At
Wolsey's beck, be sure her satellites would scatter wildfire
through the court, and blast the recreant King with "——

" Anathema, Maranatha.",

The woods shook the wind like a thunder-peal, and a
gaunt woman in red and white started from the bush,
and stood erect before them. In her eyes gleamed a

magnificent, yet half-demoniac frenzy, as with a sort of hysteric laugh, she screamed—

"We meet at last, Thomas of York, here in the land of the Philistines.   But the ban is on thyself, lord Cardinal, the rankness of Kitty Boren hath tainted the purple in thee : I tell thee, an thou swelter still within her wanton arms, the veil of the Temple will be rent in twain, and the hot lips of the heretics slaked with the blood of the saints.   Awake, awake, lord Cardinal, that painted doll will bring the curse of Rome on you and us.   Lip no more with Dalilah, or thy limbs be withered and thy locks shorn by the Philistines, aye, beyond redemption.   Wot you, they spare not e'en the saints ? · Becket is branded, un-canonized, his bones laid bare, his jewels filched—"

"Say'st thou," exclaimed Wolsey.

"Why, look you yonder, two massive chests—an escort is coming, rich as the Cloth of Gold, along the Pilgrim's Way,—there his shirt of camel's hair, the bloody knife, and the skull in sainted silver, all, all despoiled ! aye, and the blood of the Saviour from our Abbey of Hailes. The deluge is at hand, be sure : hush, hark, it comes— orbs, ears, both blank, but *my brain*, so !"

Elizabeth Barton stood like a sybil, waving an osier wand.

"Mine is the rod of Moses," she cried : she stamped her foot, and water gushed from the ground.*

---

* The Winter-bourne in Stoneham Lane is an intermitting flood. It is curious that it flowed at the Restoration of Charles the Second, on the outbreak of the Plague in 1665, and on the very hour of the Revolution in 1688. Its flow is still deemed prophetic.

"A miracle," murmured the Acolytes.

"And what," said Cromwell, "doth this portend—good or evil?"

"Evil to him," she screamed, "who hath pawned the angel of Arragon for the rank Lutheran of Hever. I, the Noune of Kent, did call God's wrath on Clement in thy behoof, and Katheryn and little Mary did bless thee with their prayers, despite thy malice : we may not save thee now, Wolsey. Speak Bocking, speak William Hart, speak Scott, thou who had famished, but for the holy bread in Mary's lap, tell it in Gath, how the Virgin spoke in my belly while I winged to the saints; and how I wrestled and kicked the devil from my cell, despite his hoof-mark on my arm, and his reek of stinking smoak, Maranatha!"

Elizabeth Barton stood for a moment in cataleptic silence, while Wolsey sunk into the deepest thought. He was roused by the sybil's scream—

"Home, home, to Hampton, Wolsey! Holmsdale is no home for thee, the hornet's swarm is round thee—look ayont the valley, look what seest thou there."

"The King! 'tis he."

"Aye, hot from the judgment-seat—they have weighed thee in the balance, and found thee wanting: we wear the purple now—so to our Court at Street."

As the royal cortége came on the brow, she grasped the scarlet hat and flung it on her raven locks, and towering like a rebel angel, she tore the cloak from her shoulders, and then waving the cap over her head, she again screamed out "Anathema, Maranatha! Woe to the blood of Cadwallader! woe, hear the revealing, Henry Tudor! By this mystic ring of Julian,* that I fling to earth in defiance: if thou procedest in this divorce, thou wilt not be Kynge of this realme one daie nor houre."

"What mummer is this?" asked the King, trying to smile.

"The mad Noune of Kent," replied young Boleyne: "'tis Wolsey's trick, never did cardinal bring good to England."

"A truth, a truth, e'en from a heretic!" cried the Sybil, and she stamped on the hat like a fiend in masquerade: "to Becket's shrine, King of England, kneel on the stone of Plantagenet and repent thee, disgorge thy sacrilege: off with thy slaves to Jerusalem, and like thy namesake, in sackcloth shirt and barefoot tread bloody footsteps from Venta even to the martyr's tomb, and bare thy shoulders to the lash!"

This was too much, the King raised his hand, and all were mute for a moment. Then the "Star-chamber" and "Tyburn" were cried aloud, but Anne whispered the King, "Paul's Cross for mercy," while the Sybil screamed, "Death, death—he is waiting for us all! Fire and faggot for me,—your neck is white and tempting, Nan. Boleyn, 'tis worth the lopping, Nan."

The fanatics were carted off at once to London, and this was the warrant of their doom: "Stand ye at Paul's Crosse in the sermon time, where ye with your own hands shall severalye deliver ech of you to the preacher a bill declaring your subtill craftie and superstitious doings. Thence to Tyburn tree."

* The ring found 1738, by Sir Marmaduke Gresham, was in-scribed, Jul. nazaren. rex.

The royal cortége passed on to London, the King bestowing the slightest bow on Wolsey, who, after a transient homage at Becket's Shrine, found on his table in York House the Papal sentence.

There was wooing at Hever and at Ankerwyke, and Anne Boleyn was Queen of England. Yet the place of her marriage was, like that of her birth and burial, a doubtful point, whether Rochford, Hever, Blichley, or Sopewell, where Julyans Bernes penned her "Boke of St. Albans." "The lady marchionesse (Holinshed and Grafton), was married in the closet at Whitehall, in the presence of many, on the feast of St. Erkenwald, 1532, by Dr. Lee, and her maid of honour was Jane Seymour."

From the conduit of the Chepe the while flowed xeres and claret from noon to night.

And ere many months had gone, a decree went forth that Elizabeth was the child of Anne daughter of Lord *Reujafort* and her brother! and so her *lyttel necke* was lopped by the sword, the first adoption of the French mode. As it rolled on the ground, the tapers on Katherine Shrine, in Peterborough, lighted up spontaneously, and after matins went out. Her body was taken by stealth to Sallechurch, by midnight, and then to Hever.

And the fallen Car^lis Ebor. died in Leicester Abbey. It was a gracious mercy, else he had been tried for treason, and then——aye, what then ?

THE Saxon finials, ham, field, stede, ton, ley, are common about Holmsdale. Here is Nutfield, Notfelle, Nuffield, or Northfield, noted for its fuller's earth and baryte.

There is Godstone, Wachelstede, Walkenested, Walkham-
stead below Winder's Hill and the woods of Rooksnest.
There is Oxtead, Acstede, and lonely Lympsfield, closing
in Surrey Holmsdale, once the home of Savage and of
Eugenia Stanhope, both associated with unhappy stories.
You may find the finest flies on the sand common, and in
the woods of Trevereaux and of Titsey, once the house of the
Greshams, their grasshopper being richly carved on the
oak panels.   Yonder on the slopes is the disfranchised
borough of Bletchingley, Bleachingelee, Bleachingleagh,
retaining but one of its seven churches.   On a mound,
where Aubrey saw great graffs, are the mere fragments of
one of the noble castles of Holmsdale, bits of firestone,
blue bur, chert, Kentish rag and chalk-marl, are yet to be
seen in the fosse.

> " Her palaces are crumbling,
> And music meets not ever now the ear."

Yet Bletchingley was once the abode of royalty, and
not long after Buckingham's attainder—it was a gift to
Anne of Cleves.   Its highest pride, however, was when
the " stout Gloster" of the bard was lord of the castle,
when every oriel lighted a costly chamber.

> " Oh for that pencil erst profuse,
> Of chivalry's emblazoned hues,
> That trac'd of old in Woodstock bower
> The pageant of the leaf and flower !"

Then might we tell in less homely phrase than our own,
how a lord's daughter may be nonsuited in the court of
Cupid by a gipsy, the coronal of gold eclipsed by—

𝕿𝖍𝖊 𝕾𝖈𝖆𝖗𝖑𝖊𝖙 𝕳𝖔𝖔𝖉.

"I love but only one, and you are only she."

EDWARD the Second had espoused at Boulogne, Isabel, the she-wolf of France, and the marriage was graced by five kings, France, Navarre, Almaigne, Sicile, and Edward himself, and four queens, Mary of France, Margaret of England, Navarre, and the royal bride. The king's best men were young Spenser, and Piers Gaveston, but he looked coldly on Spenser and smiled on the other, as he leaned on his arm on his way to the altar. So Spenser soon cut the court and travelled by himself, and in dudgeon. It was some time after this event that a young man, in the guise of a Templar, was wending his way over the beautiful chalk hill on which is now spread the demesne of Marden Park, and came down upon Wachelstede, now Godstone. Over his gambron he wore a shirt of thin chain-mail, and over that a surcoat of baldekins from Babylon, embroidered with a black cross, a small gorget was round his throat, and he wore a light cylindrical helmet. His cowled paltoque was thrown over his arm, and on his heels were fixed the spear-shaped spurs by thongs of gilt leather. He carried a small *martel de fer* or wedge pickaxe, and a small embossed target hung on his shoulder, and so he journeyed on, armed, as it were, *cap-à-pie*, although peace reigned around. He had alighted at the hall of Alicia de Dammartin, who held Laggaham

of the king, by service of a pair of gilt spurs, price six-
pence.

"So hast thou done with tickets-of-leave and games of
bo-peep. And why come you in battle array, Hugh
Spenser?" she inquired. "Jealousy, I guess?"

"If you will, noble dame, this upstart king-bane is
beyond endurance."

"And, prythee, which of you hath the king's ear now?"

"Faith, I know not, the queen doth play us off like
shuttlecocks, one 'gainst t'other. First, I was sent to my
Marche in Wales, recalled and Piers was bundled off, and
now, spite of Dionysia and De Vallance, of Notfell, and
the dying mandate of the last king, he bore young Edward's crown, not I. I am from Malta, too, and prick for
Temple Elfand in the Weald, for you must know when the
knights of St. John kicked the Turks from Rhodes, De
Elfande gave their cell to the Templars, and St. John's
tythe free for ever, therefore wear I my helm."

"'Twere well, but fear not Piers Gaveston. Hearkye,
'twas he set up Voidras, who swung at Northampton for
swearing he was king and Edward a baker's boy—'twas
he played booty to the Scot at Estrivelyn—'twas he stole
the tressels of gold that brought down the Arch's excommunication—then Warwick his 'black dog of Arden'
is his enemy."

"And yet the king would force him on Marguerite de
Clare, but we'll cut the cockerell's comb and lop his spurs :
he'll mount the white feather, as he did at Mytton, but
the twilight fades, so thanks, lady, and adieu."

"And no love for Elinore !"

"Love ? 'twas but her father's will to pledge our hearts against our lands. So long an exile I, I have forgotten her, tell him from me."

" What, know you not that Clare is dead ? "

" Dead ! poor old Clare, and Elinore ? "

" If thy heart answer not, neither will I, Hugh Spenser."

The knight bowed and rode from the gate.

" Now, Elinore," he said, " we are free to choose—both free—yet for the honour of Clare—no, here ends my wooing ere it be begun."

A pale crescent was gleaming over Holmsdale, and heat-drops were falling fast as he sat musing at the Roman Hypocaust at Pendhill yonder, and night came down ere he was aware. He was making towards a cottage light, as he thought : but, after dancing and flickering in a zigzag, it settled on the sedge. He was turning from this will-o'-wisp in something like anger at the illusion, when a soft moaning fell on his ear, and he saw a fair boy lying exhausted on the edge of the marsh. He leaped from his saddle and raised the boy in his arms, and, leading his horse through a tangled coppice in the direction the boy pointed, he reached a very humble cot : the door was ajar, and he entered and laid his light burden on a truckle-bed of rushes, already occupied by an aged crone, to whom he heard a gentle voice whispering, "Hush, hush !" He poured some drops of malvoisin from his flask on the lips of the fainting boy, whose lustrous eyes thanked him with an eloquence far more expressive than the syllables of the lips.

But the knight knew not yet the treasure that was to open on him in that dark chamber. There were eyes more deeply blue and lustrous that were beaming on him from the corner. Kneeling by the bed was a fair girl dressed in the coarsest woollen, her face half-hidden beneath a scarlet hood. She had an open volume in her hand from which she had been reading prayer, and she was now bathing the wrinkled forehead of the aged crone.

The girl was seemingly about sixteen, and when her half-hidden eyes were lighted up, even by the pale glimmer of a burning rush, their expression was angelic. She blushed maidenly as Spenser looked on her, and, rising from· her knees, she whispered softly, "Bye Goody, the bell of the *bankero* (sheep) *hath long ceased*, and 'tis close on curfew, we must douse the fire and light, for, though my caste may be Egyptian, I am a true Norman in this, you know."

" And will you douse my sister's light," murmured the boy, " that I have followed till I am weary, weary, oh ? "

" Hush, darling," she whispered, " God made that light, none dare to douse it but himself."

" Ah," he said, " 'tis the angels' light, I know."

Spenser looked bewildered, and the girl whispered "'Tis ever thus at twilight with that *bittas chave*, this jack-o'-lanthorn is to him his sister's spirit, and he follows it o'er marsh and mire. But hark, the curfew, yek, dool, trin, staur, pange, shouv, efta, okto."

So she unhooked the *cacave*, and trod the burning rush beneath her foot.

" Good night."

" What," said Spenser, " alone and in the dark ! "

" Oh ! 'tis not far, but a short mile to the *gav* and
Romany blood fears not, and I am never in the dark. God
lights the cottage chamber and the welkin for the poor.
See how the moonlight kisses his cheek."

" Aye, believe her, sir," whispered the boy, " angels are
ever in the light. Hush, 'tis *his* step, but he's your sister's,
and I forgot he loves but pretty gipsies. You're better
far than pretty. Heaven has made the angels' souls even
on earth more beautiful than their faces.'

" If she bears that, she is indeed angelic," thought
Spenser.

The girl smiled, and telling the boy to " lip her fangaste "
(kiss her fingers), and, drawing her hood close, she was
gone.

" Why, what a heart and soul this gipsy has ? " said
Spenser to himself, " her eyes, the music of her lips—yes,
the boy was right. Why, what is't ails my heart, I
that have been weary e'en of the gaze of beauty ? Well,
well, she's gone and ther's an end on't." And so he sat
still, believing the dame to be asleep. As the boy roused,
Spenser asked the maiden's name.

" Angels have none," he lisped, while his thin lips
quivered with a smile—oh, such a smile.

" Ah, I thought Ellen the last that went from earth.
I shall meet her soon, and I will tell her there is an angel
yet on earth fit for a seat in heaven."

" Shall we keep a place for you, sir, by our side ?

" Hark, hark, a woman's voice," and Spenser rushed from

the hut, and in the darkness he could yet discern two forms.

" Shame, shame," she said, " you of all earthly beings, I dare not tell my brother, or—"

As Spenser rushed and flung off the man with whom she struggled,

"No, stranger, no," she cried, "you ruin me at once if you do quarrel here,"—and she was gone.

" How dare you this ? " muttered the man, " a gipsy-girl is fair game for all the world, besides I've charter and free warren here, knight's fee and manors."

" Manners that disgrace you—nay, you're mine—till I know she's safe."

It was long ere Spenser relaxed his hold, and shook the man from his grasp, and, when he returned to the cot, there lay the old crone dead, and her knell was tolled in the last peal of the curfew.

" She is dead ! " he whispered in the boy's ear.

" Oh, I knew that," he murmured : " I heard her go, and there she sits with my sister up in heaven."

Spenser watched until morning broke, and when the gossips had *laid out*, the child kissed his grandam, and dressed in his Sunday suit—a whim of many in the last stage of consumption.

" Aye, this is a rare creature," thought Spenser, "and new to me—nature pure and true—worth all the gawds of fashion, all the painted dolls of the harcem." Then musing for a moment, he kissed the boy's forehead, and mounted the Chert Hill of Tilverstowe, the road that Cæsar took over Holmsdale. By the mound over the Castle mill, he hears—

> "A noise, as of a hidden brook,
> In the leafy month of June."

An icy spring bubbles up *through* the water of the infant
Medway, beneath a rock, green with *witches butter*—it is
he *Fountain of Diana*, and faith, a dip in such a bath
might chill a Phryne down to chastity. Quaffing the
diamond drops, he murmured a blessing on the scarlet
hood, and was stretching o'er the weald to Temple
Elfande, when twang went a bow-string, and a wounded
roe dropped at his feet. A man in Lincoln green started
from the covert, and bade him "Good morrow!"

"So," he said, when he had blown his bugle, "my
arbaleste is sure as ever, look ye; 'twas Cœur de Lion's
once and Edmond Crouchback's, it suits me best, though,
in my boyhood, Robin Hood taught me the long-bow,
when he pricked for venison in my woods of Chelsham
and Wattville."

"Methought," said Spenser, "these were all the lands
of Clare?"

"Clare! oh, ay, from Hants to Kentland. I ought to
know, I was a pet of Clare's."

"Why so was I, though ne'er in Holmsdale till yesternight. Know you his son?"

"Know him, no: but, wherefore, do you ask?"

"Because I honour Clare."

"Why, so do I: but where do my verderers loiter?"

"No matter, like Robin I can dress my own venison, so
my whinger—ha, forgot—wilt lend me thine. What,
a noble opal, faith! Why, how, 'tis very like—aye,

at the Mise of Lewis? Leicester, aye? 'tis Norman, hey?"

"A birthday gift from noble Clare."

"I knew 'twas Norman, like these walls of Holmsdale. Hearkye, I've suit and service there, and favour with its lord, he'll make a Templar welcome, so follow me Red Gilbert of Holmsdale—for so they call me here. There's Meun the Rhymer, who dreams of shrines and pilgrims—you'll come with me to Holmsdale?"

The *invite* was too tempting to refuse, and, as they reached the castle-gate, the bowman said, "Here, Wilbert, to the Gloucester chamber, this Knight of the Cross is an honoured guest of thy master," while Spenser looked on the carved escutcheons and badges with something like bewildered recognition.

Well, at noon next day, Gilbert de Clare received the homage of the warenners in the court-yard of his castle of Holmsdale in Bletchingley, within a rank of serving-men, with badges on their sleeves, three chevronels gules. In the suite stood John de la Meun, who finished the *Roman de la Rose* of William Lorris, or (some say) of John Clopinel, afterwards Englished by Chaucer. He came over with the English court after the marriage of Isabella.

> "Wrought was his robe in strange gise,
> And all to slyttered for queintise,
> In many a place lowe and hie."

and he gloried in embossed and painted boots.

There was a swaggering fopling too, on a horse, in a party-coloured suite, half blue, half red.

> "His swerdes sheth of ivory,
> His helme of latoun bright,
> His sadel was of rewel bone,
> His bridel as the sonne shone,
> Or as the mone light."

And he was hailed as "Noble usher or Huisser," or, as *we* should call him, "Master of the Revels" : and the serving-men bowed the knee before him, but they who knew Piers Gaveston whispered slyly, "ah—

> 'Long beards heartlesse, painted hoods witlesse,
> Gay cotes gracelesse, maketh Englonde thriftlesse.' "

But the fopling's "make-up" requires a more minute colouring, for he set the fashion of the day. Beneath his surcoat or cyclas of sable and vair and minevair he wore

> "Of cloth of lake fin and clere,
> A breche and eke a sherte,
> And over that an habergeon
> For piercing of his herte."

Round his brow he had a double garland of gold, and the back of his hair was shaved in true Norman fashion.

But here, flanked by a bevy of lackeys, two ladies were ushered to the court-yard by Piers Gaveston, who smiled and bowed, but they gave him frowns in return. One wore a robe and *cyclas* of Damascus, on her head she wore a veil and wimple, and on her feet square-fretted boots, a boar's head at each knotting of the fret : and she laid her wimple aside and displayed her glossy tresses folded in a gold *cam* or net, and pendant from it there was a fire jasper on one side and three amulets of gold on the other. The other maiden was enthroned on a chair of state,

and John de Meun has thus described her in the " Squier
of low degree."

> "And yede my daughter in a chare,
>   Yt shall be cover'd with velvet red,
>   And clothes of fine gold all about your head,
>   With damask white and azure blewe
>   Well diapper'd with lilies newe;
>   Your mantle of rich degree,
>   Purple pall and ermyne free."

At the same moment the noble host, in his robes of state,
led Spenser forward and introduced him to his uncle the
Duke of Brabanys, who married Marguerite of Acris, his
mother Joan's *suster*.

And the fopling came forward to usher the stranger to
the Queen of Revels, but, when their eyes met, each
started as he had seen a ghost—and, indeed, Spenser was
bewildered, for the lady, on hearing his name, was trembling on her sister's bosom : the knights still looking
daggers at each other. To Spenser she curtseyed low, and
whispered to Gaveston, " Dare not for your life, for my
sake, for your own.   And, prythee, why that frown, good
stranger ? "

" E'en that I know him well, fair lady."

" Aye, we *have* met—at court methinks," said Piers.

" And in a cottage too—last night—"

" Nay, nay, I do pray you both, be friends, Piers is
yours, sister—curb him, or you'll rue it."

" Ah, may I know your name ? " said Spenser.

" We call her Elinore: I am Red Gilbert, as I told
you."

" The noble Gloster, pardon : dolt that I am, I might

have guessed it all, but I have drunk of Lethe and forget a friend, you remember one even unknown."

"Nay, I did know you by your knife, it hung on Leicester's girdle once, but come, you'll tread a measure, Hugh, with Elinore. How now, Sir Piers, why stand you posen there? Marguerite, hast clipped his tongue—bestir thee man, or faith you'll shame your office."

" You have been wandering far?" said Elinore.

" Into the lands of the Sun."

" And last?"

" From Araby."

" The blest—you were happy there."

" Nay, I was wanting that would make me so—hope, love."

" Methought in Araby that love was ever on the wing."

" Aye, like the butterfly from flower to flower, he lives his day and dies."

" So sings yonder pensive poet : hither De la Meune, this gentle knight will listen to your lay."

Elinore caught up her chitar, and this is the chaunt they sung :—

> "Tell me where with hope and love,
> Felicity hath made her home,
> In Tempe's vale, in Cintra's grove,
> Or Shiraz' golden dome?

> "Lady, in desart, cloud or storm,
> Love wantons in his wild caress,
> E'en icy rocks his torch will warm,
> And light a wilderness.

> "Tell me where love with love is blest,
> In what enchanted cell he lies;

Is it within a jewell'd vest,
Or in a Houri's eyes?

"Beauty may lure love's burning vows,
  But beauty is their lightest part,
  Her lips are but his pleasure-house,
  His home is in her heart."

While the revels went on, and Piers was flirting with his all but affianced Marguerite, and De la Meune was pattering rhyme to the maidens, Hugh Spenser was wooing Elinore as in duty bound, but it was a cold and formal service.

Clare had been watching them intently, and had just resolved to *absolve* him from his suit and service, when the curfew again rung through Bletchingley, and with hand-pressing and embrace the guests departed, and Gilbert de Clare beckoned Spenser to his Gothic closet.

"You have talked with Elinore," he said, in very solemn tone, "you love her not."

"Our father's word is law, and I *must* love her, nor stain the honour that I owe to Clare."

"Love is not so pliant, Hugh, he will rebel, and marriage they say is made in heaven. Now hear me, Spenser. I am a fond and truthful brother, and do love my sister. *Must*, sayst thou, no, no, we will not make a mockery of love. Hugh Spenser, you are free, 'twere best for both, for troth her heart is icy as thine own, her eyes downcast from him we hoped might woo and win her, and tears bedewed her cheek. Yet, 'tis strange, that in her sleep *your* name—(so whispers me her sister)—but 'tis naught to you, your heart is still your own."

" It was, till yesternight, and then 'twas stolen by a gipsy from me. Aye, from *me*, whose heart hath spurned the wild girls of Araby, and all the diamonds of the desert. No, noble Clare, I am not free, my heart is *not* my own, and it were sin and shame to tempt so bright a thing as Elinore, so, 'twere meet I crave forgiveness and begone, where—"

" In the cloisters—seek her there, alone : one parting word to Elinore, and then, good night."

In very pensive mood, Hugh Spenser entered the oratory, one only object filled his thought, the scarlet hood, and when he reached the altar, who shall paint his wonder, the scarlet hood herself was kneeling there and weeping, for the boy in his Sunday suit lay on a cushion dying. As Spenser knelt beside them, the boy started up, " She loves you, I know she does," he whispered, " I will not die yet, not till—" he whispered in her ear, and her cheek was in a moment crimson-flushed.

" Yes, your vesper hymns shall go together there, I know some of the angels, and *they* will sing them too, will they not, Lady Elinore ?"

" Elinore ! you the girl in serge," exclaimed Spenser, while the boy uttered a scream of delight as he caught her to his breast with a kiss so pure and holy, as not to profane even the sanctity of the oratory.

There was a silent trio, for a moment, when Clare, who had heard the scream, entered the chapel.

" Is this a Templar's troth, Hugh Spenser ? This for

the honour of Clare. I thought you truthful, Hugh, but from this hour—" While Elinore rushed to her brother's arms, as the boy exclaimed,

" They love, they love! believe it, noble master. Ah! I'm dying now, dying. Oh, so happy! Sister, I'm coming to you, you will joy to know there are two angels yet on earth that love. Let me look on you once more."

They both kissed his forehead.

" You are too good for earth. Oh, Lady Elinore linger not too long, too happy here, I know, to wish for heaven, but I will fly down and fetch you if you tarry. Ah! a shadow—'twill be light enough in heaven, the shadows there are light. Why, look, the stars are big as moons. Hush, now! and when you come to us come hand in hand together. I know you will, for souls were made in pairs."

Elinore again kissed his forehead, and—he was dead. Poor boy, they laid him out in the chapel where he died, and it was an emblem of his purity that marble white which we call the half-mourner, at the moment it was flitting o'er his bier. Elinore was lost in thought, for the boy was her darling, and she started and blushed when Clare whispered,

" So, Nell, you were the gipsy, hey. Why, I might have guessed as much. Noble Spenser, the Homage shall grant you for this wench's sake suit of court in Holmsdale, she'll seal the bargain with her lips, take your knight's fee, Sir Templar—nay, that were exaction, Hugh—enough, enough, or we dissolve the court of homage and send thee back to Palestine."

Be sure there were bishops and deans, and lords and knights of fame, and dames and damosels of birth and beauty, that flocked to Bletchingley to do grace and honour to the marriage of the Scarlet Hood.

You see the purple moors of the sand-range yonder, across the weald; thitherward our course is bent. As we wander on, one of the choicest elements of beauty is around us—contrast.

The charm of Rembrandt lay in the magic of his *chiaro scuro*: a century ago, courtly vanity herself was wont to spot with black plaster her forehead and her cheek, as a foil to her lilies and her roses. Even the swarthy Æthiop has learned the secret, and hangs around her rich brown arm the precious pearl and noble opal. The charm is displayed by Nature herself, in the transitions of chalk, malm, and green sand in this accomplished district. We see the chalk dotted with beech, yew, juniper, box, ash, chestnut, and sycamore, the sand with linden, birch, beam, and pine, the wealden with oak and elm, and the malm with the willows.

Contrasted with the paps of the chalk, are spread yonder moors of the Leith range, their eastern brow Redland, the Holm, or *Locus Florentius*, rising abruptly from the Holmwood.

The prettiest sand-lanes lead from Dorking thitherward to the wildest beauty in Surrey, by the dingles of the Rookery and the vales of Mereden, the Holmsdale of the olden maps (where you may find the intensely cold spring of Megs-well), or by valley Lonesome, or the woods of Wotton, and in your walks you may gather the native ferns of the heath-hills—hart's-tongue, and polypody, and spleenwort, and shield-fern, and adder's-tongue, and moonwort, and .brake, and, by rare chance, a tuft of *osmunda regalis.*

Here and there peep out from the sand-banks the most grotesque roots of the old beeches. You may, perchance, light on one of which we present a faithful sketch.

The prestige of antiquity, too, is around us. There is Winter field, where, fifty years since, Saxon and Frankish coins were discovered. You lofty mound, Heanstige or Ansticbury—the grand Roman station of *Stanestreet*— is a polygon of twenty acres, the vallum and fosse being

traced by Britons and Romans, and remodelled by the
Danes. Stanestreet was the line of incursion from *Reg-
num*, or *Cissaceaster*, by Oakwood to *Noviomagus*, or
Woodcot on the Downs.

Seen from Anstiebury, the green sand, over the hamlet
of Cold Harbour, is finely contrasted with the rich greens
of Mereden. In autumn the long shadows, the failing
notes of the evening birds, the faded petals of the wild
flowers, the tinkling of the falling leaf, and the chill of
early twilight, present to the contemplative mind a
chastening symbol of decay.

From the wood-crown of Anstiebury the *coup d'œil*
over to Kent and Sussex is magnificent. On the descent
along the meadows the scenery is more *artistic*, enriched
by its foreground. There is *Kitlands* embosomed in its
nest of trees, and beyond it lies fine old *Berehurst*—a
gnarled and giant oak of four centuries standing sentinel
at its gate. The peeps over the weald are exquisite, and
the lawns the very spot for a Decameron, where we might
linger throughout many a summer's day,

> " Framing as a fair excuse
> The book, the pencil, and the muse,
> Something to give, to sing, to say,
> Some modern tale, some antient lay."

We may, perchance, remember an antient tale of Berehurst, the modern lay we will leave to the feathered choir,
for Bere is a very paradise of birds.

The pine-woods are oft the haunt of three rare things—
the *hawfinch*, the *pine bullfinch*, and the *crossbill:* the
waxen-chatterer, and even, we believe, the *hoopoe* have

fed on its arbutus. You may hear, in early summer, a
special concert of the song birds : *soprani*, the goldfinch,
greenfinch, chaffinch, siskin, blackcap, the warblers, and
the larks,—*contralti*, the blackbird and the thrushes,--
mezzo-soprani, the bullfinch, the redpoles, and the linnets,
and the *prima donna* of the woods, the nightingale. We
desire no fitter symphony to our story, than its trill—no
fitter flowers for its garland than the roses of Berehurst
There, on one stem you might see *maiden's blush*, and the
cloth of gold, like the cheek of beauty, and her jewels on
a royal birthnight. Be sure the blush-rose is the
favourite,—

> " To it, the live-long night, there sings
> A bird unseen, though not remote."

We have often listened to the lay, and have thought it a
love-chaunt as passionate, even, as that of the bulbul in
the gardens of the blue Ægean. However that be, as we
listen we are ever thinking of a certain story-teller of the
olden time, most accomplished in his art, who has told us
how a pair of pretty creatures were once bewitched with
this romaunt of the bird and the flower. 'Twere vain,
however, to look for it in the " Boke of his Cronycles,"
for Sir John Froissart, its *auctour*, would have blushed
for shame to have blended with the loftier legends of his
history, the babyism of

𝕿𝖍𝖊 𝕷𝖔𝖇𝖊-𝖑𝖎𝖕𝖘.

> " In the time of my childhood, 'twas like a sweet dream
> To sit in the roses, and hear the birds' song."

OUR tale is of peace, yet its date is close on one of the most
martial eras of England's chivalry : the age of Syr Ber-

tram de Clesquy, of De Foix, of Bruce and Wallace, and
Prince Edward the model of chivalry, and eke of the
Lady Philipp of Hainault, the queen of England, who,
at Neville's Cross, vanquished and led captive David of
Scotland, to grace, with two other kings, the pageantry of
Windsor Castle.

It was many years after the field of Poytiers, that I,
Syr John Froissart, sometime chanon of the church of
Chimas, and erst clerk of the chamber to Philipp, one of
the godlyest ladies in the world, crossed the waters, with
letters from the Count of Hainault to the Duke of York
in Engellond, and honoured with the sacred trust of
Phillipp Rouet, bride-maiden to her illustrious sister
Katheryn Swynford, who was to win rank for her base-
born, with the coronet of the high and mighty prince—
Lord John of Gaunt. From Becket's shrine to the lintel
of Berehurst, where, for the triumph of Creci, all was
Plantagenet and glory — Sir Richard de la Bere, its
master, was he who saved the Black Prince, as the
Frankish martinets called him, and won five feathers
for his crest: he held his casque at Poictiers, when
Edward, between Montjoye St. Denys, and St. George
Guienne, received King John from Syr Denyse Morbech,
Knight of Arthoys, for that he would resign to none but
his cosyn of Wales : it was he who bore the cup of wine
and spices that Edward served " on day of the batayle' at
the supper, in Malpertnesse," to his captives, who hailed him
le gentil Seigneur. Here also housed two noble dames, once
jealous rivals, now bosom friends, and though Berehurst
was almost of Saxon rudeness, their style was semi-regal,

M

and though their shield was crossed by the baton sinister,
they were linked with the blood royal, being the relicts of
the prince's sons, Sir Roger Clarendon and Sir John
Sounder. They were in royal weeds, one

> " in widowes habit large of samite brown,"

and of the other

> "her clothys, everych one,
> Shall blacke ken in tolequin herte swete,
> That I am as oute of the world agone."

Their chamber was picked out with Edward's field-
colours, blue and red, with golden lions crowned and
langued blue. There hung the tiny helm and gauntlets
the prince wore at *hastiludia*, and Sir Geffery Charney's
gauntlet, the French banner still in its grasp, while on
the walls and on the server's sleeves, blazed the words
Ich dien, and *Houmont*—the mottoes on his feathers and
his tomb.

The real jewels of the widows, however, were their
boy and girl, and in truth they were like nothing earthly,
and could be painted but with a feather of the Peri's
wing. It were a gleam of paradise to see them wandering
hand in hand among the ferns and fox-gloves of Leith
Hill, weaving coronets of sun-roses and cuckoo flowers, or
fast asleep upon the mosses, fanned by the winglets of the
blue and copper flies that haunt the heath hills. One
evening, while the pets were feasting on the rich illuminated missals, and the scribbling of Meun and of one
Master Froissart—save the mark!—so royally wrapt in
leather by Mouthell, the dowagers were deep in council as

they sat on the edge of the rich silk bed bequeathed to Lady Sounder by the Black Prince.

"My cousin of Clarendon," whispered the Lady Sounder, gazing on them with that ecstasy that none but mothers feel, "ours is a chequered life, yet happy beyond all women in our darlings!"

"Aye, cousin, let Edmond frown, we are content. Look at the jewels! Poor Joan may well be jealous of our kids, with her puny boy Prince Richard. The Maid of Kent would filch these little bastards an she could, but we will keep our lambkins from the world in all the sweetness and purity of primæval life. But, Gossip, I have a thought deeper than thou wilt guess."

"But I do guess, Gossip, ere thou speakest it : look at the darlings, are they not made to love and be beloved? And yet they love not as we would have them love."

"Thou hast said it, cousin—aye, we must *make* them love. Yet, faith, they scarce seem human things—far more like nympholepts than boy and girl."

And how, think you, did the dowagers set about their task of *forcing* love on sheer simplicity.

"Roger, my pet," said Lady de Clarendon, when they were alone, "I do delight to see you so joyous and content. Yet I do wonder, aye, that you never have a wish."

"A wish, my mother!—a wish! Why, what on earth is that?"

"What—why, to long for something more."

"More than I have! Have I not all I want?"

"Not all—not *quite* all Something to love!"

"That something have I got already, mother."

"Already !   So—is she good and beautiful ?"

" Very."

" Then I am happy, sweet one.   Gulnare, is't not ?"

"No, not Gulnare : you make me smile, my mother.
What, want Gulnare ! why, she is ever with me.   What,
love Gulnare ! why, she is but my cousin.   You are my
mother—my nearer, so my dearer, kin : so, as I ought, I
love my mother all."   And he threw himself on his
mother's bosom.

Yet they who looked on Roger de Clarendon, might,
once in a way, catch him very deep in thought, as if he
longed for he knew not what.

And Gulnare—was she thoughtful too ?   So guessed
her mother, and she spoke :

" You are wishing, my child."

" Yes," replied Gulnare, in a whisper, " no—yes—no
—why should I wish ?   Have I not you, my mother ?
What want I more ? "

"I thought you might want—I thought—I thought
of Roger."

" So have I thought of Roger—but want him ?   No.
Why, he is ever with me—morning, noon, and night."

" And that is why you love him not ? "

" I said not so.   Yet why should I love him, mother ? "

" Why, is he not a man, sweet one ? "

" Roger a man ?   Oh, I hope not !—methought all men
were monks or devils, for so they're painted in the missal.
What, love a thing like that ?   Why, they fright me even
in my dreams !   Roger is *not* a man, or long ere this he
would have eaten me ! "

"Eat you, my child, an angel like your cousin ! "

" Angel !—oh, worse and worse ! The naughty angels, came they not down to the daughters of men—no good did come on't, mother. Bid me not love an angel, or a man, or I shall think you're tired of poor Gulnare."

" Yet promise me."

" Oh, yes : I'll promise all that you desire, so it be not to love a man."

Believe not that Gulnare, even in this solitude, was unknown. Gentles and nobles in plenty sought to woo and win her, for the fame of her beauty had maddened half the gadflies of the Court, even the noble bastards of Lancaster, who now came down to Berehurst to gallant the Lady Philippa to Windsor. There was John Lord Beauforde, the Erle of Somerset, the idol of John of Gaunt, who loved his son entyrely, and Henry the Cardinal, and his Grace of Excester : and in their suite, fresh from his embassy to Genoa, came one Geoffry Chaucer, who rhymed in the purest Saxsen English.

It was the morrow of Poictiers, so let me dash off a pencil sketch of the scene. There is De la Bere in full suit of mail : there sit the widows in royal pourpoint of scarlet ribbon, and deeply pouched and buttoned down the front, their hair rolled up in cauls of gold : there is a group of noble girls dressed in holiday, as Master Chaucer whispered in mine ear,

> " everich on her hede,
> A rich net of golde, which, withouten drede,
> Was fulle of stately net-stones sett.
> And everyche lady had a chapelet
> On her hede of braunches fair and greene."

But the beauty of all was Gulnare glittering

> "as it were a mede,
> Alle fulle of freshe flowres white and rede."

And her neck of snow was circled by a deep blue ribbon, clasped by a golden buckle.

Then I, Sir John Froissart, in my cotte hardie, given me by Amadeus of Savoy, Count Verde, kneel and lay at the lady's feet my illumined boke of "Meliador," in crimson velvet starred with golden roses. Even as I am kneeling, my Lord of Beauforde is flirting with Gulnare, and, reckless of her frowns and blushes, is playing with the ribbon round her neck.

"Nay, nay, my lord," cried Sir Richard de la Bere, "profane it not: that sacred thing, was the queen's once, and graced a royal prince: it doth bear a royal legend too fine for our rude lore of Surrey. Hither, Master Geoffry, the theme may grace a poet's lip. But here is Master Froissart, we forgot he might be in presence there: and so, Sir John, though Wickliffe frown on us—and Wickliffe is a holy man—tell to these gentles here the secret of that holy ribbon."

"I obey, Sir Knight: I do remember me — 'twas in Windsor Hall of State, the brawl and revel at its height. Even the king and queen did leap like wildings in the dance, and her Grace, not Joan of Salisbury, as the story goes, did make a leg. When, lo! down drops that thing of blue down on the floor—I say not whence it fell. Then blushed the queen deep red, the Court, aye one and all, laughed in its sleeve. And when the king did take the ribbon up (another dare not, it were too proud

for any touch but his), and bound it on his leg, the
laugh was loud throughout. But, in a flash, the king
did frown them down to modesty: 'Now, by the rood!'
quoth he, 'this were a graceless slander on our State and
Queen, *Honi soit qui mal y pense.* Listen, lords and
ladies, to the King. Now, by St. George, we swear that
sovereign honour be done to that silken tie: that zone
shall be the high emprize of Majesty, the brightest star in
the constellation of honour. Aye, by St. George! who won
the holy field in Palestine. Remember, lords, how Cœur
de Lion, under *Acre's* walls, bound thongs of leather on his
choycest knights. So doth the King of England here, in
Windsor. Kneel, kneel, my son, thou flower of chivalry
—as e'en our Frankish foe doth name thee yet—I dub
thee with the blade that flashed at Creci, and we unbind
the precious fillet, that it may grace thy leg, my son, to
encorage and shewe alle nobil hertis ensample of mater
of honour! So rise, Sir Edward of Wales, first knight of
the blue garter.'"

The shouts of "Edward, more brave than Ribaumon or
Gasson de Foiz," made the welkin ring. As the echoes
died away, had you peeped among the purple clematis,
you might have seen two pretty pairs half hidden in the
virgin's bower. There sits Philippa Rouet,

> "with a wildness flings
> Her fingers fine across the strings
> Of her kitar."

And with an orient grace trills away with her virelays,
or green songs of Provence, and roundels, and *chaunts
royeaux,* and the nightingales overhead are singing, too,

in very jealous rivalry, and Master Chaucer recounts
a very charming story of Araby the blest,—how, in the
gardens of Gul, the nightingales hovered over the roses
of Sharon, and wooed them with their song into the very
ecstasy of love.   And there are listening, with lips wide
apart, Roger and Gulnare, bewitched and bewildered with
this Romaunt of the Rose.   With all this enchantment
the lids of Philippa had closed in Araby, and just as
they opened in England, and they had told the rhymer all
he longed to learn—lo, the boy and girl were gone !   And
we must follow them with Chaucer and Philippa, or our
story will halt just where it ought not.

"We are in the rosary now."

"So," murmured Roger de Clarendon, "a dream is it ?
'Tis a heart, then, that beats against my ribs.   Methought,
good lack, I gave it to the rose.   Ah ! I see a beauty
yonder,—I'll cover it with kisses, and then Gulnare shall
have it for her pillow : but first I'll make it love me.
There, that's my love-chaunt, pretty rose, and now will
you kiss and blush on me, I wonder."

So he crept to a rose and laid his cheek on a flower, as
he thought—"No ! why, where's the good of dreaming ?
the rose won't kiss me.   No, I am a boy, and not a nightingale—I'll try another, so."

And Gulnare, *she* had dreamed too, of something leaping in her bosom.   "Why 'tis alive, I'm sure.   The
gracious ! how it leapt when the bird came down to kiss
and woo me."

"Oh, what a nice warm game is kissing, and Roger
never played it with me.   Yet, gracious me ! what a

naughty little thing am I. The pretty bird, methought
—Woe's me: Gulnare, you're not so good as you were
wont to be. Yon foolish bird, that's singing there, doth
love the rose—why not a rosy lip? And you, foolish
girl, only to *dream* of nightingales. Nay, nay, he *shall*
love me as I ought to be."

So she laid her lips on a rose, as she thought.

And pray, now, how long this game of love-lips in its
playing? Marry! until their conscious eyes first met—
and then they took to lisping thus:

"What, you a nightingale?"

"What, you a rose?"

"Why, who'd have thought, though lips are red and
ripe, they were so very, very good to eat—did you?"

"Not I, but the rose hath taught me now to relish
lips and feed on kisses."

"I've learned a lesson, too: the bird hath lessoned me,
Roger. Yet odds! my little life, how hard and fast our
hearts are beating—feel. Oh, Roger, we must part, an'
you come not and try to quiet mine. It hurts me—doth
not yours? Come, try to still it, there's a duck, or our
hearts will kill us dead: so part we must."

"And is it really pain, Gulnare?"

"I'm sure I know not whether pain or pleasure, but
I'll run and ask mamma: so now we part."

Yet the simpletons kept closer still, and Roger whispered—

"Why, I do think, Gulnare, we were made for one
another."

"Why, so do I: and yet I ache again—keep off, keep off."

"And not to love, Gulnare?"

"Love!—how learned you that?"

"Our lips have taught us, Rosebud."   .

"Pretty, naughty lips! How often have I kissed my own, and yet I never loved! But yours are so sweeter, Roger."

"We *do* love, then, Gulnare."

"Aye, if liking lips be love, I suppose we do. And not to know their use before! No, Roger, no—we must not part 'em now."

"Well, if they must, they must, 'twere pity to part them now."

But a truce to all this twaddle, for the boy and girl are quiet now, and you are smiling, or what is worse, are frowning on our folly. And there stands Master Froissart, and there the dowagers themselves, who, trembling for their darlings, had stolen into the rosary just as the bird, that had been hanging on an orange blossom, and bending it down to the brow of Gulnare, opened its wings for flight to the Rainbow-field.

THEY who, in our day, gaze from yonder noble terrace of *Brome Hall*, so magnificently overlooking the glory of the Weald, and so beautifully backed and shielded from the northern blast by the great Morss Wood, never dream of the dense and tangled forest that lay around it even in the fourteenth century. It was the verge of the once great forest of Andredswald : a few precious and venerable relics of its acorns being yet preserved at Leith, Berchurst, Tilford and Knole. It was the nearest spot to London where real wild sport could be found : for the wolf, and the boar, and the hart came up out of the wald and made their lair in the outwoods. From the terrace we gaze, in bird's eye, on many a place among the rich meads and copses of the Wealden enriched by incident. On a mound of yonder bosky ridge, beyond the Roman gate on Stanestrete, stands a lone chapel richly endowed. In addition to its early revenue of 200*l.* a year, Queen Elizabeth granted 368*l.* from the Exchequer : and the benefaction was increased in the eighteenth century by Evelyn, Millar, Godolphin, and Offley, and lastly, with Queen Anne's Bounty. With the history of this chapel is blended a tale of sadness—a love story most unhappy in its catastrophe, wrapping in the deepest sables three fair families, and even to this day casting an historic gloom over

Okewode.

> " A document in madness,
> Thoughts and remembrance fitted."

It was in the depth of this Okewode Landwode. "Tremble not, my precious one," said Edward de la Hale, folding his arm around her waist : "trust me— my wire-haired lurcher, Brindle, will pull down the gauntest boar in the Landwode, aye, as he did the blood-hound of De la Brome : as he were conscious that the brute's master were the rival of his own in the heart of Yolande."

"You have no rival, Edward," she replied softly : "you

are all and everything and alone with your poor Yolande.
Yet I do fear me there are evil spirits around us, even
now, that will blast our fondest hope of love. That love
is stolen and stealthy, Edward, and I have nightly visions
—oh, how dark and joyless! and they foredoom us, I do
fear, to something very sorrowful : but we *must* love, or
life is o'er."

"What were life itself, without it, sweet one ? "

"Aye, what !" and Yolande dropped a tear of penitence
for her conscious disobedience to her father's will. But
her woman's heart was full, and creeping to her lover's
side, she murmured again—

"Alas ! what were my father's house but a cloistered
cell, without Edward de la Hale ? but, hark ! the bell !
the banquet waits, and we shall be missed ! "

"Well, our love shall be no longer secret," he whispered:
" I will kneel to the prince this very hour : trust me, he
will gain Sir Walter, for he loves me very graciously."

"Love you, who loves you not ? there is none : ah !
yes, there is one—William de la Brome : but I will tell
him how dearly I love you, and he will give me up, be
sure, for *my* sake."

Edward de la Hale heaved a deep sigh, and Yolande
answered with a smile : for she was unconscious of its
expressive import, and so they wandered homeward.

Yonder, in Highlande, was perched the hunting chalêt
of William de la Brome, the lord of many acres hereabout. The retreat was now honoured by royalty : no less
a personage than Henry, Prince of Wales, Duke of Cornwall, and Earl of Chester, had come into Surrey from the

great city to hunt the wild boar in Okewode Landwode—
for as well as a merry wag and a brave soldier, Prince Hal
was, like Nimrod, a mighty hunter. To meet him, were
bidden Sir Walter de Fancourt of *Yolande* under Holmbury, and Edward de la Hale, steward of the Landwode.
The hut was rude as those at the æra of Edgar, or Athelstane, but Brome had decked it out superbly with hunting-
spears, and poles, and bugles, and knives, and boars
heads, and antlers of the Red-deer. And there was a sort
of heraldic state too, for the Prince had brought with him
John Wrythe, the man who, in after years, as Chester
Herald, claimed France for him when he was a king and
a conqueror. The banquet was half over, and the wine-
cups were passing freely round. The prince had more
than once looked about and asked for his favourite, when
Brome inquired what his grace could see in the wishy-
washy losel, De la Hale.

"Let not Yolande hear you," said the Prince : "the
lightning of her eye would strike you blind : her heart,
my word on't, beats for the Landwode, William. But
your wine-cups, gentles—here's to Yolande de Fancourt
and Edward de la Hale."

"I am her father, noble Prince :" muttered Sir Walter.

"And I her lover, sir," added Brome, "spite of—"

"No thrift in either of you," muttered Sir Walter :
"mark me, Master Brome, he who wins my Yolande must
first win a golden spur in the course of chivalry, or
do some special service to the house of Fancourt : so
an equal chance for all, and that a poor one."

"And where hides this cynosure of eyes, this mighty

mistress of hearts ?" cried Henry: "we long to look on
her: not that *we* care an ace for a rolling eye or a luscious
lip ourselves,—but, see, they come. Wishy-washy ! what,
so giant-like in form, so eagle-eyed : no, no, William Brome,
so bright a creature could never affection a coward."

"Yet some may doubt him, sir : nay, even I will tell
him so to his face, I, William de la Brome : now by the
boar's head I swear—"

"Who swears by the boar ?" cried De la Hale as he
entered the hall : "the boar is the emblem of our house,
take not his name in vain."

"Silence, silence, we command you," exclaimed the
Prince : "we are not here to foster feuds. My brightest
Hebe, fill the cup of peace with crystal from the spring—
kiss but the brim with thy lip, and 'twill blush ruby in a
flash of light. We greet thee, mistress of beauty, and
swear the boar shall be the fortune of De la Hale."

"Perchance the *fate*," muttered Brome, frowning on his
rival.

The feast was over in the chalêt of Highlande. That
morning, at the dawn, the yeoman prickers of the Prince
had emerged from a cot in the Landwode, where a horse
can stand with its legs in four parishes, and were beating
about for a monster that had long haunted the coverts, laying waste the district around. The prickers knew him
by his footprints, and had laid him up in Okewode, awaiting the Prince and his suite from Brome. And hither
they are coursing along Stanestreet, with spears and
bugles, and Yolande on her jennet on the right hand of
the Prince. As they came on the wood—

" 'Tis a boar royal," said Hubert the head pricker,
" we shall tread him up anon. Your grace had need of
the toughest ash in the weald—his tusk is two feet long :
look to the lady, gallants, an' he should break loose now."

As he spoke, there was a loud crash among the boughs,
and the boar bounded like an elephant from the wood,
and before the lurchers could be loosed from their slips,
he rushed at the palfrey, and Yolande fell toward the
ground. But Edward de la Hale caught her, and plant-
ing himself against a giant oak, confronted the monster,
with his spear in the right hand, while Yolande, trembling,
grasped the left. The boar *ripped* one lurcher after another
as they charged him, and then, although a prick from
Edward's spear made him reel, it made him frantic too,
and with a furious leap he bounded against the tree,
transfixing the wrists of Yolande and De la Hale so firmly,
that they were only released by the slaying of the boar
and the sawing of the tusks.

" You have saved her, Edward," said Sir Walter de
Fancourt, " the boar *has* been your fortune."

" And his fate, said I not so ?" muttered Brome to himself, while Edward knelt on the spot, and said, " Blessed
be the ground for ever : we will build a house of prayer
and thanksgiving." And in that hour De la Hale decreed
the chapel in Okewode, of Saint John the Baptist.

The hunt was thus in a moment ended, and as Sir
Walter and his escort bore Yolande to her home, and the
cortége wended along to Brome, the sun went down red
and fiery over Holmbury.

And what happened now ? William de la Brome, as

they clomb the hill, had beckoned a beetle-browed creature from his suite, and had dismissed him with these broken sentences—' At the midnight hour—no blood—the oven —close—close—remember—"

None heard them but the slave.

The wind howled and hurtled among the pines of Anstiebury, as Edward de la Hale left his prince for his own house, that he might make it a home fit for Yolande de Fancourt.

Ere the hour of noon, he himself was gone, none knew whither: indeed, there seemed to be a *centrifugal* spell around Brome, for it was noised abroad that Edward de la Hale had a mission to the French court, and had hurried off without even a parting kiss for Yolande. Her lips quivered incessantly, yet she wept not, spoke not, and a fixed stare was all that told of her depth of feeling: her consciousness of a partial fulfilment of her foreboding. At the second midnight she arose and wandered in her sleep to Highlande, and was found in the morning, her icy cheek pressed close to the oven of the chalêt, and in cataleptic unconsciousness was borne back to her home.

Prince Henry was slumbering on his pallet, and William de la Brome sat alone, a wakeful, watchful man, until the morning dawned, when he started like a spectre from the tomb and staggered to the prince's chamber. And the hunters, as they assembled one by one, whispered of moans and unearthly sounds, as if

" Spirits were riding the northern blast."

Indeed, some secret spell seemed to haunt the guests, so

one by one they slunk away, leaving William de la Brome alone in his chalêt.

From this hour a strange mystery seemed to enwrap the chalêt of Highlande, and strange noises were ever and anon floating on the wind, but no one knew whence they came. Indeed, the place was well-nigh deserted both by friends and domestics. Yet with all this desolation, the spot seemed to possess a wondrous attraction for Yolande : night by night, even in storm or pitchy darkness, she wandered from her home to Highlande, and listened, with her cheek against the cold stones, and none held her back, as it was clear that after the night-wandering a state of quietude ensued that had mocked all the leeches' art to induce : and so it was whispered she was love-lorn and moonstruck. The crones of the Sandhills had almost ceased to whisper or to wonder, and had well-nigh forgotten *the bee in her bonnet,* when one morning the hour of noon had struck ere Yolande returned from her night walk : and then it transpired that a peasant, passing Wotton church at midnight, had seen two men shift a heavy load from their shoulders, and inhume it carefully in the chancel of the church, while a form as radiant as a spirit from another sphere knelt by the altar stone unseen by the men—the chief mourner over a desecrated sepulchre.

It was strange that William de la Brome about that hour called on Sir Walter Fancourt, and as Yolande glided in, knelt at her feet. But she stood, after her return, for awhile icebound, and taking a sprig from her bosom muttered almost in Ophelia's phrase, " there's rue for you : " and then, waving him from her presence, retreated to her chamber.

N

That night she went not to Highlande, and when in the
morning she saw Brome in the breakfast hall, she aimed at
his breast with her gold bodkin, and pricked him deeply,
but instantly drew back : and folding her arms and im-
printing her lips on the space between them, as if there
were an intervening object, she smiled upon it and held
her bodkin behind her, as if some thing or thought had
averted her aim and saved a life : and so she vanished
from the scene.

From that day, William de la Brome was laid in his
chamber a weary month, with the festering of his wound,
but it brought him repentance : he confessed to his priest,
though none knew for what, yet Yolande shook her head
with a solemn significance, as she could have told an awful
truth.   But her lips were sealed by some paralysing force,
and writing was a myth to the country girls, even of high
birth, at that age.   The last scene of this mystery was in
the consecration of the chapel of Okewode, which had
been raised at the cost of Sir Walter de Fancourt : and in
memory of the lost lover he had directed a marble slab
(still perfect) to be indented with an effigy in brass,
the hands clasped, and a scroll from the mouth inscribed—

J'hu mercie MCCCXXXI, Edw. de la Hale Armiger.

And there was Yolande, in deep mourning, although no
one had told her of that ceremony, kneeling with her lip
upon the name.   And that lip moved for a few moments as
in silent prayer, and then she lay like a blighted lily in
the arms of her father.

It was believed around Okewode that Yolande knew

the full secret, and some even whispered their more than
suspicion of Brome. The fate of Edward de la Hale was
yet a mystery, when one night Sir Walter de Fancourt
was aroused for the deposition of a dying man, but only
disjointed words fell from his lips in his delirium. The
last word that had been oft repeated, was *Wotton*, but it
led to no discovery, yet it was thought to point to the
grave of De la Hale. The other day, the bones of a
gigantic skeleton were exhumed in Wotton Chancel, not
far from the *brass* of John de la Hale, and from their size
we may fairly believe them the relics of him who was
immured at Highlande to his death, and secretly flung
into his grave on the night of Yolande's stealthy pilgrimage to Wotton.

It is among hills varied like these, that we are most
deeply impressed with the *archæology of creation*, through
countless ages of transition, perchance tens of millions of
years. The rock of the globe is our text book. Geology,
indeed, is the first great natural truth of the Bible, when,
having remodelled this beautiful world from a shapeless
chaos, "God saw that it was good." It is a subtle point
whether fire or water were decreed to map with all these
undulations the surface of the globe. We will leave the
Plutonist and Neptunist to argue this point on the summit
of Leith Hill, as they proudly glance on the grand display
of the chalk formation, which encircles as a frame the
Wealden, so rich in Saurian Giants : *iguanodon*, the lizard :
megatherium, the sloth : *mastodon*, the mammoth : *glyptodon*,
the armadillo : and *pterodactyle*, the bat : all predecessors

of man, ere the globe was perfected for the special home
of the intellectual animal.

When Dennis the critic once stood on this magnificent
brow, 1,000 feet above sea-level, this was his rhapsody :—

"I thought it the beautifullest prospect I ever beheld,
it would transport a stoic, a sight of enchantment, a
vision beatific,—forty or fifty miles off, downs awful and
venerable, their tops in the sky. A more transporting
sight than any in England or in Italy : even Valdarno
from the Appenines, Rome from Viterbo, and the Cam-
pagna from Tivoli and Frescati."

Lith, Leth, or Leith Hill is the *Liteffeld* of Domesday,
the "Hill of Feru." From the summit of the tower,
where Mr. Hull, the friend of Berkeley and Pope, is
buried upright, we may discern forty-one churches, and
points of ten counties. In Kent, Westonell and Holling-
bourn, the church of Frant in Sussex, Highclere or Beacon
Hill in Hants, Nettlebed in Oxfordshire, Walbury in
Berks, Wendover in Bucks, and Dunstable in Bedford-
shire : from one single point are visible St. Paul's Cathedral
and the Sea. The country directly below us is one wide
verdant carpet in spring-time : was " sweet Auburn " we
wonder, more fresh and lovely than yon village green :
was it circled by so neat a group of gables as this Ockley,
Ocle, Oclea, or Hocklei, " the Field of Oaks ? "

Ever look for humble happiness on a village green like
this, remote

    " From mad ambition and the pride of kings : "

where human nature is content to linger on in primitive

simplicity, rich in the wealth of poverty, for contentment
is the riches of nature.

The rural spot is peaceful now as an infant's slumber :
yet, once on a time, it formed the head quarters of the
Saxon host, and on this tented field, according to the
chroniclers, they "won the Greé."

The Battaile of Okeley.

> " Ere the ruddy sun be set,
>   Pikes shall shiver, javelins sing,
>   Hauberk crash, and helmet ring."

THE Danes had routed ·Beorthulfe, king of the Mercians,
and then marched from London over the Thames into
Surrey, we believe *about* 850, although Matthew of Westminster and the Saxon chronicles differ regarding the year.
Hynguoar and Hubba, the sons of the beautiful Lothbrock
of Lochlyn, had come over in the fleet of Rorie, nephew
of Harold Klack, and were esconced "on a down called
Oclea," and here in Southrey they pitched their battle.
This down was Anstiebury.

They had raz'd *Entons* in Capel yonder, and had
brought away the bell and the gates with which they
barred the fosse of Col Arbor.   They had carried off the
Saxon women, too, for the Pagans ever thought it a trick
worth gold to fire the Christian fanes, slay their men and
boys, and deflower the virgins, who often cut off their ears
and noses to save themselves from the clutch of the Danes.

They had called in their scouts from Holmbury to
defend their station on *Heanstige*, for they were now

bereft of their famous and enchanted standard the
REAFEN, which it was almost death to lose.   This
magic web had been woven by their three sisters of Abo.
It eclipsed even the Scout, or Spy Rafen of Woden, the
sire of Thor, *Alfadir* or father of all the *Sacæ*, whom the
Gauls call *Suesones*, the Cymbri *Sausen*, the Scotch *Sacon*,
the Irish *Sassenac :* and it was believed they sprung from
Saeya or *Buddha.*

And now the shadows were falling, and the Danes had
formed a *Valhalla*, or hall of the chosen, where they
made ready to bathe their senses in mead.   The beautiful
Valkas served it up in golden cups, for the Danes were of
the Teuton or Gothic tribes : so as Mahomet had his
Houris, Odin had his Valkas, even in *Gimlé* or the second
Heaven, when the Valhalla had passed away.

The scene would have charmed Salvator, for the men
let down their long hair in honour of Harold Harfiger,
and so they drank and howled till "night dew-lapped
came, and every gleaming star."   The song had ceased,
and by the side of Hynguoar sat his little fairy Leman
Olafe : her eyes like large blue globes cut out of the
firmament, and rolling those lustrous orbs, she hung on
his lips until the noble Dane yawned and hiccoughed—
" Fresh beauty, ho, pure fresh lips untasted : yet give me
fresh kisses : fresh lips for every hour : lips dropping
honey, and breathing song."   As he spoke, the twang of
a harp was heard outside the tent, and an air wild as the
west wind.

" Ha, Odin hath blessed the prayer," cried Hubba,
starting from his seat : "hark, hark ! 'tis Hero Hogen."

As the cadence fell, the chief whispered a fair boy. "Forth, Sweyn, we would fain look on the angel who sings thus to the soul of Hynguoar : by Odin, my ear hath not drunk such sweetness since the rouse in Krönberg." The boy glided from the tent, and in a moment returning, thus spoke (for beauty may inspire poesy in a breath) :—

> " Her mouthe ys lyke the rosen rede,
> Her eyne lyk the refen gray,
> And everyche worde she utters,
> Ys lyken a mynstrell's laye."

Olafe had also stolen away in a very jealous mood to look on the song bird, and she too, beauty as she was, seemed bewitched, and, as she stood again on the dais, she whispered, " 'Tis a Saxon woman, Etheldritha, of the noble blood of East Anglia, behold her ! " and in a moment the bright Saxon was kneeling at the feet of Hynguoar. She wore the Saxon *gunna* or gown, and a scarlet cloke of her namesake, the princess, and lappets of gold and emerald rings with costly pearls, hung on her ears. She was bright as the Judith of the Fraga, "the maid with the twisted locks," and sweeping her rude harp, she sang like a seraph this runic rhyme :—

> " Up wak'd the Queen of Danmark,
> In her bower she lay :
> O whilken o my ladies strikes the harp soe.
> It is none o your ladies,
> Whose harp ye hear,
> It is Hero Hogen,
> Singing soe clear."

The Danes rolled their eyes in rapture while she sung. "Thou hast ravished our ears, bright Saxon," cried

Hubba, clutching the noble maiden in his arms, while the chiefs, holding their golden cups aloft, swore by Odin no throat so deep and clear were among the Valkas of the Valhalla.   In short, so did Etheldritha charm the Danish chiefs the livelong night, that they were still reeling and rolling as the sun arose over the weald of Kent, his beams streaming into the tent like the *Regnarokr*—the twilight of the gods.   Then Olafe, at her master's nod, took a golden amulet from his wrist, and with a jealous scowl clasped it round the arm of Etheldritha.   And now it was time for slumber, yet even when the women retired, the men of Lochlyn drank mead, and hiccoughed until they sank into a drunken stupor.   Etheldritha was watching for the moment, and rushing out she roused the Saxon women in their tents : the amulet, even more potent with the sentinels than a pass-word, opened the gates at once to their husbands, who carried off the Enton gates and the bell to Capel Steeple, and with its triumphant clang roused the Saxons on the green. .

The king of the western Angles, Æthelwulfus, also called Æthulf and Ethelwolfe, had marched from Horsaham in the glades of Coit Andred, or Andredesweald, or Andredsuada, in Sud Seaxnarice, and he entered Sudric, the land south of the river, by the great Stany Street Calceway, to Arseste, now Evershed's Place, and he had rested on Aclea, the fosse and mound of which may be traced near Ockley Church.   Tents were pitched on the *feld* of *okes* by Elderslie, and there were ranged, according to their rank, the noble, the free-born, the freedman, and the bondsman.   The king wore a solemn brow,

for he had been elected, if not consecrated, to the See of
Winchester, and was but now released from his holy
orders by the Pope, that he might mount the throne
of his father, the great Egbert. He wore a robe of cloth
of gold over a tunic of padded linen : a collar of gold with
a *breast-beorg* defended his broad chest, and a Phrygian
cap shaded his brow. His two *Theons*, or body-guards,
also wore the cap, and the *yehrynged-byrn*, and torques
of gold. Their beards were forked like the Hebrews,
and the hair was dyed of green and orange. They bore
targans, shields of embossed leather, and in the belt was
thrust the *twi-eced-seax*, or double-edged knife. The men
carried long seaxes and a *twybill*, or double battle-axe,
hung in chains over the shoulder. And there was Wada,
or Huda, Eorlderman of Surrey, bearing a white shield,
his felt hat studded with one rich jewel. And by the
king's side stood young Alfred, his fourth son, then five
years old, in a fine linen shirt, a tunic falling to his knee,
beautifully embroidered in blue, red, and green by his
mother, lately dead,—Osburga, daughter of Oslac, the
King's cupbearer—and on his feet were *slype sceos* of silk
and gold. Around his neck was the famous amulet, hung
there by the Pope himself (when at four years old he left
Mola), to save him from shipwreck. It was the *bulla* of
gold inscribed " Alfred, me haet gewerchan," since found
in the Isle of Ethelyngay, where " Aluredo " had been in
exile.

On each side of their pet stood Swithan of Winchester,
the boy's tutor, and Alstan of Sherborne. Round the
neck of Swithan, hung by a golden cord the MS. copy of

the Gospels of Eadfred of Durham, illuminated by Ethelwold, and writ in Anglo-Saxon. Alfred held the rich MSS. of Alshelm, and Cædmon, and Roland, the gift of his mother Osburga, not of Judith his young step-dame, the king's doll-wife. The prince opened the book of Roland, and he and Swithan tried in vain to read, when a youth whispered, "I will teach you." Alfred smiled and accepted. 'Twas Alstan's turn : he kissed the prince, and hailed him "perfect peace," and talked of Roland.

"Think of your grandsire, prince," said the youth, Asser, afterwards his life-writer and Bishop of Shireburne, "of the great Ecgbeornt, the Bretwalda," and he told him he should himself be great, and Alstan promised the unction of the Pope, and then they retired to read "Erygena and Boethius' de Consolatione."

The king sat in council of war with Wada, for the neighing of his stallion, held by the Saxon as a battle-cry, had fired him to rush at once on the Dane. It was, moreover, the *glory* month, *milke-monat*, when the cows thrice in the day yield their milk : and the day itself, Wodnesday, was propitious too. William de Regibus, a writer of historyes, sayeth, "the Saxons worshipped a god named Woden (Mercury), and a goddesse Fria (Venus), and called the thirde daye in the weke Wodnesday, and the fifthe daye Friasday, or Freesday," while the fourth was Thorsday, in honour of Thisa, wife of Thor : all these were lucky.

But Wada had counselled Ethelwulf to wait for his son, Athelstane, whose ships had just beat the Vikings' fleet at Sandwich. For Wada had tried the judgment of

the *Iodhain Moran*, with which the Irish judges were wont
to encircle their necks ere their decision : this remained
unclosed on Wada's neck, and his faith told him his
judgment for delay was a right one. "The foe," he said,
"was thick and in array on Col Arbor : if they drop
down on the Hamwode—"

Wada was interrupted by the king. "Behold!" he
cried, "Mars the great planet beams on us brighter than
the moon, aye, even than yonder *Stahl-nufus*, glaring on
the Danish camp : the planet-God hath ever shone on the
fortunes of Ethelwulf, aye, and so was it even now, when
Erlecorle beat the Northmen at Wenbury. Well hath the
Druid proclaimed, 'Stars dispose the affairs of men.' So
noble Wada, down, down with the Vikings, wer't but to
avenge the rape of Etheldritha."

At the moment a collared thrall rushed without ceremony
into the presence, and shouted "the gates are won, the
women free:" and then it was Etheldritha herself that
glided in with stately grace, and knelt at the king's feet.

The Saxons shouted, and Asser proclaimed a miracle.

"And art thou safe, fair Dritha?" cried the king :
"we deemed thee stained and lost."

"It was my own ruse, Bretwalda," replied the lady.
"I played the drunken Danes to sleep : even yet they
may be snoring in their honey-cups."

"Sayest thou so, maid of honour, in glory as in name,
then are the men of Lochlyn lost : to prayer, to prayer,
holy Swithan! they shall swear on their holy braslet
fealty to the Saxon—*nemed eure Seaxes*, men of war, and
down with Lochlyn, unfold the Reafen, *vorwart*."

(We may hint by the way, whether Odon of Devon-
shire, or Alfred himself, in after time, took the *real*
Reafen from the Danes.)

While thus the Saxon camp was arousing, on Heanstige
the chiefs were awaking from feverish slumber, and bind-
ing their burning brows with wetted rags, had girded on
the *brynio*, or rynged byre, and assumed the round helm
with the nef-biorg, or nose-guard,—and they brought out
the stallion, and Hynguoar swore on his golden braslet
that the Romish king should eat of it, in token of his
conversion to Paganism. At that moment the alarm was
sounded : they snatched their white and gilded shields,
but ere they could *form*, a body of the Saxons had gained
the brow, and dislodged the Danes.

Roric was pouring oath on oath on the sleepy soldiers,
and thrice sent the Saxon wench to *oud skrahg* (old
scratch) : but order there was none in the ranks.

The fight was a series of skirmishes, yet the Danes
smote away in wild and reckless despair. Hunguoar
dashed with his guard. through great Mors-wood, and
some floundered down the steep of Leith Hill like the
toparchs of Macmurragh of Leinster, and drew not the
rein till they fronted their foes on Ockley Green. Then
echoed around the cry of "nemht ihre saxes," or "owd
iur saxes," as a Saxon or a Briton led : and soon was the
green sward soaked with the blood of Denmark. (It is
the loathing of this blood that has kept the mole from
earthing on Ockley Green to this day).

The flying Danes divided on Hamwode, the footmen
taking the weald to Slaughterwyke, the chariots along

Stane-street. There was a stand by Bury Hill, since called Warfield, and on Standard Hill by Bookham, where the Reafen was taken and regained, and where the bones of the Danes were recently exhumed.

The Saxons, tired of pursuit, halted on the downs, and hiding in pits made by the Britons, lay in wait for the flying Danes. There, on the east bank of the Mole, on the morrow of St. Michael the Archangel, St. Swithin consecrated the chapel of Michaelhams: and coins were showered in honour of the victory—*stychas feorthlynge penynges*, the fourth of a penny.

To oust the Danes who skulked in Eldburi, Laore and the Lord's Nore by Waldtone, Ethelwulf encamped at Kœnigswald, we now call Kingswood. As the Danes fled on, Warcoppice was their last halt in Surrey, and here fell the brave old Roric. As he was dying, they flung over his shoulders the charmed mantle of Regner Lodbrog—to whom alone he was second—worked by his wife Aslanga, and spotted with his blood: and this was Roric's death chaunt :—

" We struck with our swords : in fifty and one combats have I fought, and summoned my people by my warning spear-messenger. There will be found few kings more famous than I. From my youth I loved to grasp the red spear, but the goddess invites me home from the hall of spoils. Odin has sent for me, and laughing I will die."

This was the warrior's last breath, and as his soul mounted, Hynguoar cried aloud to the host,—

" Rise, spirit of Heimdal, thou God of the golden teeth : sound high the Gjallar horn, a hero is gone from earth."

Now you must know this Heimdal, the child of nine virgins, was the watchman of the gods, and, from his watch-tower on the rainbow, blew a blast on the passage of a hero over the bridge of Heaven to Valhalla.

Roric was laid in his barrow on yonder downs, the mere ceremony of *Hoygold* or burying : their hurried flight forbad the *Roisold*, or burning.

Thus ended the Battaile of Okely, of which you may read in many an odd chronicle.

This is the epitome of Asser :—" Here Ethelwulf, son of Ecgberht or Athelstane, at the head of the West-Saxon army, fought with the Danes at Ochley—they descending from Anstie and Holmbury (after sacking London), and made the greatest slaughter of the heathen army that we have ever heard reported to this present day."

And this of Florentius, in " Wigorniensis Chronicon." " Nunquam in aliqua regione in una die ante hoc post ex iis occisum esse audivimus. Sanguinisque fluvios capita et membra cæsorum secum volvere."

And this of Hardynge :—

> " And in the yere eyght hundred fifty and one,
>   The Danish hoste in Thamis did arrive.
>   Kent and Southray Sussex and Hāshire anone,
>   Distroyed sore and through the south gā dryne.
>   Whes muche folke thei sleugh, both mane and wife,
>   Which host yᵉ kyng with battaile slewe doune sore,
>   That home again retourned thei no more."

> " He smote them hip and thygh with a grete slaughter."

And this is the quaint augury in Guy of Warwicke,—

"For Sir Anlaf, King of Danmark,
  With an ost store and starke,
    Into England is come.
Fifteen thousand knights of priis
To this land thai stroyen y—wis,
  And mani a town han nome.
A warke it ys as easie to be done
As tys to saye Jacke Robyson."

IT is at the early hour, the sky being clear, when

"The besey larke the messenger of day,
  Sale with here songe the morwe gray,
And firy Phœbus riseth up so bright,
  That all the orient laugheth at the sight,"

that you should look off westward from *Starveall Corner*.
The brown bronze of the heath fields is finely backed by the
chalk downs and the ultramarine of the remote distances :
there was, however, a darker aspect when Evelyn wrote
thus to Aubrey of "The Sugar Loaf mountains of Wotton,
which with the boscage upon them, and little torrents
between, make such a solitude as I have never seen any
place more horribly agreeable and romantic."

At first we may smile at this inflation, for it is in truth
wild enough for the Val-demone at Ætna's base, yet from
one aspect Holmbury and Coneyhurst are cones, and we
have seen them come out in deep purple shadow as the
cloud is hanging o'er them, and the pinewoods of Felday
and Tanhurst are black as jet. Are we sure that the
memory of John Evelyn was not brooding then over some
solemn incident of the time? There was one, now, well-
nigh forgotten, but which was in perfect harmony with his

picture, and with the gloom, which even now is flung
around us by this present shadow of

The Passing Cloud.

"I came to the place of my birth, and cried, 'The friends of my
youth, where are they?'" An echo answered, 'Where are they?'"

THIS fanciful sentiment of the wild Arab was echoed by
the lips of a young soldier, who had missed his way amidst
the lurid shadows of Blackheath felde.   He rode

"on a brown stede,
And a pendaunte behind him did honge
Unto the erthe yt was so longe."

He wore a shirt of mail and over it a surcoat with very
long hanging sleeves, and on his head a round skull cap-
bascinet with a hollow boss for the panacke or plume :
his long blade was curved, and a lance at rest hung under
his right breast, and with it a fragment of a casque.   As
he threaded the dingles of Stoney Moor, the night was most
unpromising, and might make even a bold campaigner quail.
Thunder was booming deeply among the hills, as an old
dame hobbled from the pinewood towards the rudest hut
in the corner, and as she was bobbing curtsies to the
stranger, he begged a crust and shelter for the night.

"Aye," she croaked, "a bist mayhap we can, but a
crust, mercy on us, not one left in all Starveall Corner :
wot ye not of famine in the land."

"Then how far to Abinceborne?"

"To the Hatch, a mile and a mossel, but 'tis shut afore now."

"But I am for the Manor, dame."

"The Manor? wus and wus, all wreck and ruin there— blight, blight, more elynge now than ever,—ruined all : at your peril go not there, or anywhere to-night, for darkness is coming round us, and the flood is rolling down the gill, and—hark, there's a stroke might waken doomsday," and at the moment lightning blazed bright around the cots of Felday. "I'd offer you my truckle-bed, but I'm a lone woman, and have a character to lose."

The soldier- smiled at this coquette of eighty odd, and pointed to a spark of light just glimmering through the blackness.

"That," she muttered, as she threw her hands aloft : "No, no! 'tis like yon blaze of heaven, 'twill sweal you an you dare it : yet, poor old soul, he was once as good as gold."

"He? who, what name?"

"Hush, he hath himself foregone his name, and dares us all to utter it. A dark cloud is on his name, as that now bursting overhead, but like that cloud 'twill pass away, I wot. But, gad's me! there's no hope for you to-night *but* that : so try him if you will, they'll take ye in, aye, and mayhap they'll do for ye —an ye will dare it, ye *will* dare, for ye've *kissed the hare's foot*, I ween : but look, look — a ball of fire over Holmbury, so bright and blue : that's death, death to you or me, though which of us——"

As she spoke, the bolt struck her to the earth, and

O

the poor old crone lay dead at the soldier's feet. As he lifted her from the ground, his horse bolted with affright and ran wild across Hurtwood. There was no help for it now, so, laying the withered corpse on its truckle-bed in the hut, he groped his way toward the flickering light.

Now in this dismantled hut, as the crone had hinted, dwelt an aged pair, careworn and misanthropic, and as proud as poor. Though once in luxury, their state was now the most abject poverty : cresses from the oak runnel in Pasture wood, and earth nuts and sorrel salad, and a grey hen when the springe was lucky, this was the sum of their larder : even the blue of heaven was to them a cloud, its light, indeed, was their shadow. And now they sat by a peat fire, shivering and famished, a greasy rush emitting the faintest light.

" Ah !" muttered the man, " were *he* alive, his youth might redeem our blighted fortune, but age and want have sunk us too deep ever to rise again."

" He may be living yet, old man."

" Dead, dead, or long ere this—well, well."

He grasped his knife, and his eyes glared on his wife, and the words " death, death," fell from his lips.

" Death ! no one to kill : death—whom prythee ? "

" Whom ? ourselves, better than maundering here—no one can see us now."

" Yes—One !" and she pointed her shrivelled finger to the roof—" hope, hope, Felday."

" Hope—ha, ha ! *we* hope !"

His wife tried to smile, but her hope was despair. Yes,

" The hope in dreams of a happier hour
That alights on misery's brow,
Springs forth like the silvery almond flower,
That blooms on a leafless bough."

" Aye," he still muttered, " even those we housed and feasted have left us now to our fate—even the very rats have cut us : so our last black loaf, and then, starvation—not a mite to buy another."

The woman drew from her bosom a golden knife, but instantly returned it.

" Why, this may save awhile—but no, never, never : his last birthday gift—no, no, starve, perish first ! " and they burst into tears, and sat mute in their desolation. At this moment the wicket was pushed aside, and the soldier with his dog entered the hut, and bowing low, he flung off his cloak.

The man glared on, the woman coaxed the dog, but he growled and slunk away—yet he was a noble and a generous fellow too, but dogs of that breed are deep physiognomists.

" Ye've sought a barren crib," muttered the man, as the soldier placed a gold noble in his clutch—"black bread and cresses all we have to spread : yet hold, here's the breast of a grey hen for you." But the soldier gave it to his dog.

" You are taken with this relic," said the soldier. " Aye, 'twas a jewel once, the helm of Louis of Bourbon," as he held up the gold-bossed casque. " I struck him down *mortz*, as they said at Azincourt : while Harry the King closed with Alençon, just as Guillaume Martel, Sire de Bacqueville raised aloft the challenge flag, the blood-red

o 2

oriflamme. By George, 'twas a sight to see—here, look, is
a leaf Alençôn struck from Henry's arch crown of gold
that surmounted his helm—that Henry laid at Katheryn's
feet.   That day I won my golden spurs—knight banneret
on the field, and when I've entombed my lord the Erl of
Suffolk at Ewhelme, then to kiss hands in London—but I
tire ye, so if you can spare a shakedown in your sheeling?"

"And your casket, sir," whispered the old man, eyeing
a· small but richly inlaid box : "'twere best I loke it,
'twere safe there as at—the manor-house!" (the stranger
started at the word) "oh! no one would dream of robbing
us, hey dame!"

She nodded assent with a curl of her lip.

The stranger settled the point by securing the casket :
"*We* fear not robbers, do we, Lion? aye, you saved me
once, brave Arab, and will again, if need be."   And so
the soldier and his dog lay down in the penthouse, and
fell asleep.

As they sat in the gloom, single words dropped like
minute-guns from those aged lips : "golden spurs—jewels
—nobles—didst hear?" and they looked at each other
with dark significance.

The woman glanced at the knife that the old man was
clutching convulsively.

"What art fumbling at?" she muttered.

"Fumbling, sayst thou? what, oh, the knife—look, it
will point to the penthouse, look—canst guess?"

"Guess, are you ready then?"

"Ready, ready—for what?"

"Said you not we'd die together?"

" Die ! nay, nay, that were suicide, the worst of mur—
hush—*we* are not fit, *he is*—he'll go to Heaven, we to—"

" Hush, hush," muttered the crone, " you fright me :
hark, their sleep is deep," and then as the man crept
toward the penthouse, she listened to the heavy breathing,
for she had time to think. There was silence for a moment,
and then a gurgling of blood—a stifled moan, a faint
struggle, and all was still.

As the man rolled staggering into the room—"the
casket," she growled : " the casket—open quick."

" I dare not—I dare not !" he cried : " would I had not
done it—take-you the knife."

She clutched the bloody blade, and wrenched off the lid,
and for a while they both stood motionless, the blaze of
the jewels dazzled and bewildered their sight—their hearts
throbbed wildly, and they half forgot the deed in their
delirium,—one demon, mammon, filled all their breasts,
and they sat fumbling the jewels in mute enchantment,
until their glance fell on another golden knife, the fellow
of their own, and they were at once transfixed with horror.
So passed an hour, when, bareheaded, the soldier entered
the room. The woman fell on the floor, and the man on
his knees.

" You ! you !" he screamed, " and living — you, no,
thou'rt a spirit sent to drag us to our doom."

" Ah !" cried the stranger : " *my* knife, as in my dream
—blood—quick, tell me quick, *whose* blood is this ?"

" My son's—my own—thine."

" Son, your son, I !" exclaimed the soldier, snatching
the bloody knife which the old man was about to plunge

into his bosom. "My father, you! Heaven's mercy, dream I still: yet there is blood—ha!—"

The stranger rushed back to the penthouse, and there lay his dog bleeding, dead.

"My son, art thou indeed in life? blessed be Heaven I killed not thee!"

"Thou hast killed me, old man, there in my Arab, *there:* he was more than life to me. Father, mother, ye have wrung my heart with despair—what, betray, murder the stranger within your gate!"

"My son," sobbed the old man, "we were starving—frantic—mad."

"No more, no more! but, father, mother, on your knees, in abject supplication for grace and mercy! 'tis a murder of the deepest dye, for the blood of fidelity is on your head. Yes, twice my Arab, twice thou'st saved my life, now by the forfeit of thine own, and when I forget thy sacrifice, may my right hand forget its cunning, my poor, poor Lion."

In a roll of the battle of Azincourt is blazoned the name of John Feldè, for he was among the foremost in the charge against the French noblesse, on which Hardynge thus quaintly rhymes:—

> "On ye Frēch partie ye dukes of Barre and Lorein,
> And of Alaunson in battaill thei were dedde;
> And takō were of chiefteyns in certain
> The Duke Lewes of Orliaunce their hedde,
> The Duke of Burbone on that stede,
> Therle of Vendom, and Arthure als of Brytaine,
> And Sir Burisgalde, Marshall of Fraunce certaine."

Thus, by his daring, the soldier revived the fortunes of

his house, and even enrolled its honour, but his heart never again warmed to his boyhood's home. The story is almost forgotten now, yet among the boors of Pitlande and Tralee, you might perchance catch a whisper here and there anent the death-cloud which on that night came down and passed over Starveall Corner, our own memory is even now haunted by the tale as we stand by the *Hatch* of Abinger : for it is rumoured that in its well, 150 feet down from daylight, still lies the bloody knife of Felday.

A BY-WAY village of a right primitive aspect is this Abinger, its· antient name, Abinceborne or Abingcire, (Upper Shere). On its tiny green still stand the stocks, with a whipping-post, a rusty iron chain and a broken rivet. The quaint gables and porch of the Manor-house are in perfect keeping with its church of St. James, the highest, except St. Martha's, in the county. The wild commons about Abinger are varied by bosky dells, and heath-brown hillocks, with rich clumps of that golden furze, at sight of which Linnæus fell on his knees in a fit of rapture. Around us are ranks of stately pines glowing like shafts of porphyry in the sungleam, and dwarf-oak stems dotted with *cornicularia*, the white discs of *placidium*, and the pale green *parmelia.* In the dingles we find the glutinous *collema*, the club moss that yields the sulphur-dust for lightning, ferns and mosses coloured gold by *lecidia* : the female of the Blechnum fern we have seen a full yard high.

> " Down by the hamlet's hawthorn-scented way,
> Where round the cot's romantic glade are seen
> The blossomed bean-field and the sloping green,"

are the dense copses and skirts of the Pasture wood—in
the sand lanes may be gleaned the finest wild plants,
orpines and teazles, and thistles, docks, borage, and
bugloss, and hemlock, mullein and foxglove, all teeming
with insect life. *Io* and *Atalanta* are sipping the honeydew
from the flowers of the Archangel, on the stem of which
their larvæ will feed. The heath is alive with whites and
blues, and coppers, and hoppers, and grizzled skippers.
Here is a sudden transition from the barren to the
beautiful. It is a joy to come down from the wild moor
into valley Lonesome, rich and green as a vale in Thessaly.
Its romantic seclusion tempted the rich Jew, Jacobson, to
erect his lodge of Tilbrook. and this is Talfourd's eulogy,
"Nothing so fine, nearly London than Westmoreland."
A runnel ripples from the high woods, falling sixty feet
into pools where the crimson spotted trout is leaping at
the mayfly. There is a special poetry around us,—

> " The gush of springs, and the bend
> Of stirring branches, and the bud which brings
> The swifter thoughts of beauty."

Here spring the ivy ranunculus, the scarlet Adonis, and
orchis mascula, and golden lunaria, and clematis, and on
wild thyme feeds

> " The bee with honied thigh,
> That at its flowery work doth sing."

In Lonesome many a garden-flower grows wild, and
there the Admiral displays on his wing the red ribbon of
his order, and the Tiger moth his scarlet vest and under-
coat. We are treading now on classic ground. The Till
brook ripples down from the lawns of Lonesome into the
green leys of Wotton, that so beautifully underly the

beech-woods, and where it is joined by the runnel in the
dingle of Friday Street (Fria Stede) there stands half-
buried the honoured home of Sylva Evelyn. The quaint
brick house, now, we believe, condemned, is in keeping
with its Saxon name of Wodentone. But the prestige of
John Evelyn is paramount, as we wander beneath the

columnar majesty of his own favourite beeches, so richly
laced with lichens, and so densely overshadowing the
moss-grown alleys. In summer time you will light on
many a truthful painter at his glorious study, Redgrave or
Cole or Warren, perchance. Two centuries ago, you would
have encountered Sylva himself, planning his *Elysium*

Britannicum, or deep in thought on the very spot selected for his own grave: a circular group, something like a Druid's temple, now the very spot

> " For those whom wisdom and whom nature charm,
> To steal themselves from the degenerate crowd,
> To soothe the throbbing passions into peace,
> And woo lone quiet in her silent walks."

Yet hither wandered with him a little world of intellect: there was Aubrey the antiquary, and Oughtrede the pious, of Albury, and Grinling Gibbons, the carver of the screen in St. Paul's, whom he caught by Say's Court cutting orchids on an alder stump, and who now might be cutting " J. E." on the beeches, not yet erased. The noble Howards, too, were ever visiting the great virtuoso, and we may fancy them at the pastry board, a plank of oak, ten feet long—the banquet, game trout from the Till, a grey hen from Holmbury, and Albury venison, roasted by his own smoak-jack, and eaten with blackberry jelly. With the king-pine, the gift of Charles himself, was served the sap-wine of the birch, and that of the wild bird-cherry or merry tree, and arrack punch in the silver bowl of Wotton.

In the drawing-room and the closet, " a raree show for all the country round," there lay Evelyn's etchings, "taken in perspective from the top of the grotto," the folio of his "Sylva," just printed by desire of the Royal Society, of which he was President elect, its arms gracing the title, and for which the King thanked him on the day of his coronation: there were the family portraits of Lely and Kneller—his MS. "Diary," still in the library of Wotton,

from which many a choice scrap may yet be gathered : there
were the mezzotintos of Prince Rupert, a carved skull by
Albrecht Dürer, and the crucifix and cartoons from Tin-
toretto by Grinling Gibbons. From their gossip we might
learn of the demolition of the Crosse in Chepe, and the
proclamation of *Unkingship* in the portico of Paul's : and
the decree of the Barons to wear coronets : the promise by
Howard of the Arundelian marbles to the nation. The
descent of Evelyn is not of yesterday. Avelyns traced to
Plantagenet, and even to Lusignan, king of Cyprus, and
one was taken at Azincourt. In 1634, Richard Evelyn
was the last sheriff of Surrey and Sussex, and marshalled
the judges with 116 men in green and silver, with javelins,
and thirty gentlemen, of whom he was uncle or great uncle :
and in the hall they were wont to keep Christmas, *more
veterum*, with a group of 300 bumpkins.

The melancholy that ever inspires us, while prowling
among these

> " Arched walks of twilight groves,
> And shadows brown, that Sylvan loves,"

is even enhanced as we cross by the ancient hostelrie of
the Hatch, and stand within the rustic porch of St. John
the Evangelist, where John Evelyn, when four years old,
learned his Latin of one Frier, and this mood is deepened
in the sepulchral chapel, where he is laid (1705) among
the Darceys, Leslies, and De la Hale.

You cannot imagine a spot more picturesque yet solemn
for a country church than this, embosomed among majestic
chestnuts, and on the verge of a valley perfectly Tyrolean.
It retains the prestige of its *Leper's Window*, and there, in

the grass, stands the urn of Gulielmus Glanville, who left money that boys, about February, might assemble at his tomb, and recite the Lord's prayer, creed, and commandments. There are scenes of ancient interest withal, lying around the church-yard of Wotton. There is the *Deer-leap Wood*, carpeted with campions, cardamines, anemonies, hellebore, wood sorrel, and blue bells. It was wild enough in the olden time, but even then it was gilded by a gleam of romance, for oft

> " The muse hath found
> Her blossoms on the wildest ground,
> And noxious weeds at random strew'd,
> Themselves all profitless and rude."

Bear this wood in mind while you look over the valley on one of the choicest indents of the chalk hills—*Piquet's Combe*. It was no common creature that gave the combe its name, it was no common creature that he dared to worship, it was no common incident that here in Wotton Wylde brought out the confession of that love, so passionate yet so pure, and told in one brief moment the deep secret of

The Dere-lepe.

> " She loves, but knows not whom she loves,
> Nor what his race, nor whence he came."

THE girl was sweet as the wild rose in June, and like the rose she bloomed among the briars. A scarf, as green as the leaves that embosom the flower, was round her, and on her brow gleamed a small but very costly jewel, in strange contrast with her tattered robe,—it was like the star of hope gleaming above poverty's cell. In her hair was woven a fresh-blown flower. It was on yonder green mound, near the mill by the Rookery, still called the *Castle Bank*, and, according to Aubrey, the site of a fortalice, and there is a form leaning over her in the strange garb of a savage! We may not guess who he is, for she knows not herself, yet there is, be sure, some latent nobleness about him, or so bright a creature as Edyth had never smiled on him, or the melancholy Master Camoys housed him in his hall at the *Bury*. He had just whispered in the ear of this peerless girl a thought, since so sweetly echoed by Moore—

> " Where the bright eyes of angels only
> Should come around us, to behold
> A paradise so pure and lonely.
> Would this be world enough for thee ? "

As he read in her eyes all he hoped for, she started, and whispered " my father," and in a moment the youth leaped the fence and was gone. He who came on was of the sternest visage, and the maid loved and feared him, as a father and a monitor, so, e'en now, he frowned daggers on the boy, and smiled lovingly on his daughter. He threw off his cloak of faded cloth, and his cap, that was graced also with the golden broom, for you must know they were sprung from the blood of Fulke, the great Earl of Anjou.

" It grieves me, my own Edyth," he said softly, " to see thee, that wast but now the light of King Stephen's court, immured in this lone cell, the sport of the rude elements, with little else than cresses from the brook, or sorrel from the wood."

"Grieve not, my father," she said, " be sure I am happy, for I am with you."

"And lovest thou thy father all ? " he asked.

"As deeply as daughter can," she replied, and a blush (we may guess why) was burning on her cheek. "I do own, when first we lost those joyous springs of life—"

"Aye, my poor lorn flower," continued he, folding his daughter to his breast, " it were a loss indeed. Oh, 'tis ungracious, unroyal, this proud young Henry, this new-fledged King of England, hath forgotten all. Heaven, how my royal father petted this duke of the curt-mantle, this Henry Fitz-Emprice, call him what we will. Why, how he feasted him, adopted him—aye, there's the rub, and now he cuts me out, *me* William Plantagenet, from my poor heritage, and then lodges me here within four ruined walls. But as to keeping, it is not : nay, we are half famished, and all because I will not kneel in homage to Henry. No, I will perish first. You know, I was in succession, though Maud and Beckett frowned, nay there was even a buzz of my *crowning*, if the Bishop of Rome would deign to do it. But 'twere now safer to keep aloof, for there is foul play a-foot, be sure. Eustace poisoned at Edmondsbury, and drowned and earthed at Faversham "—

"Yet Maud and Adelais ! "—

"They ! they despise us, Edyth, we are base : the truest love were a shame, they say, if sworn without a priest."

"Yet Maud hath sent me tokens, father."

"A feint, a feint, my child: William of Surrey dead, I was the only man of the name: but for the queen thou wert a princess, Edyth, and princess you are to me: those golden crescents, that star, your gown of russet, are yet as bright as Eleanor's. Henry may vaunt his mingled blood, Saxon and Norman, for aught I care,—he may be Earl of Anjou by his sire, Duke of Normandy by his dam, this *domina Anglorum* forsooth, and Earl of Poytowe by his wife—let him—yet *we* wear the broom, too, that Fulke, our grandsire won, as bright a jewel in our cap as the opal on thy brow of snow—nay, nay, my Edyth, weep not, weep not."

"My poor drowned mother—'tis her only jewel left me."

"Aye all in the bosom of the deep, with the noble boy who saved thee: thou wouldst love him, Edyth."

"My holiest prayers are his, 'tis all we have to give."

"Yet were he kneeling at thy feet, as stricken and as poor as we, thou wouldst redeem my pledge?"

The maiden hung her head, and blushed deep crimson.

"I—would fain obey you, sir—but here is Master Camoys."

As she retires, an old man in his dotage comes toddling on the scene, and greets the noble recluse, who raised his hat, and acknowledged the honour of the visit.

"Nay," replied Camoys, "I ever honour worth, sir, and I love beauty, but how's this, she weeps."

"The old story, sir."

"Piquet: marry—well thought of, I have a suit—"

."Nay, spare me, Master Camoys, to you this masquer may be a paragon—to me he is a traitor, for he hath dared, spite of my frown, to love my child—you have no child to cheer your hope and hearth."

"No, true, hope is a blank to me, my hearth a desolation, my boy—alas, alas !"

"Dead "—

"An exile from his home is he—oh, could I unsay the word that parted us !"

"Your hand, sir, I, too, am a banished man, and e'en for sympathy as for his noble daring I might honour him, but that he dares to win a child of Anjou !"

"Yet, if love "—

"Love ! who would not love my Edyth ? lordlings and fops in plenty wooed and kneeled in vain—there was, indeed, but one—the saviour of her life—hear me, Master Camoys, 'twas on a rock of the deep sea at midnight, the moment a wave, on which he bore her to my arms, rolled back, and swept him and—my wife— my wife, Master Camoys, from my sight : all lost, even the hoard of jewels in his grasp: to him, my only jewel now, my child is pledged, but he will never claim her, for recognition were impossible.   Yet ere the wave had clutched him, I flung around his neck a chain of gold, gemmed with her mother's beauty. That chain might claim the love of Edyth, but he is lost, aye lost."

Master Camoys was silent from that hour, and from that hour, heart-frozen by the father's frown, the wild boy vanished from the Bury.   And Edyth was changed, her lips ashy white, her eyes lustreless,

" Her soft pensiveness of brow
Had deepen'd into sadness now,
And boding thoughts that she must part
With a soft vision of her heart,
All lower'd around the lovely maid,
To darken her dejection's shade."

Her only solace now was to dole out the alms at the
chancel loophole to the lepers.

While her father was watching her wasting in the
deepest sorrow, on a sudden her eye began to brighten,
and her lips to redden : it was a mystery, and her father
of course suspected—yet the wild boy was never seen, and
he at length believed that time and charity had worked
her resignation.

So—one day he found on the lawn a scrap of scribbled
paper, and this was the rhyming on it.

" Is it true, that diamonds shine unrivalled in the blaze of day :
Yes, save when those eyes of thine the heart's wild dreams of
    love betray
Then, sweet, a mirror shines as bright, for both reflect but
    borrow'd light.

Is it true, the lily blooms in Flora's lap her fairest blossom ?
Yes, save when Zephyr's wanton plumes unveil the beauty of thy
    bosom—
Then, love, the lily droops, for, lo ! *there* gleams a purer—whiter
    snow.

" So," he muttered, "know you the scribbler, Edyth :
another lover, hey ! "

" No, my father, not another lover—it is a poor lone
leper, who haunts the hill, and lives on meal, and milk
and cresses, and plays with wildings, and takes alms at the
windows here.   Hast not seen him, father ? "

P

"He, poor Naomi, white, white as snow—well, well, no fear of him, and yet you blush, Edyth! I do fear that savage still—no, no, I may not think you love so base a thing. You must forget him." .

And Edyth blushed the'more.

"Have I not forgotten; sir," she murmured, "have I not ceased to think of him—this very morning I was thinking how odd it was I never now did think of him." The only fib she ever told.

"And yet he or some one thinks of you," and he picked up another scrap beneath the leper's window, tied to a bunch of wildings. "A fair conceit, i'faith, the fellow paints thy beauty daintily."

> " Love's emblems all, but, oh ! his fairest blossom
> Is woman's ever-blooming excellence ;
> The witcheries of her life-breathing bosom
> Fall like a sunbeam on the panting sense :
> Her eye of light, the soul's pure evidence,
> Beams mild as Hesperus—

"Sublimity itself ! why, 'twould win an empress, girl."

Edyth was silent: she laid her hand gently on her father's arm, when, lo ! the leper himself came limping along to the window.

"In good time, i'faith: here, sirrah—where learned you this? Methinks your fittest theme were charity, not love."

"Charity, noble sir," said the leper humbly. "Charity is the fount itself of love—this beauteous lady is charity to poor me. Sure a poor leper, like me, may love even as brighter beings love—but, woe's me, he must adore as the ghebir doth the sun—his god—his life—at awful distance from the orb he worships. For my poor rhyme, noble sir,

I have tramped the wide world—a troubadour in the
north, in Italy a trovatore, a trouveneur in Florence, where
all is poetry—for this Norman-French is ever the breath
of love—we call it *romance*, coming as it does from old
Rome—yet it is written in the Gallic idiom."

"A scholar, too, why thou'rt a riddle, boy."

"I am an outcast, noble sir, yet have I haunted courts
ere now, and knelt on the steps of honour.   I was a boy
in Winchester when Maud was crowned by Henry the
bishop, brother of Stephen the king: 'twas I who brought
her in a coffin on a litter from Devizes to Gloucester: it
was her life: I was her page when, like a white angel, she
glided from her arrest in Wallingford.   But I shall tire
you out.   Your servant, noble sir"—and so the leper hobbled
off churchward.

Watching his retreat the recluse muttered his misgivings.
"Hear me, Edyth," he said, after a long pause, "be warned,
the bucks are wild at rutting time, even yesternight in
twilight one leapt yon paling as I passed,—twelve feet, by
Jove, and yet like a chamois over went the deer.   You
need not blush at that, but keep from the fosse-way by
the barrow Edyth, there is danger imminent.

Now it was twilight once again, and Edyth, with all her
warning, wandered, unconsciously, round by the barrow,
just as her father chanced to cross the fosse-way.   There
was a rush and something leapt the fence at a bound, but
it was instantly caught by the forelock by a stalwart arm,
that dragged him to the light.

"A buck!" exclaimed the recluse, by the lord! my eyes
deceive me—a mongrel hound, by Jove, down dog, down,

or by—" In the struggle a wolf's hide was torn away, and a youth, perfect in manly beauty, was displayed, and Edyth fell on her knees before her father.

"No fooling, girl," he cried, "thou hast played thy father false—my curse be on him."

"And I have sworn to love him, my father, our troth is in Heaven, and father—I am—your child!"

"Mine thou art, rash girl, but as thou knowest, not mine to give away, a father may not be perjured even for his child: be quiet, boy, for her prayer alone hath saved you —I say, be quiet, hound as thou art!" In the grapple between the two stalwart athletes the links of a massive chain around the youth's neck were snapped in twain, and a casket fell to the ground. A yell burst from the recluse as he glared on the jewel case, and he unloosed the grasp of the young savage—for it was he.

"Where, how, how got you that?" he cried, "Edyth, Edyth, look!"

But Edyth had fainted on the turf.

"We cannot be awake—my child, my child. Ah, Master, Camoys."

But Camoys, who approached, stood aloof, and regarded him not.

With streaming eyes, and in silent wonder, he gazed on the boy, who had lifted Edyth from the ground, his face being now for the first time free from his dishevelled hair.

"Piquet, my father, both," she cried, falling on the breast of the youth, "oh, happy, happy chance!"

"What," exclaimed the recluse, recovering his voice,

"and thou hast kept this casket holy throughout all thy pains and poverty—guessed thou what was in it?"

"Guessed! I but knew the casket was another's."

"And it is with thee, thou noble boy, that I swore unconsciously to break my pledge, as I did break the chain. By St. Hubert, thou art an hart royal, boy,—thou hast made a wondrous deer-leap, faith from doom to blessing, for I *had* doomed thy life: but my curse is void, and thus I redeem my pledge."

Edyth's cheek was crimson flushed, of course, as her father joined their hands, for this parental hint was ratified by the burning pressure of their lips, and their locks were interwoven in sad confusion, as if Nox and Aurora were already weaving love-knots for the bridal.

But the wonder and emotion of Master Camoys, who chanced to enter on the scene, were intense: in one moment, when the perfect disguise was cast off, he saw that the wild boy, even he who kennelled and slipped his lurchers, and was the idol in his hall at Bury, was in truth the very child whom he had doomed to banishment.

The intensity of the double discovery had yet kept him silent, but the heart of a father could no longer be restrained.

"My son, my son!"

'Twas all he said, for the truant boy felt that he was accepted, and rushed from the bosom of his love to that of his father.

The spinning out of a story is often prosy as an old wife's tale, or we might tell at length, how, at this blissful moment, the cortége of the Empress Maud chanced to be sweeping along from Adeliza's Castle of Arundel to West-

minster, how she caught up her pet and her protegé, and,
taking French leave, bore them both off to King Henry's
Court, how Edyth Plantagenet was at once the joy and
idol of every eye, and how St. Thomas A'Becket, assisted
by one Hymen of Olympian birth, did work the miracle
of converting two beings into one.

But our story is told. Yet you must know that the
haunt of the wild boy was henceforth named *Piquet's Combe*,
and that, year by year, on one especial day a brilliant group
came down to Master Camoys, in Wotton Wylde, and kept
high revel in the coverts of the *Dere-lepe Wode*.

To a kindred spirit even the barren moor is an inspiration.
The Range of Leith presents a picture in little of

> " Caledonia, stern and wild,
>   Meet nurse of a poetic child."

It is one of the rare spots in Southern Britain where

> " The moorcock springs on whirring wings
>   Among the blooming heather."

A few years ago there were some packs of them, we may
now very rarely spring a solitary grey hen or black cock.
Three species of heath cluster here together, *cinerea, tetralix,*
and *calluna*. Among the green alleys flourish furze and
broom and juniper and tufts of cotton rush. The old bark
of beech and fir is embossed with lichens : white rot and
marsh pennywort lie on the yellow green of the brooklet
mosses. Towards Laylands, by the pines, sprout a profusion of fungi of all colours—*Telamonia*, bronze-capped,
veiled, and fringed : *Tricholoma*, white-gilled and purple-

ribbed: *Agaric, boletus edulis, muscaria*, studded with golden asteroids: *Coprinus atramentarius*, fairy ring *Champignon*, and puff balls. On these heathtufts we have seen the webs of giant spiders tough enough to be wound off like silk.

Broadmoor is the wildest glen on the southern hills, and, shrouded by purple shadow, it deepens into perfect sublimity. It is precisely the waste on which we might expect to encounter the weird-sisters of Macbeth, or the wizard of Lochiel, or the Black Dwarf. Indeed, yonder mouldering cabin might be his hut.

To us it shadows forth the early life of a moor-boy who once hovered about these hills, and the fate of

The Girl-Mother.

> "Sire doctoure of Physike, I pray you tell us a tale."
> "It shall be don if that ye wol it here."

IT was about the middle of the eighteenth century, that Mr. Richard Hull had invited three select neighbours to eat whortleberries and cream, and counsel him on the site of a prospect tower on the hill: the Earl of Macartney, of Parkhurst yonder,—N., the physician, from Eversheds Place in Ockley,—and Jeremiah Markland. Hull was pointing out the objects of the weald.

"Ah," said Markland, "when first I trod this hill I was a mere boy, and intended to be ninety on the faith of this my cherished habit,

Lever a cinque, diner a neuf,
Souper a cinque, coucher a neuf,
Faite vivre d'ans nonante et neuf.

But, alas, I am an old dotard before my time."

"Then go to Sloane, man," said N., "he'll make you young again, as he did the king."

"Rather *mummify* me, or pickle me for his museum."

While thus they gossiped, a sudden change came over the scene—a dark purple cloud floated along the hill, and a whistling blast came whirling up through the windy gap.

"Let us back," cried the Earl, "if the cloud bursts on us in Broadmoor, wet jackets be sure, and rheumatics for us all, or worse still if we be weather-bound, for I am bid to Jacobson's at Tilbrook, and his perch and *water-souchy* will be spoiled."

On the instant down came the pitiless hail, while thunder rolled and lightning was flashing athwart the moor.

The landscape had changed from smiling green and amethyst to one sombre suit of sable.

"We have but one refuge," said Hull, "yonder half-roofless hut, it is a dark dilemma, so we must take French leave : here is the hut, and dismal enough it is, in sooth, 'tis solitude itself : I have long had misgivings that the place is curst."

"Why, aye," said N., "I never pass this hut without a shudder myself, I know not why. I fear no witches or wizards, and yet here am I half-possessed, a sort of animal magnetism, like pins and needles in the brain. Aye, I do believe the hut is haunted." And so they crossed the threshold, and crouched down to a dull peat fire.

" If there be witches," said Macartney, " they are not at home, not a breath stirring, 'tis an awful silence."

" And yet," whispered Hull, " it seems to me that we are not alone in the hovel. Hear ye not a breathing low and laboured ? "

"Fancy, fancy," replied Markland, "Meg is out whorting, be sure."

" Meg ? " inquired the Earl, " who is Meg, I pray ? "

" What," answered Markland, " know you not Meg of Mereden ? ah, poor wench, more sinned against than sinning, I ween."

"And yet the wonder goes," rejoined Hull, "that you, so good and pure, should consort with one so withered and so—"

"Nay," interrupted Markland, "I will tell you why: my poor dumb boy loved her, doted on her, as his mother. Oh, he would hang on her, kiss her skinny fingers, and drop a tear on her dewlap neck : and yet, I do confess— though I cannot divine it, there must be some lurking secret, some strange mystery, as if a dark and dreary destiny impelled her toward the poor dumb castaway."

" Forbear, good neighbour," murmured the Earl, " we are all of a shiver already, an ague-chill is creeping over me, whether from storm or story I know not."

" Nay," said Macartney, " the words of Master Markland chime in well with the gloom around us, and I would fain learn more of the shadowy creatures."

" Listen then," said Markland, patting the burning turf with his cane—" 'Twas in the Foundling Nursery, in Dorking, an off-set, as you know, from the Hospital in

London—ah, that most excellent gift of charity. Well, this dumb orphan became its protegé : he was a thing of beauty, music was breathing in his face, and yet his tongue was tied, and his accents were a mere monotonous *bark*— faith, 'twas a strange boy. Although he seemed to loathe mankind—all but Meg and me—he doted on dogs, that would fawn and crouch at his feet, the pigeons winged around his head, and they would settle on his shoulder, and feed from his lips, the small birds flitted in flocks at his whistle, and he caught them and fondled, and then let them fly again. He was an expert 'Merops apiaster' too, catching the wild bees, extracting their sting, and sucking their honey-bag. He was my pet, my solace at Milton Court for many a long evening : I read to him, and, when at death's point he was left by the doctors, I watched and watched until Hygeia breathed into him, as if in triumph, a fresh spirit of life. Aye, I ever loved those most dearly whom God, in his wisdom doubtless for some mysterious end, had marked as outcasts or waifs in the world."

" And yet no converse ? " inquired Macartney musing.

" Not in *words*, yet he was intensely eloquent, his eye-flash after awhile told me all he wished. I was oft on the eve of learning some secret it was clear, but on the instant the boy looked down as if he was groping in the dark. I was enraptured with the study, and at length half-understood him, and could well-nigh guess a name : and he was noble too, noble by nature,"—Markland paused, for the physician was restless, but he continued—"for when I spoke of thoughts sublime and deeds of glory, methought his eye glanced with living fire. Yes, I loved him, for he was my own child by adoption. Yet there was a spice of selfishness in me, I fear, for I hoped my love would bring a holy light to my death-bed."

"What! and your Tasso and your Statius, by which the most learned hail you as a brother—"

"Hold, hold," exclaimed the sage, "the Devil hath already tried that dodge of flattery, and failed, thank heaven. We are but steward and minister of God's bounty upon earth : the world itself is but a porch of the universe, where the poor are waiting for alms, and we the almoners of the Creator.

"Now the haunt of my poor boy was—is now, perchance —this wild valley, this very hut, where the old crone, Meg of Mereden—rest quiet, doctor, I pray thee !"

"I thought," muttered the physician, "that I heard—"

"Yet, sooth to say," continued Markland, "it were not love pure and true for her, nay, he even barked and frowned when she fondled him, and still some mystic spell lured him to Meg's hut: aye, away from me and good Martha Rose of Milton, who loved and cherished him. But he has left us, and now herds with Meg in a hut which is, you see, poverty itself. And Meg this while asked not alms of any, and even received the holy communion on last Lord's day, and dropped a golden guinea in the plate. One special thing has raised my deepest wonder, gentle friends; a brass-bound casket given her by the young lady at Elderslie, on the green, of which she averred the key was lost, was ever in her grasp. And so the boy would glide up yon dark and

broken stair, and sit rocking in the chamber, while Meg
was bringing water from a cold spring over the hill, they
now call it Meg's well, a sort of Lethe, as 'twere, for her:
one sip, she affirmed, and she forgot her woes: dip but her
hand, she was in a breath cleansed of the leprosy of sin,
and if Macbeth's dark lady had dipped therein, the damned
spot would out like a flash of light.　One night—why,
Doctor, what is this to thee—one night the water failed
her—her spirit groaned—some deep and awful *mystery*—"

At this moment a deep groan, as of one in mortal agony,
was heard over head.

"'Sdeath," exclaimed Hull, "there *is* some one in
the hut."

"In the throes of death," added Markland: "for the
mercy of heaven, Doctor—" but the good leech needed no
spur save his own heart-beat, and he blundered up the
broken stairs even at the risk of his neck.

"This is passing strange," said Markland in a whisper,
"so intensely dark has been this mystery to my mind:
why, hark! there is a fate, an awful destiny at hand, at
this moment and in this house!"

"In harmony with the elemental strife without.　I
thought the secret would go to the grave with me.　I must
go, I must go, a soul is departing: hold me not, 'tis my
duty, 'tis my call!"

"Stay, stay, dear Markland," said Mr. Hull: "so dark
a bed of death *we* may not look upon.　Go not, I pray
you."　Markland stopped at the foot of the stairs, and at
the moment a bolt fell on the chimney and struck the
hearth at their feet.　The groans were deep and terrible,

the four good men were paralysed with fear, and sat in mute wonder and suspense, waiting for a messenger from the bed of death : and the groan grew deeper and louder, and then a scream, and then a frenzied howl, and then— all was silence for a few moments, and the Doctor almost tumbled down the stair, the brass-bound casket in his hand, the dumb boy hanging on his arm.

"This, then," he cried, "is the secret. There is a skeleton in every house."

"Aye, something in my dream of this," muttered Markland. At the sound of that voice the boy rushed to his arms, and buried his face in his bosom.

"Listen, gentles, listen," said the Doctor, his lips tremulous with his emotion, "for my heart is too full to be quiet, an' I speak not out—that staircase," and he glanced at it with horror: "but listen to my story. On that staircase there is the skeleton of this house." They all crept close together. "Look—the stains of blood on the wall to this day—*my own* bloody marks!" (Markland felt the boy quiver in his arms at the word). "But you shall hear. One night, 'twas fifteen years ago—"

"The very age," muttered Markland.

"I was roused from my bed by a young man of noble mien and address, he had heard of my skill, forsooth, and he needed it. 'Your lancets be sure,' he said, ''tis some two miles off, the carriage waits at the door.' We entered it, and he directly told me I must submit to be blind- fold : and so he wound a fillet over my eyes. We bounded up hill and down dale, and round and round for many miles, yet something whispered me that we were even then not far from home, for the very air I breathed was familiar to me. At length we stopped, and I was led up a staircase into a dark chamber, and there lay a fair girl, almost a child, pale and beautiful as marble, in the very pangs of childbirth."

The boy fell from the shoulder of Markland and almost articulated a sound like "mo," "mo."

" Well, after a pang or two, a babe was born. I thought my solemn task now ended, when the two brothers stood each at an elbow with drawn swords, and even presented their richly ornamented Highland tacs, and swore by Dian, the Goddess of Chastity, I should not leave until I had bled their sister unto death : she had disgraced their house by this degraded issue, and she must die !" Markland could scarce keep the boy from bursting from his grasp, and his eyes glared on the Doctor. "It was life for life : I knew it, but, alas, I did evil that good may abound—I murdered her with a lancet, yet in her agony, 'ere she died, she smiled like an angel on me, and she beckoned her maid to her side, who groaned out 'Alas, the sin is mine! 'twas I that—lady, lady, all I can do is this,' and she took from a cup water from the spring at Mereden, and crossed her icy forehead.

" ' You can—you must do more, Meg,' the lady murmured: ' swear—swear—my darling as your own—the casket— the ingots—the jewels—all *his*, when fifteen years have passed—' and then she died. A weighty bag of gold was offered me, but I flung it on the ground in despair, and, truth to tell, could have stabbed the men who offered it.

" I descended the staircase, and pressed a bloody hand

on the wall. Come here, here—look—the stain's as fresh though faint as when the bloody print was done. And so this deep and dreadful secret, that has rankled in my breast till this moment, is brought to daylight, and there lies my partner in this dark and devilish service—hers, alone, the plot of the seduction—lies stark and stiff.

"Yes, now the hand of fate is on the curtain and brings the whole scene to light. In that chamber of death but now I found the dying crone and the dumb boy—ha! he is striving to speak. He was watching by her side, and she was trying in vain to make him hold the casket, while he instinctively pressed her trembling head to his bosom. The creature burst into tears. 'The first,' she cried, 'for fifteen long years, since—you—and—I—nay, since I brought the ruthless seducer to my fair young mistress.'

"Hush, hush," I exclaimed, "why the boy might hear: look, look at his eyes.

"''Tis true,' she cried, not heeding my words: 'oh, that I could make a clean breast of it, that I could from her cold, cold grave recal my—no, no, hush—no name—she lies yonder in the corner of the churchyard: for the boy, I've dipped him in the well in Meredin, 'tis a holy spring, and his tongue will—hark! they call me—hark! the casket—the boy—promise me.' I rushed to the staircase and the boy followed, and, as he gazed on the crimson stain, an air of mystic intelligence stole—like a halo, over his visage, he hit his forehead, he strained his eyes, he pressed his lips on the wall. You may think this unmeaning: it means a mystery deep and spiritual, for thus the angels of the Almighty commune with man more than we wot of. Well, we were again at the couch, and the dying woman drew my ear to her quivering lip. 'Hush,' she whispered, 'I dare not tell his father's name—'tis among the titled of the land—but—no, no—I dare not—'

"I thought so," muttered Markland.

'Closer, closer—hush—in the churchyard yonder—in the corner—at high midnight—' and then with a deep gasp, and a sob, and a shiver she died."

"Heaven's mercy," said Markland, "on his soul. Yes, the divine will rant on this titled father's honours and virtues! and a coffin, with scutcheons of gold nailed on its crimson velvet—the deep and damning colour of his crime: and oh, unhappy boy! the only record upon earth of thy mother is—her blood upon the wall!"

The boy, who had listened open-mouthed to the doctor's story, rushed to him and, frowning, flung him with super-human force, and dashed the casket also to the ground, and while its costly jewels were rolling on the floor to the wonder of all, he cried aloud "My mother's blood—he killed my mother," and he fell in agony into the circling arms of Markland.

"A miracle! a miracle!" exclaimed the Earl.

"Nay, a law of nature," said the doctor: "the physiologist has learned that an intense shock which might destroy another, will shoot an electric spark of reason through the apathetic brain, even as the blaze of fever will light up a momentary gleam of intellect in that of an idiot: such the solution of the wonder in old history of the scream of the dumb boy of Lydia, 'Kill not Crœsus.' The boy was still in the arms of Markland, who wept and murmured "looked but the libertine on this solemn scene, and reflected on the woe and the curse he had woven for human hearts, would he not fall to earth and call to heaven for mercy : but who may fathom the mystery of moral evil ?"

"Nay," whispered the Doctor, "'tis to prove the sterling gold, Markland—to give the loving, Christian heart like yours a time and place to heal the wounded soul and turn evil unto good."

While he was yet speaking the storm passed away— even with the spirit of Meg of Mereden, and the friends wended their way in silence over the moor.

The roses that grew years after this over that stone-less grave in a corner of Ockley Churchyard were the choicest of their kind, they were planted and worshipped daily by the moor-boy, in pious memory of his Girl-mother.

YONDER wilderness of *Blackedfelde,* or *Blechefelle* (the field of blae or peat), was once the haunt of stags, and wolves, and bears, and "wild boares heretofore" (writes Master Aubrey)—witness their memorials at Boarehill, Hindhead, Hartswood, Buckland, Wolvens, Wolvers, Berchurst. Then of the forest primæval there are patches yet—Pasturewood, Hookwood, Heraldswood, Coverwood, Coneyhurst, Ewhurst. The sand-rock of this moor is tinted fawn and black, and is cut into the wildest dingles, cots peeping up here and there among the heather and gorse. On the heath near Albury there is the site of a Roman temple, called in the Loseley MSS. Aldbury

Q

Camp, where coins have been exhumed. Of this *toft*,
Aubrey remembered the "ground-pinning of the square
and the circle," but the mural fragments have been
worked into churches and cots!

The green paths of Hurtwood Common beautifully lace
the mosses, heaths, and ferns. Scale, if you will, the
mighty Himalayas' giant throne, supreme in its proud
magnificence, and teeming with blooming things pre-
eminent in beauty : yet in its jungles floats the poison
film, and bloated with venom beneath its balm-breathing
blossoms coils the hooded snake. In these quiet wilds of
Surrey there is, at least, the joy of being safe and at home.
On the summit of Holmbury, or Home-borough, are the
fosses of an oblong vallum of about nine acres, irregularly
zigzag, tending north and south. The ascent of the hill
displays many a lofty object of interest—the churches of
Abinger, St. Martha and Ranmoor, Ewhurst Mill, the
towers of Leith and Holmbush. The panorama of the
extreme distance compasses Hollinbourne, Frant, Crow-
borough, Firle, Ditchling, Wolstonbury, Chanctonbury,
Bury, Petworth, Blackdown, Hindhead, Hascomb, Highclere, Cruxbury, Cæsar's Camp, Nettlebed, Harrow, Hamp-
stead, and Dunstable. Encircled by this wild beauty,
there will ever be an expansion and elevation of thought :
indeed, the rudest heart must feel and love in such a
scene, and friendship will be more pure and true than in
the ovens of slavish fashion. Yonder, below the cone of
Coneyhurst, lies Ewhurst or Iwhurst, with its old church
of Peter and Paul, and its fine rectory, and the gleam now
crossing the weald lights up many an old place worthy of

illustration. Near Vachery Pond, that is glittering in the distance, you may discern the oak-woods of the Tudor-house of Baynards, specially noted in Evelyn's "Sylva." Had you looked on its solemnity in its olden state, you will not marvel when we tell you, that for many a long year it was famed far and wide about the weald as a haunted spot, especially when you learn that it was, in reality,

The Place of a Skull.

" Was this a face to be exposed
Against the warring winds."

AMONG the fine paintings at Baynards may be noted Zucchero's picture of Queen Elizabeth with her four courtiers, Leicester, Burleigh, Essex, and Raleigh, and it is deemed the best portrait of the queen. There are relics of former days—a steelyard, presented to the City of London by Sir Thomas Gresham, when Lord Mayor—it is inlaid with gold and figures of Romulus and Remus. But there is a relic still more precious—the charter-chest of a High Chancellor of this realm. It is beautifully bound in metal, and coloured, and has four locks and a secret keyhole, and, moreover, is blended with a mystery that is still whispered around Baynards. In the middle of the sixteenth century, Mistress Margaret Roper, the mother of Lady Bray, was drooping here in sorrowful retirement. But the household of her relative, Sir Edward Bray, were keeping a merry Christmas in the servants'

hall. The windows were darkened with holly from
Holmwood, and from the black oak-beam, that stretched
across the ceiling, hung a huge bough of mistletoe, and
kissing, be sure, was the order of the night beneath it.
Even the prude pouted her lips for a blessing, consecrated
by custom of the season. Nay, old Tabitha, the Puritan,
confessed that a kiss on Christmas Eve smacked of devotion. The long hall-table groaned with cakes and ale,
and there was the wassail-bowl reeking with hot raisin-
wine and brandy, saturated with the richest spices, and
sugar, and lemons, and floated with hot roasted apples.
And there were snap-dragons, and hot cockles, and then
the dance of Sir Roger de Coverley, and the cushion-dance
—a mighty favourite with the girls of Surrey, as each
couple knelt on a cushion and embraced at the bottom. The
queen of the night was Dorothy Coley, a favourite even
of the maids in spite of themselves, and the boys were
over head and ears in love with her.

She was " Maistres Margaret Roper's Mayde," her pet
and confidante, and, though all were therefore jealous,
still Doll was the darling. Even Poll's sweetheart was a
truant to Dolly, at which Poll, like *a bochant* wench, as
Doll called her, tossed her head, and said :

" 'Twant for the waliation of the thing, neither doth it
magnify, ony one 'ates to be composed upon. So I'll turn
over to Phil Flummox, and I expees un to-morrow, tho'
I'm sure he-won't come." And then she threw sheep's
eyes at Tom.

Yet Dolly frowned on all alike. Even when the powdered lacquey made a leg before her, the little gipsy

cocked her nose, and good "morning to your nightcap."
She did, however, half smile on Robin Mayweed, a half-
witted boy, who was set down a *muff*, because he never
kissed a wench, and never talked big, nor clenched his
fists, but went maundering about mumchance in sly
corners, and, like other caves-droppers, set folks by the
ears and did a deal of mischief. 'Twas said, as how
Robin ad'nt a mossul ov elburgrease, but a monsus kit ov
gapeseed. Yet Dolly was sartin that, because he thought
small beer ov 'isself, he'd take a first-class ticket for
'eaven.

It was now hard on midnight, and the owls and the
evejars were at it round the caves, and the wassaillers
were standing knee-deep in snow, snorting out, "A
worsel! a worsel! a worsel! we begin," and so on. But
there was a call for Betsy Figg, and so Will Wiffin, in the
true Surrey slang, brayed out,—

> " Oh Betsy Figg was a nice young cretur,
>   She was a barmaid down at the Bell,
>   She was a cherrybum in her form and fetur,
>   And all this here—vy, she knowed werry vell.
>   Her greshing nose vos 'ooked like a parrita,
>   And her lushy lips, they vos vet, and thick,
>   And her golding locks was the colour of carrits,
>   Which they e'en-a-most kivver'd all her lillyvite nick."

Just as the twentieth verse was ended, some strange
noise was heard without. All looked scared, and muttered, "What's that?"

"No wonder," said Doll, "such wanton trash as that :
and Madame Margaret so woe-begone and heart-broke.
'Tis a parlous shame, isn't it, Robin?"

But Robin, as it seemed, had made himself scarce.

"As I live and breathe!" cried Poll, "there's a light in the oriel chamber."

"Pish!" said Dolly, "I have the key myself. The oriel has ever been kept holy since my lady died, and lay in state there."

"'Tis the chest," muttered the lacquey.

"But you look so wise, Miss Dolly, as though you knew more," replied Poll: "set the wassaillers to work, and you will be rid of these crotchets. Come, the Carol, the Joys of Mary."

They had just finished the verse,

> " The next good joy our Mary had,
>   It was the joy of five,
>   To see her own Son Jesus
>   To raise the dead alive."

when Robin, pale as his shirt, rushed in, crying out, "Gemini, crimini, oh!" and stood staring aghast, while all were open-mouthed, and held their breath.

"Why, Robin," screamed the scullion, "is it you or your brother?"

"Why, what hast found?" cried the groom, "a mare's nest, hey?"

"What hast seen?" inquired the gardener. "Why standst there quaking like doddlegrass?"

"Or rayther like green-gooseberry jelly," echoed the still-room maid, "why thou'rt flabbergasted, Robin."

"Pheugh, sich a sight!—O Lord!—pheugh!"

"Sight!" cried the lacquey, "why, how dare you?"

"Oh, crikey! sich a thing——"

"Thing!—what?—where?"

"The sperrit—there, there, there, in a sherte and gyrde of haire!" and Robin burst into hysterics, "though 'twas funny, too."

"Funny! why thou wicked horesbird—but tell us, tell us."

"Why, pheugh!—it pulled out——"

"Pulled out—hey, what? what? The Lord preserve us!" screamed the cook.

"A bleeding skull!"

A shudder and groaning throughout the hall! You should have seen the horror in their faces, by the livid light of the snap-dragons. None but Dante or Milton could describe it. Dolly alone was in her senses:

"Think of Madame Margaret—shame on you, Robin, grinning away like a Cheshire cat in breeches, and croaking like a toad in a hole."

But Robin had not done: "'Twas in a napkin— pheugh! like John the Baptist in the Bible, and the thing hugged it in its hairy arms, and then—pheugh!"

"And what then?" cried they all.

"Why gi'd a buss," blubbered the boy.

"Why, we must uncork the mystery!" said the butler.

"We'll find the key to it," said the housekeeper, fumbling the bunch at her girdle.

As she spoke, a huge barn-owl came hooting and flapping down the chimney, filling the hall with soot. This was a clincher. Some fell on their knees and tried to pray. Others put their tongues in their cheeks, and winked, and shook their heads, and in a few minutes all had slunk to bed but two—Dolly and Robin.

The next day whispers were rife about Baynards, and it was a scarecrow to great and small. A ghost, as tall as a *popular* tree, sat on every window sill, though none could " kitch more nor a shimper on him."

In a few days there was a clear house : they dropped off one by one, except the shoeblack and the chambermaid, who said, in a breath, that they would brush away together. The valet "set a high *vally* on his precious life," so he cut the valley of Baynards. The housekeeper would no longer keep the house, so Dolly and Robin were left to take care of the cats together.

But Robin, like Cymon, was an altered man, or rather he had grown a man in a pig's whisper, and Dolly found out that he could, on occasion, even love a pretty girl : as to kissing, as she whispered to her gossip, why—she taught him that herself. And so it turned up that one evening as the sun set over Blackdown, she led Robin, who was ever dodging her heels, to the oriel chamber, telling him to " keep up his pluck, and give a good gulp if his heart should come into his mouth." He had need of the injunction, for there in the oriel sat, not in a hair shirt, but in a suit of sables, and with the bloody head lying in her lap on a napkin, Mistress Margaret Roper.

Robin was distilled to jelly, not only with the head itself, but that the lady and the *thing* were one and the same.

Mistress Roper sighed deeply, and lifted the skull to

her lips, and, beckoning Robin, she said in a solemn tone,
" You love this girl, boy, be true to her and me. Now
look on this precious relic, 'tis the head of an angel done
to death by devils—Sir Thomas More, my father.   There
is the hoary clotted beard that he put aside with a smile,
for—*it had done no wrong*. Aye, there thou wert, thou
holy one, on London Bridge for evil eyes to mock and
scoff : blessing on Edward's head for the relic his ruthless
sire had doomed !   Listen, children : before the chopping,
he sent this *precious handkercher* to his darling Meg—and
here, look ye, his last words writ with a *pist le cole*—and
here, hung on a chain of pearls and rubies, the King's
medal, faithless, thankless Tudor !   Hide it in your bosom,
girl : and, hush! when I am dead, be yours the duty,
boy, to bear this sacred head to Canterbury.   Let not
day's light nor man's eye look on a thing so holy.
There, in St. Dunstan's aisle, will Margaret's body lie :
and there, close by, will be an iron grating, and—the
smith will rivet the bars around it—boy, see it done ! "

And when Margaret was entombed, Robin bore the
skull to Canterbury in the *handkercher*, and there it is
to this day.

After due mourning, Robin and Dolly, one winter-morn-
ing, were man and wife. So intense was the cold, that,
as Dolly's tears were freezing into icicles, she vowed she'd
never more be married at that time of the year, at which
Robin, as in duty bound, shivered the more.

The parchment picture of Margaret Roper was kept in
the gallery in Baynards, until the time of the Mores
of Losely and the Evelyns.   It may be there now.

The legend of the "gory skull" is kept alive to this hour, and there is many a Surrey boor who durst not venture nigh to Baynards after nightfall.

THE chalk over Abinger Hall, and West *Gomeselle,* or Gumeselle ("the Chief Hall"), is rich in mosses and lichens, and finely sprinkled with beech, ash, and beam : and there, by the woods of Netley, or Letely, are the Lomax-firs, that won the gold medal of the Society of Arts. Thereabout may be found the bee, the butterfly, the musk-orchis, and the pasque-flower. The banks of Till, here gently gliding between the chalk and the sand, are fringed by river botany : *Epilobium, Dianthus,* or Deptford-pink, called here codlings and cream,—*lithrum, Salicaria,* the flowering-rush,—*Sparganum,* or bur-reed, the green spikes of arrowhead, sedge, and willows, and alders, so useful for dye and gunpowder,—*cniicus palustris,* and spurges, on which feed the Acromyctæ moths. The yellow bull-moth, and the crimson underwing haunt the cat's-tail rush, and the black-spotted copper hangs on the wild oat. To lend subject to the scene, the neatest and quaintest cots, with picturesque gables and chimneys, fringe the margin of the stream : it is the village of Shere Eboracum, *Essira* (the clear stream). Its well-trimmed flower-beds, enlivened by the ripple of the rill, form a perfect anodyne on summer evenings, even to an unquiet mind, especially during the tinkling of sheep-bells from the green hills around. Those brows are exquisitely planted and command very accomplished studies, with gorgeous foregrounds and purple distances.

There is every element of beauty on the hills rising over Shireburn Spring, that forms its liquid mirror in solitude, and ripples down to the Till by Albury. The very venerable church of St. James, in Shere, displays very antient bits of transition Norman, and there is a fine doorway with three zigzag mouldings, and *fleurs-de-lis*, a rose, and a flamboyant window. There is a quaint and massive old font of Sussex marble, an effigy of Lord Audley, and images of the Rood, of St. John Baptist, St. Anthony, St. Roche, St. Nicholas, and St. Mary de Miserecordia. There are six bells, "a fine ring, which the echo of the hills do much meliorate."

In such a vale as this, that seems the home of peace,

"where all but the spirit of man is divine."

we would fain record a tale of joy and gladness, but we must stain our page with a prominent and darker theme. Woe's me! that the love of woman, inspired to soften and to bless the heart of man, should be so often "begun in folly, closed in tears,"—that the fire of jealousy should so oft inflame and degrade man's noble nature, and light up in his breast all the wild and savage instinct of—

The Bloodhound.

" Downwards he rode by death's spectre realm,
He met a hound coming from Hela."
VEGTAM QVIDA.

KING JOHN had been disporting on the brown moors of Blackhethfelde. Many a wild hart of the forest had been hunted to the death, and more than one soft heart that beat in maiden's breast had been left desolate by the wiles

of the wanton king. He had been the guest of Sir John
de Braose, to whom he had lately granted the manor of
Gumsele Letely on the demise of Eustace de Lys : for
Lady de Braose was a daughter of Llewellyn, Prince of
Wales, so related to Joan, John's base daughter, who had
espoused a Llewellyn, so she wore before the King a
semi-regal costume, a *mandelion*, with sleeves of gold
broidery hanging down the back.

Yet was De Braose in deep sables for his brothers, or,
as some have it, the wife and son of William Braose, a
rebel subject of the rebel king, who had starved him to
death in Windsor, Sir Tristram of Elbric hardly escaping
the like, but that he was so well beloved. Many of the
gay cavalcade who met the King were still lingering
about the woods, pricking for does about East-Chertshawe-
Paganels, and Charpenvilles, from Abinceborne, who
claimed *soc, sac,* and *sol,* free warren and frank pledge :
Walter de Burg Lord of Connaught and of Shyre, with
Richard, Earl of Ulster, his son by Aveline Fitzjohn,—
Roger le Savage de Pecco, who had bought Tower Hill
hard by, of Braose—John Fitzjohn—Geoffrey Fitzpiers,
Earl of Essex, who in right of his grandmother Aveline
was Earl of Vachery and Cranely, with Isabel de Lacy his
beautiful bride.

It was a holiday in Shere, and all the cottagers around
were *out,* for the village had ever been noted for gambols.
Dugdale in his legend of "St. John the Baptist," tells
how "the pepul fell to lecherie, songs, daunces, piping,
and to glotony, and sinne." And we read, too, in the
churchwarden's books (Henry and Elizabeth), of "drynk-

yngs and wakes at church festivals." The presence of De
Braose, and the Rector weeded these *agapœ*, or love-feasts,
the *vigilia* and *Evyns*, of their impurity. Yet, as a sop to
Cerberus, "church ales" were still sold by the wardens !

The hunt had come from the woods into Shere to the
festival of the " Kyng-game," for which it was renowned :
not the pageant of the three kings of Cöln, nor the game
of chess, but the installation of the "Kyng of the Beane."
They drew up just as the sweet bells were pealing, and a
bevy of fair girls issued from yon south porch, led by the
rector, Elias de Bechyngham, in full canonicals. Then
came in a row the *Assart* tenants, or renters of the woodlands, in homespun, straw-hats with green bands and
oak-leaves, and each had his *Kibbling-axe* in his belt.
The house-girls were all at the windows on the gaze—for
young eyes are ever curious. Then stalked along a tall,
rough fellow, Ailric the bailiff, whose haunt was in
Kingsdown. He was the slave of the King, or rather of
his minion De Mauley, who had the reversion of De
Braose's grant. In the Court-roll, Ailric, himself, "had
keeping of the green after seisen, given by the King's
precepts to Peter de Mauley." He cast a withering scowl
on the serfs who crowded round him, and especially on a
ragged boy, who gave him scowl for scowl. The boy was
shaggy as Edgar in "Lear," yet truly beautiful, looking
like a beggared prince, and his frowns would oft shoot
forth a radiant glance, as if two spirits—the *Kitchi*, and
the *Matchi Manitou* — were trying each to get him.
Oliver's only crony was an imp, nicknamed Loup, for
he had once pulled down a wolf in coverwood.

. There were, however, two black eyes ever looking through their tears on Oliver, wild as he was, and the beautiful gipsy that owned them would look abashed away. 'Twere hard to say whether love or pity were the dominant passion of her heart.

. "So Ailric is not himself to-day!" muttered one of the Assarts.

"Or rather he *is* himself," observed the steward of the royal copses : "were he not a brute, 'twould not be Ailric. He was born in sin, we know, and, faith! he's no regenerate. Well, he'd be no great loss to us, say I."

"Bosh!" grumbled a dirty boor, who aspired to the hangmanship, "an' 'twa'nt for chaps of his kidney, what call for the gallows, mates ? He'll swing on't one day, as sure as a gun, for he's the deepest in the drinkings, and the loudest nutcracker in church at Michaelmas, and that's a sartain sign, or I'm a Dutchman!"

With a covert sneer Ailric bent to De Braose, who whispered his lady,

"That man is my fate, my Azrael, be sure—see how he clutches his knife. He yearns for his title on the roll, and De Mauley would lift him there at once, barring me."

"Nay," said De Burg, "you've *sac* and *soc*, De Mauley has reversion only.".

"Well, well, my knife is sharp as his. Cœur de Lion and I were match at dagger play, but I beat him at short sword."

And the Assart tenants set up a madrigal, and then there was a wrestling bout. Ailric and Loup were quits, but Oliver floored the bailiff three to one, amid the cheers of the boors, and the smiles of the girls, and Gwyneth above all.

"She loves him," muttered Ailric : "yet I drugged her warden's ale with bark of the Wytch elm. His blood !— no, I dare not. His dame would curdle *mine* with her infernal mandrakes."

He was checked by the huge cake, dressed by the girls with blossoms and ribbons, in which Lady de Braose had dropped the bean, and this was to be cut for by the men, and he whose slice contained it was chaired by the tenants, and was free to kiss the lips of all the girls in Shere. The bean was Oliver's : and there he stood erect in triumph, during his installation as Kyng of the Beane, and he chose, of course, the beautiful Gwyneth for his queen. And such a pair was never seen yet in Surrey. No wonder : the boy from morn to dewy eve was breathing health on Holmbury, and the girl every May morning took her beauty-bath in Shereburn Pool, and the maids of honour to the Queen of Faery, with their *asperges* of cotton-rush dipped in the kalydor of Shereburn, had sprinkled her into so bright a beauty, that Paris, who always had an inkling for pretty women, dropped one day from Olympus down to Shere, and swore, had she been on the piny top of Ida, he should have thrown the apple into her lap, and not into that of Venus.

Would we might still harp on this theme, and forget Ailric—but we must tell out our story.

Red and pale by turns, the bailiff growled and clenched his fist, and shook with jealous fury. And when the burning kiss was pressed on the girl's lips, he rushed like a fury on the boy, and plunged his knife in his breast. The victim fell on the maiden's bosom, and they both fell prostrate to the ground. The folk all seemed paralysed, so Ailric had full time to bolt, and, as he was fleet as a fallow-deer, he was out of sight in a moment. Sir John de Braose dashed off on his horse, while the ladies grouped around the dying boy. He was borne into the church by Loup, and there beneath the image of St. Mary de Miserecordia, one of the five saints embalmed in Shere, he died. The rustic girls chaunted a requiem for his passing spirit. And there Loup was left alone with the body.

Ailric fled over the moor straight as an arrow towards Hurtwood, and then doubled on his track, De Braose then close at his heels, when the steed stumbled and threw his rider, and his foot hanging in the stirrup, he was dragged across the dingle, and there he lay inanimate. Ailric, throwing up his cap, cried out :

"De Mauley, now, is Lord of Edwinstone! See how I'll clutch the slaves. Well, I played a deep Kyng-game at Rouen, and won—for Hubert, like a fool, refused—and now there lies De Braose stark and still. So where's your free warren now, Sir John—six feet on Shere heath, ha! ha! Yet be sure, Ailric. So out! my trusty knife, I have kept you for this. Here's the blood royal still gilds the blade. Now for the blood of—hark!"

The bay of a hound, louder and louder, arrested the knife, and it only made a surface wound.

No sooner was the boy fallen, than this bloodhound of

De Braose yelled and broke his chain, and, rushing off,
came up to the spot a few seconds after Ailric had fled.
A moment the dog lay by his master, and licked his
wound, and then, by his wondrous instinct, followed in
the murderer's wake, who was in full flight by Tralee
toward Holmbury. He reached the Roman vallum with
throbbing heart and burning brain.

"She's my enemy," he muttered, "but the hell-hound
is at my heels—the devil's whelp is worse than his dam!
So casting his knife into Pitland Spring, he stood a
moment over an overgrown hole in the ditch, prepared
to leap down, when the dog caught his shoulder, and
tore away a mass of bloody flesh, and then recoiled in
terror : but the taste of blood urged him again on his
prey so madly, that the two bloodhounds rolled together
into the den. There, beneath a rowan, or witches' tree,
sat a form, withered, yet beautiful, the lustrous eyes of
youth mocking the wrinkles of age.

"Avaunt, avaunt!" she screamed, "what want ye here?
Know ye not 'tis hallowed ground : hallowed by spell
and curse. What, De Braose's hound! then thou must
be his enemy, as I am of his Welch wife, who hath
cheated my boy of his Gwyneth, and made him mad."

With that she held the lip of a bitch to the dog, and
he lay crouching in a moment.

"I know the dog," she muttered, "but who is the
brute? What, by Pluto! Ailric—thou—thou! Then
fate is closing on us fast—fast." She whistled thrice.
"What," she cried, "nor whelp, nor boy? Hold! is the
slave dead? No, he stirs—saved for *me*. So, here's

R

moonwort gathered at the full in Cold-Kitchin yonder,
'tis singular to heale greene and freshe woundes."

So she poured the *lunaria* down his throat, and
chaunted wildly,—

> " The first leet night quhan the newe moon set,
>   Quhan alle was douffe and smirke,
> We saddled our naighs with moon-fern-leif,
>   And rode to old Elbrie kirk."

The man opened his eyes, and muttered, " Mercy!
Mercy!"

" What for *thee*—the fiend who dragg'd me to the bed
of the libertine? I cried to you for mercy then—did I
get it? no! Say, who lost me my soul? who peach'd
me at the drynkyngs? who call'd me ' beldame-witch'?
Thou, Ailric, thou! Aye, thou shalt feel my witch-
craft! But wait for my Oliver—my royal boy, who hung
with Henry his brother on my woman's paps."

The man sent forth an hysteric chuckle.

" What meaneth that? Some hell-work, slave!" And
she wrenched his bleeding shoulder, till he groaned for pity.

" Aye! thou shalt have it: 'twill match thy mercy.
Thou shalt live awhile. Look on me, that thou hast
blasted even in her prime of beauty : on me, Olive of
Oakhurst, that thou didst mock when John flouted *my* boy
for Miss Warenne's brat : and now—Ha! what's here
on thy wrist?—Blood! purple-black!" And she smelt
his arm. "Faugh! faugh! Yet there's another smear—
scarlet—royal! What! what! hell-kite!" She pressed
her nose on the blood-spot, and kissed it frantically.

The lich fowl croaked as it hovered in the air.

"Owlet, my night-raven," she screamed, "there's death! And who's the flesher?"

The bird flapped its wing over Ailric's head.

"Ha! he is dead!" she bellowed: "dead! mine own! my beautiful!—down, down, spawn of Gehenna, down!" And she rolled Ailric in the dust. "Where is my boy?"

"Oh, let me die!" he groaned: "that grin of triumph is torture to me."

"Die now! No! no! Your life is a priceless jewel. Wait! wait!—I'm thinking how to torture more!"

All this while the hound was mumbling his mouthful and growling: but he saw the man prostrate and powerless—and he was still.

"Well, art better?" she muttered again. "Revive, revive! Not half alive yet! Hold!—here's water from the spring," and she held it to his lips.

"'Tis poison to me! poison! Forbear!—there's blood in't. Let me die without it!"

"Die! why—look! thy wound is healed—oh, precious moonwort!—and thy senses brighter than ever. Mandrake and nightshade would have deadened: so thou art ripe for vengeance. Hark! hark! Who comes? down dog—down? So Loup—at last—and alone!"

As Olive sank on a sand-block, Loup raised his burden on the wall, and it rolled into her lap.

"My boy! my boy!" she cried, straining the corpse in her arms. "Vengeance! vengeance a million-fold! Ha! a red-ring adder! So——."

The reptile struck Ailric with its fang, and, coiling back to its hemlock, writhed and died.

"What!" she cried, "a worm to cheat me of my prey! No! no!"

And she directly smeared the livid wound with juice of adder's tongue, screaming wildly—

> "For them that are with newts and adders stung,
> She seeketh out an herb that's called Adder's tongue,
> As Nature it ordained its own-like hurt to cure.

Ailric, thou hast shed blood royal, and I will honour thee. The green withs, Loup: look! Ailric, look!"

"I am blind, beldame."

"Blind! nay, thou must see thy torture, or I lose my sport. Here's eyebright.—Well done Euphrasia. His sight is clear again. Now for thine honour. There lies my noble boy: he shall hug thee, Ailric—aye, in thine agony!"

"Cruel! cruel!" groaned the writhing creature.

"I save thee from Gallows-lane yonder, and thou callest me cruel! Now, Loup, now!"

She held the bleeding corpse of her boy, while Loup lifted Ailric in his arm, and with the green withs they bound the two together, and laid them on the ground.

"I doom my boy to shame. Thou didst mock him in his pride: now on his shroudless bier he shall glut his ghost with vengeance! Look from thy throne, John Lackland—another death-spot on thy soul!" And she sank exhausted to the ground.

And there, day by day, lay Ailric, writhing in convulsive throes, ever and anon wiping away with a dock-leaf, the slaver from the purple collops of flesh that rolled over his lips. And the deadly nightshade, and the darnel twined around his neck—they are the garlands of a sinner's soul. And after many days, the whiff of the bloody slime that curdled on the ground was so intense, that even the adder and the eft writhed, and hissed, and crawled away.

Days and days passed by, and Sir John de Braose lay at a cottage on the moor, called *Hound-house*. His wound healed : yet he lived in sickness and languor. One day it chanced, as he was out a riding with John Fitzjohn Fitzgeoffry, Lord of Shere-vachery, that they passed over Holmbury, where a blast of tainted air—as from a city of the plague—almost struck them to the earth : and there, on a mossy stone, sat a creature almost unearthly.

" So," she cried, with a smile, addressing Fitzgeoffry, " *you* are here !"

" Olive of Oakhurst ! you ? " exclaimed he.

" Aye, Olive the harlot, she ! John and Osbert de Warenne, and Joan Llewellyn, I tell ye, *my* bastard was worth ye all. Follow me : there—there he lies !—once so beautiful, now so loathsome ! and by his side Ailric—the bloodhound. Hark, hark ! 'tis his death-ruckle. Ay, you *may die now*—slave of my woman's vengeance ! Wilt confess ? "

" No ! "

" Then die in thy deadly sin. Yet—hold ! we may be merciful : so, then, extreme unction for thee with the rankest *witches' butter* ! "

Ailric moved his blackening fingers, as if to ward the demon off : but not even a groan escaped him—he was too weak, and in a moment he was dead. The suite of De Braose bore off his body in dismal silence. The other mass was too loathsome to be touched : yet his mother sat by it night and day, while kites and ravens gorged themselves with the carrion, the bones bleaching on the hill.

One night, as Olive sat watching a star, she started and exclaimed : " The mandrake !—Look ! John, the king, is on his death-steddle ! I know it. None but this—the murderer's mandrake—bred of the slime of the grave, can tell the degree of putrefaction and rank of a corse, and give quietus to a witch or a tyrant. We must, we must ! "

The weed grew apace, and the withering flowers around it waxed pale and shrivelling. And Olive, at midnight, pulled the mandrake—though she knew herself *must* die— and sent it by Loup to the court of King John.

" Seek the nameless priest," she said : " he is my brother : he knows—he knows ! " And in a moment Olive herself was dead.

Now this priest was the king's confessor : and what did he with the mandrake, think you ? Holinshed affirms that the King died " at Newarke Castell of new sider : " Gisburne, that he was poisoned by pears at Swineshead— proved by the tarnish of his jewels : others, that he died of green peaches, and sweet ale. There may be another story. Simon Swinstead received his sister's mandrake. " A monk," write Grafton and Caxton, " was in the abbey with the king : and *he* took the king's cup to the closet, and he was commanded, as *Dapifer*, to sip the ale, and in an hour the monk was dead ! And then the king shi- vered, and muttered, ' The Lord have mercy, then, on me ! ' And so he went to Newark and died." The Abbot, who confessed and absolved the king and the monk, has

left no record of confession : but who will doubt that the
mandrake of Olive was the poison of the cup that killed
the king ?

They hung Ailric's body on a gallows on the heath.
This passage in the "Perambulator of the Manor of
Shere" (16th Henry VIII.), may point to the spot :

"... In the middle of the valley unto a stone hepe lying in the
hethe, by the hygheway that ledeth from Guildeforde to Ewherste,
where lately stode a payr of galowes."

The nameless priest, who found home and favour at
Elbrie was long seen to haunt the dyke of Holmbury : and
he took the bleached bones of his nephew and laid them
in the ground in Shere-lane : the upright stones may point
the unconsecrated spot where the refuse of poor Oliver
was earthed. The pride of the legitimate Plantagenets
forbade inscription : but the *Gules*—three lions, *passant
gardant*, in the south window of the chancel, may be
Prince Henry's memorial of his bastard brother.

De Braose died early in the reign of Henry III. : and
'tis he, probably, that lies in Horsham Church. The tomb
was renewed in the reign of Richard II., and is even now
in fair preservation. Close to it, on the chancel floor, is
a brass effigy of the nameless priest.

The rich sombre house of Albury, on the margin
of the Till, is perfectly in keeping with the deep golden
greens in which it is embosomed, and it is graced by
oriels and very ornate-clustered chimneys. A very ancient
pile is chronicled in "Doomesday"—Elberie, Elbrie, Ald-
burie, Oldbury, Albergune—Saxon and Roman names,

derived, perchance, from the Roman temple on the heath.
Hollar's view of it shows an ugly gabled pile, and they
called it a *mansio frequens* of Henry, Earl of Arundel,
who, with Thomas Howard, Lord High Marshal, made it
their pet. It was once the home of Heneage Finch, Earl
of Aylsforde—the friend of Evelyn and Aubrey, the 'silver-
tongued,' whose acuteness saved the seven bishops from
the clutch of James. The spirit of devotion should hover
over Albury, the valley of the trine churches, for it stands
on the line of the Pilgrims' Way, and is consecrated by three
holy fanes. The screen of the Cathedral, or Irvingite
church, imparts a mystic air to the transept : there is a
fine stone altar, a crucial orient window, beaming with
colour, shrines and sedilia for the apostles, prophets, and
evangelists, and a throne for the presiding angel. It was
here that Irving and his proselytes held conference on the
Second Advent, resulting in his book, " The Coming of
the Messiah, in glory and majesty, by Ben Ezra, a Con-
verted Jew."

There, close to Albury House, beneath sombre shadow,
stands the dismantled fane of Peter and Paul, in which
ministered Horsley and Oughtrede, whose tomb is preserved. The square cupola tower is probably as old as any
in England, the bases of the columns being, we believe, of
the stones of the Roman temple hard by. There are fine
lancet windows, a rude Saxon font of Sussex marble, a
very ancient screen, and tables and brasses of Westons and
Drummonds.

The emblematic roses that once gemmed the green turf
are long since withered, and so is the young cypress that

drooped over a form—once fresh as the flowers in their budding, now, alas! slumbering in the cold grave.

Memory fades not like the flowers : and we have led you to this tomb of young beauty, that we may tell her story. Yet, look—there is a grey man kneeling, weeping there : his thoughts lie deeper in that grave than you wot of. Approach him, and you shall learn even from his own lips the secret of

The Worm i'the Bud.

"Oh, fairest flower, no sooner blown but blasted!"

So whispered the grey man, and with a deep, deep sigh, he went on thus mourning—

"Yes, you shall learn the story, for the heart is ever lightened by breathing its sorrow to sympathising ears, and such I know are yours.

"I will tell you how a young life was withered in its core, even while hope and love were bounding in her bosom. She was the sweetest flower in Albury, when a poor student, who now weeps before you, came down from the great city to rusticate in his boyhood's home. On yon green lawn—but a few short paces from her grave, we had wandered hand in hand, a boy and a girl, and there, years after, my eyes were dazzled by the maturity of that soul breathing beauty I had once gazed on in the child. It was then all blushing, now pale—pale as the snow-flake, yet so intense was the lustre of her large blue eyes, that they seemed to kindle a maiden blush upon her cheek.

" Emmeline "—and he breathed a deep sigh—" *she* was
in that buoyant stage of life when the rose-tint colours
every object around us, and when joy is the very element
of our being, when even physical suffering is slighted
or forgotten in the blithe moments of juvenile excitement.
Ah, that excitement!—it is the woeful secret of half the
maladies of maidenhood, though ever disregarded! nay,
often nourished by parental love from the very cradle : it
is the canker in the bud, lighting up the latent germ of
that dire disorder that so quickly drops many and many
a maiden into her tomb, even in the brightest lustre of
girlhood. The while the doating mother, unconscious of her
fatal error, is watching her child with fond delight, as she
is floating like a zephyr through the mazes of the dance,
the latent seeds of consumption are bursting into its own
parasitic death-dooming life within that delicate bosom.
While the hectic blush is mantling on the cheek,
many a heart is dreaming of love and joy ; but the sapient
eye detects at once in that roseate patch the outward sign
of disease—stealthy and sure as the pestilence that walketh
in darkness. Alas, that I must recall that evening of
spring when Emmeline was my partner in the waltz!
and with the purest confidence of innocence in one who
loved her—was leaning against my side. After a while we
paused in our whirling, and in a moment I felt the tumul-
tuous throb of her heart, and heard her tremulous
breathing almost as rapid as the pulses. The truth flashed
on me like lightning. 'You are not well,' I whispered.

" 'Quite,—can I be ought but well in such a paradise,
and—with such a friend ?'

"'Yet your heart is throbbing, your cheek is burning?'

"'Oh, yes! but that's nothing, it is ever so when I delight in the dance, as I do now—oh, how much! Come —another round!'

"It would have been a crime in me to have obeyed her wish, and I led her directly to her seat, not without her playful frown at my cruelty. But a group of worshippers flocked around her, and resisting my urgent entreaty—my almost severe rebuke, this joyous creature was whirled away dance after dance, spite of all my prayers, to the ecstatic pride of her mother, and the delight of her companions. To me the wreath of lilies around her brow was but the votive chaplet hung on a marble in the grave-yard—yet she was to the last moment the pride and life of the ball-room.

"Morning was coming on when Emmeline dropped on her pillow. Sleep? repose?—no, no! her heart-beat forbad it, it was wild and throbbing still, as in the whirl of the waltz: how could sleep steal over the senses of a being in such a state? Morning came, and when I listened closer, I was aware at once that, like the latent worm in the bud of the rose, disease had secretly crept on to that confirmed development that clouded every gleam of hope. Yet so fresh and joyous was even now her expression, so exquisite her smile, that my effort was vain to raise even the slightest fear or apprehension in her friends: they only echoed her own words, 'Oh, that's nothing.'

"But soon a change, a doleful change, came over the

scene, even sooner than I thought. One little month
confirmed the truth of my suspicion to all but herself, yet
it were a cruelty, they murmured, to dim by solemn
warning even a spark of such radiant enjoyment. But
now her fair round limbs began to dwindle, and her form
to bend, yet her eyes were more lustrous than ever, and
she was still the loveliest girl in the vale of Albury, and
in her own thought, strange paradox, she was fast pro-
gressing to perfect health : alas ! alas ! she was hurrying
fast another way. Another evening came, and her smile
though languid was still so beautiful that for a while a
gleam of hope became even confidence in all—but one.
He was watching her with the most intense anxiety, for
he knew the truth, he was marvelling at that wondrous
elasticity that will conceal the inroad of disease, and even
triumph for a while over the very onset of decay. When
they laid her lute on her lap, I was awe-struck by her
raising herself on her couch : then, with something like an
unearthly effort, she took up the symphony of ‘The
dying Christian to his Soul,’ and began chanting in tones
perfectly seraphic—

> ‘ Lend, lend your wings, I mount, I fly,
> Oh grave, where is thy victory ?
> Oh death—where—where—’

The syllables hung in a murmur on her lips, one
tremulous sob—in which was a whisper of her Saviour's
name—one long-drawn sigh—one upward glance to Heaven, and her lids closed, her long silken lashes drooping on
a cheek as icy cold as a frozen lily in the bosom of early
spring. Dear, dear Emmeline ! ”

THE demesne of Albury lies between Chalk and Sand?
on the fertile galt, so rich in every fly and flower—

> " A populous solitude of bees and birds,
> And fairy form'd and many colour'd things;
> Who worship God with notes more sweet than words,
> And innocently open their glad wings,
> Fearless and full of life.

Sat Childe Harolde in Albury when he wrote this?
There is the lappet-moth lying like a leaf on the
catkinned willows, and there the giant cossus, called the
goat-moth, its crimson leopard-spotted larva, having the
goat odour: there are the hawk, the privet, and the hum-
ming-bird moths, and the *macroglossa stellatorum*, thrust-
ing his long tongue into the nectary of the dionæa—we
have caught him: so be it with every wild rake who rifles
thus the sweets of beauty.

The highwoods are interlaced by the softest moss-alleys,
skirting the dingles that cut down into the valley. They
are exquisitely planted and gemmed with golden *hyperi-
cum, calycinum,* and *androsæmum,* and with thee legant
helianthemum, the sun-rose.

As we walk the green terraces by the cave cut by the
stream from Shereburn, we remember Sylva's diary :—

" To Albury to see how that garden proceeds, which I
found exactly done to the designed plot I hadmade with
the crypta through the mountain in the park: such a
pausilippo is no way in England besides ! "

Aubrey aided in this work.

Evening is near, there on the water-brooks lie the
lilies, nymphæa and nuphar, closing for sleep upon the

water, while others are going down to scatter pollen.
Thus some lilies dive into the watery shade, like Nereids,
to hide their bridal blushes. The female blossoms of
Valisneria are held on the surface by long green threads,
the male flowers come up to fructify, and then dwindle and
die like the ephemera, the female directly retiring, like a
shy matron, for her widowed parturition in the grave.

We may be deemed ultra-fanciful to declare that
flowers have their characters, and play them too. *Clytie*,
the brazen coquette, looks the sun full in the face, and
challenges with a blush his burning kisses : *Dionæa*, opens
her bosom unblushingly to her insect lover, and like the
Syren, glories in his fall : the *Mimosa*, like a modest
maiden, shrinks even from the gentlest touch : the *Evening Primrose*, still more discreet, closes in her charms as
the hour of burning comes on, while the night-blowing
cereus and the high-born *Victoria*, like "maids that love
the morn," only begin to bloom when night is near.

> "As Nightingales do upon glowworms feed,
> So poets live upon the living light,
> Of nature and of beauty."

ARGAL, in this sweet Valley of Albury, where the light
of beauty illumines nature, lives the erudite writer of
" Proverbial Philosophy." There is romance even in his
husbandry. Twelve grains of *mummy* wheat, taken by
Sir Gardner Wilkinson from sealed vases in the Thebais,
were sown in Albury : a sample, perchance, of that " full
and good corn," kept 3,000 years ago by Joseph—then
master of the household—during the famine, and found in
Benjamin's sack. Only *one* precious grain germinated, the

rest, by worm or rot, or east wind, were blasted like the seven withered ears in Joseph's dream.

This little romancy vale was peopled in Aubrey's time by a commonwealth of powder-monkeys, black as negroes, and in *Lythie* or Collyer's hanger, fringing the leys of *Celeonde,* still grows the logwood that is charred for the finest powder.

The velvet woods of Albury and Wonersh are in high relief from the fine combes of the chalk-hills hereabouts: select those on the ascent to Clandon and Effingham, or that rising over the deep clear spring of Shereburn, that ripples down in its solitude to the Till—the turf is carpeted, and the hedgerows and banks gemmed with

wild flower, *twayblade* and *aceras* spring beneath the
beeches, and the downs are profuse in thistles, cotton,
musk, milk, dwarf, plume, tuberous, and Carline. As
you ascend to the finest point, Newland's corner, may
we not fancy that the white-fleeced flocks around those
grotesque yews of centuries, may be in direct descent the
lambs of that very flock once folded by a shepherd, who,
as the story goes, won unconsciously and without wooing,
the love of

The Not-browne Mayde.

"For thy name, that is no part of thee,
Take all myself."

It is curious to note the varied modes by which love
steals into a woman's heart, and how, unconsciously to the
angel herself, one little incident may first impress, then
soften, then subdue.

When Rose May first felt this influence—when, indeed,
she first dreamed that she had a heart for a lover,—we
may but guess, for every word and action implied that she
loved her father all—and yet there was, with all this devotion, a spice of affection for all who loved him, and it is
this sentiment that may unfold the deep secret of her
maidenhood. With all her maiden softness, you must
know there was yet a dash of chivalry about Rose May,
for she had indeed dived deep into the chronicles with her
father, Ralph May, who was a rich widower, and worked
the manor farm of Tytetinge yonder, an old stone lodge of
St. Martha's Chapel on the hill, noted in "Domesday," and
even now displaying three lancet windows in the ironstone

walls. Henry was Master May's shepherd, and as he
never mentioned his family name, the very concealment,
of course, excited suspicion, and so his society was cut,
and he was left alone with his sheep. So when he had
folded his flock for the night, he crept silently to his cock-
loft, yet not without a sigh and a tear. These, however,
ever ceased when Rose came near him: yet he was shy of
all, and all he did was his duty, and this was simple
enough.

It chanced one night that Rose had read herself *out* in
the Wars of the Roses, and thereabout, where York was in
the ascendant, and father and son were fighting in opposite
factions. Ralph May was yearning for the climax, yet he
would spare his darling's eyes, so he summoned Henry to
talk of this and that about the farm. And then they gossiped about the chronicles, and Rose, though her eyes were
burning, would have read on, but her father closed the book.

"Nay, my own child, we must leave Clifford and his
fate for this night still in the dark, nor tire this poor boy
with the lore of chivalry. *His* blade is his crook, I ween :
his cymbal hangs on the neck of the bell-wether."

But Henry's eyes flashed as he spoke, and he stammered
out an offer to read through the chapter.

"*You* read !" exclaimed the master : "why, 'tis black
letter, boy. Even Rose, scholar as she is, has often found
her match : and where, prythee, learnedst thou ?"

"I scarce know where or how—in the wilds of Cumber-
land I picked a crumb or two—ay, and in Craven : but I
pray you let me try."

So he took the volume of Grafton, and read of Towton

8

Field, while his eyes flashed, and May and Rose listened and looked on him in perfect wonder.

As he read, his voice faltered, and a tear dropped from his eye, Rose watching him the while with deep emotion : " Men alyue pass'd the ruyer vpon deade carcasses, and that the greate ryuer of Wharfe, the greate sewer of all the water coming from Towton, was coloured with blood." He closed the book, and said, " Westmoreland, North-umberland, Dacre, Welles, Neville, Trollope. Oh, I could tell how Edward rode to York, and took Lord Clifford's head, muttering curses on him who stabbed young Rut-land ! Oh, noble Clifford, that, like Æneas, bore thy father on thy back—ah, Towton was thy grave ! Pardon, my master—pardon, my bright mistress, you wear the white flower, and may scorn a Clifford, be he ever so humble."

" A Clifford !—you ? "

" Ay, Clifford, yet orphan and outcast. On that bloody field of Towton, e'en at the moment Lord Clifford fell, my father's spirit also rose to heaven, and then 'twas down with Lancaster, and proscription : 'twas death to a Clifford in the south, so Maud, my mother, hid her boy in the fells of Bolton till I was hunted out, and then I tended flocks, and learned my horn-book of the monks of Bolton year after year, till traitors tracked us home, and then—and then—and now I am your shepherd, master."

Rose stared with all her eyes, and the yeoman was utterly bewildered, and the poor shepherd crept weeping to his truckle-bed, and there he thought of days long agone—bright shadows, be sure, for the young brain is intensely reticent of early scenes. That night there were two sleepless beings in Tyteing, and their night-thoughts were on one theme, for both had lost a doating parent, and their hearts were in the closest sympathy. It was just at the dawn, as the shepherd rose to tend his flock, that Rose's lips murmured, "Poor boy, poor boy!" and in the echo of those syllables she fell asleep and dreamed of Henry Clifford. With the morn,. as ever, came her lovers to Rose May, while Clifford watched on the down : but he loved his lot, for he was watching for Rose May's father. Yet, ever and anon, a sigh burst from his bosom. Grafton had opened a spring that had well-nigh run dry.

The lovers, they went as they came, and Clifford, did he aspire to hope? He dare not—his passion was worship, not love—she was to him a planet to be adored at distance, as the star by the shepherds in Chaldæa. In her presence, he scarcely breathed : yet we may guess what he felt, even by two lines scratched with chalk on his closet wall :—

" Browne is my love, but graceful, and each renowned whitenesse,
  Matchd with thy lovely browne, looseth her bryghtnesse."

We may whisper that a myriad of rhapsodies of a like intensity may be found in Clifford's book, ycleped " A Divine Centurie of Spirituale Sonnets," and be sure he ever thought of Rose when he scribbled.

And Rose May's feeling towards the. shepherd-boy—oh, the purest pity, 'twas clear. Were there a spice of love in't, she would have *smiled*, would she not? for is not love a joyous thing? But Rose wept and sighed instead, and she was sure there was no shame or peril in such a feeling. So night after night they called in Clifford to recite the chronicles of Grafton, and his rich voice deepened ever with the intensity of his subject.

Ralph May felt, had Henry's lot been cast in a nobler sphere, he would have won a hero's fame, and Rose looked on him as a martyr, and, spite of his rude garb, thought of Bayard and Gaston and Guescelin : and as for the Yorkist lovers, they looked suspicion, as if they had an inkling, but further thought about a poor shepherd was clearly beneath their notice.

He who fulfils the humblest duty well earns our esteem, and he who faithfully works out his mission, though his heart and life be lone and dreary, earns our pity—ay, and our love. And so the nut-brown maid did love with a pure intensity this humble shepherd-boy. And Clifford, this while, seemed in his very labour all content—the secret *this*, the consciousness of doing his duty in that sphere in which God had placed him, and this for Rose May's father. True, he was enduring the penalty of sin, but he was as near heaven in thus enduring patiently, and looking up to his Creator, as a Howard in a death-cell or lazaretto.'

Winter was again in the world, the floods from the melting snow had rolled down into the valley of the Till and drowned the water-brooks, even the homestead of Tyteinges was deluged, and it was the fortune of the shepherd, even at his life's peril, to save the pet lamb of Rose May. Although she called not her neighbours together, like the woman in Holy Writ, yet, be sure, heart-breathings were lavished on Clifford in profusion as they sat around the fire and sipped the warm and luscious *elder wine*, for

which even Speed eulogises this vale of Chilworth. And
so the days wore on, and Rose would breathe a night-prayer
on her pillow for the shepherd, for she knew he was gone
cheerless and sorrowing to his truckle-bed, instead of keeping merry Christmas in the hall. Then she wished he had
been her brother, and then—oh, the perverseness of woman's
wishes !—she was glad he was not. She wondered herself
at her depth of sympathy, but she thought, were he not in
sorrow and forlorn, she had not felt that soft sweet pity
that was akin to—Rose left even the thought unfinished.

"Poor boy," said Ralph May, as one evening they had
been talking—"poor boy, I do love him, and that's truth."

"And so do—" but Rose again bit her lip, and wondered at her own words. And then she bit her lips again for
their indiscretion—the worst thing she could do, as they
only blushed the deeper, and felt the warmer. Then she
looked for her father's frown, but he was really smiling—
that was very strange, but it told Rose at once that she had
done no wrong, and then, like a flash of light, she knew
that—she loved.

Ralph May must have seen it all, but he still sat mute
and smiling. One would have thought 'twere best to send
Rose away to Guildford or Godalming, but instead the
shepherd-boy was even allowed—nay, desired—to wait on
Rose to yon Chapel of Martyrs on the hill, where, after
matins, Rose often sat sketching, and Clifford, apart in his
lady worship, writing ballads. One stanza will display
the intensity of his love-dream :—

> " Oh, she were aught of beautiful, and shining
> Bright as the phantom of the lover's dreaming,

. A lily on his bounding breast reclining,
A star of peace o'er all his sorrow beaming.
She were his life, her radiant beauty gleaming
Pure as the snow on virgin lilies lying:
She were his soul, her holiest tears, ystreaming
From orbs down gazing on her red lips sighing,
Soft as an angel's kiss, unblushing and undying ! "

Now you will wonder, perchance, at Ralph May's implicit confidence and trusting, but he knew his boy well, and his honour and humility, and Clifford held his trust sacred to the very letter. Yet, though he was giant-strong in his resistance, his love was pure and true as that of the maiden. Day after day, however, he stood, like the Peri at the gate, without daring to hope : and so he might have lingered on till his doomsday, but devotion brought out a climax and a confession that romance had failed to do.

Ralph May's spirit went to heaven, and they laid his body in the Martyr's aisle, by Morgan of Chilworth. A month had elapsed, and Rose May, as the hills were empurpling in the sunset, was kneeling on the cold stone in the Martyr's cell, breathing her prayer to heaven, her shepherd-boy standing aloof and gazing on his mistress with all the worship of a devotee.

" Kneel with me, Clifford," she murmured. " My father loved you, Henry, and I—I— " The red blood lighted up her clear brown cheek *Titianesque*, and with averted face she added, " I—am my father's child."

" Then you will pity me, lady, as he ever did."

" Pity," she exclaimed—" pity ! showest thou *me* pity ?"

" I know not what you mean, lady : pity, said I. Nay, I implore your mercy, rather."

" I would be merciful even to my enemy."

" Yet you show not mercy now—even to a—friend."

" How meanest thou, Clifford ? "

" To lift your poor boy so high, whence he must fall again to earth. Lady, I do implore your mercy : yet even to look on the glance that kills me is a blessing."

" Say, then, only say you love me, Clifford, or I may indeed blush a bold and forward girl. Say but you love me, or I cannot look again, and tell you this. Love must be mutual to consecrate this fellowship of ours : there is my hand."

Clifford took not her offered hand, but, trembling, knelt by her side, and whispered " Why do you love me, Rose May ? "

" For your humble faith and truth to my father. Am I not his child ? Give *me* the truth thou canst not give to him—say but you love me, and I may look you in the face again."

" How dare I love ? " he exclaimed wildly : " a shepherd-boy—an outcast—a banished man—my very name a shame-spot in the land : how dare I love my master's daughter ? you that are wooed and worshipped by wealth and honour, to wed an outlaw who must hide his shame from the world ! "

" My bosom were your world, Clifford," she answered tremulously. " Oh, hide your sorrow there, for now I know you love me."

" Would I had fallen with my sire in Towton Field ! ' he cried. " Rose, Rose, bid me, and I will die for you— live for you I cannot ! Oh, were Richmond—pshaw ! " .

"Then 'tis done," she murmured : "without my shepherd-boy 'twere desart all."

> "Her soft pensiveness of brow
> Had deepened into sadness now,
> And boding thoughts that she must part,
> With a soft vision of her heart,
> All lowered about the lovely maid,
> To darken her dejection's shade."

Even as their tears were flowing fast, Clifford started up and stood like a statue.

"'Tis the hunter's horn," whispered Rose.

But the bugle sounded nearer, and a cry of "Richmond, Richmond!" rent the air, and a troop of horse were scouring o'er the hill.

It was a meeting as lucky as it was joyous.

"George Stanley," cried Clifford, "my boyhood's chum, embrace a shepherd-boy! Henry is king?"

"And Gloucester in the dust : the banner, ho."

"The Rose of Lancaster," shouted Clifford, raising his woollen cap : "hail to the peerless flower! Peerless, said I : nay, behold its match, a Rose—more precious to me than the brightest in Henry's court—a nut-browne mayde, who stoops to love her shepherd."

Stanley bowed.

"A truce to compliment now : Clifford hath a sterner work than dalliance, so, noble captain of the guard—nay, nay, here's your commission from the king, *Lord* Clifford."

Rose May, who was folded to his breast, gazed for a moment wildly in his face, and, turning ashy pale, slid like a melting snow-flake from his arms. As he raised

her to his breast, he whispered, "Clifford may claim
you now, my beautiful—

> "For ye have wonne an erle's sonne,
> And not a banysshed man."

That same hour witnessed the betrothal of Henry
Lord Clifford and Rose May, at the altar of St. Martha's
Chapel. Alas! it was only a betrothal : the sudden gush
of joy was a pang in Rose May's bosom. Clifford felt her
heart throb, for a moment, wildly against his own, and
then, convulsed by the intensity of its ecstasy, it ceased
to beat, and she lay dead in the arms of her shepherd-
lord, the last of all the martyrs !

And in the Martyr's aisle was Rose inhumed, and some
of the iron-stones, even now scattered on the hill, are the
relics of her tomb.

After this awful incident did Henry Lord Clifford,
Baron de Vesci, of Brougham Hall, in right of his mother,
Margaret of Londesborough, do loyal service to the king,
and then harboured awhile in his beloved fells of Craven,
and there grew deep in astronomy with the Canons of
Bolton, who addressed him as "Lord of the Percy's fee,"
and when tired of Bardon Tower he again came into the
world and wedded Anne Saint John of Bletsoe, and
secondly, Florence Perdry, after his return from Flodden
Field.

The romaunt of "The Not-browne Mayde," and Prior's
"Henry and Emma," sprung from this slight episode in
the life of Lord Clifford, and not from a ballad in a book
twenty years later: "London from the Time of Kyng
Richard, called 'Cure de Lyon.'" Whitaker has adopted

as the hero the *son* of the shepherd-lord : but he was
too young then, scarcely in his teens, and a sad losel
withal, and the shepherd, although not an erle's son (nor
Rose a baron's daughter), was the only *banysh'd man.*

ST. MARTHA'S, or the Mound of Martyr's Hill, now the
site of a humble chapel-of-ease, was once crowned by a
church of Bishop Odo of Baieux, of the manor of Celeonde,
in Beolege, and the chantry was the shrine of a pilgrimage
in the time of Edward IV. according to Bishop Wayn-
flete's registrar, 1150. The tomb of the knight and the
antique coffin-lids were, we believe, of the thirteenth cen-

tury, when it was noted in the *compotus* of Henry VIII.
Coleonde, Martyr's Hill, and Firma ecclesiæ.

The cone of green sand forms a sort of buttress to the
chalk-hill and commands a panorama of surpassing
beauty. The vale of Albury seems blended into one
mass of woods and emerald meads of tufted velvet. The
western view is magnificent, exquisitely composed of the
purple heights of Hants, Berks, and Oxfordshire : the Till
is gliding gently along the meadows to the Wey, that
directly cuts through the chalk-hill at Guildford, in its
course to the valley of the Thames.

Guildford.

Vadum Aureum, the golden ford, was a Roman station on
a little island or heap of sand, and on its site rose up the
Guild on the Ford, Geldford, or Guildford. The town is
rich in old things, especially its three parish churches—
Trinity, St. Nicholas, and St. Mary's—its chapel of St.
John displaying very curious frescoes on the spandrils of
the groined arches. There is the Guildhall in High Street,
with its grotesque balcony and the Stoke mantelpiece in
the Council Room. There is Abbott's Hospital, in
which Monmouth was lodged after Sedgmoor : the family
of Israel is painted on two windows. They may still
show you the site of the old king's park, and tell you
of the *Parker* and the knock *pynne*, and of the spring
tasted by Queen Elizabeth, and noted in the Loseley
MSS. "in a corn-field under a'hedge N. Est fro' ye Freary
house."

Of the Castle of Guildford there is no mention in
Domesday, yet we may believe that on its site, even in
the time of Alfred the Great, some pile was standing, as
he left Guildford by special deed to his nephew Ethelwald.

The square keep now standing is of the Norman era
and we may trace the outer walls of chalk. In the south
west corner on the second story is a curious circular room

its basement of chalk and flint : its walls are ten feet
thick, and are incised—it is asserted, by a prisoner—with
very rude figures : an infant Christ on the arm of Saint
Christopher, a bishop, a crowned king, and the Crucifixion.
We enter by a stone arch of the oratory, looking like a
window, high up from the ground, there being no other
opening, not even loopholes. The pile is rich in historic lore
of the Norman time, especially in the reign of John, and
it was one of the castles held in the name of the Dauphin.

We believe that circular chamber, with its scratches on
the wall, may have been associated with a record of
Heywood in his "Life and Death of Robert, Earl ot
Huntingdon " - (era of Elizabeth). It tells how Lady
Bruce was lodged with her son in this dungeon, and how
King John threatened to burn the place, gave she not
up the boy as an hostage for his father's fealty.

But Guildford Castle possesses an interest far deeper
and darker than this.

There was, years and years ago, even in the Saxon era,
another young innocent, whose very dreadful destiny Grose
has located in this very keep.

In Hastell's "Pastime of the People " of 1529, we read
the record thus :—"In the yeere of Cryste, MXLI. the
two sons of Egelredus, Alfridus and Edwardus, cam from
Normädy into Englond to vyset theyr moder Emma, and
brought with them a gret cöpany of Normäs, wherfore
one yerle Goodwin councellyd the king and the lordys not
to suffer those Normäs to be within the realme for
jeopardy—by which meanys he gatt auctoryte to order
the matter hymself, wherfore he met with thö on Gyl

Downe, and there slew Alfridus and the most part of the Normā."

This is " brief as the posy of a ring," and only whets our curiosity.

On the eve of this tragedy, however, there were two prating sentinels, who were keeping watch and ward in the guard-room of this Guildford Castle. From these chatterers we may, if we will listen, learn something more regarding

The Doom of Ælfrede.

"Oh death, made proud with pure and princely beauty,
The earth had not a hole to hide this deed."

" So," whispered one, grounding his double-bladed axe : " some freak of Harold the king, I guess."

" Harold the tyrant; rather."

" Is't true he keeps the real Athelyngs in foreign thrall with Richard of Normandy ?"

" Worse—worse—hark ye, Herouard : Queen Emma, their mother, the once bright *maid of Normandy*, hates them for their blood of Ethelred, and she would rather set the crown on her pet Hardyknute, or Harthocnut, by Cnutz, or Canutus, or Cnute, or Knut, whiche'er his name, who is trifling his time in Denmark."

" And Harold ?"

" Hush ! he has forged letters in Emma's name, in this wise : ' So fare ye well, my dearest bowels and very in- wards of my heart.' "

" The harpy ! And what—"

" Oh, Ælfred hath taken the bait, and is coming hither-

ward, poor innocent lamb, with six hundred men of
Flanders, by Sandwich, in ships of Godwin: the sly old
fox, hung round with gold bossed shields, now a gift to
Hardyknut."

"And Ælfred trusts to Harold, hey?"

"Why, look ye, the Lady Editha comes with the Abbot
of Croyland to pray for him, for she is love itself. As
the rhymer has it—

   " 'Sicut spina rosam genuit Godwinus Editham.'

Yet 'twas a brave sight, Herouard—the fine ships rounding
the foreland, the men with gilded mail and rings and
braslets: and then the homage on his knees at Canterbury, and then the progress along the Pilgrim's Way to
Winchester. Ah, well-a-day, your ear for a secret. The
poor Etheling will not leave this keep alive! 'twill be—
hush—his cell and his shamble-house. Seest thou those
red pennons o'er Harold's camp on Gyldismore? Trust
me, their stain is blood."

"Blood!"

"Ay, the Earl is jealous of the boy, and his wife, the
daughter of Cnute,—he would crown himself, or wed his
girl to Edward. Hush, hush! they come! and by Saint
Hubert, Harold himself."

   "And Godwin at his heels."

"And Emma in all her pride."

("The lustrous pearl of Normandy," though Anglo-
Danish, was the daughter of a duke and the widow and
wife of a king: so she was clad in tunic and mantle of
costly tissue, a veil of gold pendent from her brilliant

diadem. As Beowulf records, " Mindful of her descent circled with gold, and so she walked with her boys yboth.")

" This," said Godwin, addressing Ælfred with a smile, "this is *terra regis,* your own demesne, in line direct from your namesake, noble prince."

So passed the pageant on to Guildsdown, as the sun shot his fiery beams athwart their revelry.

'Twas midnight now, and the soldiers were lodged in those deep chalk caves or chambers, we yet see in the quarry still called Whitehall—the entrance in Quarry Street, and the portcullis grooves are even now visible.

Well, at midnight, the Saxon brigands arose, and in came Harold's villains, and they decimated the Norman host : only the tenth man was saved. Some were dragged to the crypt—the cellar of the Angel, toward the new church on the east bank of the river—and others were hamstrung, or scalped and chained, and brought to the High Street, and one and all murdered in cold blood.

But the people were wroth, and rose on the assassins, who fled to Wibbas Dune (Worplesdon), to 'hide themselves in the sanctuary, and then " the king's bailiff had no demand on that account."

Prince Edward (the Confessor) started from his couch in affright.

" Where, where is my brother ?" he cried. "Strange, strange, I see him not, yet I do feel his spirit on my breast : his heart is throbbing wildly against mine. Ah ! blood, blood—his eyes, his eyes—look, mother, look !" and the Prince fell back in convulsions, his palms pressing on his eyelids, while burning tears, ay, like drops

of blood, were streaming over his cheeks, and his whole
frame was writhing in agony. Yet none could divine the
cause, until the doom of Ælfrede was whispered from lip
to lip, amid the execration of the kingdom.

It was the wondrous mystery of the *sympathy of sense:*
the boy, whose head lay in the lap of his mother, Emma,
was feeling, pang by pang, the agony of him who was, at
that moment, writhing beneath the fangs of his torturers.

The doom of Ælfrede was a dreadful truth: yet so
varied are the records of the chroniclers, that it might
seem but a coinage or a myth.

The chronicle of John Harding is in this wise—

> "Some chronicle saieth he putte out bothe his eyen,
> Fro which he dyed sone for pain and woo:
> Some others sayin he slette his wombe full keen,
> The lengest gut to a stacke he nayled tho,
> Led hym about the stacke (ther with muche) wo
> Till all came out that was his wombe within,
> Thus sleugh thei hym with (sobteltie and) gyn."

In the *Polychronicon* of Radulf Higdon, it runs
thus—

> "Alfred Hely missus,
> It was decreed
> They shoud him
> To Ely-bury Fen,
> But soon their royal prize
> Bereft they of his eyes."

Grafton tells us "they put out the eyen of Alphured,
and sent him to Ely—wyndynge theire guttes out."

This is the record of the Abbot of Jervaul, in York-
shire:—"He was put on a hack-horse, his legs tied under
him, to Gillingham, in Kent, and then to Ely Monastery—

L'isle de Hely." And Speed :—" His bowels were cut open, and tied to a stake bit by bit."

Little thought the great Alfred that his tented field of Guildown would be so basely stained with the blood of his namesake : and little thought the demons who played chief parts in this tragedy, to what degradation they would come at last. We would fain believe that Emma was guiltless of the blood of her offspring : yet this lofty creature was doomed to an ordeal by her son, the Confessor, for her share in it, and for another high crime— adultery with Alwyn her cousin, nay, it was even whispered with Harold Harefoot her reputed son, but, in truth, the bastard of Cnute and Elgiva. .

The Queen had fled to Bruges, where she was fostered by Athela, or Adela, the daughter of Robert, king of France, and wife of Baldwin of Flanders. On her return to England she was adjudged the ordeal of the plough-shares in Winchester. The test was, indeed, a triumph of her innocence and chastity, for she passed over un-consciously, her eyes being bandaged, and calmly asked " When do I come to the ploughshares ?"

These are the words of Fabyan, " Vpon the morne she was blyndefelde, and lad vnto the place bytwene II men, where ye iron laye glowynge hote, and passed the IX sharys vnhurte." One chronicle imputes this judgment to Harold, whose body was exhumed in the Confessor's reign, and thrown into the Thames, for this cruelty to his mother Emma.

Then followed the doom of Godwin, the arch traitor, at the banquet of the Confessor, who had taxed him with the crime. So Godwin took bread before the king, and said : "I eat holy bread before thee, O king, and my eating thereof shall be the probing of my innocence, so I beseech you bless the morsel." Then Edward blessed the morsel in his hand, and Godwin with great solemnity took the bread from the King, and placed it in his mouth, and did essay to eat, but was therewith choked.

This is the record of Hardynge—

> " Full well and trewe I fynde it dayly nowe,
> Had ye ne bene, thus had helpe me my brother
> Therl then to the Kyng on side gan bowe,
> And sayd if I wer cause, I praye God nowe,
> This breade passe not my throte, but dead I bee,
> And straungled here anone that ye maye see
> At his prayer anone with that he died
> For with that breade straungled was he, ey stound
> It might not passe his throte."

And yet, in the " Mirror of Magistrates," of 1610, Godwin thus pleads gently in his lament for Alfred—

> " The more his virtues were, whose blood I spilt,
> Remorseless wretch, the greater was my guilt."

Then of Hardyknut, who was King of Denmark, while his brothers Sweyn and Harold ruled in Norway and England, it is thus written :—" Sone after Hardyknutus, beying merry at Lambyth, sodenly waxyd downe, and wythin viii dayes after dyed."

Here endeth the doom of Alfred. Yet furthermore is writ in Latin and Norman French, in a book now in Gonville and Caius College, Cambridge, thus marked on its title-page :—" Ci cumence la Estoire de Seint Ædward le Roi translatio du Latin."

> " At famed Egdean meets many a proud Queen,
> At Adversane they meet again,
> At Catherine Hill they bid farewell."

So runs the rhyme, and this sand-rock is St. Catherine's or Drake Hill, the site of one of the statute fairs of the South Saxon country.

It is crowned with the iron-stone chapel of "St. Katheryn in Ertindon," or Artington, the Roman *Ardoneon*. It was founded by the seventh Henry, although tradition affirms it to be one of the chapels built by sisters Katheryn and Martha.

Yonder great house of Shalford, beyond the Wey, was graced in the olden time by two very bright creatures, that shone on their green meadows like pearls set in emeralds. The "fair Geraldine" of Henry Howard, Earl of Surrey, was long worshipped, like Laura and Beatrice, in the burning lays of her poet lover : her wooing was a pure platonism. The love of Isabel de Vipont was as pure and as glowing as the passion of Juliet or Viola, yet was it smothered in her bosom, as she thought, for ever and a day.

You would never guess the charm that broke the spell which seemed to seal her fate, and raised the latent spark of love again into a flame.

An echo from the chapel—

"The Ruse of the Ring."

" If you had known the virtue of the ring,
  Or your own honour to contain the ring,
  You would not then have parted with the ring."

AN evening in autumn, early in 1300 : a flood of golden
light is bronzing the woodland greens : the moon's pale
disc is just tipping the beeches with a coronet of silver,
and glistening on the grey walls of Guildford Castle.
As the evening shadows were falling, and the wood-
doves were cooing themselves to rest among the elms
of Braboeuf, and the last drowsy tinkling of the sheep-
bell was echoing on Guildown, a young traveller, about
twenty, with cheeks glowing as those of Clytie with the
kisses of the sun, was standing in the northern doorway
of the chapel. Beneath a white cloak, he wore a mantle
of the finest cloth of *Baldekins*, fresh from Babylon : his
hat was of low crown and broad brim, with cockle shells
and relics of Mount Sinai in front, and he was shod with
the Doric shoe, a leathern scrip hanging from his shoulder.
And there he stood, leaning pensively on his knobbed
Bourdon-staff. As the twilight was fading fast, he was
looking down in deep thought on the valley, when he
heard a plashing in the Wey that winds at the base of
the sand-rock, and beheld a light shallop on the bank,
which a girl, bright as the moonbeam, had paddled across
the Pilgrim's Ferry. She moored the shallop to a willow-

bough and, light as a fairy, leaped on the bank, and
having thrice crossed her brow at the spring bubbling
from the rock, and drawing close her hood, she mounted
the hill to the chapel-door. As the stranger retreated to
the newel staircase, a fragment of which yet remains,
she warbled in the most plaintive and seraphic tones—

> " Oh, the heart is chilled like a frozen flower,
> That is curdled by frost in a maiden's bower,
> And its freshness is withering, hour by hour,
>   If love's not there !
>
> " But it bounds like a joyous thought in Spring,
> Or the tremulous pant of a love-bird's wing,
> Or the trill of a wild throat carolling,
>   If love be there !"

With a sigh she entered the chapel, while the stranger,
with palpitating heart, watched the beautiful devotee
thus stealing on his solitude. She kneeled awhile at the
shrine of St. Katherine, and if we had listened closely
we might hear on her lips the subdued cadence of a rude
hymn, one line of which still embosses four of the five
bells in Shalford Church :

> " Lord, plead my cause against my foes,
> Confound their force and might;
> Fight on my part against my foes,
> That seek with me to fight."

Hearing the rustling of the stranger's cloak, she started
and exclaimed, " You are early, Master Walter, yet am
I right glad you are here : I have told my beads, and

breathed my vespers in my closet, and now I do lack
your solemn counsel sorely, for my father will want
you an hour hence : oh! save me, Master Walter,
save me!"

Now, this Walter Herman she spoke of to the stranger
was a very devout young man and fresh to the priest-
hood: we believe he confessed half the catholic girls in
Ertington. Well, here was a dilemma for an ardent
youth, yet the most delicate alternative, he thought, was
to fold his cloak over his brow and listen patiently,
though we do fear that a spice of curiosity had some
share in the ruse.

The maiden raised not her eyes from the floor while
she thus spoke, *sotto voce :*

"I do claim your deepest pity, holy father, and your
blessing. My sire hath pledged my maiden hand to a
very fool, a golden calf, that his uncle John de Brunyfeld brings here to woo me. E'en were my heart yet
free, *he* knows not how to woo a lady, but he would win
me, forsooth, by the broad acres his cousin's death has
thrown into his lap : that cousin whom, even as my life—
Ah! I shame to tell you, yet, forgive me, Master Walter,
for I have a woman's heart, that once warmed to love and
truth : but Ernold is an icicle doth freeze me with his
touch : 'tis but the memory of my blighted faith that
keeps my heart alive. 'Tis a sad story : ah! that I
should live to tell it. Yes, when my lover kneeled and
asked me of my sire, woe's me! that father swore an
oath against his suit couched on some deadly feud of
family. Wretch that I was to check my smiles : and yet,

like a duteous child, I might not stain a father's oath in
heaven, however shame it were to look coy and cold
e'en while my heart was bursting. Oh! I have sorrowed
for it deeply : hour by hour have I wept and wailed for
him who fled and fell at Ascalon : and now his idiot
cousin doth wait to wed me, and bear me to the halls
of Clifford. Yes, you do pity me, I know it : even from
your sigh : then, tell me, is it fair, is it maidenly, to
cheat a father's will ? Yet I, too, have an oath in heaven.
Wilt shrive me in the rankness of my falsehood, prythee,
speak !"

The stranger spoke not, but sighed and assented with a
nod.

" Then must I whisper closer, Master Walter, for even
the night-moth must not hear the secret of a frozen heart."

No wonder that of the stranger was throbbing wildly as
the beautiful girl still whispered with her lips close to his
ear, " The heart of a maiden is a pure and holy thing :
'twere better sure devote its love to Heaven in its vestal
purity than breathe a truthless vow and taint its homage
with a broken faith."

She paused a moment and trembled like an aspen leaf.
" There is one only way—come closer, Master Walter : 'tis
you alone can save me—you alone must wed me : nay,
you need not tremble at your proselyte."

" Yet," whispered he, " how will your lover—"

" Told I you not he fell at Ascalon : ah, my cheek, I
blush to think on what I've said, but thou wilt listen
still ! There is *a ring*—Lord Vipont keeps it holy e'en as
'twere a relic of a saint : its legend were too long to tell

—yet know you that it is absolute on our destiny : once placed by man around a maiden's finger, 'tis an espousal true and holy. Wilt thou do it? I know thou wilt—thou wouldst not wed me to a fool ! "

" Yet I— "

" Still listen, holy father, for I do trust thee with all a virgin's faith. The rites of marriage will suffer no desecration by our transient plighting, for thou art a priest, and sworn to singleness of life : that moment over and we part—for ever. The senseless wooing of Ernold will cease at once to my inmost joy, and a cell will be the home of *sister Isabel*. Thou wilt save me, bless me, Master Walter, wilt thou ?—ay, I knew thou wouldst ! And now away to Shalford straight, for I do fear that Ernold hath the ring. Were we not discreet and bold, one little hour may yet seal my fate—let us away, and I will tell you— Hush—! "

As Isabel de Vipont paddled her confessor across the Wey, Walter Herman himself entered the chapel, but there was none to meet him, or greet him. The prude will frown of course at all this treachery, but they who revere the sanctity of woman's heart and its pure love will smile away the frown in a moment : however, the stern moralist, sitting in judgment on this stranger, may bring *him* in guilty upon his honour. We shall see in the upshot.

Two fair sisters were trembling with anxiety by the rich mantelpiece and firegrate in the dining-room, when they were summoned by Lord Vipont to the chapel of Shalford House. The baron was richly robed for the solemn occasion, and Brunyfeld and Ernold de Tangley in waiting by his side, when missives were sent to the hall for Master Walter Herman, and the stranger entered the chapel, his hood concealing his visage, and he at once laid his hands in blessing on Isabel and Idonea de Vipont who were kneeling at their fauld-stools.

"Welcome, Master Herman, welcome," said Lord Vipont: "so thou hast shrieved my wayward child, and thy holy lips have taught her to obey. Give thy father thy last virgin-kiss, my child, and then the rites of the ring. Know ye all this jewelled circlet is sacred as the oath to Heaven on all in whom courses the current of our noble blood: e'en without the Church's pale it seals a maiden's vow of plighted faith, and cannot be revoked. Yet the holy Church is my honoured mother, and Vipont will not shame his creed by maimed rites, so, holy father, art thou in presence here to sanctify: bless thou the ring."

The priest took the glittering hoop from Ernold's clutch and pressed it to his lips, and in a moment it circled the virgin's finger. Ernold de Tangley shivered, and waxed pale as his shirt, though he scarce knew why, and Lord Vipont became scarlet as the altar-cloth, for he knew the mighty magic of the ring: he grasped his dagger-hilt with one hand, and the priest's arm with the other, while Isabel fell prostrate at his feet.

"Pardon, my lord and father, pardon for Master Walter and for me: I am still your truthful child, and my soul is saved by him. Father, I am the bride of Heaven: the spousal robe of sister Isabel will be a frock of serge, her bridal chamber a cell of stone in Newark Abbey, and then, Clifford, I am thine for ever!"

"Ay, for ever!" echoed the stranger as the hood fell from his shoulder and displayed the gear of a gallant knight. "Thou art espoused of Heaven, Isabel, for Heaven ·hath blessed the ring that made thee mine. The cloister! no, the Hall of Clifford will henceforth be the home of sister Isabel."

In a moment the truth flashed on all, for all knew Roger Clifford: without greeting his cousin even with a word, Ernold had vanished from the scene, and Lord Vipont obeyed at once the judgment of the ring, and staunched the death-feud of Vipont and of Clifford by blessing the heart of his child. We need not tell how Shalford and ·Aldefaud, and Skipton, and Egremont, were again a happy brotherhood: we need not tell, for every maiden will guess how, on many an autumn evening, sister Isabel did paddle her holy father across the Wey to Katherine's aisle, and how—but the rest shall be a secret still.

THE secluded demesne of ancient *Loseley* and the deep green of its oaks and elms are in perfect keeping with its heavy gables.

It is among the very topmost boughs of these old manorial trees that the rare Purple Emperor, *Apotura iris*, loves to haunt, his little humble satellite *Thecla*, the purple hair-streak, flitting far below. The royal fly feeds more like an alderman of old: the game flavour of a dead pigeon will ever draw him down to earth.

It is in these richly wooded districts that we may see

the special beauty of every season, the pale green of
spring, the rosy bloom of May and June, the golden
bronze of July and August, and the sombre hues of fir,
yew, cedar, juniper, and holly, like beauty spots on the
cheek of the snow in winter.

Lothesley is the "*Lot of the Pasture.*" We may revere
it as a special memory of the Tudor and the Stuart, when
the Mores held their high state within its chambers :
would that every stone of the venerable pile might last for
ever ! If we study the archæology and the legend of these
old houses, as specially illustrated in the annals of monastic scribes, we at once regard the sacred recesses of their
muniment chests in which these treasures are stored, as
the precious reliquaries of historic truth, the holy-wells
from which the streams of incident have been so
copiously drawn.

You see yonder gateway in the western wing : had you
stood beneath it one evening in the seventeenth century
you might have heard the wailing of a fond old father
echoing along the gallery. The secret of his sorrow is an
old story, but all may not have read or listened to the
legend of

The Lady Lift.

> "It is too true an evil, gone she is.
> And what's to come ? "

In yon mullioned window a taper-light is burning dimly :
it is little more than a glowworm spark, and you would

scarce note its flickering. There is one, however, to whom that glimmer is an evening star of the brightest promise, like Hero's torch to Leander as he floated across the Hellespont. The young clerk had watched the window for an hour or twain, and his heart beat quick as he caught the dancing light in the long gallery : the next moment a lady glided from the postern : she was yet in the fresh prime and bloom of womanhood, and, like Juliet's—

> " Her beauty hangs upon the cheek of night,
> Like a rich jewel in an Æthiop's ear."

" Be silent, for mercy's sake," she whispered.

" Nay, I spoke not, sweet one."

" Your eyes *looked* as you were speaking, and I will believe them, for eyes do never fail in truth : lips, alas, too often—nay—hush ! hark !"

" 'Tis nothing but the eve-jar's murmur."

" Ah, whatever it be, 'twill wake the house, and this cruel door to creak on its hinges, thus : haste, haste, or Margery will catch me yet—her ears are quick when she is wide awake. Heaven grant the poppy water lulls her into slumber : but my father, too, he is in the green chamber —hark, hark, she stirs, and I must answer an' she call.

" Why, lady-bird," screamed a voice, " what, Anne More, I say : ha, an open door ! What wakest thou, sweet pet ? why so late in the gallery—why so late ?"

At the moment she was folded in the arms of her lover, and he kissed her lips audibly.

"Be quiet, foolish boy," she murmured: and then more loudly, "It is only a night-owl, my honey nurse."

"Owl, owl!" exclaimed the crone: "I vow I heard—"

"Nay, an owl, I assure you: so prythee be quiet, sweet Margery. Quit not your warm bed: leave the owl to me: he'll soon be off if you let him alone. I'll silence him, I promise you."

"Why, what have you to do with owls, a maid like you? you should be sleeping—not watching, pretty one. The midnight bell hath struck, and you lose your beauty sleep, and I have dreamed of danger: the night is chill —to bed, to bed."

"Nay, I am safe, be sure—safer, ay, and better where I am : and I am warm as a toast—very, very warm."

Her lover had lifted her in his arms, and in a moment she was strapped on a soft pillion at the postern door. One moment more, over the turf and through the gate, and they are off in a canter, leaving Loseley Park far behind.

"How can I thank you enough, sweet Anne," exclaimed the youth : "what do I owe you ?"

"Your true love, John," she replied, in glowing accents: "mind I must have it all, *all*—you are rich in it : there is no debt in love's schedule, you, his steward, cannot pay, and yet I should doubt you, John—I saw your scribbling scapegrace—

      "' He is stark mad, who ever says
        That he has been in love an hour '—

Is't so ?"

"That was before I knew Anne More," he said.

" Well, well, John, you see I *do* trust you with all a maiden's confidence."

This dialogue and more was breathed as they flew by Brabœuf Manor, a fine old place, to the lone village of Compton.

" So, thanks to our steed," he cried, " we are here, and there are *they*."

Donne lifted Anne More from the pillion, trembling like an aspen, as he whispered, " We must not linger, sweet one : there be fleet steeds will follow, trust me." At that moment they were at the porch door of Compton Church : at the next, the shade of a dark lantern was drawn, and a dim light streamed over the ancient mould-ing of the arched rood-loft of the very quaint chantry-chapel, now the Loseley sitting, and lighted up the deeply splayed stained window.

" You are true and good as gold, Samuel Brooke," said the lover to a young priest, robed in his surplice, " and where is Christopher our father ? "

" Why, how now, sweetheart : fear not, fear not."

Anne More was trembling with her lips wide apart.

" Hark ! " she whispered : " heard you not? I do fear me that the night-owl boded evil."

" Nay, my love, 'tis the wind in the pine-grove, nothing more."

But at the instant a bell was heard faint in the distance.

" Nay, pretty trembler : why, that is nought but the sheep-bell in the Ley."

" No, no, they are up in Loseley, and we are lost."

"Then off with your glove at once—tears ?—nay, nay, we'll foil them yet—off, off, the ring—quick, and then away."

So the marriage rites were slurred, the service hurried over in disorder, but at the moment the ring was on the lady's finger, Sir George More, with a posse of menials, rushed into the chapelry.

The bride fell into her husband's arms, and then on her knees to Sir George, and sobbed out, "I have sinned against my father, alas, alas ! "

The baronet, choking with emotion, exclaimed, " Ay, you have played me false, Anne : you—so pure, so maidenly, and I so fond a father. But 'tis well : we are in time " (he dreamed not love were quick in ceremonials as in its making): " thou art still Anne More." The lady's silence confessed a negative, yet he continued, " And who hath dared seduce my darling ? "

The bridegroom lifted his eyes.

" What, thou, John Donne, thou traitor : in chains with him, and off to my Lord Ellesmere : we'll teach him to keep his clerks at York-house, nor let them loose to pick and steal from honest men ! My good brother, blind as a bat is my brother of Ellesmere, and so is my sister Bess, to lose my jewel thus : but thou art still Anne More : and so bind the varlet tight, and quick for Loseley. Nay, my wild girl, no airs :" and Sir George dragged her into the coach, and they were soon again in Loseley Hall, and so ended the bridal.

Margery was awaiting in deep anxiety, for she loved her pet dearly.

"Here," muttered Sir George," "here's your truant, madam: this is your watch and ward is it? so off with your keys, quick:" and he snatched them from her girdle, and opening a chamber door, he thrust in his daughter, and then having double-locked it, he gave them to a waiting-maid at his elbow, the falconer's daughter. "Here, Janet," he said, "young eyes and ears are more alive to mischief than blear and blight: keep thou ready watch, and call your brother, girl."

"I am here, sir," said the falconer's son.

"Lie you there, sirrah, at her chamber door, and for your life, nor sleep nor stir till cock-crow, and then gird you up for London: for a boy, thou art the surest guide in Surrey."

And so Loseley Hall was once more sunk in quiet, Sir George esconcing himself in the green room, close to Anne's chamber: Margery was in dudgeon and disgrace, the only expression of her lips being a sort of sensual smack when her tansey pudding and mint-cup were brought to her cell.

The moon was still regent of the sky, when our group of actors in this night piece were in the courtyard. Sir George, who had for a moment retired to his library, held in his hand the committal he had drawn of John Donne, for abduction, to the Marshalsea or Fleet, until the Star-Chamber or the Ecclesiastical Court could sit in judgment on his crime.

"And now, young Merlin," said Sir George, "you have a sacred trust—see you are true to it."

The young falconer bowed low, but kept his face

U

averted, his eye fixed on the hawk on his wrist, the
feather of his cap falling completely over his cheek : for,
like the Newhaven fish-wives with their Sunday creels,
the falconer never rode even to prayer without his hawk.
So busy was he with his bird that Sir George, as the
cavalcade started off, grumbled in his ear—

"Hark ye, hark ye, young shaver, see you to your
charge and not your hawk : if either flies away, let it be
your bird, if not, tremble for your ears, varlet—so off with
ye, and round by Pirford : nay, hear, and Master Wolley
there will join you straight for London."

And now a day is gone by. Sir George More sat in his
drawing-room that had been just renewed and beautified
in very early Tudor for the Queen's visit, but the richly
panelled ceiling, deeply embossed moulding, and gorgeous
pendants, had this morning no charm for him.

"So," he muttered, as he crept to his breakfast, "treason
will not escape me." Yet for once he looked not in his
folio Shakspeare on his lectern, without which he rarely
broke his fast. In gloom and solitude he passed two days,
the falconer's girl in all callings, especially in the missives
from Sir George to his daughter, the substitute of Dame
Margery.

"So," said the Baronet, "the old girl is in dudgeon, is
she—the dullard, she should rather joy for the cageing of
her nurseling. All safe, eh ? "

"I hope so, sir," said the girl.

"Hope so: you know it, slut !" growled her master :
the door is locked, and you have the key : she must be
safe, so close too to one who loves her, eh !"   ·

Sir George caught not the roguish twinkle in the girl's eyes, for his own were wandering to the shield of 1568, even now in the window, and then anon to the device of the mulberry tree on the cornice.

"*Morus, tarde moriens cito moriturus.*"

"Prophetic," he muttered, "aye, prophetic : clear as daylight : faith, I guessed it not before. Well, our lineage may endure for ages yet : George More, like the blighted berries, will drop before his time, and all from this wild girl's folly. Why, what's this ? " (taking the packet that the wench, with downcast eyes, had presented to him). " Esperance ! from Northumberland ! eh—why, how, how came it here ?"

" My brother, sir—is just now—here—"

" Back already, impossible ! " exclaimed Sir George, tearing off the seal, then, starting from his chair, he screamed out, " Married, married ! Call Margery this moment."

" She's taking her mint-cup in the buttery, sir."

Sir John heeded not the boy at his elbow : his eye was transfixed on the letter till Margery entered.

" Out with the truant, woman ! " he exclaimed. " Why, you're drunk, beldame."

Margery shook her head, and pointed to the motto over the buttery door, " *siti non ebrietate.*"

" Out with her ! " she mumbled, " out from whence ?"

Sir George seized the keys, and rushing out flung wide the chamber door, and found the room tenantless.

" Blear and blight ! " the dame continued, " why, that's rich, i' faith. Whose else, I wonder ? an thou hadst

u 2

peeped *under* the falconer's broad hat, with half a glance thee would have seen a braid of golden locks, and a marble brow, not the burly cheek and red crop of a bumpkin like that. Oh, where were your barnacles, Sir George?"

The truth flashed on the Baronet at once.

"You cockatrice!" he cried, "why the ducking-stool in the mill-mead at Guildford were too good for you."*

"Degraded, worthless," and many more isolated words burst from his lips, and then he chopped out the sentences of his letters: "Wolley to watch her—reconciled — never — dismissed by Egerton, so far well. But a thing of seventeen — cruel, cruel. And what blurts out my fool of a sister? Heard him recite — pshaw! a loose ballad about Phryne, I warrant me. George More you're a fool—an Oxford boy, that, like Picus Mirandola, was born, not made wise, has filched you of your green girl, Sir George."

Another lapse of time.

Months had passed, and Sir George sat in his muniment-room, his coffre-fort unlocked at his side, displaying those choice MSS. and precious deeds—the Loseley papers. There lay the autographs of Lady Jane Grey, as *quene*, and Elizabeth, and James Stuart, and others, on which the Baronet glanced with a listless eye, for he was very ill at ease, and then he unconsciously opened a doleful letter of some months' date (the seal—Christ on an anchor,

---

* The remains of the ducking posts were in Guildford in 1710, and there is the record of the ducking of one Margery—a scold—in that same year.

the crest—a sheaf of serpents) sent to him with a copy of Donne's *Biathanatus*, or Self-Homicide. The letter was subscribed "J. D. A.D. undun, from my lodginge by y° Savoy."

Thither he had retired on the resolution of the Ecclesiastical Court, his wife being taken to Pirford, whence he instituted a law-suit to recover her, and failing, fled to France.

"Self-Homicide," murmured Sir George: "sad, sad— all-prophetic, and I *her* sire. A thief in the dark—'tis monstrous!" and he grumbled till he slept.

The suit failed of course, while Anne Donne was wandering about forlorn by the Sheerwater Lake and the pinetum and the decoy at Pirford, and watching her wasting baby.

One night Sir George had been dreaming of his daughter, when he was awoke, as the midnight bell was striking, by the rolling of a thunder-peal, and the gate-bell was pulled, and the porter announced a benighted stranger.

"Shelter of course. A More never closed his door to distress." The wanderer flung his drenched cloak aside.

"Donne," exclaimed Sir George, "the despoiler, and you dare—"

"Pity, pity!" entreated the clerk, in a subdued tone.

"And why art here, thou traitor?"

"I sought *her*, sir, my wife, by her own desire."

"And she has written, eh?"

"She came herself, sir."

" Art dreaming, knave ? "

" I was dreaming, sir, when she came—may I tell the tale ?

" I was in my chamber in the embassy, and drowned in sleep, when, in the hour of darkness, Anne, my beloved, glided to my bed—her hair dishevelled, and pale as marble, and a dead child folded in her arms, and she laid its little lips to mine—— "

" Varlet ! " exclaimed Sir George, rising from his chair, " thus far I have endured what grief alone could force on me. I look on thee with loathing, John Donne, and might well thrust you forth from a house where you have stained my name and scutcheon, but mercy pleads for you at this dark hour. Yet mark me ! a dry suit, a manchet, and a stoup are all these once honoured walls will dole out to a traitor. So with the dawn, see you to it, Ferncombe : " and he waved the intruder off.

Master Donne retired with the groom-in-waiting, and at sunrise he was wending his way toward London, where the day before his wife had *borne a dead child !*

And now it was the year 1603. The Queen was dead and James had mounted the throne. About the middle of August, Loseley and its lord were in their holiday suit, and no wonder, for soon galloped into the court-yard a courier heralding the approach of royalty : for James also was fond of progresses. The whole posse of retainers lined the hall, and Sir George himself stood at the portal, his plumed cap in his hand, as a king and a queen stepped down from a coach of state.

Anne of Denmark was ushered at once to the chamber

of Elizabeth, and old Margery's eyes were riveted by the Queen's vardingale.

"So you have more taste than the sultana, woman," said Anne, "for when my lady Wych was presented to her, that slave of the seraglio laughed aloud."

The King, in his suit of sables, first eulogized the last proof copy of More's "Demonstration of God in His Works," and then the rich chimney-piece, still in the drawing-room, caryatides and a tablet of shields supported by fluted corinthian columns, over a pillar with entablature in high relief.

"Why, your place smacks of the old Norman, mine host," said the King.

"An't please your Majesty, we boast even of the *Saxon*," replied the Knight: "Osmund held of the Confessor long before the Conqueror gave it to Roger Montgomery of Arundel and Shrewsbury, for his prowess in the field of Hastings, and, certes, our own family have not shown the white feather. But, the Queen, the Queen !" as Anne was marshalled to the chamber in high state.

"We are beholden to you, Master More," she said, "your very floors savour of royalty. Elizabeth of Tudor once pressed our couch, my King."

"Ay," rejoined the Baronet, bending low, "and Henry her sire, and Katherine Parr. Yonder, on the wainscot, is their monogram, 'H.R. K.P.' That bed hath been a sacred thing with us ever since the Tudor pressed it. Yet, certes, your Graces are more trustful in George More, than good Queen Bess with his ancestors."

" As how ? "

Sir George opened his ponderous oaken coffer where
some leaves of the precious Loseley MSS. lay enshrined :
and the royal pair laughed aloud as they read the letter
of Sir Christopher Hatton, Master of the Horse : "Uppo'
tewsdaye next wich shalbe the xxvii of the moneth
dine at Okynge, and that night go to bed to y^r house—
to th' end you may take order to see it made sweete and
meete to receave her Ma—tie."

" And sweet it must have been : for the Queen, madam,
often slept four or five nights at Loseley, so that Wyng-
field, one of our jealous pates, thus warned my ancestor :

" ' She is now detirmened to come into your hous, and
for thatt ytt shalbe the grete trouboul and a henderenes
unto you, inded a grete bore, as the host is counseld
t' avoyde his family.' "

And royalty laughed again.

" But, prythee, good Sir George," said Anne, looking
around, " your lily of Loseley—why greets she not her
queen ? "

" She is stolen, Madame," replied he. " Know you
not ? "

" Stolen !—and the thief ? " said the King.

" An't please you, a poor clerk of Ellesmere's."

" Fore George ! the very boy—worth his weight in
gold, Master More—fitter to serve a king, so said old
Egerton.   Is't he ? "

" May be, sire," replied Sir George, " but for a More,
he should be a dean at least."

" Well, well, we'll see—we'll see ! "

"And for our maid of honour, we will wait the morrow," added the Queen, winking at the King. "So, Master More, your hand." And Sir George led the Queen to the banquet, wondering the while what the royal lips could mean.

As the Queen sat at the banquet :

"It joys me, thrice honoured Madam," said Sir George, "to see your Majesty in the chair worked by the virgin queen."

"Ah!" replied James, "she knew I was to wear her shoes and press her seat :" and then he whispered to a lacquey, "Ashton—the cockaleekie."

As the banquet was served, the King addressed his host, "Thanks, thanks, Master More. And now your zeal in the Overbury case might make you Lieutenant of the Tower, but Baby Charles begged it for Steenie. Wait awhile, wait awhile, 'twill be yours anon, for Steenie——Ah, the cockaleekie !" And the King set to with his dish in real earnest.

"The wisest fool in Christendom speaks truth, George," whispered Sir Edward Zouch, the court-buffoon, in the Baronet's ear, "Buckingham's star is waning. Why, listen ! Taylor, the King's waterman, will tell you.

> " He wears a farm in shoe-strings edged with gold,
> And spangled garters worth a copyhold,
> A beaver band and feather for the head,
> Prized at the Church's tythe—the poor man's bread."

But the King's eye is on us—hush !"

The feast was over, and the night was waning when the royal guests arose, and Sir George, with lighted tapers,

led the way to the Tudor-chamber, and, as he bent his
knee at the door, the King hung round his neck a jewel
pendant on a blue riband, and said, in very gracious
accents, "A good night, Sir George More, Chancellor of
the Most Noble Order of the Garter."

The morrow came, and Sir George was in his study
arranging his copy and his proofs, for even with the
slumbering of royalty overhead, he forgot not his sheets
of proof for which he left those of his couch. On this
privacy a man booted and spurred stalked in unannounced.

"Why, man, how darest thou?" exclaimed the baronet,
when e'en the Lord's anointed——"

"'Twas the Lord's anointed sent me," interrupted the
man, as he took off his cloak and bowed; "ay, under
hand and seal—*ecce signum.*"

"What again, thou thief and traitor, see'st thou this?"
and Sir George pointed to the motto over the door.
"*Probis non pravis.* Ah!—an apron! Why, what in
Heaven's name means all this mummery? Art mad,
John Donne, or scullion to the devil, eh?"

"That I wear not borrowed plumes, sir, as this will
tell you."

"Eh, the King's own seal, I swear! What, invite
thee to dinner? A hoax—a hoax! Thou'lt not get it,
John. Put not thy faith in princes, John. Why, even
I was promised Earl at least, and still but a poor red
hand on my scutcheon."

"Well, you found it all a joke, eh?"

"A mighty pleasant one, sir, tho' the King did frown
a bit when I did take my seat."

"Nay, nay," he cried, "my cockaleekie is for crowned heads, man. A bishop, look you, might edge in his apron : but a dean!—no, no—even of St. Paul's. I dropped on my knee, sir, for I guessed it all, and his Majesty went on : 'Doctor Donne, though I called you to dinner, you sit not down with me. Yet I will carve for you of a dish that I know you love well—for knowing you love London, I do, therefore, make you Dean of St. Paul's, and when I have dined then do you take your beloved dish home to your study, say grace there to yourself, and much good may it do thee : and so when you are in lawn sleeves, perhaps—there, that will do, the cockaleekie will be cold.' But here is Anne, sir."

"Anne, Anne, where ?"

"In her father's arms," replied Anne of Denmark, stealing from the closet, as her namesake sank on his bosom, and bathed his cheek with tears.

"My child, my child ! Well, well, as my royal mistress smiles on thee, shall a father frown ? But we must have thee wed *again*, Anne : ay, in broad daylight, Anne. And then your sermon, Master Clerk, and your text—let us see—what shall't be ?"

"' Put not your faith in princes,' sir."

"Nay, nay, ' the King's name is a tower of strength.' Be that your theme for ever more, Master Donne, for it has gained you that you might else have whistled for, my forgiveness, Master Donne."

"Aye, and a silk apron to boot," chuckled the King, "so quick with your *pseudo-martyr* man, and then come to St. James's for your cockaleekie, man, and then you shall read the proofs of King James, *Basilicon Doron.*"

They who would read the love-letters of John Donne to Anne More, his sermon on his wife's death, and the epitaph on her marble, must search the records that lay hid for two centuries in a large oak-chest in Loseley, and have been arranged by Kempe, with the title of " Loseley Manuscripts."

We cannot traverse the County of Surrey without think-ing of its chronicles. This quiet old town was the home of Owen Manning, whose notes were so well worked out by William Bray. They may well be proud of their minister of St. Peter and St. Paul which preserves the initials of Henry VII. in one of its mullioned windows.

Godalming, God-helming, or Godelminge is *Englished* by one wiseacre, *Godiva's Alms:* and by another the *Shadow of God's Gift.*

Among the antient crones who stand beneath their lintels, wagging their tongues from morn to night, you may of course glean many a wondrous tale, such as the unblushing story of " Mary Tofts, and her *Litter of Rabbits,*" a miracle yet believed by many who should blush to own it. In the more enlightened circles it will go hard but you may be favoured by a tale of more historic dignity. The most fertile era in national interest is often the eve of a new dynasty, or the dilemma of a State.

At the dawn of the eighteenth century the deepest secrets of State policy were oft the pet theme in many a lone house with illustrious men in decadence, who were seeking a covert or a sanctuary. Even in this fine old Godalming, then half out of the world, they might wander with their angle by the gushing Wey, that rolls along and fertilizes the leys, or sit quiet and fearless in their oaken pew, as once was wont to do Master Theophilus Oglethorpe in his Westbrook Chapel. The death of Anne Stuart's son, the Duke of Gloucester, of James her father, the king *de jure*, and of William of Orange, the king *de facto*, set the Court of St. Germains on the *qui vive*, the slang toast being "the little gentleman in black velvet," meaning the mole, whose earth-hill tripped up King William's horse. Yet Anne was quiet on her throne, for James's bastardy was noised abroad, he was nicknamed "Mary Gray's warming-pan," and was even proclaimed *trayter*.

It was during this dilemma that Master Lewis Oglethorpe was returning from his travels, and blended with a choice morceau of British history and of British mystery too was this advent to Godalming of

Little Master.

"The boy is, hark ye, sirrah, what's your name — oh, Jacob, aye!"

IT was along yonder lane, still red with the dust of the clinkers, that two young horsemen were galloping through mire and dirt toward Westbrook. They were clad in black velvet, their cloaks trimmed with sables, and their small triangular hats with feathers, their hair being tied with a broad, black band.

The youngest, who wore a blue ribbon with a pendant jewel, flung himself from his horse in the court-yard, and dropped on his knee before the Baronet, who embraced him and bade him welcome to the heart of a father and of a sister.

"My sister," exclaimed Master Lewis, "Ha! more beautiful than ever—bright as the morning star. Oh, who would not love so sweet a sister?"

The ardent youth pressed the girl's lips so warmly, that her cheeks in a moment blushed ruby red.

"Enough, enough," cried the father, "fie, fie! spare her lips, boy—have done, have done! And so you are an envoy: eh?"

"From Mary of Modena, to Anne of England, sir, and, by Jove, well nigh forgot, from Mary Beatrice and Eleanor d'Este in Chaillot cloisters—though faith, Wharton here beat me hollow in ruffling the young nun's feathers. So sister dear" and Florence was doomed to a second batch of ardent kisses, and, in the effort, the jewel was flung from his cloak.

"What! a badge of honour?" inquired Sir Theophilus.

"The pass-key, sir, to the queen's closet at Kensington, though faith, we are too late a-field, I fear, for Byng is on the sea, and Stirling up in the north."

"And the king—eh?

"Your pardon, the chevalier, sir," whispered Wharton.

"Ay, ay, 'twere safest," said the Knight, "hedged in as we are with Protestants and Mohawks: yet Heaven

save him, for he has a precious gift, a wondrous grace of
mercy, that child of many prayers. But haste there : be
fiddles in the hall—so take your girls and be merry."

The revels opened in real earnest. Little Master danced
like a fairy, and as they walked the final Polonaise, he
whispered Florence that she was fairer far than the Stuart
girl that all were dying for : and were she at Hampton
Court, she would cut her out with Hamilton in half an
hour.

At early dawn the cavaliers arose and rode off north-
ward, and for three days Westbrook was in dull repose,
although 'twas clear that, for some cause or other, its lord
was in a desperate fidget : when, on the fourth evening, the
cavaliers returned jaded and chop-fallen.

"A blank, a blank, Master Oglethorpe," exclaimed
Louis.

"Sir, you forget," whispered Wharton in his ear.

"Pshaw, a truce to masking now," interrupted the
other : "my sister flouts my suit, sir—the exchange is
against me : so I am sent back to Germains as a counterfeit
—think of that, a counterfeit : and faith, had I staid
longer, I had been nailed to the counter itself, like a
clipped Jacobus forsooth. Here, Wharton, tell my father
all, while I go kiss my sister Florence."

"So, my lord marquis," whispered the Baronet, " our
ruse is baulked."

"Baulked, sir," grumbled Wharton, " bitched out and
out : for though we were safe and snug in the closet at
Kensington, and were biding our time to be touched for
the evil by Anne, as the heir of St. Edward, they all twigged

us at once. Swift, the mad parson, raised his shovel hat,
and old Richard Cromwell, the octogenarian, who is even
yet a dangler about court, smiled and winked, and Rochester,
fresh from Dublin, and Buckingham, the seal—"

"Nay, the closet, the closet, my lord!" interrupted his
host.

"Oh, full as the ark of Noah, sir! beasts of all sorts
and sizes—Whigs and Jacobins cheek by jowl: there was
Mistress Morley in her state chair, and Sal Jennings, and
Marlborough himself, who has ratted, and Burleigh, and
Mordaunt, and Dymoke, all curious as to that green boy
of mine—and then there was a scene.

"'Methinks, uncle of mine,' said the queen, as she
took the pen from Rochester to sign the bill of attainder:
'methinks this *Pretender*' (so Anne called him first),
'hath a right *regal*, if not a right *divine*—yet must we
play the Queen, therefore, give me the warrant, uncle
Rochester. There, 'tis done!' and Anne Stuart wept like
a child.

"And then she snatched the packet from Little Master,
who was kneeling at her feet: 'So,' she muttered, 'an
angry scrawl! what, flout our father's blood? no, no! yet
we *will* save our Church, howe'er the Pope has shut the
gates of Heaven against our heresy. And now my Lord
Marquis, *your* suit, ha! I guess it by your *Steinkirk*.
Art not cruel, Wharton, to trust your poor James with
that sly fox who kept the daughter of a king, *our grandam*
and her girl, without a spark to warm their frozen fingers?
But hither, hither, Rochester! raise this pretty boy, and
let me look on him. How, a blue ribbon and a jewel. So,

herœdes deerunt ! Alas, alas, my own poor Gloucester.
But hide, hide your jewel, boy—yet stay, what's here?
Innocent, to our dear son in Jesus, the most illustrious King
of Great Britain ! God's mercy, and all this barefaced
treason blazoned forth in the very conclave of cardinals
in the Vatican. Let the closet be cleared. James Stuart,
thou art passing fair (as she held him before her eyes),
fain would we believe the Queen of tears, thy mother—
pshaw, the crown must not wear weepers. Hide, hide your
jewel, boy—Anne Stuart drops her lid on its treachery :
still, *'tis* a leprous spot, and may mark thee to thy doom.
We would fain skin it over, James, but to purge thy
heresy is beyond even the confessor—this cancerous sore
of papacy.'

"' My gracious sister—'

" As little Master spoke, there was a hubbub in the court.
''Tis the train-bands,' cried Madame of Marlborough,
rushing in—'the mob cheer D'Aumont and Fingal, and
his Irish at the Sun swear oaths for James and the Pope,
heard you ever, Madam? bray out the king shall have
his own again.'

" Anne Stuart started to her feet :—' Be wise, Wharton,
be wise ! away with him at once, Kirk's lambs are in the
garden—the soldiers hold to the test, and a thousand
pounds are on thy head, James Stuart—remember Monmouth, James—away, away !'

" The king dropped on his knee, and would have
lingered still, but Anne's word was law : so we took French
leave, and here we are."

James Stuart unbuckled the garter from his knee, and

x

bound it round the arm of Florence Oglethorpe, then galloped off with Wharton to Rochester Castle, and directly sailed for France.

Now this may be the secret of the story, still remembered in Godalming, that Louis Oglethorpe of Westbrook, and James Francis Stuart, were one and the same person.

The Macpherson and Lockhart Papers affirm Anne's wish to place the *king, her brother*, on Scotland's throne : Burnet Leslie adds, even on that of Britain.   Swift and Pope assert her intense hatred of the *Pretender*.   No marvel this, for Anne was ever kept aloof by Mary of Modena : and although Catharine of Braganza, the dowager, had faith in his legitimacy, and the Pope, his godfather, sent over the consecrated clout by Barberini, yet the warming-pan mystery was never so cleared up, as to favour the notion of belief in James Stuart's birthright, or of Mary's miraculous conception.

The Western Wey forms a *crook* by Tilford, *ripa de Tyllesford*.   There, on the green, yet stands a very noble monumental oak, of one thousand years, noted in the charter of William of Blois, and there is a legend of its early spring even years before that.

In the year of grace, 1066, there was a tent of torn banners beneath this tree over a group of very noble creatures—a majestic woman, a youth of lofty bearing, and two holy men, and on a pallet lay an athletic form, wounded and prostrate.   Wherefore so rude a shelter for beings of so noble a nature ?

As we were about to sketch this legend, we dropped

our quill, for a soft whisper came to our ears, whether of fancy or of conscience, we know not.

> " right well I wote,
> That all this famous antique history
> Of some th' abundance of an idle brain
> Will judged be, and painted forgery."

We confess the rhymer may have reason on his side, and our own courteous reader may, perhance, knit for a moment the brow of reproof : yet, when we remember the varied readings of *his* destiny, who is our chiefest subject, we may venture with more confidence to resume our pen, and you shall learn the secret of that noble group that stamps even a right royal impress on

The Cynynge Hoc.

" Under which king, Bezonian, speak or die."

In the vale of *Senlac* or *Sanguelac,* now called Battle, seven miles from Hastings, on the Eve of Pope Calixtus, the Saxon Thanes had quailed to the Norman invaders in deadly contest, as the chronicle has writ,

> " Deraye the rught in the feeld,
> With helm, hauberk, and bronde bright,
> On strong stedes good and lyght,
> Whether is more power,
> Jesu, or Jubyter."

In plain words, Harold, the second of his name, and last Saxon king, had fallen before the star of William the Norman. " And indeed," quoth the astrologer, " a

star had forewarned him.   On the calends of May, 1066,
a light from heaven, some said a comet-starre, or long-
haired starre, first appeared on eve of *Litania major*, and
shone all the week."

Well, the battle—*Senlachium bellum*—was done, William the Conquestor, or Conqueror, as he is now styled,
was resting after the fatigue of the fight in the town of
Hastings, awaiting, indeed, the decision of the people,
and there he esconced himself, doubting, almost fearing
his scant of credit in the land, and uncertain whether
an ovation or a judgment.   He had already, with great
solemnity, thanked God and St. Valery, and they had
chaunted as an *Io triumphe*, the song or hymn of Roland
and the Paladins of Roncesvalles, that had been sung by
the Knight Taillefer as the war-cry of the Normans, when
they rushed to battle in the morning.   William had
decreed the building of a castle on the field of his triumph,
now called Battle Abbey: on the very spot where stands
the high altar at this day, was proudly waving the ducal
banner called *Mora*, embroidered by Matilda.   Missives,
however, soon came from the provinces, that set his mind
at rest, and he felt he was now king *de facto*.   While the
Norman banners fluttered o'er the field, the Saxon flags
were torn and trodden under foot.   Still the collared
serfs, and thralls, and soldiers of the vanquished were
roaming and peering around, for it was decreed that they
might remove and bury all *but* Harold the King: and so
they wandered about muttering, as a half-holy aspiration,
"Holyrood, God Almighty!" which had been shouted
as their war-cry in the morning.   Harold's skull had been

transfixed by a barbed arrow through the left socket, and it pierced his brain, and his body, and those of his two brothers, Leolyn and Gurth, lay somewhere among the dead and dying.

It was now midnight, and the torches of the "seekers of the slain" danced like meteors about the bloody field, for it was known now that a huge guerdon was promised by Githa, the mother of Harold, for his body, the Conqueror having decreed that it should be inhumed without any solemn rite on the sea-shore. She had knelt to Geoffrey Martel, who had fought in the van of the Normans, and had offered for it its weight in gold. At length her tears and despair prevailed, and it was granted to her gratuitously, and so her scouts ransacked the field, but they found not the body of the King. Indeed the corpses that lay naked around had been so gashed and torn, and so many skulls transfixed with arrows, that recognition was almost impossible, and they gave up their task.

In a remote part of the field there was another and a very different group. Among them a fair woman, bright as the day-star, and clad in cloth of gold. She knelt in silence by a naked body, when, on a sudden, she screamed aloud, " 'Tis he! 'tis he! look at that precious mark on his breast—'tis my own lord." She raised the bloody head on her bosom, while two majestic monks were anointing the noble soldier with holy unction, and one was drawing out an arrow, for the monks were the leeches of that age. The lady bound a banner-scarf around the forehead, " brondet," as we learn from Robert of Gloucester, "with fygur of a man fyghting, biset al about with gold and precious stones." On his knees, his hands clasped before him, was a youth, a mere boy, whose soul beamed through his lustrous orbs into the face of the soldier, regardless of a wound gaping in his own neck.

At the moment two Saxons were about to fling the body on a horse, when one whispered, "Hark you, Rollo, there is but one form like that—hush! he is not dead, so leave him to his leeches."

The lady had cried, "Mercy, mercy! I am his wife. Ah, now they leave us, thou art saved beloved. Osegood, Cnoppa Ailric, Childe-meister, ye are blessed, sure he will live, and Ulph, my noble boy, thy father will bless thee yet."

"Eadgytha," muttered the soldier faintly, "my own *Swansheils.*"

"Hush!" she whispered, "there is no safety but in silence and repose, the spies are slumbering round us: I knew thy heart was beating, though all believed thee dead."

"And how —— ?"

"Care not," she whispered, "twas the precious mole on thy breast, my cheek so oft hath slept on—hark! hark! they come."

It was a sumpter mule : and so, lifting the soldier on to a rude litter on his back, they journeyed on through Western Sussex, the least suspicious route. They halted by the green mound of Hydon yonder, and obeyed this injunction of the fairies to ensure their blessing on the balmy water :

"On Hydon's top there is a cup,
And in that cup there is a drop,
Take the cup and drink it up,
And leave the cup on Hydon's top."

Again they halted, in Oxenford, by Pepper-harrow Park,
which Pugin has adorned by a groin-arched cell. At
length they pitched their tent at Ilvethamstede, and
here the lady and the boy tended the soldier night and
day, while the monks kept vigil and knelt in prayer for
God's blessing and for life.

So passed many a weary hour, when one morning a
cortége halted on the green, nobles, and scouts, and
men-at-arms.

"By St. Luke's face!" exclaimed the foremost of the
train, "we are forestalled in our camp-tree. Yet, look
you, Henry, a noble creature, faith! But spread the
feast, we may feed with keener gust in the sunlight of
such beauty. So let her lout of a mate snooze on, an' he
will, mine own lips shall keep hers from cooling."

"Nay, Rufus, seest not the man is wounded?"

"What of that? He is a Saxon, I know it by his bare
pole, and his casque there dangling o'er his lair."

"Saxon or Norman, friend or foe, Rufus, he is in
distress, and pity were but his right : and, bethink thee,
here is our ward, Edgar Atheling, the scion of Saxon
blood, forbear, brother, forbear!"

The lady had been eyeing them askance, "'Tis they,'
she murmured, "God of Mercy, we are doomed!" Yet
bending her knee, and drawing her wimple over her lofty
brow, she whispered her thanks to her advocate.

"Nay," cried Rufus, "thank us by thy service, my

bonny Hebe, or Fria, an' you will, for so your Woden
dubbed his Venus. You're bright enough for either, for
bluer eyes or browner hair—"

He paused, as he looked on Ulph, who was recoiling
for a spring like a young lion, but the monks held him
back, and Eadgytha whispered, "Hush, for the sake of
heaven!" Then spoke she aloud, "Gentle masters, my
lord sleeps, and—"

"Lord," exclaimed Rufus, "a Saxon lord!—ha, ha!"

"So while I serve these nobles here," she whispered,
"your father's head upon your bosom, boy."

"We rob him," said Rufus, "ay, of his downy bed:
'twere pity so soft a pillow were unpressed," and Rufus
drew the lady to his side.

But she tore herself away, and played the servant to
perfection. On a whisper from his brother, Rufus called
for the bourgogne, and rising said, "Fill high the cups,
we pledge you, noble Athelyng!"

"*Royal*, brother."

"The noble Athelyng, whose gentle craft, I wage, joys
more in wald and covert than in battle-field, trust me
thou'lt lead a quiet life in Norman England."

"*Norman!*" muttered a deep-toned voice.

"Who grunts there?" asked Rufus: "but your cup,
your cup, Edgar Athelyng, we have shown you how a
Norman can fight: ye'll see anon how a Norman can pull
down a hart royal in our New Forest yonder by Hanton
water. And now, look ye, how a Norman can drink—
come, no jealousy, boy, hail to the Norman right!"

"*Right*," muttered the voice, "what right?"

"The right of victory, base croaker, what collared serf art thou?"

"I am Erl Waltheof, Rufus: I dare the leopard in his den: my collar 'tis but iron, my heart is steel—ay, right of victory! Shame on thee, Edgar Ethelyng!" and he held his gyved wrists aloft, "shame on thee, to link with proud, usurpers—thou art *Bretwalda*, thou our Cynynge, now."

"Sir Erl," murmured Edgar, softly, "King Edward did ordayne before his death that Harold should after him be King."

The wounded man tried hard to rise, while Waltheof drew a 'scroll from his bosom: "Hear this, then, the scribe hath writ,—

> "But fyrste he made Duke Harold protectoure
> Of his cousyne to governe to aysse
> Edgar Athelyng, full yonge a gouvernoure,
> Whome he ordayn'd to be his successoure,
> As very neyre to Edmonde Ironsyde."

So thou art Cynynge, Athelyng: for Norman right, William is no son of Odin, nor hath the voice of the *Witan*."

"Peace, varlet," cried Rufus, drawing his dagger, with more than his wonted stammer, "by Luke's face!——"

"Grace for the lady, brother," interrupted Henry, as he saw her flushed with emotion, "I pray you peace, Sir Erl. Brother, is this wise?"

But Rufus went on:

"Tell me, for thou art yclept Beauclerc, tell me, what is your Saxon now, where their witan, Eorlcundmen, and Thanes, and Knights, and Ceorles, and Viscounts?—fine names, and nothing more. And now set they up their idol Edgar : warning, boy, remember Hereward, and Roger de Hereford, and Ranulf de Guader, Earl of Norfolk, his daughter's fool. And hark you, Sir Earl, keep your wanton Judith at her spindle, or by fire or water! as she will—— "

"Shame, brother, shame! I blush, yon wounded man's in agony."

Suddenly a cry burst from the lips of Waltheof, "My King, my King!"

"Thy King, thou Saxon churl, lies festering far away, with blood base as his own, for Athelyng—— "

"Mercy, mercy!" exclaimed the woman.

"The crown, the crown!" cried the Saxons, with one voice, "all hail! Childe Edgar," Wulfstan, the bishop, raising the scroll aloft.

"Thy staff protects thee, slavish priest," muttered Rufus, as he strode across and snatched the scroll : "thus tear and trample I the rag, and now who will gainsay the Norman?"

"I," shouted the wounded soldier, and the Saxon Athelyng started.

"Thou?—pshaw : e'en if thy pigeon-livered craven Harold—why down, boy, down."

Ulph was starting forth from his corner.

"Were Harold in thy tent, I would howl in his ear this roll of the Norman, the noble of the world, Barons and Sheriffs, for Erls, and Viscounts, and Vavasours. Good night to your Saxon lingo—be quiet, man."

The soldier was starting again from his couch.

"Why, what is't to thee, and thou Waltheof, thou
toad of Harold, down—what ho, there! we would lip the
cream of Burgundy. Hither, my Hebe, kiss, kiss the
wine-cup, e'en our Falaise boasts not a lip more ripe and
luscious than thine own, sweet, sweet, as the honey of
Hybla!"

Folding her in his arms, Rufus pressed his burning
lips on hers.

The wounded man uttered a deep groan, and tried to
spring from his son's grasp: but he sunk back on his
couch, and the banner fell from his brow.

Ulph rushed and caught Rufus by the throat.

"Down, dog of a Saxon," grunted Rufus, "down, or
thou diest. What! would'st throttle the heir apparent?"

But Ulph held his throat until the purple blood oozed
from his nostrils.

"Bind the hound with thongs of iron," cried Rufus,
as he rolled writhing on the ground, while Eadgytha
rushed back to the couch, and Waltheof stalked forth
and glared on the prince.

"Such," he exclaimed, "be the fate of all who flout
the sons of Woden: base libertine! a bolt shall reach
thy heart, even while thou art sinning: even this arm,
now gyved and manacled, would crush thee as it did
thy brother, who would have stained my Leoline—my
curse on thee and thine!"

But Rufus heard him not: he was gasping, and his
eyes were blood-shot. Eadgytha whispered low in Wolf-
stan's ear, "Start not, it is over—look, look! he is
dying."

The man gazed on him with a smile, and held his hand as the priest approached.

"Wulfstan," he gasped, and then he sank back exhausted, "Wulfstan, and Waltheof, my last Prelate, and my last Erl."

"Be silent, or we are lost," whispered Eadgytha, "pray for us, Wulfstan, prayer and shrift are all thy king will need of thee here."

She kneeled, and Ulph dropped down by his mother's side, and the Bishop of Worcester gave his blessing with the extreme rights of the Church.

The prayer seemed for a moment to reanimate the dying king, and he leaped almost from the couch.

"Royal! ay, by Woden's star, and Saxon ever! I'm dying—call Edgar hither."

Athelyng entered the tent, and Harold kissed the brow of Edgar, and the banner dropped upon *his* breast.

"To horse! to horse!" cried Beauclerc, entering, "we are waited for, noble Athelying."

"Royal, royal, he is the King now, for I am dying, call *him* King." With the effort a torrent of blood gushed from the socket, and Harold was still.

Eadgytha rushed to the opening of the tent.

"Proclaim it! Waltheof," she cried, "proclaim it! Harold, the king, is dead!" and she was about to wind the clotted banner round Athelyng's breast. "No, 'tis a mere rag to thee, Edgar Athelyng, 'twill be a charm to Ulph." And she kissed it, and bound it round the broad chest of her son.

"Hide the boy," whispered Beauclerc, "an' Rufus

learn his birth, he will be stark as thee, Harold Infelix."

"Harold," screamed Rufus, entering, "did I hear, Harold, by Jove, 'tis he! lift him slaves, we'll crown the dog at Winchester ere noon."

"He will not wait," cried Eadgytha, "he has won! and wears a crown of glory in a higher sphere."

So closed the royal scene beneath the oak of Ilvetham-stede. At that moment, four kings by right or conquest were there : Harold, the dead,—Adeling, or Athelyng, the rightful and testamentary heir of the Confessor,—William, surnamed Rufus,—and Beauclerc, Henry the First : deserved not the glorious tree the name of the *Cynynge Hoc !*

Yon purple cone of Cruxbury, *The Mount of the Cross*, contrasts finely with the bright green leys, and the gold and amethyst of the furze and the heather around the Abbey of Waverley.

Monastic Waverley,

> "Altho' the wild-flower on thy ruined wall,
> And roofless homes a sad remembrance bring
> Of what thy gentle people did befal,"

yet within the precious volume of thy "Annals," the book-worm will still pore over many a mystic fragment in monkish Latin, even of the early Plantagenets. We might record the wondrous *mythi* of Alienora, the royal Countess of Leicester, but as we are treading the turf of Moor Park, our thought is absorbed in the memory of the accomplished, high-minded William Temple, whose heart was inurned beneath yonder sun-dial; and his accomplished, yet low-minded clerk.

We will call this clerk before us, and tell you how he played with

𝔚oman's 𝔥eart.

"Man's love is of man's life a thing apart;
 'Tis woman's whole existence.'

WITHIN yonder cot, once loaded with roses and jasmines, there was a blossom, fair as the jasmine, and sweet as the rose. She was fifteen years younger than the clerk, her hair raven-black, her eyes dark and lustrous. They had been watching the crimson-spotted trout shooting like a golden arrow among the water-lilies, when he opened a little book, the gift of his cousin, John Dryden, and scribbled by little Alexander Pope, who lisp'd sing-song even in his cradle.

As he read, he stole his arm around the girl's waist, and she tried to remove it, but the moment his eyes gleamed on hers, she dropped her arm.

"These are unholy words of Eloïse, Master Swift," she whispered, "they breathe not of pure love—no more, I pray you,—'tis unholy."

"Why, 'tis the love of Paradise, Stella, when Adam's heart was throbbing on the bosom of Eve."

A lady in weeds stole abruptly on this *tête-à-tête*.

"So, Master Clerk," she said, "ever getting my foolish girl into a corner."

" We were reading, Madam."

" Holy lessons, doubtless ; would I could thank you for
your teaching ; why, what is here ? "

" 'Tis Abelard and Eloïse, platonic love.

" Platonic trash ! you know your master hath denounced it, Master Swift, you are playing a deep game
with a woman's heart ; be this. your course of study,
heaven help my child ! "

" Mother," murmured Stella, gazing on him with the
eyes of a worshipper, " mother, I—"

" Unhappy girl ! " murmured Mrs. Johnson, you have
raised an idol, and challenge me to worship. Cadenus—
Stella ; oh, I have read your scribbling, Master Swift,
your 'Broomstick' we may smile on, but for your *Latin*
slang—call my daughter 'Hester,' and I'll believe you.
Remember poor Varina."

Stella wept as he whispered, "Miss Waryng, Madam,
was a jilt, and I had seen one fairer than she."

A smile dried the tear on Stella's cheek.

" Ah, silly girls," said the widow, "smiling on falsehood, unconscious that you will be the castaways of the
next chapter. Master Swift, forget us, you have nought
in common with my daughter."

So, a year or two have passed, Stella and Mrs. Delaney
were followed from Ireland by Swift, ill, and ill at ease.

He had been plucked in Dublin, and, although in his
chamber at Moor three kings had slept, and he had eaten
strawberries with William of Orange, who petted his
sketch of the "Tale of a Tub," yet his hope of a silk
apron was blighted.

Waverley was then the haunt of Swift and Stella, and one morning as they wandered thither, her deepest thought hung unconsciously on Stella's lips, : "Woe's me, woman's heart beats but to be broken."

The words foreshadowed the scene of another heart-blight, now to be enacted before them.

Within the crypt there was a group of joyous creatures, all but one, and she the chief of all, the bride of the morning.

In the centre of the ring was a very eccentric tripod cauldron, that is still kept in the vestry of Frensham church. The bridesmaids had secured it for the day by knocking at the porch, and curtseying and turning five times round before the clerk, and a vow to the fairies of Borough Hill that it shall be restored at sundown. Ther was a stranger youth gazing on the scene from the ivy.

"Is it a dream?" he murmured, "a vision of her that is gone. A bridal! Such might ours have been, if fate—hark! the lay of love she sung when in Alyce Holt I hung my cross upon her bosom. Julia!"

The bride turned pale as death, and, looking wildly on the youth, seemed to search for something in her bosom, unconscious of all else, until the stranger rushed from his covert, and pressed his burning lips on hers. Spite of the bridegroom's grasp, he folded her in his arms, and the cross fell from her bosom.

"Mine, the cross is mine," cried the youth.

"You are mad, fellow!" exclaimed the frantic groom.

"Mine, both the cross and Julia; off, off, or by the Hell you merit—off, I say!—what, you will have it, fool!" he drew a blade from his pouch, and the bridegroom fell bleeding, dying, to the ground.

As Swift and Stella loitered homewards in the saddest mood, one only sentence fell from her lips: "Another heart is broken."

And one word, unconsciously, from those of Swift, "Vanessa."

There were missives lying on the cottage table from Ireland,

Y

" What then," whispered Stella, laying down her letter,
" what *my* destiny? she was but twenty, I am thirty-one."

" *Was*," exclaimed Swift, taking the letter, Vanessa's
hand; " nature abhors a vacuum, fill it."

" There is a darker passage still, read on."

" Heaven's mercy ! " he cried, " dying—dead."

" Yes," and Stella echoed her own words, " another
heart is broken."

And Swift spoke no more during a melancholy hour ;
but, ere he maundered home to Moor, his conscience
scribbled thus, his last sad thought :—

> " Bright sunset bathes in glistening dew,
> The rose's swelling blossom,
> And deepens with a ruddier hue,
> The blush within its bosom.
> But if a sunset of the heart
> Of blighted passion speak,
> How blanched and cold the living rose
> That bloomed on beauty's cheek."

A brighter day seemed at length to dawn, and there
was, ere long, a gleam of hope that the rose might blush
again on the cheek of Stella, even blighted as she was, for
she was wedded to the Dean of St. Patrick's, in the garden
of the Deanery, yet the orange flowers were but a
mockery on her brow. She was, indeed, a forlorn and
virgin bride, yet her last parting thought was this worship
of her idol, sent to him at Moor :

> " Long be the day that gave you birth
> Sacred to friendship, wit, and mirth,
> Late dying, may you cast a shred
> Of your rich mantle o'er my head,
> To bear with dignity my sorrow
> One day alone, then *die to-morrow*."

During the Dean's hurried flight to his wife in Dublin,
the words " die to-morrow," were ever on his lip, and his
shaggy eyebrows were even wet with tears, and when he
crossed the threshold of her chamber, Stella lay fast
asleep—in her shroud! Another woman's heart was broken.

His romantic sorrow impelled the Dean to seek once
more the cottage-home of Stella, and here, on the spot
where we first found him, was completed the circle of
incidents from the morning in Waverley.

Yonder in the sand-rock is the cavern which Britons
named Leod-wel, the profane moderns, " Mother Ludlam's
Cave," but the monks of Waverley, " the Prophet's," or
" St. Mary's," or " Holy-well," for with its water they
worked their *Hygeian* miracles.

There is even now a cleft in the cave, called " the Fox's
den," and it was many months after the scene in Waverley,
that, as the legend tells us, one Master Foote,

> " A wretched, ragged man, o'ergrown with hair,"

slunk into this hole in remorseful mood, to hide himself
from the world, but as no one could recognise in him
the blood-stained being who had escaped pursuit from
Waverley, he was left unmolested, skulking from the
daylight, and coming out with the owls and bats at nightfall. A hollow sandstone was his lair, but no rest for his
conscience, or slumber for his eyelids : he was a mere
breathing idiot, doomed to die by inches. One evening,
as the moon rose over Cruxbury, a stifled groan startled a
wanderer, even the Dean of St. Patrick's himself, who
had sought, at early hour, the spring in Mother Ludlam's

cave, and there lay the creature dying. He was borne to the town, and, with rude and unholy rites, was laid in his sepulchre of sand within the cavern. The skeleton is now crumbled into dust, yet the cast of his face may be yet preserved in Farnham.

We may not affirm that the malady of the Dean of St. Patrick's was excited by these incidents of mortality, yet Jonathan Swift will ever remain a psychological enigma: so chaste in his converse, especially with women, yet oft so utterly disgusting in his writing. Varina's hopeless devotion, Vanessa's fatal despair, and Stella the maiden wife, dying in the wreck of her idolatry, compose a tissue of hapless mysteries, never to be cleared.

When we contemplate an intellect so lofty and so bright, yet so deeply dark and so desolating, as even Lord Orrery, and his great-grandnephew, Mr. Deane Swift, confess, we are impelled to one of two conclusions: either to believe in *possession*, one dark spirit striving with the better angel for man's heart, or in the antagonism of healthy and diseased hemispheres of the brain, thought and word and action all displaying, as either hath the mastery, a shadow or a glory of the soul.

The secret source of his pollution of thought, ere Swift "expired, a driveller and a show," may, indeed, be traced, and displayed by anatomical demonstration: when the corpses of Swift and Stella were exhumed in 1835, in the vault of St. Patrick's, that of Stella was even beautiful, and teeth more pure and white were never known, the skull itself was a model of symmetry. The skull of Swift was morbidly thick and thin in patches, much of it completely transparent; an indication of intense *compression* of the bones, by an *effusion* of scrum within the membranes of the brain.

THE halls of this antique pile of Farnham, that frowns so majestically on the site of the *Vindormis* of Antoninus, may be, for aught we know, of as holy a memory as the cells of Valombrosa, for it has long been the rural palace of the Prelate of Winchester. Moreover, it was the resting-place of an anointed Queen in her progress through the south.

The whirligig of time brings round its changes: the progresses of Elizabeth and of Victoria are very different things. Our gracious Lady, whose descent heralds trace to Alfred, and Teuton sages even to Odin the Scandinavian demi-god, can time her flight to Balmoral almost by minutes: the routes of the Virgin Queen were toil and trouble, especially through the merciless ruts of *Mudshire*, or the weald of Sussex. A few miles' transit were a summer-day's journey, and secretaries of state were often posed to find a sleeping-place for majesty, after a month's diplomacy. Even when Philip of Anjou visited the Queen of England, bush-faggots were laid down by Haslemere and Busbridge, just before the carriage, and even then the boors were often set to drag it through the mire.

The great hall of Farnham was oft the scene of regal festivity, and many an incident of the Elizabethan age, there and elsewhere, was filched from the truthful records of history, washed in with brighter colours, and tilted into

the pages of romance. Who knows not that Elizabeth,
with all her proud and lofty spirit, was deeply tinged of
the romantic? The magnificent creations of William
Shakespere, and the myths of Edmund Spenser, were
sketched off in fairy colours, to tickle the fancy of the
"fair virgin throned in the west." We may not marvel,
therefore, that many an incident of that era comes down
to us *coleur de rose :* so were tricked off the rivalry of the
Tudor and the Stuart Queens, and the intrigues of Essex,
of Leicester, and of Howard.

We pray you bear this in mind, while you listen to
a chequered melodrame, the memory of which weighed
down the heart of Elizabeth, for even a Queen may weep,
when she has lost

The Precious Moment.

"Headsman, hold thy hand!"

ONCE on a time, in the month of September, the Queen
had slept at Sutton and at Loseley, whence William More
had brought her to Farnham. Here she was welcomed
by a flowery speech of the Porter at the gate, and with all
the solemnity of homage by the Bishop of Winchester,
who ushered her Majesty to her chair of state in the great
hall. The pope had been her theme with the bishop.

"As for the thunder of the Vatican," she exclaimed—

' Tantæne animis cœlestibus iræ.'

We're up in our Greek and Latin, hey, Burleigh? witness
our *ars poetica !* 'Twas mother tongue with poor Ned

and me. Mary burnt *her* books, and cut Roger Ascham for her monks, so he took up and cottoned with the scapegoat, poor Jenny Grey. Wilt hear us in our Latin ?— here are the Gospels, now," and she felt for the little gold-bound book, enamelled by George Heriot, which commonly dangled at her girdle. "Ha, forgot !"

"An't please you, Madame, here is mine."

"Ha, Tindal !—God's light ! our mother's book ! Why, thou'rt my mother's pet : Anne Gaynsford, this *was* my mother's, then : where got you it ? "

"Madame, on Tower Hill, the last——"

"Spare me, spare me," cried the Queen, as Lady Zouch of Codnor fell at her feet.

"Yet blazon you this precious book, lord bishop "—and the Queen dropped a tear on the title-page—"aye, to the world, and shame these painted dolls of Monte Cavalho and Holyrood. Apropos, here's Norfolk, from his keep at Arundel, 'tis something yet to see him in the south. Hither, my lord, think nought of Burleigh's frown : sit, sit you here, we'd have thee in the seat of honour still, however they whisper of the Tower. What, *my* Howard, my own blood royal, in a cage ! yet counsel we to keep thy thoughts from Nor'ard."

"Your counsel is my law, my Queen."

"Well then, as we ride along, lisp me a stanza of contrition. Helicon runs in your blood, my lord of Norfolk."

"Ah, would my father's craft were mine. He clomb Parnassus, to charm the glory of that smile : I could but lag behind. Yet I may improvise by proxy : here is a boy from Avon's bank, even from cock-crow to sundown he

lisps in numbers. William, come forth, kneel to your
Queen."

A fair youth crept from the crowd. The Queen laughed
at the baby poet, but little Shakespere, nothing daunted,
in a moment carolled thus :—

> " When Cynthia smiles,
> And roses blush beneath her eyes,
> As deep as sunset paints the skies
>   Of orient isles,
> And whispering joys and balmy sighs
> Breathe soft as murmurs from the dove,
>   I kiss my love.
>
> " When Cynthia frowns,
> While passion's burning fountain flows,
> And the bright lustre of the rose
>   Its torrent drowns,
> To woo those lips t' again compose,
> That wreath of smiles affection wove,
>   I kiss my love."

The Queen turned on her saddle. " Methinks, the boy
hath read your thoughts, my lord. Now where shines
this Cynthia of thine, o'er Holyrood, or Windsor, hey ?"

" Can you ask me, madame ? There is a planet faintly
gleaming on Holyrood, the moon herself doth shine on
Windsor."

> " Aye, chaste as the icicle,
> That's curdled by the frost from purest snow,
> And hangs on Dian's temple."

These and other syllables fell like honey from young
Shakspere's lips.

The Queen's eyes sparkled : " Thou lispest sweetly,

boy," she said, " thou shalt be our's anon : poor Ben is waxing old—your cage shall be at Sheno ! "

So, calling Raleigh to hold her stirrup, she dismounted.

" Why, gad's me, master Raleigh ! " she cried, " there is the print of our shoe on thy cloak yet. Well, well, we have not forgotten thy gallantry: there is a jewel for 't."

There was a pleasure-house and garden on the keep in that day, and when, some minutes after the Queen had mounted, Raleigh was writing with the Queen's diamond on the casement,

> " Fain would I climb, yet fear I to fall."

then as the Queen read it, he blushed and fled.

"Poor boy," she said, "Heaven's mercy it be not prophetic ! " And then, drawing the duke's jewelled hilt, she completed with it the couplet :

> "If thy heart fail thee, climb not at all."

Raleigh crept to the window, read the Queen's rhyme, and blushed deeper still. It chanced, as the Queen re-mounted, came an aged man, and a pale girl, leading by a silken cord a milk-white fawn : and two bright things they were, so phantom-like. And then came riding in a youth, booted and spurred, with a despatch of state.

"Missives from Spain, madame," said Burleigh.

" And what from the Escurial, now ? " cried the Queen, still sitting on her jennet. " Ha ! Burleigh to die, and Mary crowned: God's life ! 'tis a black scroll. Stand

forth, my lord : how say you, guilty, or not guilty?
knowest thou this hand?"

Norfolk took the scroll, and started at the sight—

> "Your most obedient Wife,
>
> Mary of Scotland and Norfolk."

"Why, she's the wife of Bothwell!" screamed the
Queen. "The wanton! three husbands, and we not one.
You are a bold man and a graceless. Thou dost shame
thy Saxon lineage, Thomas Hoffwerd. What, grant thee
pardon, *life*, e'en when the headsman's at the gate, and—"

"If I have erred, Madame," said the Duke, dropping
on his knee.

"Erred, you have *sinned*, my lord, 'twere to stain our
grace, indeed, to pardon thee again : penitence, pshaw!
prove us thy innocence. Even then, to let such a traitor
loose, unseal death-warrants for one smirk of penitence,
why, e'en those rebel Nortons might bend a knee and
hope for mercy then, despite of Burleigh's frown."

The pale girl came trembling from the crowd, and fell
prostrate at the feet of the Queen, while the fawn laid
her cheek on the latchet of her golden shoe.

"Why, what means this?" cried the Queen. "Shall's
have a play, extempore? yet, faith, ye're a pretty pair
of puppets, and your name?"

"Norton, of Rylstone, Madame."

Norfolk started at the name, and tried to speak.

"Silence, my lord, we listen, girl : but art thou innocent?"

"We are *all* innocent, gracious Queen, my father,

brothers, all : 'twas not the crown, 'twas the fair woman they would win for him : ah, gracious madame, is she to forfeit love who wears a crown? Ask your own noble heart, your nobles love you, madame, you have a right, and beauty to be loved, aye, as a bright and gracious woman should."

Elizabeth blushed, and glanced, unconsciously, at Leicester.

"The sovereign of a state, thou'rt more my gracious Queen—the monarch of all hearts, how deeply, dearly, are you loved : then, mercy, lady, mercy on those who love you thus, and would lose their precious life-blood for your grace."

The Queen changed colour, and her heart throbbed and told her had she not been a crowned Queen, she had been now a loved and loving woman : yet she merely murmured, "too deep, too deep, my lord," in Norfolk's ear.

There was a pause, Emily fell on her knees, and was about to speak.

"Madame," said Burleigh, "this wild and wayward girl—"

"Nay, nay," interrupted the Queen, "when fresh young nature speaks, we care not for bearded lips."

Emily took the hint, and murmured softly,—

"Oh, madame, be what you are, come down from your throne, and be a gracious woman, not a Queen. Oh! ask your heart if there be one on earth that's worth so bright a jewel: oh! would he love and honour you the less, because your grace had spared the blood of the Nortons : mercy, madame, mercy!"

There was many a tearful eye that wept for her, and many a maiden echoed her prayer for mercy.

Norfolk nodded aside, the urchin from Stratford lisped forth some words about "mercy being twice blest," and so forth. (You may see them imprinted in his play.) And then he fairly forgot himself, for he kneeled and kissed the hem of Emily's robe : he would have kissed her lips, but they were too pure and sorrow-laden to be touched.

"Thy words have charmed me, maiden," said the Queen, "'tis eloquence and truth."

"Were justice blind, madam," whispered Burleigh—

"Justice, my lord : true, thou'rt my councillor, yet this once we do reject thee, that boy doth learn us better : we will be loved : *mercy* were the Queen's pearl, now—see thou to it, for 'tis a precious moment."

"Madam, too late," murmured Cecil, "the warrant is despatched : ere two suns set, ten headless trunks—"

Emily Norton sunk on the ground, and the fawn bleated and butted against Burleigh's knee.

"Why knew we not this ?" asked the Queen, scowling.

"That nothing sad might shade this happy progress."

"Happy ! what, 'tween life and death ? 'tis the curse of crowns, my lord—God's light, when shall I cease to sign my hand to that my heart condemns ? What ho ! the fleetest steed in Farnham, ho !"

"She is here," cried the booted horseman, rushing from the group, "she is here ! by one good act Oswald may yet sponge out the stains of a wanton life. Fleet as the whirlwind, Bess will clear the counties at a bound, and by the second dawn—but your warrant, madame, and I fly."

The Queen beckoned Raleigh to her side, and signed the pardon on his shoulder, while she sat on her jennet, and, that it might at once be read, her name was on the top, like that of Jane Grey.

Richard Oswald kneeled at Emily's feet, and whispered, "for thee, angel of light,"—but directly rising, he muttered, "shame, shame, Richard, forget thyself!"

Oswald placed the warrant in his bosom, as he threw himself into his saddle, and his steed was seen, like a black eagle, cleaving the wind toward Bagshot.

Emily still lay on the ground, murmuring the words, "Blight, blight!"

"Blight, indeed, poor wench," and the Queen tore a pearl from her stomacher, and dropped it in down the maiden's neck. "Wear this, for my sake, poor wench, 'twas the nearest my heart, wear it next thine own, for thou art e'en as pure a thing as that. For thee, Mary Stuart, thou hast much to answer for. For you, my lord, we marvel not remorse hath struck you dumb, your creed we might o'erlook, for we may both be in error before the throne of light, but a woman—"

The Queen paused, and frowning darkly, pointed to the bracelet on her arm.

"Beware the edge, my lord, roost in your solitary keep, for there be sleughhounds abroad—there's my hand, Norfolk, we part friends, farewell. Heaven grant you sleep in peace, and for that surety, 'mind *on what pillow you do lay your head.*'"

Norfolk tried in vain to smile, for he remembered his father's fate.

"Ecbert," he whispered to his henchman, "look to your dogs, and load to the muzzle your patron of steel."

Ere nightfall the duke was in his castle at Arundel.

That evening Burleigh was closeted with the Queen until midnight. He told her the duke had, for certain, sworn his plight to Mary, as he hung round her neck the rosary of gold (now at Corby), and he finished a long argument with two words, "the Tower." But the Queen was firm, for she had four times signed his death-warrant and revoked it with a tear.

"Then, look you here, madame," continued the earl.

"Why, who wrote this?" she screamed: "so Mary that's your game, a bairn born in Lochleven! why Both-well is away: God's light, it flashes on me now, yet 'tis but a wench I see, and sent to Soissons—yes, thou'rt right, Burleigh—the warrant, quick, lest we again repent: there, 'tis done, the state, we hope, is satisfied, would the Queen were so too."

The doom of Thomas, fourth duke of Norfolk, followed hard on this incident: and now for the unhappy fate of the Nortons.

As the second sunset was gilding the walls of York Castle, a black filly, lathered with foam, was pulled up at the foot of a scaffold, the rider falling as if lifeless from its back, even as the noble animal snorted and dropped dead. At that very moment, Edward Norton's neck was on the block, and the axe was raised aloft, but the headsman held his hand, for the angel of mercy whispered him for once to *spare* a life. Dropping the axe, he lifted Richard Oswald from the earth, when the precious warrant of mercy fell from his breast. The sheriff read the pardon on the seal, and in a second broke his wand asunder, while Edward, yet unconscious of the scene, was still kneeling. It was a hair's breadth, in ten seconds his head would have rolled away among the bleeding trunks of a father and eight sons. For them, alas! time was no more, for him, alone, it was indeed the precious moment.

Attended by Cuthbert, Emily, unconscious of her orphanhood, was treading her way back to Rylstone, for she was a true Catholic, and worked out her pilgrimage to the letter. The raven croaked, and the northern wind whistled shrilly over the fells of Bardon, as Cuthbert flung wide the gate of Rylstone Park, and the fawn was bleating piteously, as ominous of ill, for instinct hath a wondrous knack of prophecy. Yet there came one gleam of joy, as Edward met his sister at the door, and she fell weeping on his neck. And there was another figure in the moonlight, and Edward whispered, "bless him, my sister, he well nigh lost his life in saving mine."

"*Your* life, Edward, and where is my father? where, where my brothers, where?"

The youth's averted face told the truth at once, that they were orphans. Many months of the deepest sorrow were passed in Rylstone, you may be sure.

The fairy fawn, as she is believed to be even to this

day in Craven, trotted every Sunday morning over the
fells to Bolton Abbey—

> " Where soft the dusky trees between,
>   And down the path thro' the open green,
>   Where is no living thing to be seen ;
>   And through yon gateway, where is found
>   Free entrance to the churchyard ground,
>   Comes gliding in with lovely gleam,
>   Comes gliding in, serene and slow,
>   Soft and silent as a dream,
>   A solitary doe."

And there, on the grave of the Nortons, she lay listening to the organ's peal and the chorister's chaunt, and
when they ceased, she bit a daisy from the grave-turf,
and bore it home to the mourning girl in Rylstone. And
Emily, and Edward, and Oswald loved her as a sister :
it was a precious sympathy, and this, courteous reader,
is our secret.

True, the maiden's heart throbbed for him who saved
her brother's life, but the fawn, by its bleating and its
fondling, was oft a very happy medium, and, indeed,
made the match.

The orphans had worn out many a long day in weeping,
when mournful tidings came to Rylstone. The head of
the fair Queen was *lopped*, and Bishop Wickham offered
thanksgiving for "the happie dissolution of Marie, late
dowager of France," the church bells ringing out right
merrily in Lambeth.

At the same hour ('twas a strange contrast), there knelt
in Bolton aisle, a maiden, two youths, and a monk, and

a creature like a virgin lily, for at the dawn she had bathed her silken skin in a crystal spring, on the margin of the Wharfe, and on her velvet collar hung the Queen's pearl. And then, the holy rite of marriage, yet no merry peal was rung that day in Bolton tower, no bevy of maidens to kiss off her tears, and the only bridesmaid of Emily Norton was the white fawn of Rylstone.

Our pilgrimage is ended, as the golden gleam of beautiful nature is fading into twilight, yet the memory of the heart, more lasting than the hour, will be ours for ever.

We have been joyously gathering, here and there, a flower in the field, and a leaf from lips and chronicles, while a dark frown, perchance, hath been gathering on the brow of the critic. Well, there is no hope, no memory, without its shadow.

LONDON: R. CLAY, SON, AND TAYLOR, PRINTERS.